LIFE MEANS NOTHING BEHIND THE GREEN WALL

LIFE MEANS NOTHING BEHIND THE GREEN WALL

a novel

by PROFESSOR Z

Physician's Publishing

Printed in the United States of America
ISBN 0-9665240-5-5

This book represents a work of fiction. All names of
characters and institutions are the product of the author's
imagination. Any resemblance to actual persons, institutions
or events is entirely coincidental.

The anonymous author of *Life Means Nothing Behind the
Green Wall* owns all legal rights to this book but has
delegated custody of the book and oversight of all matters
related to copyright protection to Physician's Publishing
Company.

Dedication

This book is dedicated to all
my past residents.

—Professor Z

CONTENTS

Dedication v
Author's Note viii
PROLOGUE ix

PART I: New York Park Hospital
1 The Hospital 3
2 Minor Procedure 9
3 Adverse Outcomes 31
4 All You Need is Love 51
5 The Launch Pad 55
6 The Cousin 61
7 Politics and Pasta 68
8 Gathering Storm 86
9 A Stubborn Group 114

PART 2: The Hunter and the Hunted
10 Skirmishes 123
11 The Investigation 147
12 Whistle Blowing 159
13 The Lists 175
14 The Virus 187
15 Witch Hunt 204
16 Unnecessary Operations 217

PART 3: Wheels of Justice
17 The Matching Game 229
18 Pressures 234
19 Going Down 237
20 War of Attrition 254
21 The Feeding Tube 265
22 The Beginning of the End 274
23 The New York Report 299

EPILOGUE 307
Glossary 315

Author's Note

Most surgeons I know are hard working and honest doctors—deeply committed to the well being of their patients and dedicated to their profession. Occasionally they commit mistakes, but to err is human. This book, however, focuses on a different group of surgeons, a group that creates much harm but remains almost unrecognized by the public and practically uncontrolled by the surgical and medical community.

You may be curious whether the story recounted in this book is "true." I can assure you that the surgical-medical-scientific component of the story is as accurate as I—a weathered surgeon in active practice—could produce. All the rest of course is purely fictional. Whether similar characters and institutions described herein exist at all, or can exist, I leave to each reader to decide.

The author wishes to acknowledge the significant contribution of Chris Meister, Ian McLeod and Joyce Griffith to the writing of this book. He is also grateful to Joan and Yuval Gelfand, Paul Rogers and Heidi for their criticism. Many thanks to the friends and colleagues who were supportive from far away: Ahmad, Armin, Avi, Gabi, Phil, PO, Bob, and Uli.

PROLOGUE

"There's a sort of decency among the dead, a remarkable discretion: you never find them making any complaint against the doctor who killed them."
—Molière, 1622-1673

It played out in an irritating slow motion. I would take a deep bite in the edges of the laceration, and then throw a careful knot. Every time the suture would tear out of the thin, friable muscle.

I tried again.

And again...

The pink blood blobbed noisily, then gushed out of the large rent in the left, upper chamber of the heart. From there it leaked into the overfilled suction bottles and sloshed onto the floor.

"We are losing her," the senior anesthetist commented calmly. This was not the first time he'd seen a junior incompetent surgical resident losing a patient. I was desperate and paralyzed. *Hell, this atrium is as soft as shit. I can't close it. She's finished.* I took another bite...It lasted perhaps a minute or two but later on I would re-play it in my mind for hours in slow motion.

I had seen more than a few stabbed hearts during the first month of my surgical residency in Lady Mercy Hospital. I even operated on a few under the expert supervision of Yorgus, my senior resident. Already he was known for having boasted the largest published personal experience with injuries of the heart in the literature. But on that day, I was without him. This was my "solo flight" on an injured heart.

Only twenty minutes earlier, when I was dozing with a few interns in the pit, after a bloody night, the young lady was wheeled in, drenched in sweat and already defecating. The pulse was barely palpable and a large stab wound was present left to the sternum. Another drunk and jealous lover. At this time of night, it went without saying.

"Let's go," I hissed to the interns who weren't moving fast enough to my liking. We wheeled her to the OR shouting, "Stab heart!"—a local battle cry. This instantly woke up the anesthesia and nursing team. Lübscke knife to the sternum, the pericardium opened, a finger onto the left atrium wound, a suture of silk. But this time it was different and the sutures kept tearing off the thin muscle of the atrium.

"It's useless, she's gone," the anesthetist said with contempt when I finally got one suture to stick. "You can continue practicing but she's lost twice her blood volume. She's empty. Let's stop!" He switched off the ventilator and left the room.

I looked at the corpse that I had created; the remains of red lipstick still on its lips, the red-nailed fingers motionless on its side. No words were said as I sutured the skin incision overlying the gaping chest and helped the nurses remove the pipes and tubes. I also helped wash the body. I then crawled to the next stretcher in the corridor and fell immediately asleep. When I woke up I realized immediately that I could have saved her. *I have to learn to deal with the atrium.*

Since that horrific event I've found myself sporadically dreaming in slow motion. My hands are moving, I use instruments, but I do not progress at all…again and again.

Lady Mercy Hospital is located at the heart of a multi-million crowded South African township. It was an urban battle zone twenty years ago and probably is so today. Fridays used to be the worst because that was when everyone got paid. With cash in their pockets and cheap wine and homebrewed ale a fearsome mix in their bellies, the locals feasted on fury. There were only two types of citizens on Friday nights: Victims and perpetrators.

Mayhem persisted through the weekend, and the tide of horrendous injuries often overwhelmed us. The surgical receiving area, locally called "the pit," resembled a dressing station in Stalingrad: patients on stretchers, on chairs, on the floor, crushed skulls, stab wounds, shot abdomens and mangled vessels spilling blood everywhere. The contrast between the day and night was striking. During the day academic professors taught us surgery. At night they departed leaving us junior trainees to king the stormy nights.

A line of stretchers along the long and shabby corridors ended at the doors of the pit's shock room. On the stretchers lay stoic young males to whom suffering was no stranger. Most of them were semi-comatose, if not from intoxication then from loss of blood. At first I'd run from stretcher to stretcher to see which of the victims, wrapped in thick stained woolen blankets, was gasping to death from a thoracic wound, forming a red pool under his stretcher.

"Marc," I was told by those older and wiser, "you can't save 'em all. Don't waste your time. First come, first served..."

And thus number eighty-nine in the line of stretchers would be found cold dead when it was his turn to enter the brightly lighted shock room.

Life means nothing in these parts, I concluded in silence.

During the endless nights we would operate continuously on an incessant stream of wounded men and sometimes women. Occasionally we dealt with natural causes: a woman with acute appendicitis or an old man with a perforated ulcer. But for the most part we would mend punctured hearts, suture lacerated vessels, and push back eviscerated guts. Young and brazen, we would attempt to do more than we were trained to handle, accumulating our own list of dead.

Life means nothing, I would remind myself after losing another patient.

Then at the chilly dawn, groggy, blood stained and weary down to our bones, we would round on the numerous patients admitted during the night. The critically ill lay on stretchers near the nursing station. We had nowhere else for them because intensive care was always full. Others were on beds and mattresses between the beds and even under the beds. Those with more minor injuries such as a simple puncture of the lung would spill into the corridors. They sat patiently on hard, wooden benches, smoking hand-rolled cigarettes made of coarse, black Zimbabwean tobacco, coughing and bubbling air into the water bottles connected to their chest drains. For two hours we would move from patient to patient. Sometimes we'd find a corpse under a bed—a "missed injury."

"Zohar," the Professor said, kneeling at my side to view yet another ashen body. "You saw this gentleman?" The Professor lived in another world. He had slept at home the whole night and would soon be chasing balls around the golf course.

"Yes, Sir," I replied, trying to decipher the crumpled piece of paper representing the dead man's medical chart. "I suppose it was me."

The Professor stood up and looked down on the naked body, which had been turned around to expose a tiny stab wound on the right side of the back. He did so very carefully so as not to soil his white trousers. "Zohar, you managed the left pneumothorax all right but missed the one on the right. You have to examine the whole patient, every square inch of him. You've got to learn to be thorough."

First come first served, I thought to myself. The Professor shrugged his shoulders and continued pacing down the isle of that huge hangar-like room. The golf course was waiting.

Life means nothing.

After grinding hours in the hospital I would drive home along the manicured lawns of the suburbs lit by the late morning sun, trying not to fall asleep behind the wheel. There was no accountability here. People died easily preventable deaths without anyone paying the price. Not even an academic soul searching and mind improving mortality and morbidity conference. Nothing.

Life means nothing.

Little did I know that there would be times in my future so bleak and so unexplainable by comparison that I would be yearning to be there once again, twenty years back.

Back where chaos was a daily tornado that consumed life with an appetite that I knew I would never experience again. That was, at least, until I arrived at New York's Park Hospital in 1995. Then my whole perspective of what life really is changed.

I realized it was even cheaper.

PART I

New York Park Hospital

1

The Hospital

Every hospital should have a plaque in the physicians' and students' entrances: "There are some patients whom we cannot help; there are none whom we cannot harm."
—*Arthur L. Bloomfield, 1888-1962*

New York Park Hospital (NYPH) stands in the midst of a quaint brownstone neighborhood of Brooklyn. Its solid complex of buildings has dominated the neighborhood of Park Ridge since the late nineteenth century. The Park, as it is more commonly known, proudly serves the ever-changing Brooklyn community, adopting itself to the shifts in time. From the posters exhibited on the wall of its grandiose lobby-like entrance, one can learn about the history of the NYPH. When founded, around the same time that the Brooklyn Bridge was completed, it was called the Park Hospital—not "Brooklyn's Hospital" and not "New York Hospital." The "New York" suffix was added more than one hundred years later when the hospital merged into one of the giant medical hospital complexes organized by the city's ivory towers.

Actually, the new name sounds a little more trustworthy and even appealing in a commercial sense, particularly with the new subtitle: "Affiliated with the New York Center-Manhattan University Medical School." But even without the bombastic titles the old Park Hospital was a grand institution, nourished by the great Brooklyn of its time and providing state of the art medical care for citizens.

Over the years the Park changed with the community. After the WASPs left, the Irish arrived, then the Italians. Ambitious sons of immigrants went to medical schools, specialized, and returned to Brooklyn. The demography of the hospital staff and the community were alike. Jewish doctors and patients seemed to avoid the Park. Instead, they preferred the nearby Ben Maimon Hospital or the Jewish Hospital, where in 1942 Albert Einstein underwent his aneurysm operation by the great Rudolf Nissen.

The post World War II era brought significant changes to the Park. Sponsored by generous federal and city funds, the training of young doctors and specialists became increasingly profitable to hospitals. Not only could they enjoy the cheap labor provided by the trainees—previously available only to the greatest university hospitals—but in addition, the government paid—and still pays—the hospitals handsomely for each resident. Consequently, teaching programs mushroomed across America, spreading into Brooklyn and eventually the Park.

At the same time the neighborhood became poorer and less attractive to young American doctors, who preferred the ivory towers of the great cities or the more affluent hospitals in suburbia. To feed the numerous available vacant training positions, inner city hospitals, like the Park, had to recruit foreign graduates who flocked in masses to the US, mainly from the Third World. Between 1950 and 1980 the vast majority of the young doctors the Park managed to attract were Indians, Pakistanis, Iranians, Arabs, Tai, and Filipinos. In fact, recruiting teams were sent by the hospital to India to import residents. Rumors claim that the recruiters—Americanized Indians—earned large amounts of "backshish" money paid by the families of prospective residents.

The typical face of the hospital departments in those days consisted of a chairman and senior doctors—aging white Americans—and an isolated face of an Italian American or a Jew in a sea of immigrants from Asia or the Middle East. With time, the foreign doctors graduated from their training programs to become specialists taking over senior faculty positions. During the late 1980s the Park became a multinational tower of Babel, the Department of Medicine being predominantly Indian with an isolated pale face, who

4

to the occasional visitor, looked like a tourist in Bombay. A few Iranian-born surgeons controlled the Surgical Department while Oncology became a pure Egyptian oasis.

The 1990s brought another change. As the communities surrounding the Park yuppie-fied, the hospital had to upgrade to remain competitive. A new CEO added a modern wing to the hospital and a doctors' office block just above a large bookshop. An underground parking lot completed the deal. Now you could visit a NYPH doctor, park your car and sip a cup of Starbucks coffee at the bookshop. Why go to Manhattan?

Concurrently, tougher accreditation requirements by the various specialty boards began to prevail, with the undeclared intention of eliminating "Third World-like residency programs" and decrease the number of foreign graduates entering the country. In order to save the failing residencies programs, better qualified department heads and faculty members had to be imported from the outside, creating new tensions with the pre-existing old guards.

From the street level, the Park has never looked so good. Step inside and see its ample, fully carpeted lobby with mock Edwardian furniture. One of the many renovated elevators will take you up to the patient floors. The corridors are polished, the walls covered with reproductions of classic and modern artists. Peep into the patient rooms—a five-star hotel!

Finally, after all those years Manhattan has come to Brooklyn. No doubt this is the place to bring your mom, wife or child, or even yourself. It is nearby and convenient. They say that the food is excellent, and the nurses smile and talk in broad Brooklyn accents. Sure, everybody knows that for the treatment of cancer the Memorial Hospital on the East Side is the best in the world, but try to go there—*what a schlep*. Yes, all those medical web pages on the Internet talk about the advantages of university hospitals, but we trust the Park, and besides, it is now affiliated with the Manhattan University.

No wonder that the *New York Monthly* listed the Park among the "top ten" hospitals in the greater metropolis.

Although the Park Hospital in this story is purely a concoction of my imagination, there are numerous facilities across the US just like it.

▲▼▲▼▲

As with any hospital in America, the New York Park is a micro cosmos—a small almost self-contained political and financial system. Although the hospital is formally designated as a "non-profit" institution, the chief ambition of those who govern it is to make it as profitable as possible—and not, of course, for altruistic reasons.

Michael Howard, a lanky Irishman with a small skull impelled over a stooped six foot, seven-inch frame, was the hospital's almighty president. An astute financier and health care administrator, he also served as chairman of the State's Association of Hospital Presidents and was elected by a leading financial journal as the most successful Hospital President in the city. Howard ran the hospital with the help of a small army of Vice-Presidents. The only physician among them was the Senior Vice-President for Medical Affairs, Dr. Albert Farbstein, a late sixty-something internist who was born, raised, educated, trained and promoted in Brooklyn. White haired, balding, bearded, eagle-nosed, and very short, he looked as if he'd jumped straight out of a Nazi propaganda caricature.

As the CEO, Howard held the keys to the hospital's purse, and he knew that the fatter the purse the bigger the bonus to be added to his already high six-figure salary. Naturally, Farbstein also had a financial interest in the well being of the purse. The more doctors and nurses he employed for the money, the more generous Howard would be with him. From any management's perspective a hospital is a business: a large factory that employs doctors and para-medical staff. A factory that processes patients.

6

Two bodies control and limit the power of management. The supreme one, at least in name, is the Board of Trustees, which consists of non-medical dignitaries from the community. The trustees appoint—and fire—the CEO and control his performance. At the Park Hospital only two MDs have voting power on this board: the President and Vice-President of the second controlling body, the Medical Board. The members of this physician-controlled group are elected each year by their fellow hospital physicians. Theoretically, the Medical Board is a democratic body, with a book of bylaws and associated committees and subcommittees elected for various functions. One of the Board's chief roles is to assess the credentials of physicians who wish to practice in the hospital and to approve the privileges granted to them by the chairpersons of the various departments. The Medical Board represents the higher level of the hospital's quality assurance mechanism and is responsible for maintaining an optimal level of quality care. At the same time, the Medical Board functions as a doctor's union to protect professional and financial, interests of the doctors in opposition to hospital administration.

With the authority to appoint, punish, supervise, and protect, the Park's Medical Board is almost omnipotent. It can decapitate or force into resignation a chief of department and even the President himself, which was the fate of Mike Howard's predecessor. In the end, a group of physicians control the Medical Board, the hospital and a large portion of its purse. For many years the domination of the Medical Board at the New York Park rested in the hands of a triumvirate of two surgeons and a physician who had alternated as chairmen and deputies for years.

The oldest was the Vice-Chairman of Surgery, Dr. Joseph Mantzur. In his late sixties and fragile looking, Mantzur was the typical "do-it-all" Brooklyn surgeon. Name it, and he'd do it: general surgery, vascular bypasses and chest operations. Born in Iran, he immigrated to Germany with his aristocratic family before the downfall of the Shah. He completed

7

medical school in Heidelberg, and a surgical residency at the Park Hospital long before "New York" was added to its name. For thirty years he was considered the leading local private surgeon, gathering immense influence and wealth. The showpiece of his wealth was an oceanfront mansion and a large boat on the tip of the Island. This was where Dr. Mantzur used to escape each Friday night after a strenuous operating week, far from his dying patients and their anxious families. It was common knowledge among residents that during long weekends and holidays old Mantzur was unavailable. Emergencies, true or otherwise, had to wait until Monday.

The second surgeon in the ruling triumvirate at the New York Park Hospital was Dr. Mahmud Sorki. Sorki, son of a Persian Ayatollah, studied medicine in Iran and trained in surgery at the Park under Mantzur's wings. He married a local Italian nurse and established himself in private practice. A real "cowboy" surgeon, for many years he was considered the "top knife" by the hospital medical community. He, too, became immensely rich.

The third in the triumvirate was Dr. Herb Susman, the only real American in the leading group. He was a half Jew born and bred in Brooklyn. As a graduate of a Caribbean medical school he completed an Internal Medicine residency in the Park where he met and bonded with Sorki. Energetic despite his immense size, Susman became a Clinical Professor of Medicine with two publications on his curriculum vitae. He and Sorki, both in their late fifties were as close as brothers and socialized together at top Manhattan restaurants and Bahamas casinos, with women in Atlantic City, sharing jokes, loud laughter and a lot of booze. Their old mentor, Mantzur, a widower, did not drink, did not look at women and did not overeat. Always calm, controlled and poker faced, he was the gray eminence of the New York Park and, as I would soon learn, my true nemesis.

2

Minor Procedure

If you want to be on the staff of a hospital, lad, pretend you're a fool till you're on it.
—Lloyd Roberts, 1853-1920

September 28, 1998

Breathe—come on, breathe. You know how. For God's sake, breathe!

A silent, dry gulp. The mouth opened, but the chest didn't move. Something's jamming. Something is seizing this engine.

I noticed rapid eye movement. Oxygen level in the blood was depleting rapidly. I'll give it another thirty seconds max before the brain goes blank. That is if the lungs don't burst first—an absurd but interesting possibility.

Then I realized I knew the symptom; I've witnessed it often enough in dying patients. One moment they're fighting with unexpected determination, the next they drift past the point of no return. I began to register in cold blood every minute detail as his body methodically shut itself down with the grace of a medical Three Mile Island.

The head rolled to one side. The oscillograph's amplitude bounced on the screen, leaving a hysterical pinball's amber trace, the raw score sheet of life performed by the monotonous whine of an electronic beeper. Remarkably steady, an unerring beep-beep-beep said that the heart seemed intent on going on, brain or no brain.

Stunned, I sensed my own heart rhythm merging with the thumping of the heart in the dying form below me. Emotional gravity pulled me down to the abyss. I was being sucked into the last throes of this struggle for life. It was not his life oozing away, but my own.

Then colors exploded before my eyes and the rhythmical electronic pulse was replaced by a chaotic ring. *An alarm? An instrument malfunctioning?* Darkness swallowed my mind and confusion consumed my thoughts. Something was pumping moist sand into my lungs. I popped to the surface like a buoy from the bottom of the dark ocean, cold sweat on my forehead. Only the ringing remained.

It's the phone. I'm in bed. The clock on the radio showed that it was ten after four in the morning. I took a moment to recalibrate my systems before answering the phone. A call that early in the morning could have only meant one thing, so it was worth the extra ring to make sure my head was screwed on right. I took a deep breath before reaching over. Despite my best effort, I still somehow managed to knock over the glass of water on my bedside table as I groped for the receiver.

"Hello?" I said, a hint of irritation spicing my voice.

"Dr. Zohar? Good morning!" It was the cheerful voice of Mike Silverstein, our fourth year resident. A part of me was refreshed by his early morning blast of happiness. The larger part of me figured it had no business anywhere near me at four a.m.

"Morning Mike." I coughed to shake the grogginess out of my throat. I didn't make much of an effort to be polite about it, either. *Why the hell so early again? This is the third stupid call tonight!* I detached myself from my wife's warm body and took a deep breath.

"Sorry to wake you up," Mike continued, oblivious to my discomfort. "I have a nice case for you. Are you up? Can I continue?"

I stretched before answering, no doubt filling the phone with a loud primal sounding groan. "Go ahead." I listened with my eyes closed, my left hand scratching my balls periodically. Years of practice had taught me to produce a mental image of the case under discussion through the voice on the other side. Yes, a case—not a patient yet. He'd only be a patient once we'd had our personal encounter.

"Fifty-five-year-old male. Smoker, drinker. Myocardial infarction two years ago, no congestive failure, no medica-

10

tions—oops—he is on aspirin. Presented yesterday five p.m. to the ER vomiting fresh blood. His blood pressure was low. Responded to a few liters of fluids. GI scoped him, found a large ulcer in the duodenum. It was oozing so they injected it. An hour ago he vomited a pint of clots and his pressure went down to eighty." I sat up on the edge of the bed and tried to rescue my glasses from the puddle of water that had spread over the table.

The case needed an emergency operation. Silverstein was our best resident. Perhaps even the best surgical resident the hospital had ever seen, or would ever see at the rate it had been going. I respected his intellect and trusted his skills and judgment; I could see and feel the patient over the phone as he explained.

"Hey." Silverstein hesitated for a second. When I'm deep in thought I have a habit of becoming absolutely motionless. Sometimes, my wife says, I even stop breathing. "Are you with me?"

"Yes," I said, careful not to lose the image forming of this case in my head. I knew if Silverstein saw a problem, there was a problem. In contrast, when our chief resident from the Ivory Coast would tell me that someone needed their belly opened there was a good chance it was something silly like gastroenteritis. I didn't press the panic button until he said the patient is well. "OK, Mike. This guy needs to be done soon. By soon I mean now!"

"That's what I thought Dr. Zohar. I booked the OR; it is ready. Radezki is busy inserting a central line. Blood is on its way. When can we start?"

I did a quick calculation in my head. "I'll be there in forty-five minutes."

"Dr. Zohar, just one more thing you might want to know. The patient's name is Pellegrino. He owns a restaurant close to the hospital; he has good insurance."

"Mike, stop talking so much and work on the guy. We can't operate on a corpse, can we?"

"No," he said with a bit of a chuckle, "we can't."

11

"See you soon."

A paying patient? That's always nice. Who doesn't like to operate on one of them? But that was none of Silverstein's business. And besides, in an emergency case I prefer not to know about the patient's payment arrangements. Let me do the case first. If he can pay—what a nice surprise, if not—bad luck. Nothing new. Most of my patients weren't insured or were on Medicaid, which paid peanuts. Paying cases were almost never allowed to reach me; they were filtered and skimmed by our in-house surgical Mafia.

Whatever. An emergency abdominal operation would bring a few thousand bucks, and that was definitely better than the few hundred Medicare would pay. I couldn't complain. I wasn't starving, but who wouldn't want to earn some extra money? It could be compensation for this early wake-up call and another missed breakfast.

I shaved fast, one direction only. I dressed quickly: A pair of khakis, white shirt, blue navy tie with the College of Surgeons' icon. Blazer in same color, cheap—bought at Macy's last year and already frazzling at the sleeves. Heavy black British shoes. A goodbye kiss for Heidi. She opened one sleepy eye. It followed me clumsily as I moved about the darkened room.

"An emergency operation for one of your poor patients?"

I grunted at first and then mumbled to myself. This was not a patient of mine. This was a new case, which was a relief. If I had to go back and perform an emergency operation on someone I'd already operated on, that could be devastating for both them and me! It could have meant I'd made a mistake during a previous surgery. It wasn't the case this time, and for that reason Heidi's black humor succeeded in lightening my mood.

I headed downstairs, gulped a glass of orange juice and stepped into the garage. I looked at my watch—fifteen minutes from bed to car. Not bad. I took a deep breath of the crisp morning air as the automatic garage door swung open.

My black 1991 Caddy-Deville reached the top of the Verrazano Bridge and rolled towards Brooklyn. It was misty as the sun rose from Coney Island's side. I relished the sight, for the upper deck of the Verrazano offered a magnificent vista. In front there was Brooklyn, looking so peaceful with the mellow blanket of red and yellow leaves welcoming this late September day. On the right Coney Island; below, the calm blue water dotted with ships steaming in and out of New York Harbor. On the left I could make out the southern tip of Manhattan and the Statue of Liberty, lit by the first rays of sunlight. And behind me was Staten Island, where I was awakened from a sound slumber about a half hour earlier. It was a pleasant drive, unlike the routine rush-hour bumper-to-bumper morning crawl to Brooklyn. I tuned in the public radio station. It was too early for the morning news, but the classical music suited me just fine.

Driving is the only time I can think properly. Sometimes my thoughts embrace me so tightly I end up in front of the hospital without a clue as to how I got there. As I drove on, unimpeded by traffic, my thoughts drifted further and further into my memories...

...The outskirts of Johannesburg in a milky winter dawn, the smoggy air fed by thousands of wood fires on which early rising Soweto blacks cook their maize-meal for breakfast. Lady Mercy hospital with its casualty ward bursting at the seams; half-dead patients on woolen blankets groaning on bloodstained floors; knives, axes, screwdrivers, bicycle spokes still sticking out of their bodies.

Or the mist rising above Haifa's bay. The steady drumming of Israeli helicopters carrying in wounded from the northern front. They'd emerge from the black of night to land on the helipad by the sea and discharge their bloody and often noisy cargo... the nineteen year old boy shrieking as he tried to push his bowels back into his abdomen as we raced him to the trauma unit...

Brooklyn. I snapped back to the present. I took the Thirty Eighth Street turnoff and immediately started bouncing over the potholes anchored like land mines in the roadway. I was wide-awake by this time and my body was starting to feel the exhilaration that precedes going to the unknown. It is a tension at the center of the stomach that doesn't disappear until the first cut has been made. When the action begins, the focus is on the patient and the patient only. My feelings are irrelevant. There's no room for your stomach to turn anxious somersaults in the OR.

Has anyone ever tried to write about all those feelings that go on in the surgeon's mind while he is scrubbing for the operation? I wish I could, but like my dreams the presence of creative thought is erased. One minute a brilliant and creative monologue. The next minute it's sucked into the vacuum of surgical criticality.

I turned right off Fourth Avenue onto Ninth Street and then into the hospital doctors' parking lot. I inserted the electronic card, and the railing opened up. The lot for the attending physicians was empty now, but not for long. It would soon be filled with cars branded Mercedes Benz, BMW, Lexus, and of course the customary large jeeps and SUVs whose farthest off road trek would be crossing a grassy median. I cast another glance at my watch as I rushed towards the OR from the physicians' parkade. Forty-three minutes.

On time.

▲▼▲▼▲

Steam rose from the sink as hot water rushed in. Our dedicated resident Pavel Radezki and I watched the patient being put to sleep behind the glass wall and discussed the planned procedure as we washed our hands. I was calm, my neck muscles relaxed and the movements of my hands smooth. It is always the same: once the action approaches, the resentment of being bothered in the middle of the night is forgotten. Then, I'm eager to get started, sensing none of the usual tension I'd feel when scrubbing during the day for a major elective case.

With a non-emergency case the paralyzing jitteriness will subside only after the abdomen is gaping wide open. That's when the job really begins. Any error, misjudgment, wrong movement or false decision can lead to a long list of complications. If you lose him, everybody will tell you that you should have known better. Worst of all, you will keep reminding yourself that it was your fault. If he heals without incident, it's no big deal. You're a surgeon. It's your job.

On the other hand, in an emergency you operate on a dying patient—or to be more precise, on a patient who will die if you do not operate on him. He's got everything to lose, and you can win it all for him. You're the star kicker fielded in the final seconds of the game to take your team to victory, kicking from a distance never before achieved. You've been practicing your whole career to perform above expectations, but if you can't that's OK. If he dies, no one will blame you. They'll understand you did the best you could. Like a soldier on the losing side, perhaps you made a mistake, perhaps not.

If he survives, however, you are a hero. Scrutiny is blind to the celebrated.

"Dr. Zohar—" Radezki began as he rinsed the antiseptic solution from his arms. I heard alarm in the tone of his voice. Something was worrying him. This was definitely the wrong time to get sidetracked by negativity.

"What's the matter, Pav?" Forgetting that my face was covered by mask I hoped my smile was encouraging. He was hesitant nonetheless.

"Well, you know—in two weeks I'll have to present Dr. Mantzur's recent fuckup at the M&M." Thank heavens it has nothing to do with this operation! Instead, it was about the M&M, the "Morbidity and Mortality" meetings where we regularly discuss events and complications leading to a patient's death. Pavel was obviously worried about getting into trouble with Mantzur, that's all. It was not easy for a resident to present at these meetings when one of the big shots like Mantzur was involved. "I started to research the literature you suggested. I've only just begun but I must say, it looks like a pretty touchy case…"

I decided to downplay the issue—to get him focused before we enter the OR.

"A touchy case in a long series of touchy cases, Pav. Nobody gives a shit. I doubt whether Mantzur will even be present and if he will, no one will dare to open his mouth. Anyway, I hope that Winestone will let you present the case; you know that he asked us not to disclose Mantzur's fuck-ups. But we have to. Don't you worry; I'll be there to support you. And anyway; first it's Moshesh's turn. Come next Tuesday and he'll have to present that other fatality of Mantzur's—the carotid, remember?"

With raised hands Radezki turned around, pushing open the OR door with his shoulder. His eyes laughed above the mask. *He got the point. Good!*

"Entertaining piece of work, eh?"

I shrugged and raised my eyebrows. Entertaining? Radezki took refuge in sarcasm. Every surgeon does. It's a stupid defense mechanism, but it helps one to function properly. I rinsed my arms and hands as well and followed him into the room. There we let the scrub nurse gown us up. Radezki was eager; I could sense it. I knew he wanted to give it his best. Not everybody in this hospital did. Some of my colleagues provided more "entertainment" than good surgery.

Five minutes later I watched Radezki make the first cut. His hand was steady as the scalpel slid across the belly. Framed by the dark-green cloth, the flesh separated, exposing a solid layer of yellow fat. That close to the surface it always takes a while for things to get messy after the smaller blood vessels realize they've been severed.

"Just move the fucking lights," I hissed. I was getting impatient. The initial high had long since worn off. The case had turned out to be a pretty standard one. I knew what the problem was, and I knew how to fix it. Radezki stared at me above his mask, his blue eyes magnified by a pair of thick glasses. I knew he was a good guy and that he didn't get a moment's sleep the whole night, but who said surgical residents should sleep? Did I sleep being on call every other night? Did anyone feel pity for me? *Just calm down and let him continue.* "Yes, yes, yes. Shine it here. Not there. No, no, no. We work here," I pointed, my index finger drifting in a casual circle around the upper abdomen. "Up here under the diaphragm—not in the bloody pelvis. Damn it, Pav, can't you see?"

We still had a long way to go. *Probably another two hours at least.* Still, I was irritated. *How many years do I have to tolerate night surgery with double left-handed residents, semi-comatose nurses and clueless anesthetists?* As the years passed, my inner exasperation grew. I could complete that operation in an hour or so. *For God's sake! Let me only move to the right side of the table and we are out of here for breakfast.* Having dealt with hundreds of bleeding stomachs I could do this operation with my eyes closed. But this was a teaching program and Radezki had to learn. Next year he should be able to cut some poor bugger somewhere in a small American town—on his own. *He is a good chap, old Radezki. I like him. So let him continue, just calm down and teach him how to do it. That's what I'm paid for.*

"John, please open your eyes and pull on this retractor..." The junior resident appeared to have fallen asleep while leaning on the hooked metal instrument with which he should have pulled the rib cage upwards. That would have, ideally, enabled us to expose the liver and the duodenum hidden underneath. That is, if he was doing what he was supposed to.

"Yes sir," responded the somnolent resident. I was sort of fond of John. He was a disciplined and bright young man who joined our program just a few months prior from a prestigious medical school in California. He was qualified for an Ivory Tower program, perhaps not Johns Hopkins or the Massachusetts General, but a solid university hospital. *Why on earth did he choose us—a surgical program in a community dungeon?*

But who cares? He'll become a sound resident even though he is half asleep. Junior residents sleepwalk, sleepsit or sleepstand all the time. It's part of the deal; a character building exercise. I don't mind operating with a sleeping team as long as they move according to my commands. Years ago, I remembered, I replaced a ruptured abdominal aortic aneurysm with everybody around me sleeping—the assistants, the nurses and the anesthetist. I had to wake up the anesthetist at the end of the operation so he could wake up the patient. It's always funny in retrospect, provided things went smoothly. That time, at least, they did.

"OK, Pavel, what do you want to do next?" Radezki finished mobilizing the duodenum from its attachments to the posterior wall of the abdomen.

"I want to open the duodenum and deal with the bleeding vessel. A pyloroplasty incision..." He could see by my look that he wasn't exactly wrong but that there might have been something he wasn't considering. He hesitated long enough for me to interrupt politely.

"If he's stable we might as well start with the vagotomy. Dr. Cohen, how is the patient doing? Blood pressure?" No answer. "What is coming out of the gastric tube? Any evidence of active bleeding?"

Silence.

I looked behind the screen dividing the sterile operative field from the patient's head where our anesthesia resident sat, or rather, napped, apparently hypnotized by the monotonous chirping on the monitors. I saw the face mask sloppily applied over his bearded face. *Fuck it.* His senior anesthetist hit the bed as soon as the patient went under, and now this creep was dozing off—almost in as deep a sleep as the patient.

18

"Doctor Cooooohen!" I growled at him. "Hey, please wake up. This isn't an ingrown toenail procedure; this is a major operation on a sick patient. Please be so kind to monitor your patient." Nothing. "How is he anyway?" No response. I was just muttering to myself by now.

I rolled my eyes at Radezki who responded in kind. He was my only ally here in our eternal struggle against nature, death, administration, malpractice and all the non-surgical clowns, including those in anesthesia. I looked around. The scrub technician appeared drowsy, her semi-closed eyes fixed somewhere on the green tiled wall. When was the last time I operated with an operating room nurse who was wide awake? One who knew what was happening, recognized the steps of any operation better than the senior resident, and handed you the right instruments before you even had a chance to ask? It was years ago, in another country. In this hospital they were only interested in money; they wanted to save and profit. A scrub technician takes only a year or so to educate, not the several years required to produce a registered nurse. They're paid peanuts compared to what a real nurse gets. Who cares if they know nothing about the operation? They're cheap and, besides, aren't they just supposed to pass instruments—if they can do so with over-sized gloves clumsily stretched over their over-sized artificial fingernails.

"Let's start with the vagotomy, Pavel. You have fifteen minutes. Afterwards I'll take over."

I looked at the clock on the wall: it was 7 a.m. Soon the day cases would start and they'd be nagging us to hurry up.

"Now pull on your retractor," I told John, demonstrating with my hand how to do so. Radezki mobilized the left lobe of the liver and exposed the esophagus. Hiding there are the two vagus nerves connecting the stomach to the brain. You cut them to dry up the gastric acid production and thereby heal the ulcer. Radezki did it nicely; he pushed his long index finger behind the esophagus and brought up the right nerve to be divided. His face was near mine, I could feel the heat

19

emerging from his sweaty forehead. *What a guy. I shouldn't be so tough on him.*

"OK, Dr. Radezki. Great job. Your Mom back in Poland would be proud. We have the vagi. Now let's leave a large pack here, yes, here. Now deal with the ulcer. Start with ..."

"Good morning, gentlemen." Without turning around I recognized the loud accented voice of Dr. Mahmud Sorki. *What the hell is he doing here so early and in my operating room?*

"Good morning, Dr. Sorki. How can I help you?" I turned my head around with my hands still immersed in the abdomen.

"Ha! Radezki," Dr. Sorki snickered. "I see you're having fun. A big operation, eh? But you know what? You are doing it with the wrong surgeon. This isn't Zohar's case. This is my patient."

Sorki continued addressing the resident: "Mr. Pellegrino is Dr. Susman's patient, and then he was referred to me. The ER screwed up—I should've been notified. I am scrubbing up and will help you finish this minor procedure. With me you'll be out in thirty minutes. You know how fast I am. Ha!" Sorki laughed out loud at himself, which wasn't uncommon. A few others laughed but hadn't been paying enough attention to realize why. I blinked a few times, trying to digest what was happening. There was no way he would have showed up if the patient hadn't had 'good insurance.' I should have been used to it by then, but do you ever really get used to a canker sore?

Big Mo—that's what they called him—disappeared behind the white door. Mrs. McFadden, the OR nurse-manager, gave me a dry smile. "Dr. Zohar, you better leave now. Dr. Sorki is right—it really is his case. It's a dreadful mistake. I am so sorry."

I knew she was his puppy. He got her the job, just as he did for half of this hospital's staff. *He's probably fucking her too,* I thought to myself dryly. Rumors rumble here and there about Big Mo's various sexual appetites.

I removed my bloody gloves slowly, trying to stretch-shoot them into the trashcan at the corner of the room. I missed. Nobody said a word. They all knew that Big Mo was the tallest hog in the trough. Why get into trouble? I tore the mask off my face and looked at Radezki. He winked at me. He was on my side.

"Have a nice day, ladies." I bowed to the scrub technician and the floating nurse, fully awakened and enjoying every bit of the scene—two filthy-rich surgeons fighting over a patient. How amusing!

"Thanks, Pavel. You did a fine job thus far. Just try not to kill this guy." I kicked open the door towards the corridor. As I exited I caught sight of the patient's head, covered with the obligatory spaghetti of tubes, pipes and lines. I'd almost forgotten that he was a human being. His wife was probably sitting outside. *Should I go and talk to her? No, that fat pig Susman probably gave her his usual spiel already:* 'Dr. Sorki is our best surgeon. Dr. Zohar started the operation and now Dr. Sorki is performing the crucial steps. Your husband is in the best hands.' I knew the drill. It was not the first time they kidnapped a patient from my colleagues or me. *But today—what chutzpa! Stealing a patient right off the operating table!*

I removed my green scrub cap, slipped into a white coat and marched towards the lounge where fresh bagels, cream cheese and coffee were waiting. I'd had nothing since they woke me up. When the high of the operation subsides I am always starving. As I made my way down the halls towards the elevator I became angrier thinking about what had just happened.

I pushed the appropriate button and waited for the elevator to arrive. My eyes scanned back and forth from the ceiling and down to the floor. From one piece of artwork to the next. My temperature rose despite my lame attempts at diverting my attention. Finally, the elevator arrived and I found it to be empty. I stepped in and twisted slightly to pick the floor. Once the doors were closed and the elevator accelerated upwards, I gave the wall behind me a quick kick. Then another.

"Fuck!" I could have strangled that bastard.

At that hour the attending doctors' lounge was empty except for two drowsy semi-retired private physicians absorbed in the financial pages of the New York Report. The TV on the wall—permanently tuned to CNN—whispered the morning's stock exchange news as if it could guess the common interests of the doctors who frequent the lounge. On the wall were group photographs from recent hospital gala dinners: Tuxedo-clad, self satisfied and possibly drunk faces. At the corner presided a king-size coffee maker with two full coffee jars. One was regular, and the other decaf. My attention focused on the mountain of bagels spread on the surface below the window—fresh bagels from a nearby bakery. Only in Brooklyn can one find such a delicious selection: plain, sesame seeds, poppy seeds, garlic, onion, salt, egg, whole wheat, anything. I cracked a poppy seed bagel and smeared it with a thick layer of full-fat cream cheese. A mouthful—what a delight! With half a bagel stuffed in my mouth and a cup of coffee in my hand, I returned to the elevator and headed to the Department of Surgery offices on the sixth floor.

My own office was quite large and boasted a high ceiling and thick walls. This was how they built offices in the nineteenth century, not the plastic walls and hollow plywood dividers of today. The wide window invited sunshine and the sounds of life from Sixth Avenue below. I was proud of my west-facing vista: First there was a church. Behind it were the raised tracks of the F- train, which regularly crawls from Coney Island to Manhattan. A little further behind that stands the Statue of Liberty, so near but diminutive among the skyscrapers in the jagged background of the city. Staten Island bound ferries pass it all the time, full of gawking sightseers and commuters alike. On the horizon I could make out Newark Airport and the constant file of dots approaching or leaving it from north and south. One could stand at my window and be entertained for hours.

"Good morning, Dr. Zohar." I turned around to see Anne, my secretary, smiling at the door. "You arrived early today." I returned her impish grin. She was a petite blonde with a pleasant but scarred face that was heavily made up. Her scarring appeared to be the consequence of severe juvenile acne, but it was usually covered up with thick layers of face paint. But no amount of make-up could cover the blue bruise around her left eye; Anne was a chronically battered wife. She denied it but we all knew that her husband, almost double her size in height and weight, used her as a punching bag. "Dr. Winestone asked to see you as soon as you came in."

"What does he want now?" I growled, my smile forgotten. She shrugged. *Why would he tell her?* "OK, I'll see him."

"I heard about you and Dr. Sorki at the OR. I am sorry—"

"Fuck Sorki," I snapped, but not harshly. My tone was of disgust, but she knew I wasn't aiming at her. "His day will come." I smiled at Anne as I slipped out on my way to Dr. Winestone's office.

▲▼▲▼▲

"Lawrence Winestone MD, Chairman" declared the prominent brass sign on the heavy mahogany door. I knocked and entered without waiting for a reply, as usual. Winestone had a huge corner office, double the size of mine. I always got the feeling that I was walking into some medieval chamber. The windows occupy two walls and face towards Brooklyn so the Statue of Liberty is not visible from there. Exorbitant furniture cluttered with African and Asian curios and a huge mahogany desk almost made up for it.

Absorbed in his journals and books behind the enormous desk sat the Chairman of Surgery—Larry to his friends—Winestone. He was in his mid sixties, with a balding degree of thin grayish hair, of short stature and stocky,

obviously well fed, and had a pudgy but pleasant face—
Didn't my wife once say that he looks like a hamster? A nose
characteristic of our race supported a thick pair of eyeglasses
and a ponderous double chin drooped over a sharp red Gucci
necktie. The chairman was immaculately dressed in a dark
striped suit, buttoned-down white shirt, and Italian shoes. He
shopped in London or Paris, on his yearly trips, or in Manhattan's best shops—only during sales, of course.

I'd known Winestone since 1995 when he recruited me
from Minnesota. What an interesting and colorful character;
his life's story could fill a book! On a misty and lazy winter
Sunday afternoon, as we relaxed by the fireside at his mansion—just across the bay from where the house mentioned in
The Great Gatsby stood—he recounted to us an abbreviated
version of his biography. His short legs dangled over the edge
of the leathered sofa, the gray water of the sound reflecting
between the bare trees. We sipped from glasses filled with
terribly sweet Tokai wine and listened to his perfect English,
still heavily flavored by a mid-European accent.

He was the only son of the Weinsteins, a middle class
couple in Bucharest. At the end of the war he was a lonely,
terrified child hidden in a cellar while his parents hid elsewhere.

After the war the Russians arrived and then the Commu-
nists took over. Leo, or Leopold, Weinstein—that was his
name then—was shipped to Canada by his parents. Armed
with the number of his father's pre-war account in Geneva,
he was well financed. The money enabled him to enter a posh
boarding school in Ottawa. I imagined the young Leo, his
name now anglicized to Lawrence Winestone: a small, dark
and chubby boy among the Canadian WASPs, ridiculed for
his thick Romanian accent and uselessness in sports. That
was probably where he'd developed his thick skin and an
ability to survive and excel. The qualities were supported by
wit, wisdom and amazing personal charm.

Next followed medical school in Toronto and surgical
training in the première centers in England where he received

personal instruction by surgical giants. In the late 1960s he arrived in the USA with a fellowship in Boston and a promising faculty position in the Midwest. In his forties he was selected to lead the surgery department for the Jewish Island Hospital, becoming one of the youngest to hold the position of Chairman of Surgery in the USA. He kept the position almost twenty years.

Dr. Winestone put down his journal, looked above his glasses, and smiled at me. "How are you Marc?" *I am tired, I just got booted out of the operating room by that greedy, ignorant bastard Sorki and I'm still angry. Evidence suggests so far that this is going to be a really bad fucking day!*

"I'm doing well. Thank you, Dr. Winestone. You wanted to see me?"

"I just wanted to talk to you about my upcoming lecture. Perhaps you could help me." Looking up, he noticed my scrubs. "You have been operating? What did you do?"

"Just a simple upper GI hemorrhage, probably from a duodenal ulcer. Silverstein called me this morning so I started the case with Radezki." I shifted slightly on my feet as my voice changed into an angrier gear. "Then the case was kidnapped by Sorki! The monster forced me to step aside and that bitch McFadden let him do it!"

"Calm down, Marc." Winestone leaned forward over his desk and got to his feet. "Your head is turning the same color as my tie! You'll have a stroke one of these days." Winestone came around from behind his desk and grabbed my left elbow. He grabbed everybody by the left elbow; it was a part of his charm. He then guided me onto his plush leather couch that was for all accounts and purposes even more comfortable than my bed. "How many times have I told you not to take these things so seriously?"

I didn't answer, although I knew it had been quite a few times.

"Look at me, Marc. Am I excited? Am I upset?"

"But Dr. Winestone—" I said, resisting his soothing demeanor, "—we can't go on like this! They've kidnapped

25

our patients from the emergency room at night, but now they are doing it in broad daylight! Most of these patients end up dead somehow and that is not acceptable!" Winestone made a half assed shooshing motion with his hands. His next words were hushed.

"Keep your voice down or the secretaries will hear. You never know who stands behind the door. For all I know this room may be bugged. See the new ceiling?" He pointed, trying to distract me. "New lamps? Nice, eh? Only Mantzur could squeeze money for renovations from Howard. You know how stingy he normally is. I told you that Mantzur would be a valuable member of our team as a Vice Chairman. Your room needs to be re-furbished, too. As a matter of fact, Mantzur has promised to arrange for it. You'll have to select new furniture, think about the wallpaper as well—" Under more normal circumstances, the thought might have appealed to me.

"—I do not need any wallpaper from Mantzur."

"Marc, look at me. Do you think that I'm stupid?" Winestone placed his hand on my forearm.

"No, you are not." He stared me right in the eye, and my spoken truth allowed me to look at him right back.

"Nor am I new in this business. I've been a Chairman for more than twenty years. How long are you with us now? Four years?"

"Three and a half," I corrected meekly.

"Well, I'm in my fifth year here." He took off his dirty glasses and polished the lenses with the tip of his necktie. "Seems ages since I left the JIH." He sighed deeply. "Do you think I do not know who Mantzur and Sorki are?"

I was becoming impatient. I knew he was gearing up for one of his template speeches, one that I could recite almost verbatim. "So do you want us to continue to eat shit? More shit every day?"

Winestone ignored me. "Marc, listen to me, there is nothing new here. Hospitals like this one exist all over the country. A few very good surgeons, many average surgeons

26

and a few guys like Sorki." He didn't mention Mantzur. He never liked to include old Mantzur in the same category as Sorki, but I wasn't going to let him get away with it this time.

"And Mantzur, also," I interjected.

"Marc, how long have Mantzur and Sorki been operating here?"

"I don't know—twenty years or more?"

"So, you see, these guys have been killing patients for more than twenty years. Do you think that we can stop them in one day? They kill and they will continue to kill. Our job here is to educate residents and to develop an academic atmosphere which gradually, perhaps, but surely, will modify even the bad guys. This takes time. It took me almost twenty years to bring the department at the JIH to what it has become." He could see I was losing my concentration, and thankfully steered himself away from that story. Finally, he concluded: "I agree with you that Sorki is a problem. We'll have to deal with him sooner or later. But remember—and how many times have I told you this—you never fight on two fronts. You have to compromise. Even Stalin signed a non aggression pact with Hitler." *A pact that, in June of 1941, was the cause of a lack of preparation and the greatest loss of life suffered by any nation in the history of modern warfare.* I didn't remind him.

Beverly, Winestone's executive secretary, interrupted his World War Two history lesson. She entered the room without knocking, which wasn't out of the ordinary.

"Dr. Winestone," she began in a deep and throaty voice. An associate of mine, Dr. Chaudri, had once joked about having heard her voice on 1-900-SECRETARY. At least, I think he was joking. Nothing about that woman would have surprised me. "Dr. Sorki's Medical Board office called to remind you about the dinner with him and Doctor Mantzur. They want to know whether you can make it this coming Wednesday. The Marco Polo, at six-thirty. I checked with your diary and it looks OK. Shall I confirm?"

"Thank you, Beverly. Yes, go ahead and confirm. Who is next on my schedule?" She didn't have to look into his schedule book to answer.

"Ms. McFadden is waiting outside to see you. That is, after you finish this meeting with Dr. Zohar. Un-scheduled as usual, I presume."

Beverly smiled sarcastically at me and left the room. She was in her early thirties, tall, blonde, with an attractive but angular face accentuated by a beautiful smile, firm legs and a well-sized backside. A typical New England girl in Brooklyn. Beverly and I were never best of friends, but we tolerated each other. Winestone liked her; he'd always appreciated a good-looking woman around him. He had emphasized time and again that his executive secretary had to be 'presentable.' I wasn't the only one who thought she was too good to be true. She had teased me a few times in the past and played on my temptations.

I'd resisted: I had to. To succumb to one's temptations in this environment would have been suicidal. Our previous department administrator, Tamara, a black girl who was dismissed by Dr. Winestone, had attempted to sue him and myself for sexual harassment. Him for repeatedly squeezing her elbow; me for undressing and changing to scrubs without closing my door. I quickly learned that in this country, in this town, any woman who is working around you could be dangerous.

Winestone returned to his desk and waved me away after a quick wink. *"I've got things under control. Trust me,"* it said.

▲▼▲▲▼▲

"Winestone's tactic is to wine and dine with the triumvirate, the monsters," I muttered to myself as I walked towards the floors for my daily rounds on my patients. On the seventh floor Radezki walked towards me with an intern and two serious looking students in his wake. The OR cap was still

28

perched on his head; he must have just finished up with Sorki. He eyed me slyly. I was curious about the words boiling towards his lips. He looked happy.

"Hey, Dr. Zohar. Are you interested in what Dr. Sorki and I did?"

"Yes, Pavel." Clearly the two students had no idea what we were talking about. The intern almost looked awake. "What did you and that creep do together? I hope that you didn't screw the poor bugger—"

"—Screw? Your chief resident Pavel screws nobody. Even Sorki kills no one when I am with him. When you left us—when you were told to leave us—we had just finished cutting the vagal nerves, right? So next we did a beautiful gastrectomy, forty-five minutes, piece of cake. We used staplers, no hand sutures or any bullshit..."

"Pavel, what kind of gastrectomy? Billroth I or II? Did you examine the duodenum? Did you see and secure the bleeding ulcer?"

Radezki removed his cap and scratched his thin blond hair and reflected. "We did a Billroth I, chopped off the distal stomach and hooked it to the duodenum. No, we did not look at the ulcer. We did not even open the duodenum. We did everything with staplers."

"Pavel," I said with as much sarcasm as I could muster, "do you believe in God?" His confused look rebounded off of both students and glanced off the intern. "Then pray. Pray that the base of the bleeding duodenal ulcer you left untouched won't re-bleed. In fact, what you did with your new buddy Sorki is remove the stomach without addressing the problem that prompted your operation. Capisce?"

Radezki seemed puzzled. No surgeon, not even a resident, enjoys being told a few minutes after an operation that his technical masterpiece is conceptually faulty.

"Dr. Zohar," he insisted. "Take it easy, will you? You and me did a vagotomy. We cut his nerves, reducing the acid output. This will prevent any recurrent hemorrhage."

29

Stupid, stupid Sorki, I thought to myself. *What a jerk. Steals my case, fucks up the patient and misleads the resident as well.*

"Look, Pavel. If I were you I would now watch this guy carefully. I bet he'll re-bleed. Good luck."

3

Adverse Outcomes

One should only advise surgery when there is a
reasonable chance of success. To operate without
having a chance means to prostitute the beautiful art
and science of surgery.
—Theodor Billroth, 1829-1894

"I present the case of MJ, a ninety-year-old female patient. Diagnosis: right carotid stenosis. Complications: stroke and mortality. Procedure: right carotid endartrectomy. Surgeon: Dr. Mantzur. Resident: Dr. Johannes Moshesh."

It was Tuesday, 3 October 1998, 8 am. We were in the hospital's main auditorium. The weekly Morbidity and Mortality conference—known to everybody as the M&M—was starting. It is probably the hottest ritual in the life of any teaching surgical department in the country. The purpose of the M&M is to discuss all so-called 'adverse outcomes' generated by any member of the Department. At the Park Hospital, we always had a long list of cases to discuss, and a waiting period of a couple of weeks between the actual event and its eventual analysis was not unusual. But then, of course, the patients concerned no longer stood to benefit from those discussions; it was the future patients who might benefit.

The aim of the M&Ms is to educate the responsible surgeon and help him learn from his own mistakes. The best we can hope for is that repeatedly exposing members of staff to the mistakes of others will prevent them from making similar errors later on. The least we can hope for is the prevention of complications by intimidation. "If I know that all my mishaps will be routinely exposed to my colleagues," this line of reasoning goes, "I will be more cautious. I will try to do fewer

31

foolish things. I will ask for advice when unsure how to do a certain procedure." No one likes to be embarrassed in public.

In order to achieve such ambitious goals, the M&M has to be objective. The rules are simple: all complications and fatalities that occur in any patient treated by any member of the department should be presented. A complication is a complication, regardless of whether the eventual outcome is a triumph or a tragedy.

Also, the M&M ought to be a democratic forum. The boss's blunder or that of the local 'surgical giant' is as interesting—if not more so—as that caused by a junior resident. We know that in many corners of the world M&M meetings are not conducted at all and that mistakes, errors and failures are swept under the carpet to the misfortune of an unknowing public. In still other places, M&Ms exist only in name and are used to present noncontroversial cases or the latest stories of success.

Whether or not the M&M is objective and accomplishes its objectives depends mainly on the local chairman and the political environment. That day, Dr. Larry Winestone was conducting the meeting. The resident who shared the stage with the chairman and would be presenting the case was Dr. Moshesh. His huge bulk dwarfed Winestone's comparatively diminutive though not small frame.

Bashir Bachus, the head of the surgical intensive care unit, sat at my side. I whispered into his ear: "Surprise, surprise! Ol' Larry shows his face when one of the Padrino's disasters is being presented." Bachus said nothing, but I had a feeling I knew what he was thinking.

Winestone peeked above his glasses at the printed summary of the case. "Tell us what happened, Dr. Moshesh."

"This elderly woman was presented to the vascular service with transient ischemic attacks involving the right cerebral hemisphere. Arterial Duplex scan demonstrated a seventy percent stenosis of the right carotid artery. After medical clearance was obtained, the patient underwent a carotid endartrectomy under general anesthesia using a shunt. The operation was uneventful—"

"—Herb Susman cleared this poor woman," Malcolm Rusk, the director of surgical education who sat on my other side, buzzed into my ear. "Fat Herbi would clear a dead person for surgery if Mantzur was cutting."

There was a hush in the auditorium. The tense silence was not unusual when the weekly habitual complication of Dr. Mantzur, the New York Park Hospital's Godfather, was being presented. Mantzur had a hearing aid, but he didn't use it. Instead, he cupped a hand behind his right ear and appeared to listen attentively. He sat in the center of the second row.

The seating pattern of surgeons at M&Ms follows an unwritten law. Whether the M&M takes place in New York or Los Angeles the arrangement is predictable: the chairman will sit alone in the center of the first row; the person who is second in command sits directly behind him in the second row. One or two rows back, usually on the right, are the full-time members of the faculty, ready to support the chairman. In front and on the left one will find the vocal old timers. The next segment on both sides of the aisle is reserved for senior residents and less established members of the voluntary staff. The back row, just in front of the usual spread of coffee, bagels, cream cheese and doughnuts, is the domain of the 'opposition'—those who always wanted to be a chairperson and never made it. Sometimes it includes other frustrated surgeons. The center seats are occupied by a mass of medical students who consider the event as interesting as a Broadway show. One would also find a gaggle of junior residents who struggle to remain awake. Their day usually begins at five thirty a.m. with morning rounds and then snoozing through the basic science lecture.

"What happened then?" Winestone adopted his characteristic calm and objective tone.

Moshesh talked into the microphone. "In the recovery room the patient failed to wake up from anesthesia and was noted to suffer from a dense left hemiparesis. We rushed her back into the OR and on re-exploration of the wound found the artery pulsatile and without a thrombus. A postoperative CT revealed a massive stroke on the side of the operation. The patient expired the following day."

I couldn't bear to listen. In my mind I had long since nicknamed Mantzur "Terminator One." We were presented with a similar case of his every week, and yet even he was outperformed by long and far by "Terminator Two," Dr. Mahmud Sorki. My lists were full of their cases; I knew their patterns. Full names are never mentioned during the M&M, but I could have presented Mrs. MJ's story in full detail without looking at her chart…

▲▼◢◣▼▲

For six years Mrs. Magdalena Jovanelli, a ninety-year-old great grandmother, had lived in a respectable Italian nursing home. Her general health had been deteriorating steadily and she was confined to her bed and wheelchair. Much to her family's dismay she lost much of her neurological faculties, recognizing no one but her elderly son. One day after developing severe diarrhea with signs of dehydration and extreme confusion, her internist Dr. Harold Asher admitted her to the New York Park Hospital. The diarrhea promptly responded to drugs, and her mental state improved once the dehydration was reversed with intravenous fluids. A computerized tomography (CT) scan of the head was performed to check for a brain hemorrhage as a cause of confusion, but it revealed only brain atrophy, the normal shrinkage associated with old age. In fact, on Sunday, two days after admission the nurse overheard her shouting at her son: "Alfredo, bring Pasta!" It was probable that at this stage she could have been discharged to spend the rest of her life at the nursing home.

But this was not what destiny had in mind. On the admission day the second-year medical resident examined Mrs. Jovanelli from head to toe. Carefully listening with the stethoscope to her neck, he discovered a *bruit* on the right side: a hissing sound suggesting a narrowing in the carotid, one of the two main arteries supplying the brain. On the morning rounds the dedicated resident conveyed his finding to Dr. Asher.

"She is ninety," was Asher's reply, "bed-ridden, no real symptoms of brain malfunction that could be attributed to narrow arteries. And anyway, even if the arteries were narrow, who would operate on this old bird?"

The junior resident, remembering last Sunday's textbook reading, persisted. "Couldn't we just do a Duplex? You know, just to visualize the carotid artery, see the degree of narrowing?"

"OK, OK," Asher snapped, thinking about those young academically orientated residents who wanted to order any useless test they've heard about. "Order a Duplex." *But then, who cares? She has Medicare and that will pay, right?* That, and the fact that the vascular laboratory performing the test was owned by the hospital and run by Houssein Ilkadi, the chief of vascular surgery. Furthermore, Ilkadi was sort of a friend of Asher's. *Hang on—didn't Ilkadi hint at something just a week ago, in the elevator.* "Harry, we would greatly appreciate seeing more patients referred to our lab by you. They tell me that you cover three nursing homes—you surely must have suitable patients!" *Yeah, old Ilkadi's a good guy.* He had supported Asher during the Medical Board hearing last year when Asher was summoned because he had forgotten being on call and switched off his beeper...*OK. Let the hospital earn some extra bucks.*

"Listen, Rogers," Asher said. "Should the Duplex be positive, invite Dr. Mantzur for a vascular consult." He smiled to himself. Mantzur, the sly old fox that he was, would operate on anything he could lay his hands on and produced enough complications to feed all of them. Asher chuckled, relishing his own macabre thoughts. On the other hand—and this he found less amusing—Mantzur had never referred a patient to him. What a schmuck! The internist's examination required to clear Mrs. Jovanelli for anesthesia and surgery—a medical check-up proclaiming her to be fit enough to survive the process—will in all likelihood be done by Mantzur's protégé Herb Susman, and not by Asher himself. But that was life. Asher had long ago accepted that Mantzur was the local king; a sacrifice or two to him every few months was definitely worthwhile. Yes, Mantzur had aged and his surgical skills were declining rapidly. But still, Mantzur was influential. *And he is such a gentleman!*

A day later, Alfredo Jovanelli—Mrs. Jovanelli's son—was perched in a replica of a deep Victorian chair facing Dr. Joseph Mantzur, the renowned vascular and thoracic surgeon. While Dr. Mantzur studied Mrs. Jovanelli's chart Alfredo looked around, noting that the desk alone in that office was probably worth a few grand. The pink carpet was deep and soft; expensively framed diplomas and a few reproductions covered the wallpapered walls. Behind Mantzur's desk stood a huge bookshelf stuffed with impressive looking leather bound medical books. The son shifted his eyes back onto the doctor's desk, catching a glimpse of a framed picture: a younger Mantzur dressed in white with a woman and two kids, all smiling as they stood on the deck of a splendid yacht. Dr. Mantzur looked up at Alfredo Jovanelli, removing his gold-framed reading glasses. A brass table lamp lit his tanned but aging face. Mantzur toyed with a paper knife between his two hands as if it was a surgical instrument. It wasn't long before Alfredo noticed the three rings on Mantzur's long, well-manicured fingers: marriage, college and another ring of gold and diamonds. The doctor started speaking with his soft musical voice. The accent was obvious, but hard to place.

"Mr. Jovanelli, you see, the tests we conducted show that your mother has a significant obstruction in her right carotid artery. Here, look at this…" He pointed with the paper knife at a picture: A printout of the Duplex study.

"You know what this is?" he continued. "A big artery which supplies the brain with blood; and here you see the blockage. It's not unusual. You know, all those years of mozzarella, prosciutto and pasta—I bet your mother was an excellent cook, am I right? A real Italian Mama, yes? Ah, I can imagine—"

Alfredo swallowed and nodded; he was nervous though slightly relieved by the doctor's failed attempt to lighten the mood. Mantzur leaned forward and crossed his elegant dark hands on the desk in a solemn gesture. He smiled at Alfredo as he confided in him. "Besides, I adore Italian cuisine—anyway, where was I? Yes, the blockage in your mother's artery. As you know. No blood, no brain—right? You have seen the results. It is really remarkable how well your mother has coped under these circumstances—but I must tell you there is a strong chance that the blood supply of her brain will deteriorate significantly if nothing is done to reverse the process. You see…" Mantzur exhaled and leaned back again while Alfredo Jovanelli, anxious not to miss a word, instinctively clasped his hands around the armrests of the large leather chair. It seemed determined to swallow him up.

Mantzur's eyes adopted a grave expression. The surgeon met the son's anxious, questioning gaze full on. Seconds passed in silence. Then the faintest of smiles began developing on Mantzur's face again: "Well. How lucky that Dr. Asher referred your dear mother to our hospital. Because we, in fact, can help her immediately and help her avoid that risk. The signora needs a specialized operation to unblock her artery. This operation is called an endartrectomy."

The son looked skeptical. "An operation? At her age? Will she take it?"

Dr. Mantzur stood up with a swift, energetic movement, displaying his expensively tailored dark striped suit, hanging loosely on his thin body. "Oh, your mom is in great shape. Dr. Asher did a terrific job on her. Dr. Asher and me are good old friends; he trusts me. But I always prefer to obtain a second opinion. I will ask our expert Dr. Susman to assess your mother as well. He will clear her for surgery; he clears all my patients for any operation I do. He knows what he's doing. An excellent physician. A professor, you know. We're taking all precautions, Mr. Jones." Even Mantzur lost himself in his rambling.

"Jovanelli," the younger man corrected, void of all expression. He was overwhelmed. A perfect target for manipulation, Mantzur knew well.

"Yes, yes. I apologize, Mr. Jovanelli."

"But will she withstand the anesthesia and operation at her age? She is ninety years old."

"Of course, of course. These operations we do in under an hour. In fact, I perform a few of those every week."

Mantzur stepped closer to Alfredo, who was struggling to get up from the deep chair. His legs had gone numb from sitting in such an unusually low position. Mantzur put his right hand on Jovanelli's shoulder and leaned towards him. He fixed his soft dark brown eyes on the man. "Mr. Jovanelli, let me be perfectly honest with you. You and I, we do not want your dear mother to lose her mind again, or to develop a stroke—is this not so?"

Jovanelli swallowed hard.

"Dr. Mantzur, Dr. Mantzur," the overhead sound system blared its metallic announcement. "Please contact the OR immediately." The surgeon glanced at his square-shaped gold watch: "Mr. Jones, um, Jovanelli, the OR is waiting for me, another carotid endartrectomy. I'll do your Mom personally, tomorrow at eight a.m. I must run. Nice meeting you. Please excuse me." Waving his hand, the surgeon ran out, leaving the son speechless in the chair. When the secretary entered to show him out he noticed how tidy this room was. No clatter of books or journals on the huge desk or the coffee table. Dr. Mantzur seemed to be a very organized man.

A few hours later, back at home, Mr. Jovanelli spoke on the phone with his son Frank Jovanelli, a successful psychiatrist in Boston. "Listen Franco, Granny needs an operation, a blockage in her neck—yes, an artery." He recounted the whole story to his son as best as he could.

"But Dad?" Frank argued, "is the operation really necessary? And who is that Dr. Mantzur anyway? Is he good? Why don't you bring Grandma here to Boston for a second opinion?"

"Frank, the surgeon says that this is urgent; she may develop a stroke or something. He is a famous surgeon, thirty-five years in the hospital, very established! I asked Dr. Asher about him to make sure—and you know what he told me? He said that when it comes to veins Mantzur is the absolute best."

"Dad, they're not veins but arteries, a-r-t-e-r-i-e-s! And Dad, what's the rush? I really don't understand this. Please tell them to wait until next week, I'll try to fly over Sunday."

"Frank, it is a small operation, when you come on Sunday, Mama will be probably home. Ciao Franco." And that, unfortunately, was the beginning of the end for Mrs. Jovanelli.

Next morning Mr. Jovanelli accompanied his ninety-year-old mother to the OR, shouting in her ears in Italian. Mrs. Jovanelli did not wake up from the carotid endartrectomy performed by Dr. Mantzur. During the operation she suffered a massive stroke, which destroyed the right side of her brain. It was the side supplied by the artery operated upon. She died a day later, allowing ample time for her grandson to arrive from Boston to attend the funeral.

▲▼▲▼▲

Dr. Moshesh finished the brief presentation of the case. He dried the sweat from his face. He was a big guy and he sweat a lot. Dr. Winestone looked up. "What can you tell us about this complication? Was it preventable, avoidable?"

The resident shrugged. "Dr. Winestone, the operation was uneventful. We had no problems…"

Winestone leaned over and pinched the resident on his left elbow: "Whaddya mean no problems? The patient died. This is no problem?"

Loud laughter erupted from the audience, stirring the slumber of not a few junior residents. They looked around briefly, quickly lost interest and started napping on their other hand. Just about everyone else appreciated the chairman's sense of humor. They knew that Moshesh was not terribly smart and was digging his own grave. "In fact, we were very fast. We cleaned the artery in forty-five minutes. We used a shunt to perfuse the brain," Moshesh said, moistening his lips. A few of the junior residents started sitting up and shifting in their seats to get more comfortable.

"Were you happy at the end of the operation?" asked Winestone.

"Yes, we were happy!" Moshesh almost screamed.

The audience knew what to expect; this was a part of the weekly ritual. Slightly funny but predictable, that is unless someone dared open his mouth. I looked around. Mantzur hid behind his poker face, and in the back Sam Glatman was sulking. Sam was a private vascular surgeon who abhorred Mantzur. I doubted that he'd speak up.

Winestone addressed Houssein Ilkadi, the chief of vascular surgery, a Turdistan born private surgeon. "If this were your patient, would the results have been different?" This was Winestone's famous gimmick. Guest lecturers loved such a direct question. It made the M&Ms more objective.

Ilkadi, a short thin man in his early fifties and completely bald, was known as a technically solid surgeon of very good judgment. His comments at the M&M meeting were usually informative and balanced—unless the discussion involved his friends, mentors or partners. Ilkadi pronounced his words with precision. "Dr. Winestone," he said, "I had the opportunity to read the Duplex. It showed a seventy percent occlusion in the right internal carotid. This is a significant lesion, which, in a symptomatic patient—as this lady was, indicates the need for an operation. Indeed, we are told here that she suffered from transient ischemic attacks. As you know, recent prospective randomized trials from this country as well as from Europe have demonstrated that the operation would have been appropriate even in the absence of any symptoms. Therefore, I find the indication for surgery appropriate. As to this unfortunate complication, we know that the combined mortality and stroke rate after such operations is five percent in the best hands and in the top centers. Clearly Dr. Mantzur took all the usual precautions, including administration of heparin and insertion of an intra-luminal shunt. He re-explored her immediately which is also appropriate. Yes, the outcome is sad, but I do not see how it could have been prevented or better managed. Operating on these old patients is risky. We have to take risks like these. We are surgeons."

"Anybody want to comment? Anyone think that the complication could have been avoided or better handled?"

Silence. The few vascular surgeons present stared at their hands. Sam Glatman winked at me but wouldn't open his mouth. *Screw Ilkadi. What a bullshitter. To operate on a ninety-year-old bedridden woman is crazy.* Ilkadi himself would not have touched her, but he was prepared to lie in public to defend his old mentor. Another kill for Terminator One.

I raised my hand and began to talk before being acknowledged by the Chairman. "Dr. Moshesh," I said clearly, "could you please tell us a little about the exact nature of the patient's symptoms? You told us about TIAs. Could you be more specific?"

Winestone shot a look of mild irritation at me as if to say, "Shut up and let me close this case." Moshesh responded anyway: "Mmm, I guess she had TIAs. I can't tell you more. I never talked to the lady before the operation. She arrived at the OR directly from Medicine and then she died…"

Faint laughter could be heard from fellow residents. One should not say such things. Residents are supposed to know the patients they operate on. It is a key requirement stipulated by the American Board of Surgery that the operating resident evaluates his patient before the operation and takes active part in the postoperative care. Everyone knows that this is sometimes impossible and that the resident may first meet the patients when they are already deep under anesthesia, but to admit to it openly is daft!

"Dr. Mantzur, do you have anything to add?" Winestone addressed Mantzur himself, the attending surgeon responsible for the operation.

I stood up this time. I wasn't going to let this one slip so easily. *Fuck'em.* "Mr. Chairman—I asked Dr. Moshesh for information on the symptoms displayed by this patient. Could I have an answer, please?"

Winestone ignored me and looked at Mantzur, who responded in a low voice, talking quietly and swallowing words. "Dr. Winestone, this is an unfortunate case. A pleasant old lady, significant carotid lesion. The operation was routine. The shunt went in and out, no problems. I could not do it any better. Very unfortunate."

"Dr. Mantzur," I blurted out before Winestone could take over. "The symptoms. What were the symptoms? Was she symptomatic at all? What was her functional status? Could she walk?"

The Padrino turned around and looked in my direction. There was a hush in the auditorium. No one had ever directly questioned the great Mantzur about indications. For Mantzur, the indication for surgery was the desire to operate. He spoke with belabored patience. "Dr. Zohar," he said slowly and methodically, "the patient suffered from headaches and dizziness. She had a significant stenosis. Why didn't you listen to Dr. Ilkadi?"

"Because these are non-specific symptoms, not TIAs. This ninety-year-old lady was bedridden, is that not so? I do not think that there was any reason to operate on her."

Winestone held his hand up. "Let us move to the next case," he said, pointing to Dr. Malcolm Rusk, who took minutes of the meeting: "Dr. Rusk, what is our conclusion for the minutes?"

▲▼▲▼▲

Dr. Mahmud Sorki sat in the last row as usual, far above everybody. He always arrived late at the M&M and waited until there was a reason to demonstrate his presence or dissension. That particular day he stayed silent. He was not a vascular surgeon and never had much care for that field. He did not have the personality, the patience or indeed the obsession needed to successfully perform the finicky operations on tiny, calcified and sclerotic vessels. He would never comment on a vascular case, but today's meeting irritated him. *How dare that useless creep Zohar question Joseph Mantzur?* he was probably thinking to himself. *To ask Mantzur for the indication—ridiculous.* But then he, Mahmud Sorki, had known from the very first M&M meeting that I would be a troublemaker. He thought I was full of stupid comments and questions. *An academic surgeon? Professor? Professor, my ass. They are all paper shifters. They can hold a pen but nothing else. They can masturbate with their books. Useless surgeons. Slow.* No one is as fast as Sorki, he often boasted. He knew he was the top knife at Park Hospital; it was common knowledge all over town. He hadn't gotten the "best surgeon of the year" award for nothing: gallbladder in forty-five minutes, skin to skin, gastrectomy, piece of cake, a few staplers—and whoosh—the stomach was in the formalin jar. His eyes shifted from me to Winestone. The look on his face seemed to say: And that's our honorable Chairman? Why doesn't he shut Zohar up once and for all? And why did he hire that fucking foreigner in the first place? Israel, South Africa, back to Israel, some dump in Minnesota—this Zohar is like the proverbial wandering Jew. But then so is Winestone himself. The old story—Jews like to surround themselves with Jews. Back home we know how to deal with them, how to put them in their proper place. But this is America; one has to be careful, particularly when you are the President of the Medical Board and have to be popular with everyone. Sorki didn't seem to care about the racist remarks and openly talked about them, often a lot louder than he realized. Chaudri had passed on some of what Sorki had said about me the other day in the doctor's lounge:

"Look at the hospital's Vice President Dr. Albert Farbstein—the guy looks like five Jews, but at least he understands life in Brooklyn. He is cooperative. But Zohar? Forget it. Talks too much—'complications, indications, what do you think? What should have been done?' He and Winestone are probably in bed together."

Sorki was more than likely predicting Rusk's every word. Rusk put on his Midwest accent, tainted with an effort to sound Bostonian and intellectual, and responded: "Dr. Winestone, we have to conclude that the operation was indicated, that the complication was non-preventable and that the overall management of this case was appropriate."

Sorki grinned to himself. He knew Rusk wouldn't have the guts to come up with any other conclusion. He would never dare say otherwise unless the case concerned a fellow wimp. *Rusk is a chicken. Impotent.*

Sorki stretched his torso, feeling his muscular body. For a man in his late fifties, or forties for that matter, he was in excellent shape. He would sweat and puff each afternoon at his Staten Island Gym, and not in vain. He still attracted women and could satisfy hordes of them. His mind drifted to the last month's expedition to the old country. Opium and women, women and opium, what a great life. *The people here do not know how to live.*

When he returned last week he noticed that his hands shook a little, but the withdrawal symptoms were short lasting. He looked down at Winestone, short and pudgy. *Can he still screw? Sure, Winestone is filthy rich, much richer than me but can he get it up? Not him, not this pathetic sucker.* The idea that Winestone couldn't get it up amused Sorki immensely and compensated for the chairman's enormous wealth.

Sorki looked at his watch. Time to leave this silly meeting of talk, talk and more silly talk, he was thinking. He had to operate. Radezki had called him early that morning informing him that Mr. Pellegrino, the restaurant owner, had re-bled. Friday he removed part of Pellegrino's stomach for bleeding, and now he was pouring fresh red blood from his gastric tube. *Why did he have to bleed again? Fuck it. Bad luck. That idiot Zohar was fooling around with vagotomies while everyone knows that gastrectomy is the only answer to these problems. Never mind! I, the surgical master Mahmud Sorki, will solve this problem!* He'd hold up his hands to

44

assess their steadiness. Great. A gulp of Vodka just before the operation would remedy the late effects of opium. And tomorrow after work he'd start going to the gym again to get rid of the fat accumulated on his belly during the vacation. But then he remembered that he can't. God, no! Dinner with Winestone and Mantzur is scheduled for tomorrow! Oh, well. Who cares? Let's meet with the Jew as old Mantzur suggested. Herb will be there as well—someone to drink with. I imagined that between Sorki, Mantzur, Susman, they'd talk tirelessly about how they were going to quash Winestone and me like two cockroaches.

▲▼▲▼▲

Dr. Ron Gavitunyo, a fourth year resident, presented another mortality. This one was a patient of Dr. Joe Burnstein. It was well known in my circle that Joe had two left hands and a terrible clinical judgment. It was no secret. There was a standing joke among the residents. Question: how would you control Brooklyn's growing population? Answer: 'Call Joe Burnstein.'

Joe operated in any hospital where he could get operating privileges. Mid-State University Center kicked him out a long time ago. Joe was notoriously incompetent but managed to do quite well financially because he was charming and friendly to everyone and did not have enemies. Second, his affiliation with many hospitals in the area meant he never had many complications at any of them. He knew how to shuffle his big cases that developed complications or died. Third, he was a master in using the trick of discharging his cases early and treating their complications elsewhere. For example, if you operated on an old guy for cancer of the large bowel at the Park, you might send him home on post-operative Day Five. When his suture line broke down on post-operative Day Seven, you could admit him to Rabbi Maimon Hospital where the guy would eventually die. This mortality wouldn't be registered as a complication or discussed as such because the original operation was not performed at that hospital. Today's case did not permit Joe to use that trick. The patient complicated and died too early to be transferred. *Bad luck for poor Joe,* not a few surgeons thought to themselves.

Dr. Gavitunyo continued: "A very large spleen was removed uneventfully and the patient was transferred to the recovery room in a stable condition. Intra-operative blood loss was two hundred fifty milliliters..."

"Did you measure it? How do you know it was not *five* hundred fifty milliliters?"

A wave of laughter stirred the auditorium. It was another well-known Winestone joke. A good atmosphere must prevail during the presentation of major disasters. In order to survive in his elevated position, the chairman has to appear as a humorous father rather than a vindictive judge.

Ron smiled and ignored the question. "In the recovery room the patient's blood pressure dropped to ninety over sixty. This responded to two liters of Ringer's Lactate. He remained stable and two hours later was extubated and sent to the intensive care unit. His hemoglobin level at that stage was seven gram percent, and a unit of pack cells was transfused."

"What was his heart rate?" Dr. Bachus asked from the floor. "What was his pH? Was he acidotic?"

"His heart rate was around one hundred twenty per minute. We don't have his arterial blood gases but his saturation was good, therefore he was extubated."

"You don't extubate an unstable patient, and this patient was unstable, wasn't he?" added Bachus.

"Dr. Bachus, you will have the opportunity to comment." Winestone leaned over to pull on Gavitunyo's elbow. "So what happened next?"

"The patient's blood pressure dropped again in the ICU. I gave him more Ringer and blood—"

"—Let's go back into the OR when you closed the patient up, I mean before you left the abdomen. Was everything dry?"

"Yes, Dr. Winestone, absolutely dry."

"Were you satisfied with the outcome?" asked Winestone, "and, Dr. Burnstein, I assume you were happy as well?"

"Absolutely, Dr. Winestone. We were both very satisfied." Burnstein jumped to his feet. "I support Dr. Gavitunyo who performed a truly excellent job. The splenectomy was uneventful, despite the huge size of the spleen. As I said, an excellent job. Very happy indeed." Burnstein talked loud and well, albeit with a pronounced Jewish Brooklyn accent. I wished his operative skills could match his rhetoric.

"OK. What happened next?" asked Winestone.

Gavitunyo hesitated briefly, pondering the answer. "A few minutes later," he finally responded. "At five forty-five p.m. the patient developed cardiorespiratory arrest, and he coded. CPR was initiated along with vigorous fluid resuscitation. We managed to restore cardiac rhythm and circulation. The attending decided to take the patient back to the OR. Unfortunately, the patient coded again and died."

Bashir leaned towards me. I sensed his disgust before he even opened his mouth. "I was in the ICU," he whispered. "I told them that he was bleeding into the abdomen, I told Gavitunyo to get Burnstein and to run back into the OR. Gavitunyo could not get hold of Burnstein. He'd left the hospital before the guy left the table."

"Any comments from the floor? Dr. Gotahedi, would you have done anything different?"

Rachman Gotahedi was another Iranian-born surgeon. Thin, short, talked well and was always elegantly dressed. Gotahedi danced at all parties and was a personal friend and neighbor of Sorki. He was also on good terms with Winestone, so he was relatively neutral as far as the latter was concerned. He had a notorious weakness for women. At our last party for the graduating chief residents Gotahedi, apparently drunk, approached the six-foot wife of Dr. Chaudri, demanding: "Please stand up. You are so tall I wish to place my head on your breasts." His wife and friends dragged him away to avoid further embarrassment. Only two weeks ago Gotahedi had reached his hand under Beverly's short skirt and pinched her muscular butt. Saying she was furious would be saying very little. Winestone managed to defuse the fire; although nobody was sure exactly how. It was an entertaining mystery for those of us who knew about it.

Gotahedi looked at Winestone and started to lecture. He liked to talk. If you asked him a simple question he would go on forever. "Dr. Winestone," he intoned. "This was a difficult spleen. Very large. Both Doctors Gavitunyo and Burnstein tell us that the operation went well, that they achieved meticulous hemostasis before closing the abdomen. What happened then? Probably a ligature came off one of the short gastric arteries. How did you tie the arteries, Dr. Gavitunyo?" He paused, but not long enough for an answer because he wouldn't have listened to it anyway. "I hope you did not use vicryl. I use only silk. I do not trust vicryl. I remember a case, five years ago. I used vicryl, it slipped, and he bled. Never again."

Even Malcolm Rusk couldn't contain himself any longer. He whispered to me, "What a grandiose fool! Absolute crap. Always the long saga of 'I had a case…' I wish he would stop."

"No, Dr. Gotahedi, we did not use vicryl. We used silk," Gavitunyo admitted at his first opportunity.

I myself was a bit irritated, and inserted: "I use only vicryl and I have no problems. If you know how to tie properly you can use anything. Silk belongs to the Middle Ages." Contempt curled my lips and chilled my tone.

"Dr. Zohar," Gotahedi laughed and then continued. "Is this a finding based on your studies, or on a literature search?" He paused. "As I said, this was an unfortunate case. A ligature slipped or, alternatively, the hemorrhage originated from a retroperitoneal vein somewhere around the tail of the pancreas. It could happen to any of us. I had a similar case six or seven years ago. A sweet old lady who—"

"—Thanks, Dr. Gotahedi," Winestone interrupted. "We have to conclude. Dr. Burnstein, would you like to add anything? This was your case."

Burnstein walked to the side aisle. In his mid-fifties with long white hair at the back of his otherwise bald head, he was wearing the usual navy-blue suit, white shirt and boring necktie. I wondered whether he went to bed in that outfit.

"Dr. Winestone, colleagues," he said, "I cannot sleep since this sad case occurred. I played and re-played this operation in my mind numerous times, trying to figure out what went wrong. How could we have avoided, prevented that awful catastrophe?" This was another survival trick. Always be sorry. Repent and suffer in public, like in the synagogue on Yom Kippur. "Please forgive me, Oh Lord, for all my mistakes and sins."

Burnstein was never arrogant, but never openly admitted committing an error. Complications "just happened" to all of us. We are "brothers in arms," as he put it. "I have to admit," he droned on, "that Dr. Gotahedi is correct. A ligature must have slipped or something similar, causing an intra-peritoneal hemorrhage. We tried to rush him back to the OR, but—as you have already noted—unfortunately, he was unsalvageable."

Bashir murmured to me, "When Gavitunyo tried to get him to come, to tell him that the patient was exsanguinating, he was already operating on another case at Rabbi Maimon Hospital."

"Dr. Rusk, how should we conclude?" asked Winestone. "Please be brief. Our guest lecturer is here, and it's time to start the Grand Rounds."

Malcolm Rusk cleared his voice. "The patient probably died from a postoperative hemorrhage. One must admit that this—per definition—represents a technical complication. However, the overall management of this case was appropriate."

"Appropriate, my ass," I hissed to Bashir. "Another kill by stupid Joe."

Bashir smiled. No use to get a heart attack after listening to the story of yet another disaster. There were so many. I watched Burnstein head for the door out as soon as the M&M was over. He never stayed for Grand Rounds. He knew how to cut and stitch, how to remove organs. He was well trained and even board certified. He was very busy. Patients and families liked his mild personality, and he was especially popular among Hassidic Jews with whom he was able to exchange a few words from the Talmud or Mishna. He soon hoped to be included in the *New York Magazine's* list of top surgeons. Mantzur and Sorki were already on the list. His patients would have liked to see a certificate on his wall declaring him to be "Best surgeon in NY." As soon as he left the room he would no doubt forget about his now dead patient.

A friend of mine once said, "Again and again I find that there are few things so quickly forgotten by the surgical system as a dead patient." True, the family of the deceased patient may sue, but it is very unlikely. Even if they sue it will take years before the case is discussed. Burnstein always had a few active lawsuits against him, but so do most surgeons. On his way out Burnstein signed the attendance list for the Grand Rounds lecture to comply with state requirements for continuing education. Then he'd head over to the Evangelist Hospital in Jersey City where some hemorrhoidectomies were waiting for him.

His wife Shula had recently told him, "Joe, stop doing these big cases. Why strain yourself? Concentrate on the minor cases, more money and less nerves. You're not getting younger." But he enjoyed the glory and drama of big surgery. Patients died occasionally, M&M conferences were not great fun, but he was doing well. "Blessed art thou, Lord God..."

4

All You Need is Love

*How many men in a year die through the timidity of
those they consult for health!*
—Samuel Johnson, 1709-1784

Ten a.m. The lecture was over. No one bothered to ask
questions. The guest speaker was a notable Professor from
Detroit, a world expert on venous thrombosis and one of
Winestone's important surgical buddies across the nation.
But the lecture was disappointing. One wants to hear original
thoughts and studies, not a repetition of what one can find in
any textbook.

I stuffed the printed M&M case summaries into the
pocket of my white coat. This was confidential department
material to be collected and destroyed after the meeting—
with only one copy kept by the department. I was nevertheless collecting the papers for my own files. I saw others doing
the same. An "insurance policy" we called it, against potential enemies—only as a prophylactic measure, of course. In
the corridor I bumped into Sam Glatman. He put his arm
around my shoulder: "Marc, very brave, very brave. The
Padrino hated your questions. Did you notice the silence?
They were astounded. To ask the old fart about indications.
Unheard of at the old Park Hospital!"

Sam had a pleasant smiling face, a well-trimmed brown
mustache, and a perfectly matching curly brown hairdo. Our
residents claimed it was a wig that had recently been spotted
sliding down his wet scalp after a difficult repair of an
abdominal aortic aneurysm. We walked towards the elevators. "Hey, Marc," he continued. "I watched Sorki's face during the discussion of Padrino's case. Boy, he suffered. Watch
your back, though. You know Sorki and Susman are buddies.

And I can tell you, Fat Herb has some rough connections in this part of town."

"Sam, don't get carried away. This is just a hospital in Brooklyn, not a mobster joint. But thanks anyway." We carried on down the hall. A few nurses stepped aside as we sauntered past. We nodded our thanks. "I know the risks, but I won't shut up. This simply has to be stopped. I've been here for almost four years now. Mistakes and errors happen, everywhere and to everybody. But what these guys are doing is appalling."

Glatman laughed. "I am with you buddy, I am with you, but I've known them much longer than you. Prior to your arrival, the Padrino attempted to take away my vascular privileges for nothing. I mean, really. For nothing. Winestone managed to save my ass. I need to make money; you know how much my ex wife gets? You have to pay mortgage as well. You have kids in college? Expensive hey?" He pondered his own situation briefly enough for me to give my own some consideration but not long enough to come to any conclusions. "So let's be careful."

I nodded. "I wonder how Winestone will react. I'll find out soon enough: Bashir, Chaudri and myself are due to see him tomorrow regarding the residency program."

"He will give you shit for opening your big mouth. Just shut up, listen to him and swallow it. Whether you like it or not, he's the boss. Larry is a good guy. He's going to give you a hard time but just shut up." We continued on course for a few more steps before I heard this uncomfortable growl emanating from Sam's stomach. I sort of looked at him out of the corner of my eye.

"Hungry?" I asked him with a smile.

"I'm starving! Can't eat those bagels so early in the morning. Come, I'll buy you a second breakfast in the cafeteria."

"Thanks, Sam. Some other time. I have a few patients to see. But first tell me, what about Winestone? Where do you think our leader stands?"

"You want the truth?" Sam giggled. "With his tongue in Mantzur's ass. If you cannot fight them, love them. All you need is love, all you need is love..."

Glatman left me and walked towards the cafeteria humming to himself the old Beatles' song, "Love, love, love. All you need is love..."

▲▼◢▲▼▲

I ran into Radezki while doing my rounds. He looked exhausted; a large bloodstain decorated his scrub top. He looked like a murderer. A pissed off murderer.

"Hey, Pav, why don't you go and wash your face and take this filthy thing off?"

"Dr. Zohar, we just finished re-doing Mr. Pellegrino—Sorki's patient. You know, the one you said would rebleed?"

"The restaurant owner?"

"Yes, that's right," Radezki nodded, and then grimaced. "What a saga. Be happy that you are off the case."

"So that's it. I was wondering why you didn't show up at the M&M, and then I noticed Sorki leaving early, too. What did you find today? Is the patient re-bleeding?"

"Bleeding?" Radezki exclaimed, his hands gesticulating wildly. His facial expressions were a picture. His eyes were wide, and his eyebrows reached far up on his forehead. "You call that bleeding? The guy was pouring like a hose pipe!"

"What did you do?"

"We re-opened his abdomen. The stomach was huge, as big as at our first operation and distended with clots."

"You mean what was left of the stomach was huge. The man underwent a partial gastrectomy. Continue."

"Well, we chopped off another part. We went higher, completing almost a near total gastrectomy, we just left a rim of stomach and then—"

"—Just a moment." I held up my hand abruptly and stopped him cold. A part of my brain insisted I'd misheard him. The other part assured me that I hadn't, and shouldn't be surprised. "You're telling me that you blindly excised more stomach? That you did not even try to gastroscope him first, that you again did not look inside the duodenum?" My voice rose considerably. "He's still bleeding from that vessel in the duodenum, the vessel that you didn't control during the first operation after I was kicked out of the room. Do you understand?"

Radezki looked down at me, his brows drooping upon narrowing eyes. "Yes, I understand. Why are you screaming at me? Go and scream at Sorki! He claimed that the patient is hemorrhaging from erosive gastritis. You know how he is. 'Chop here, chop there, a stapler here, a stapler there, look at the clock, thirty minutes. I am so fast!'"

"Pav, how is the patient now?"

"Not so well. He lost a lot of blood."

"If you don't attend to his duodenum pronto this man will not make it. You know he had had a myocardial infarction. His heart won't tolerate the yo-yo-ing of his blood pressure for long."

Radezki shrugged. As a resident he knew he had to leave some of the world's problems to his attending surgeons. The juniors around Radezki watched me curiously. They were aware of the lack of love between Sorki and myself, and I knew that for a few of them Sorki was a role model. Sad.

Sorki was an arrogant asshole. I could only imagine what he told Mr. Pellegrino's wife today. For a moment I was glad I hadn't felt like talking to her last Friday. The case had taken the kind of turn where you know that you don't want to be part of its history. Then I realized my mistake: I was already involved, no matter the outcome.

By the end of that week, it proved to be a fatal one. Mr. Pellegrino underwent another operation. Then his heart put an end to the experiment.

Mr. Pellegrino was pronounced dead on October tenth at four eighteen p.m.

5

The Launch Pad

*The so-called surgeon who practices primarily for the
fee, who advises operation without adequate study,
who removes a normal organ without indication, who
makes an emergency out of almost every case, has no
problems or morals.*
—Edwin P. Lehman, 1888-1954

"Anything wrong, Doc? Do you see any blood?" Mr.
Potts was lying on the examination table. I'd taken off his
colostomy bag, emptied it into a basin and inserted a short
proctoscope into his colostomy. "I noticed fresh blood in the
bag yesterday. I'm very weak, Doc. Am I losing blood?" I
looked carefully up his colostomy before answering.

"I see nothing, everything seems normal. You may be
bleeding from higher up. We'll need to use a longer scope."

I placed the dirty metal pipe in the basin and looked at
Mr. Potts' horrendously scarred abdomen. One could see the
outline of the intestine under the huge, skin-grafted abdominal wall defect. Scars like those are all that's left to retrace
the steps taken in a difficult operation. You normally look at
them with the attitude of a mechanic who marvels at the way
in which a seemingly unfixable problem in a broken machine
was solved. It isn't pretty, but it works! Scars testify to an
insurmountable obstacle that was overcome by ingenuity and
perseverance, resulting in another life saved!

Yes, I had saved Mr. Potts' life. But before that I'd
almost killed him. Mr. Potts, a charming elderly African
American, previously a court clerk, was my first disaster—
and one of the worst—at the New York Park Hospital. One
afternoon I attempted to biopsy his rectal cancer and perforated his rectum. The next morning he was dying from severe
intra-abdominal feculent peritonitis. He survived after multi-

ple operations and a few months later we excised his cancer-containing rectum. Mr. Potts could have sued me success-fully but never did. I guess the bond of mutual affection that developed between us protected me. Three years later, Mr. Potts' cancer moved into his lungs. He refused chemotherapy but would see me every few weeks. He would come without notice, and his unannounced visits were the only privilege he would demand of me. We both knew he wouldn't live long.

Mr. Potts descended from the examination table and pulled the trousers up his crooked legs. I noticed the holes in his belt were not sufficient to make it hug his wasted torso. "Doc, I need some tonic to make me strong," he said to me. His expression was dire.

"Mr. Potts, all you need is a girlfriend." This was our habitual joke; Mr. Potts had never married.

"I am too tired. I went to see Les Misérables on Broadway and fell asleep during the first act."

That's a bad sign for a musical aficionado and connoisseur of the opera. I wrote a prescription and accompanied Mr. Potts to the elevator. His dark, bloodshot eyes rested on me calmly. I fought the urge to step forward and touch him. Hug him. The sliding doors of the elevator moved across his waif figure like the shutter behind a camera lens. A distant hum. Then the well-defined, narrow beam of light from within rapidly shrank towards the floor as the elevator cabin descended into the void. I could make out the faint reflection of my face in the cool, forbidding metal that bars access to the dark and empty shaft. A diagonal scratch ran across the polished aluminum. I couldn't help but ask myself if it would be the last time I'd ever take that picture.

▲▼▲▼▲

Back on the medical floor I saw a few consults. The first one was a semi-comatose, post stroke octogenarian on whom I was requested to operatively insert a stomach tube—a gastrostomy. I placed the old man in a sitting position and brought a spoonful of water to his mouth. He swallowed nicely. He did not need an operation or even an endoscopic gastrostomy; all he needed was to be patiently spoon-fed. And what was wrong with a small diameter, soft feeding tube from his nose to the stomach? "No indication for gastrostomy," I wrote in the consult note, knowing that a few days later somebody would do the gastrostomy anyway. *Another unnecessary operation and misspent money.* If only the insurance companies had any idea! Millions, possibly billions of dollars would be saved.

Similar patients were presented frequently at the weekly M&M conferences, nationwide. "How could we let him starve?" was the usual justification, or sometimes it was: "The nursing home won't admit him—or her—without a gastrostomy..."

The next patient I saw was even more depressing. Three months earlier I had bypassed her stomach and bile duct for a widely spread pancreatic cancer. I had injected her celiac plexus with alcohol, eliminating the intractable back pain. Now she was lying moribund in bed with an infected venous catheter implanted elsewhere for the administration of chemotherapy. I talked to her daughter. I wasn't terribly impressed with her at this point either. "Didn't I tell you that chemotherapy is useless in her case?"

"Yes, but they told me that it may prolong her life."

I called the OR to book this patient for the removal of infected Portocath. Another futile procedure. *Do all terminally ill patients need to be decorated with feeding tubes and poisoned with costly and mostly ineffective chemotherapy?* One of Dr. Winestone's habitual jabs to the residents was, "What is impossible to find in any hospital?" Answer: "An oncologist who refuses to administer chemotherapy."

I climbed the stairs to the surgical floor and rounded on my patients. Charts of even simple cases such as acute appendicitis were thickened with laboratory printouts. How many times is it necessary to measure serum albumin and liver function tests during three days of uncomplicated recovery from an operation? Is it necessary to draw blood for so-called routines everyday? Of course not, but I am resigned. The literature proves repeatedly that routine pre-operative clotting studies are not necessary, but tell it to the anesthetists.

"Just check the potassium," I told the intern.

"It is easier to pull an automated SMA 12 test," she protested.

The lab charges on my appendix case would sustain a family for a month, but who cares? Some laboratories thrive on such harmless excesses—*Just a second,* I corrected myself. *Harmless? How many times have I seen superfluous tests giving false abnormal results, only to be followed by further testing?* The vicious circle continues.

My patient recovering from a laparotomy for perforated duodenal ulcer spiked a temperature, but he looked happy and well. I looked at the chart. According to this an infections disease (ID) specialist had prescribed a third generation cephalosporin antibiotic. I felt my blood pressure surging. Who needed the opinion of that ID guy? This was not a bacterial heart valve infection! I was upset. I had been inside this patient's abdomen and knew that he did not require further antimicrobial treatment. But unnecessary consults are an integral part of practice. The patient's attending medical doctor obviously felt obliged to invite the ID specialist to the feeding ground.

I entered another room to remove stitches from a patient's tummy. I was handed a pack containing disposable forceps and scissors. "Made in China," I read on the handsome instruments. They probably could have been used a few hundred times. "The hospital pays only ten dollars per set," I was told. But re-sterilization would cost only a buck. I wondered how much money the import firm and distributor made making that arrangement.

Another consult: A ninety-five-year-old totally demented lady lying contracted in a pool of fresh feces; the obligatory stomach tube in place. Her "acute surgical problem" was two large trocanteric bedsores for which she was receiving intravenous antibiotics. I prescribed "local treatment" and recommended the cessation of the antibiotics, hoping for the disease to take its natural human course. I had seen similar patients subjected to major plastic reconstructive surgery, probably motivated by Medicare coverage.

The ER called me to assess a case of abdominal pain. I carefully examined the patient whose belly was absolutely innocent.

"He can go home," I said to the ER resident.

"Don't you want to see his CT?" The patient's general practitioner had referred him with a request for a CT to "rule out." It cost four hundred dollars. Often I hear medical students start a presentation with: "CT showed—" Is CT replacing clinical examination? Grunting, I viewed the CT report: "Hepatic lesion—probably hemangioma—MRI recommended."

"No wonder every radiologist drives a Mercedes," I commented to the resident acidly. I left the ER in disgust. As I climbed the stairs to my office, I recalled that last week an HMO rejected my bill because I'd admitted a patient for observation and did "no investigations" on him. In their opinion, if there was no CT and no ultrasound, how could the patient be observed?

I decided not to stop on the fourth floor. Yesterday was lousy enough with the M&M, but today was getting even worse. I guess I was caught off guard by the encounter with Mr. Potts. Perhaps I was trying to justify my own case by pointing to the blunders and selfish acts of others. Moving around on this floor would definitely not enhance my mood. The fourth floor was dedicated to chronic ventilator cases: patients who have partially recovered from a severe acute illness but still need artificial breathing through a tracheal tube. After a prolonged and costly stay in the intensive care unit they were transferred to this section for long-term ventilation at a lower daily cost.

Our residents called the floor Cape Canaveral because it was from there that cases were launched into eternal space at night. It was predictable. The tracheal tubes require dedicated suctioning and cleaning in order to remain patent. This service was seldom provided, and definitely not at night. You see your patient during evening rounds smiling and well. The next morning you were told that he or she had expired.

"What happened?" you'd ask. It would be a rhetorical question because you'd know they had suffocated, drowning in their own tracheal and bronchial secretions.

"Poor old Mrs. Santiago," the resident would say. "She was launched." No further explanation was needed. We often exchanged the tracheal tube in such patients, knowing how dirty and clogged they could get. No use to complain; management was not interested.

My biller called just as I entered my office. In order to secure my professional fees he had to deal with more than twenty HMOs and agencies, and the red tape was astonishing. Rarely was a claim paid without an initial rejection and prolonged nagging. Imagine the billions spent on such an inefficient billing system. Occasionally, my professional fees for an operation are mailed to the patient. "Forget about this check," the biller would say. "The patient needed it to upgrade his car."

Next I had to go to a hospital committee. I dreaded exposure to a team of administrators in gray suits and manager-nurses in high heels, talking a neologistic jargon spiced with words such as "proactive" and "prioritized," which I still despise. According to them "we" were doing well, meaning the budget was positive. Every launch at Cape Canaveral eventually translates into numbers in black ink, often in the shape of zeroes.

I realized that the public is also a part of the problem. Little wonder—we made them believe that more machines, more operations, more medication is better. We had justified redundant procedures on grounds of defensive medicine forced on us by lawyers who emphasized mistakes of omission more than those of commission. Who was to establish standards of care—lawyers, administrators, or us? And who cares about—care?

6

The Cousin

*It is asking more than human perfection to assume that
a surgeon's judgment may not be influenced
unconsciously by pressing financial need.*
—Edwin P. Lehman, 1888-1954

"Marc, you're late." Bashir looked surprised, and his
tone confirmed this sentiment. "We paged you already—why
didn't you answer?"

I sensed the tension the instant I entered Bashir's office.
My colleague Dr. Bashir Bachus was sitting at his desk with
Dr. Chaudri opposite, sipping his mandatory diet Coke.
Winestone was standing at the window, looking at the Statue
of Liberty under the cloudy October sky. It had begun to driz-
zle, and the moisture drew a fuzzy curtain over the outside
world. The splendor of the Indian Summer was being
drowned and washed away.

"Really?" I replied, sneering at him. "As if you ever
answer your pager so promptly—especially when your pants
are around your knees in a nurse's room."

"Are you jealous?" laughed Bashir. Winestone did not
participate in our jeering. His face was swollen with concern.
I could smell the particular mushy-sweet scent his body emit-
ted after a prolonged operation or a stressful meeting. It was
like a whiff from a two-day-old carcass of a run-over cat. I
tried not to breathe it too deeply. The room was warm and the
sent of decay more acute than usual.

"Sit down, Marc," he said. "Let us be serious. We have
to talk."

I sat down as Bashir handed me a diet Coke. I tried to
calm down. Let's get it over with.

"Marc," started Winestone, mustering great charm
despite a gloomy look. It was a good sign that this was

going to be one of his longer lectures. I emotionally bunkered down for the long run. "Let me tell you that your behavior yesterday at the M&M was inappropriate. Only Friday I tried to explain to you that we are entering a new era. Mantzur is now on our side. I made him a vice-chairman. He is an asset for us and can control Sorki. Do you know what Howard and Farbstein want? They want us to destroy each other. They want us—the full timers—to neutralize Mantzur, Sorki and the Medical Board all in one. Once they've achieved that they can control us all. And they will, you know. That is their objective. All you're doing is helping them to achieve that goal."

"OK, you've told me that before. What do you want me to do, lick their asses? You hired me to function as an academic surgeon, to mentor your residents. Now you want me to make a joke of it, to shut up while they are destroying patients?"

Winestone shooshed me. "Don't talk so loud." Winestone pointed to the closed door but ignored my vulgarities. "I certainly want you to continue educating the residents. But concerning Mantzur and Sorki, I need you to calm down. Ignore their cases. When they are presented at the M&M, keep your mouth shut. And Marc, we do not want a case of Mantzur to be presented each week. It would reflect very poorly on him."

"But Dr. Winestone, the man has so many complications and mortalities, there are more than fifty cases of his on my list waiting to be presented and that doesn't include the ones that will appear on my list between now and when we're done with the existing ones."

"What's the rush? Present one of his cases each month."

"We'll be busy into the next century."

It sounded blatantly sarcastic, but when I did the numbers I realized, given that it was 1998, that I should have said *for* the next century.

"Show me the list. Do you have it here?" Winestone snatched the list from me and scanned it rapidly. "There is no need to present all his minor complications," he then declared.

Out of the corner of my eye I saw Bashir and Chaudri giving each other looks. I couldn't tell what types of looks through my peripheral vision, but I could quite easily imagine their reaction to being told to ignore the "minor complications." What exactly was a minor complication? If it was to be presented at the M&M there was nothing minor about it. I wasn't sure I would be able to pick any one case over another. "Marc," Winestone continued, overlooking my silent appreciation of his request, "I can't tell you formally what to present and what not to present, but you understand what I mean. Let's give him a break. We need him!"

I changed my tack. *Let's talk about the present. Let's talk about the imminent disasters. Let's be adamant.* "Dr. Winestone," I said, "did you hear about Sorki's case? The one he stole from me Friday morning? You know, the bleeding one?" He appeared to have a vague awareness of what I was talking about. "He ignored the duodenum and instead performed a near total gastrectomy in two different operations. Now the patient is dead!"

Winestone looked at me through his thick and dirty lenses like an old, wise father. "Marc, Marc, stop and listen to me. I've told you this before and I'll tell you again. They have been killing patients here for many years. We cannot change it. Face the reality. Mantzur is influential, as you know. We cannot function much less maintain a thriving department without his support." It all boiled down to money. We all needed money. Hell, even I was not so naïve as to believe that the department didn't need money to operate effectively. "You do not know Mantzur. He is a gentleman and a reasonable person. Sorki is an animal, I agree, but we must establish a working relationship with him as well—via Mantzur. Mantzur is upset about yesterday morning meeting. He came to me straight thereafter. He was deeply hurt by your comments. 'Look,' he told me, 'only recently I helped to arrange an increase for Zohar and see how he treats me?'"

"A ten thousand dollar increase?" I snorted. "Big deal. I should have gotten it long time ago." Winestone thought about that for a second. His expression softened slightly.

"Only Mantzur could convince Howard to give you the increase. You'll have to accept the fact that he is now the vice chairman. I do not want you to smear him and Sorki in front of the residents. Whatever you say comes back to them. You think that the residents are your friends? Well that may be true, but they talk."

"Dr. Winestone, do you realize that Mantzur's quality of surgical practice is no better than Sorki's? It may be even worse! Can't you see what's happening here? That Mr. Pellegrino, the patient this butcher stole from me—I knew that he was going to kill him! The family might as well have called the undertaker!"

"Marc, Marc, you're not listening." Winestone raised his voice. Anger tinted his face a glossy pink. "You're being personal now. Sorki, not Mantzur, stole Pellegrino from you, right? Face it—you're confusing the issue. Colleagues are wondering about your motives in attacking Mantzur. They're not convinced your intentions are exactly kosher. As the chairman of this department I cannot afford to look at things in that way. I have to maintain an impartial point of view. Don't get me wrong: we're all human, we all have our own agendas. I accept that. But stop being so self-righteous." A moment of silence fell over the room. Self-righteous? Maybe he had a point, but I thought he was misinterpreting my concern. I was angry at the suggestion that I had ulterior motives.

"Dr.Winestone, you are insinuating that I am—" I sputtered, searching for the proper words, "—that I am opposing their actions for personal gain! I don't believe this—You know that that's not true."

"I am not talking about myself. You didn't listen. I know what I said isn't true, but you have to consider how it looks to others. Perceptions are realities. It doesn't matter what people hear; what matters is what they choose to believe. It's what they perceive to be true. And the way you behaved yesterday morning makes it difficult for them to believe otherwise. You're undermining my efforts. You're antagonizing everyone. I cannot tolerate this—and I won't. Stop confronting Sorki and Mantzur in public or I cannot support you any longer. You will be all on your own."

"Then I guess somebody from outside will have to control these butchers—"

"—Absolute madness!" Winestone jumped to his feet. Bashir and Chaudri stared at him; they had never seen him lose control before. "That would be suicidal! I warn you. You would destroy yourself and us as well. No one wins such wars."

"You are blind!"

"Please, Marc." Bashir, as pale as Winestone, tried to intervene. "This is not the way to talk to the chairman," he said. It was obvious that the two of us were escalating the problem, not solving it. They could see it because they were more or less impartial. My own views were being marred because this had become a personal interest of mine.

I left the room. It was not so much a retreat as a tactical advance to the rear. I was mad at Winestone. What was worse, I was even mad at myself. *This will get me nowhere; I've been through this before. I should know better than to lose my cool. You don't fight a system like that; you've got to have allies. I cannot afford to alienate Winestone. Strategy, tactics. Be smart, be flexible.*

At the elevator I found myself staring at the smooth, even metal surface—a passive, disinterested mirror. I closed my eyes, and then I could see it clearly again: the scar on the metal surface. The truth we both knew. Mr. Potts called for the last time today.

Yasser Sorki sat in front of my desk. Yasser was Sorki's cousin, the most recent import by Sorki from Iran to our hospital. A few other young Sorkis were employed in various capacities in other departments. Yasser, a qualified surgeon in his home country, was brought to New York by his influential relative, who promised to place him as a resident in our training program. Winestone told us that Sorki and Mantzur were pressuring him to give the cousin one of the three first-year resident spots falling vacant next July. Meanwhile, Yasser was dumped on me by Winestone to serve as a research fellow. I liked Yasser. He was a well-behaved and soft-spoken fellow. Although his spoken English was still rudimentary, he read well and understood the surgical literature. In fact, he appeared very knowledgeable. But we simply could not fast track him; it would have been tremendously unfair to the other applicants. The consensus among Bachus, Chaudri, Rusk and myself was that Yasser should not be given one of our "categorical" residency spots, but a "preliminary" one. Once he had mastered the language and proven himself he could apply for a categorical position for the following year.

"Good afternoon, Dr. Sorki. How are you doing?" I said, beckoning him into my room. "Please sit down."

"Hello Dr. Zohar! You permit—I wish to show preliminary results of meta-analysis. On local use of antibiotics in surgical wounds." Yasser smiled in the polite and correct fashion of central Asia, showing bad teeth. I examined the printed manuscript. He had worked hard at it, I could see at a glance.

"This looks fantastic," I said, flipping through a few pages and taking a moment to browse a few lines of text. His knowledge showed clearly. "Well done! It needs additional work, but as a preliminary draft it is not bad. Let me take it home and read it in detail."

Yasser smiled again. "Dr. Zohar, I have to inform—I will be one of new residents. From July next year. I very much looking forward to it."

So he believed he had the job. Straight from JFK to a surgical residency position in the USA. Thousands of US graduates compete for an approved surgical residency spot— and Sorki senior was of the opinion that his cousin could have the job because he was a Sorki.

"I am very happy for you," I said. "See me next week, and we'll go over your manuscript."

Yasser left on that note with a smile and a handshake. If what he claimed was true then Winestone had already—*No. I am getting carried away now.* I'd begun to see enemies and traitors everywhere. Winestone was right. I was being self-righteous and paranoid. You've eventually got to trust in someone. But who?

7

Politics and Pasta

*One is a nobody in surgery unless he has at least as
many enemies as friends.*
—Anonymous

Professor Lawrence Winestone stepped on the accelerator and noted with pleasure the immediate response of his red Mercedes 600 SL as it sped across the Brooklyn Bridge. Winestone loved sports cars. His current dilemma was what car to get after Christmas once the lease on the current one expired. Should it be a Porsche? His wife Rim had suggested a Ferrari, or a Rolls. What expensive tastes! Winestone smiled with satisfaction. Not only did Rim know and appreciate what was good and exorbitant, but she also had a lot of style—unlike his first wife, the mother of his children, the one he brought with him from England. An awful marriage. How he had suffered! Then those years of second bachelorhood on Fifth Avenue. The pleasures of freedom, away from his irritating wife. But Rim was different. Since he'd married her, his life had become organized; even his shirts and shoes were in perfect condition. Thank heavens he'd found Rim!

Winestone had to pick up a few dresses for Rim from their City Tower flat, the flat he'd bought for himself after the divorce. Then he visited his ninety-five-year-old mother in her grand upper east side apartment where she lived with a Romanian servant. Winestone visited his mother at least once a week, usually for an early dinner cooked by the maid: lamb kebabs—he liked Romanian food, any food, provided it was well cooked. His favorite, however, was French. Rim had introduced him to the best of Paris and the Riviera. Today, unfortunately, he couldn't eat with his mother because of the dinner with Mantzur and Sorki.

He was sad to see how his mother had deteriorated over the past year. Recurrent urinary infections were taking their toll. She hardly even recognized him anymore. When she dies—God forbid—he knew he'd sell her apartment. This together with the flat could buy a penthouse on Park Avenue. That was where he wanted to retire. He loved Manhattan; the shopping, the opera, the restaurants! They would also sell the waterfront mansion on the Island and travel during the summer months.

A minor traffic jam on Atlantic Avenue pulled him out of his deep thoughts; a taxi had bumped into a delivery van, and the drivers were arguing. He turned onto Court Street and halted outside the Marco Polo restaurant, handing the car keys to the valet. *Not such great company,* he thought as he sauntered through the front doors, *but the food will be good.* As he entered the restaurant, Professor Winestone recalled the comments about Marco Polo from the Zagat survey of New York restaurants. Winestone possessed, among many other things, a photographic memory and prided himself for knowing Zagat almost by heart. Others could recite from Shakespeare, he could quote from Zagat. He adored food. Zagat wrote something along these lines: "Marco Polo, 'Old School, old neighborhood and old country' are the three main ingredients at this 'very good' Carroll gardens traditional Italian restaurant. Spoilers suggest that there are better places at half the price in Brooklyn."

"Good evening, Dottore!" Giovanni, the veteran head-waiter rushed towards Winestone and bowed. "Can I take your coat? It's quite wet outside tonight—last days of autumn, eh?"

Winestone enjoyed the heavy southern Italian accent. All of the waiters there are authentic. He couldn't stand being served by Latinos in an Italian restaurant, not to mention Latinos serving French food—that would destroy his appetite. Maybe it was just Latinos, period.

"The other Dottori are already here, Dottore, prego—after me."

Winestone followed the waiter between the tables. The crowd was mixed. Families and professionals both go there, even Mayor Giuliani had been seen on occasion. Sophisticated African Americans would also go to Marco Polo. Winestone once saw Reverend Sharpton at one of the tables. The tacky Italian art pieces on the wall caught his eyes. Zagat gave it only sixteen points for décor, but nineteen for the food that was almost "very good." He was not paying tonight, a fact that improved the taste of any meal.

Mantzur, Sorki, and Susman were already seated at a round table. Susman should have had a separate table for himself—that large boar, Winestone mumbled to himself. *They were probably talking about me. I hate being the last to arrive at a lion's den. No, better call it a jackals' den. These cowards were scavengers, not hunters.* He nodded to his colleagues.

"Welcome, Larry," Mantzur said with a slight smile. "We worried about you. You are never late for a free meal. I do not have to introduce you to our big Mo. You and him are already good friends—"

"—Absolutely, absolutely!" Sorki laughed out loud. The laugh was grossly animated. *He can't be drunk already, can he?* "Larry and myself are great buddies. Larry decided to be late, hoping that we would take the bill before he arrived." Another laugh. "Cheers, Larry!" He lifted his cocktail glass. "How do you say 'cheers' in Jewish? 'Lechaim?'"

"As a matter of fact, 'Lechaim' is a Hebrew word," said Winestone as he tried to sit in between Herb Susman and his friend Mantzur. "It means 'to life'—"

"—No matter. Ha! Sit down, Larry. Hey, Herb, move your fat ass, will you? Give our distinguished chairman some place, you chunk of meat. Hey Giovanni! Bring our professor a drink. Larry what do you want? Watch me—when I say Giovanni all of them respond, all the Italiani! Ha!"

Is he always like this? Winestone could never understand the etiology of Sorki's manic chatter. *Well, this is a small price to pay for a fruitful peace deal.* Winestone smiled anyway and shook Mantzur's and Sorki's hands. "Joseph, Mahmud." He preferred Mantzur's handshake, more like his own: weak, flabby, and limp; he disliked that of Sorki: forceful and crushing. Winestone wasn't sure if there was supposed to be a message in that firm grip. Just in case, Winestone met the resistance with some of his own. He would not let himself be controlled.

"Larry, tonight, as you can see, we are honored to have with us our dear Herb Susman. Herb is an old friend, eh Herb?" Mantzur smiled at Susman whose face showed no expression whatsoever. *The pig never smiles,* observed Winestone.

"I am sure that tonight Dr. Winestone and Herb will open a new page of friendship. We need to work together." Winestone offered Susman his hand for a flimsy handshake. It was accepted, but turned out to be quite a sloppy effort on both sides.

"Dottore, a drink for you—or shall I bring the wine list?" asked another Giovanni.

"What are you having?" Winestone was undecided.

"Absolut on the rocks. Giovanni, could I have another one. Herb, another one?" Susman nodded. "OK. Giovanni, bring us the whole bottle, and a side dish of ice." Another staccato of laughter as Sorki turned to his colleagues to add: "Dr. Mantzur, our old mentor here, drinks only soda. That's why he ages so well: soda and no women—this is his recipe!"

"Bring me a Bloody Mary please. No wine," Winestone adjusted himself in the seat to get comfortable.

Rim couldn't understand how Americans could enjoy cocktails instead of wine with their food. But he had adapted.

"I am sorry I'm late, gentlemen. I had to drive to Manhattan and stop at my City Tower flat, and then I visited my mother just off the park. Anyway—while stuck in the traffic I was thinking about what car I should get next, you know, instead of my Merc. Rim wants me to get a Rolls, but I am not so sure. Mo, what do you say?" Winestone always started with small talk. He prided himself on his small talk, which relaxed everybody. His charming and down-to-earth manners together with his generosity had made influential friends all over the country and opened doors to the most prestigious surgical societies. "Mo, you drive a Merc as well. What about we both change for a Rolls?" Winestone also enjoyed boasting about his wealth.

"I am happy with my Mercedes. I don't get pleasure from cars only. Ask Herb. He knows what I am talking about, don't you, buddy?"

The rude animal will not draw me into one of his habitual pornographic monologues, Winestone thought. He smiled. "As a matter of fact, Mo, I'm thinking about buying a Porsche. I rented one last summer in Nice. Perhaps the new 911—she's a nice machine." Pavarotti's "O Sole Mio" floated into the room from hidden hi-fi speakers; the voice seemed to be everywhere and nowhere at the same time. Winestone was quick to pick up the cue. "We saw Pavarotti at the Metropolitan two weeks ago. It is a pity his voice is declining. Dr. Susman, do you enjoy opera?"

Susman glanced up from the menu just long enough to say, "Not really."

Bunch of primitives, thought Winestone. No class at all. The people at the Jewish Island Hospital were much, much more sophisticated. The fact that they did not appreciate his small talk was a little unnerving. *Why is Mantzur so quiet? He is the one who organized this meeting. Why doesn't he uplift the atmosphere?*

"Signori, are you ready to order?" The daughter of the owner, dressed in a black leather mini-skirt and high heels, stood over them with her pen and notebook ready.

"Let's see. I think I'll take my usual here, your excellent Penne with clams. Herb?" said Sorki eyeing the daughter from head to toe.

"Yep. The usual. Double portion please. Add cream to the clam sauce..."

"You see, Larry, good ol' Herb is on permanent diet!"
Sorki laughed loud enough for half the restaurant to hear him.
He is bloody drunk, Winestone realized. *Look at that
coarse thick nose and the silly black moustache. He's a look-
alike of Saddam Hussein.* For a split second Winestone was
haunted by the vivid image of entering his elegant office in
the morning and finding Sorki's portrait staring at him from
the opposite wall. *Absurd.*

"Joseph, what about you?" asked Sorki.

"For me the Wienerschnitzel with a small portion of
spaghetti as a side dish. No sauce, please."

"Wienerschnitzel?" Sorki snorted. "Joseph, this is an
Italian restaurant, not a fucking Austrian joint. Ha! Larry,
your turn."

Why does he have to dominate? Winestone pulled himself together and asked the lady, "What's your name? I've
never seen you here before." He tried to charm all waiters
and waitresses, which understandably irritated Rim.

"Signore, I am Simonetta, back in town for the holi-
days."

"You work on your vacation," Winestone inquired,
delighted by her enthusiasm. "How nice! Splendid! Are you
in college?"

"Yes, Dottore. I study law in Boston. What can we prepare for you, signore?"

"What would you suggest?" This was Winestone's old
trick. Waiters loved it.

"We have an excellent rack of lamb, our sea food platter
is fresh and today's pasta dish—Penne with lobster meat—is
delicious."

"Thank you very much. That does sound delicious. But
I'll have your pork cotelette. I've had it before. It is not on
the menu, but the chef always prepares it for me." Winestone
would never order what the waiters recommended.

"Grazie, signore. Can I bring you a selection of anti-
pasti, signori?"

"Of course, as usual," said Sorki. His gaze followed the waitress as she walked into the kitchen. "Cute, isn't she? Very cute, eh Larry? Did you notice her melons? Larger than Rim's, hahaha." Sorki eyed Winestone for a reaction.

Stay cool, keep your calm, thought Winestone. *Such a rude creep. He allows himself too much.* At the last annual Hospital's banquette he even tried to paw Rim. Winestone broke open the Italian bread roll and applied a thick layer of butter. He soon received his Bloody Marry and toasted his colleagues.

The pork steak was exquisite. Winestone wolfed it down and nibbled at the bone. Then he wiped the fat and gravy with a piece of bread. Not much was said while they ate except for the continuous manic chatter by Sorki. For desert Mantzur ordered a fruit salad, Sorki and Susman chose ice cream with Grand Marnier, and Winestone a warm apple pie, fresh strawberries and cream. All except Mantzur ordered cappuccino and Grappa.

"Colleagues," Mantzur began. "We all know why we are here tonight. I trust that we had a pleasant dinner and suggest that from now on we'll make a habit of it. We will dine together every two or three weeks."

"Absolutely," agreed Winestone, "As a matter of fact we could alternate between Brooklyn and Manhattan." There were so many restaurants he had yet to try.

"Larry," continued Mantzur, "I believe that we understand each other now quite well. Mo and Herb are aware of your great importance to the well being of the department, to the residency program. The residents—we need them so badly. You also understand, I believe, that the Park Hospital is not the same as your previous Jewish Island. You understand the crucial importance of our Medical Board. Larry, we need you and you need us. We must work together to maintain control, which traditionally was in our hands—the hands of surgeons. Howard wants to dominate and manipulate all of us, but together we are stronger. Herb here is on our side. Larry, you obviously remember that we—the leaders of the

Medical Board—strongly supported Howard and Farbstein when they recruited you. You remember that Mo stepped down from his position as an interim chairman, to vacate the post for you."

"I appreciate it very much, Joseph, Mo," said Winestone, emptying the last drop of Grappa and thinking he'd need a lot more Grappa to survive this social intercourse. A small cigar would come in handy, but he never carried one. *Sorki stepped down for me? What nonsense!* After the previous chairman died of lymphoma they gave Sorki a try. It was a disaster. Even his friends Farbstein and Mantzur understood that with that asshole at the helm they would eventually lose the residency. Chaudri told him how Sorki was running the show—like an Ayatollah in a provincial town, exactly the way he ran the Medical Board now.

Winestone continued. "I agree that the minor misunderstandings which developed between us and marred the atmosphere and the routine function of the department, should end. The hospital is thriving; there is enough work for all of us. As a matter of fact, during my chairmanship at the JIH the relationship between 'town and gown,' between the private surgeons and the full time staff, was exemplary. We could have the same situation at our place. You let me run the department and the residency without interference, and you have the Medical Board and the rest of the hospital to look after. Sounds all right with me."

"Larry, Larry," boomed Sorki, coming out of an apparent trance. *Is he on drugs?* The thought crossed Winestone's mind; *it would explain those manic outbursts.* Sorki's face seemed sharp and attentive to him but his brain seemed to be lagging behind half a step. "Larry," Sorki looked hard at Winestone. "There are a few points that we have to agree on tonight. First, next week's election to the Medical Board. I am running again for President, with my dear mentor Joseph as a Vice President, and Herb as secretary. Hey, Herb, wake up!" Sorki jabbed Susman who appeared narcoleptic, "Stop

75

drinking that Absolut as if it were water. Even I cannot carry your bulk into the car…What was I saying?"

"About the election to the Medical Board," Winestone offered.

"Yes. We want your full support and the votes of all the staff. We don't want any opposition. Remember that for the last seven years Joseph and myself have been leading the Medical Board without any opposition. There is no need for alternative candidates to be nominated. Am I right, Joseph?"

"Mo is correct. No alternative candidates. It would be damaging to us all. Us surgeons have to present a unified front." Mantzur whispered his points, unlike his counterpart Sorki.

He must be tired; it's past his bedtime. Winestone pitied the older man, but was thinking, *Nothing wrong with making peace. It'll do us all good.* He opened his chubby hands. "I do not have a problem with this," he said evenly.

Sorki leaned back, relaxing as if readying himself for another round of drinks. "The second point—uh, issue—is very minor. It concerns my cousin Yasser. You know Yasser? Yes, he is, in fact one of my numerous cousins. You know how many Sorkis we have back home?" Another animated burst of laughter. "Don't even ask. I am not sure whether Yasser is my first or second cousin. But anyway, he is family. I promised him a residency slot in the US. Yasser was a qualified surgeon back home, a great and hardworking kid, a top resident! I suggest you accept him into your program next July—"

Winestone's smile froze as if to say, *Forget it. Now you're pushing your luck.* His response, however, was controlled. "Mo, there's no doubt that your cousin is a bright young man. But we select and admit new residents through the national matching system. Your cousin will have to apply and go through interviews and the matching—like any other applicant. In addition, it is no longer that easy to admit foreign graduates; as a matter of fact, it is almost impossible. This is off the record, of course, but to tell you the truth, my

hands are bound. You may not know this but the current policy—not official, of course—of the American Board of Surgery is to limit the number of foreign graduates entering US
surgical training programs."

"Foreign? Foreign? Foreign?" shouted Sorki, banging
the table with a strong hand. People at the next table stared at
him. "We're all fucking foreigners! All of Brooklyn is made
up of foreigners. Foreigners—like myself and Joseph—
brought the hospital to where it is today. Look at Herb here.
He's a fucking American all right, but he's also a foreign
graduate. And you tell me that you cannot take my cousin
because, because, because, he is a fo-reig-ner?" Sorki put on
a heavy accent, imitating the stereotypical accent a New
Yorker might use to describe an Arab.

"Mo, relax." Winestone grabbed Sorki by his sleeve.
"Remember, I am a foreign graduate as well. I know that
your cousin is a good man and I will try to help. But you will
appreciate that the situation is complicated. We have to play
by the rules, written as well as unwritten ones. We may have
to offer him a preliminary position for the next year and the
year after admit him to a categorical spot—"

"No way. My cousin is thirty-five years old. I promised
him five years of residency, not six!"

"Mo, let me deal with it. I promise to do my best. As
you know I also have to consult with my other full-time colleagues who are helping me run the residency. I will have to
talk to Chaudri, Rusk, Bashir and Zohar."

"Malcolm Rusk? Malcolm will agree to anything. Show
me another surgeon in America who earns so much for doing
so little, ha! Rusk can't afford to have a spine and you know
it. He is at your mercy. Chaudri needs to make money; he'll
better cooperate. And Bashir is Joseph's boy anyhow. Herb,
what do you say?"

"Rusk is a fawckin' scarecrow," groaned Susman, his
face so heavy with inebriation he couldn't even pronounce
the words properly. *He can sound so civilized,* thought Wine-

stone, *until he curses. This is when the Brooklyn street accent resurfaces.*

Sorki brought his face close to Winestone's. A trickle of sweat ran down his right temple. His eyes narrowed. The pupils were dark and bottomless. Sorki was struggling to focus; his mind was fighting the onslaught of the alcohol, momentarily losing control over the facial features. For a split second Winestone caught a glimpse of the ruthless hatred and selfishness brooding underneath the noisy joviality and big-mouthed cowboy manners. Sorki breathed heavily. He no longer shouted. He hissed, spitting out the words.

"Zohar. Indeed, Larry. Zohar is the last point I wanted to raise with you." Sorki looked Winestone in the eye, trying to force him to blink. Winestone countered with a friendly smile, but no blink. He already knew that Sorki was no match for him.

"Please go ahead, Mo. I'm listening." He raised a hand to call a waiter. "Could I have an espresso? A double please. Another Grappa?" Winestone asked himself out loud. "Yes, why not? What about you?" He noticed Mantzur giving Sorki a warning glance while ordering a mint tea in his hushed and almost womanly voice. Sorki shrugged, grabbed his glass and emptied it in one gulp. He wouldn't have Grappa. Instead, he stuck to the bottle of Absolut. *He's like a defiant child,* Winestone thought. *Interesting. I wouldn't have thought that Zohar manages to irritate him that much.*

Sorki tried to sound casual, but after his earlier fireworks display that was impossible. "Larry, we all know Zohar is a problem. A big one. When did he start? In 1995? This guy is like a slow virus, like mad cow disease, ha! Gradually, he's penetrating the brain of our residents, poisoning them. He talks too much, asks too many questions. Why did you do this? Why did you operate on that? He's turned the M&M into a combat zone. People are afraid to operate at our hospital. They take their big cases elsewhere in order not to be criticized. Before you came, we conducted the M&M and the Departmental Quality Assurance Committee. The atmosphere was cordial. Productive, if you know what I mean. But now, with Zohar around, it feels as if we're on the West Bank of Palestine. Why doesn't he practice his evidence-based surgery in Israel, where he came from? Tell me about foreigners screwing our system!"

Winestone nodded before counterpunching. "Mo, I take your point. But cut out the personal issues for a moment. You may not like Zohar's style, but the fact is that he's essential to my program. We need an academic surgeon to fulfill the formal requirements of the residency review committee or we will lose our accreditation." *In fact, you almost lost that accreditation, you idiot,* Winestone almost thought out loud before catching himself. "Yes, Zohar can be abrupt and controversial. He is an Israeli, you know, and they are all like this. But the residents like him, and he is productive. It would be very hard to replace him, if not impossible."

Sorki considered that fact before responding. "Suppose you're right. Suppose you need him to satisfy those paper shifters, OK, OK. But then Zohar is your problem. You brought him, you deal with him. He has to shut up that loud mouth of his. Let him teach and write papers. But tell him to stop criticizing us. Joseph, he asked you about the indications at the M&M! Can you believe it?" His eyes and tone were expressive but the rest of his face seemed drawn and tired.

Sorki continued. "A fucking greenhorn like Zohar asking you about in-di-ca-tions! Ridiculous! Joseph, come on, you tell our friend Larry what he has to do with Zohar."

"Larry, you and I have been in the business long enough. I agree with Mo. You'll have to deal with the man. We know you can. We trust you. The hospital thrives on our income. The more we operate the happier the Board of Trustees is. Zohar is a troublemaker, a dangerous element. He changes the way our residents think and behave. A few weeks ago Silverstein—a good resident—refused to scrub with me on a thoracotomy, claiming that the carcinoma was not resectable. This has never happened to me before. This is a dangerous trend. What is this? Is Zohar the head of our in-house Gestapo? A surgical police?"

"No. He's the chief of our Hospital Mossad," Sorki laughed, referring to the elite Israeli intelligence service. You could call it the equivalent to the CIA, the FBI and all of the mercenaries in the US all rolled into one. "Herb, you are so quiet tonight, is it the heartburn? The reflux? How many times did I offer you a gastroplasty, eh? Herb, a forty-five minutes procedure, three staplers, boom-boom, and you are going to look like a baby. You'll be able to see your own cock again." Sorki exploded with laughter, realizing Susman's size may have been even too much of a challenge for him.

He would kill that pig if he ever operates on him and Susman probably knows it. Winestone knew. *Although...that wouldn't be such a bad idea.* Susman had a weak heart, or so Dr. Geddy, the cardiologist, had told him. Apparently his ejection fraction was less than twenty percent. His heart must have looked like a punctured balloon. It could hardly pump the blood any longer—and all that fat wouldn't make things easier. His arteries were probably as clogged as the Holland tunnel. Susman knew that, for sure. But risk an operation? By Sorki? Only a few months ago Sorki fixed an inguinal hernia on Susman's father. The man died a few days later. "Medical complications," was the formal reason. I'd unofficially called it a "kill through an unnecessary operation in a patient not fit to undergo even a shave under local anesthesia." *Is Susman too stupid to realize that Sorki killed his own father? Or did the two of them perhaps...*Winestone felt a chill run down his spine. *It's not impossible...*

Susman came to life and emptied the vodka in his glass. "I don't know what you two are tawkin about," he slurred. With the Absolut now flowing freely across his blood-brain barrier 'talking' sounded like "tawwwking." He continued. "Zohar is a subversive element. My sources tell me he has a history of gettin' hisself inna trouble with colleagues. I don't know about South Africa, but we know he created problems in Israel. I'm investigatin' it. Might be better for you," he pointed a wobbly finger at Winestone, "to deal with him before we dig up some nasty shit on that fawker. Either replace'm or shut'm up fer good. If I were you I wouldn't waste my time on foolin' around with this fawkin' yahoo. We have our methods here in Brooklyn. This is not the Island or Great Neck. We have contacts—" Susman made an unmistakable gesture. Sorki laughed, gesticulating the thought away with the flick of his right hand.

"This is not Great Neck. You kill me, Herb. Your sense of humor!" More laughter. "Come on, no need to threaten our friend Larry. He understands what we want from him. Lechaim, salute, cheers—come on, we're all buddies now!" Sorki clanked his glass—once more filled to the rim— against Winestone's and Susman's and gulped down yet another shot of Vodka. He burped with satisfaction as he slammed the empty glass down on the table and wiped his broom-sized moustache. "Joseph here is falling asleep, so let's go home. Larry, this year you will sit at our table at the Christmas party, OK? With your lovely Rim of course. Like a big family. Herb, relax, Zohar is a nobody. Larry knows how to deal with him. Giovanni, Giovanni!" Sorki shouted. Susman joined in. "Bring the fawckin' bill, will ya?"

Sorki seemed satisfied. While waiting for the bill he said, "By the way, Larry, while talking about gastroplasties— I want to offer you to join me in our new Morbid Obesity Clinic. I know that this is an old hobby of yours. I get at least fifteen fatties referred to me each month. I am ready to share them with you. Enough work for both of us. Bless McDonalds. Bless America for its mountains of fat. This is the best money I make. Forty-five minutes work brings in thousands, easy. Chop chop. Ha!"

As they left the restaurant Herb Susman held Winestone by the upper arm, keeping him back at the top of the five stairs that lead down onto the pavement as he swayed like a big ship in a rolling sea. Winestone shuddered with disgust, but let it happen—the man was obviously struggling to keep his balance. A ship without a keel, nor ballast.

"One sec, Winestone," Susman managed to say, looking at him with his eyes that swam unevenly within their sockets. Mantzur and Sorki were standing at the curb under an umbrella waiting for the valet to pull up with Mantzur's Jaguar. "Wanna tell ya something.' Anodder stupid move by Zohar—anythin' could happen. You better deal wid him soon. No more fawkin' around."

This drunken swine! Winestone thought. He ignored Susman's remark. The man was clearly out of his mind, and by morning wouldn't even remember where he had dinner.

Susman eyed him slyly. Suddenly he let go of Winestone's arm and stepped down onto the pavement, splashing through the puddles as he marched towards Mantzur's car in stiff, though varying strides. It was clear he was making an effort to look as sober as possible.

▲▼◢◣▼▲

Mantzur drove his two friends to the parking lot at the hospital, Sorki in the passenger seat, Susman in the back.

"Herb, will you be able to drive?" Mantzur tried to catch Susman's eyes in the rear view mirror. A snore was the only reply.

"Sleep apnea syndrome," Sorki diagnosed with a laugh. "No more driving for him. I'd better drop him off."

"What about you, Mo? Are you OK? The two of you emptied a bottle. The roads are wet. You must take it easy."

"I am fine, Uncle Joe. I am fine. I am always fine. I'm a strong man!" Sorki clapped on his tummy. "What do you think about Winestone? Will he cooperate? Will he behave?"

"Leave Winestone to me. Winestone is sophisticated. He is not going to be intimidated by Herb's methods. You irritated him tonight, Sorki. Winestone is strong and has a lot of influential friends. He is dangerous. Don't underestimate him. But I know his psychology. You have to buy him with style. He is aging, and this is his last position as a chairman. He enjoys himself, and this is the key to his heart. You deal with the Medical Board, Howard and Farbstein, and leave Winestone and the Board of Trustees to me. And tell Herb not to try anything foolish. We're not going to solve this one with baseball bats. We need to use our brains."

"Sure, sure. You deal with Winestone, and meanwhile I will crush the other little Jew, that cockroach Zohar. Crunch! Hey Herbie, are you still asleep? Don't be upset, you are only half Jew. We'll spare you—ha! Joseph, did you see Winestone's eyes when I offered him a cut from the fatties? I tell you, he's going to come on board—the bastard's gotta make some bucks to keep Rim happy; never mind his new Porsche. Reminds me; tomorrow morning I have two gastroplasties..."

▲▼▲▲▼▲

Mantzur is the man, Mantzur is the brain, and Mantzur is the key. Images and voices from the evening's conversation ran through Winestone's head in loose order as he exited from the Gowanus expressway onto the Belt parkway. He passed under the Verrazano Bridge, now obscured by fog. A Bloody Mary or two, a Grappa, or was it more? But he drove well and steadily; the cops never stop a fancy car with an MD number plate in any event. Hayden's Symphony number ninety-four was in the CD player. The brilliant architecture of the masterpiece's harmonies translated into movement by the effortless elegance of the Mercedes as it carried Winestone safely through the moist October night. It began to rain harder; he turned up the wiper speed.

Susman. What a pig; what a caricature. A non-entity, a cheerleader of Sorki and Mantzur. Behaved like a cheap Mafioso to impress his friends. Ridiculous.

Sorki. We have slight problem there. Arrogant bastard, full of himself. Not too smart, and not careful enough. That's exactly it: his brutish simple mindedness. Susman will back off when openly confronted—Sorki will dig in his heels. A fanatic. He belongs to a world beyond reason. Dangerous?

83

Winestone shrugged. I've come across that type before and I know how to isolate them. Sorki's manageable. *The real threat is Mantzur. He is the brain.* Mantzur was pulling the strings. Always the balancing factor, self-motivated and controlling, the manipulative diplomat. *The way to survive in this hospital is to have Mantzur as a friend—as a buffer between management and the Medical Board.* Winestone was pleased. It was his idea to appoint Mantzur as his vice chairman. A masterful move. Even Dick Kelly, the almighty president and CEO of the New York Center-Manhattan University Medical School, had congratulated him. There was a certain chemistry between him and Mantzur, a special understanding that existed between the people who control and those who are obeyed. Yet Mantzur was delicate and fastidious, not rude and common like the others. His wife Rim thought that he was a perfect gentleman. Winestone opened the window and breathed in the salty ocean air. Yes, the Morbid Obesity offer by Sorki sounded generous; a few gastroplasties could bring an extra twenty grand or so per month. Enough to upgrade all their flights to first class and pacify Rim. She hated flying business class. *The cousin, the cousin of Sorki's from Iran—what about him? Why not take him?* That thought was rear-ended by another problem...

Zohar. Yes, Zohar is another potential problem. They hate him because he irritates them in a nasty way, as their antidote. Zohar has to calm down or leave. The program has been approved for the next five years; we could do without him for a while. On the other hand... Winestone hummed along as the symphony reaches a crescendo; he held his breath, relishing those last seconds of tension about to be swept away in that beautiful closure, the pure and majestic final chords. To each his place... No, it's the other way round. Zohar actually will come in handy. He can be used to bully them, to be unleashed at any time. *He's a bit of a loose canon at the moment, but I'm convinced that I'll be able to figure out a way to control Zohar and turn him into a fine weapon.*

After all, what did they call me, at the Jewish Island Hospital? Charming Larry. Zohar is not a problem; he's an asset.

▲▼▲▼▲

He had to realize that even a zealot like me needed to survive, to pay my mortgage and send my kids to college. Not to mention be protected by my boss against ruthless enemies. I didn't know it at the time, but Winestone was gearing up to nurse my one quality he'd already tried once to change, Like a wise street fighter, using an opponent's own energy to knock them down, Winestone was going to use my search for justice to manipulate me into precisely the position they wanted me.

8

Gathering Storm

*If a doctor has treated a man with a metal knife for a
severe wound, and has caused the man to die, his
hands shall be cut off.*
—Hammurabi's Code, ~2000 BC

*(If Hammurabi's Code were in effect, almost half of
today's surgeons would be amputees.)*

January 1999.

It snowed almost half a foot overnight. The long-term forecast said that January was going to bring lots of it. I shoveled the driveway, which re-activated some lower back pain. Must be all those years of unnatural posture at the operating table. For a moment I thought about taking Heidi's brand new four-wheel drive; my Cadillac was a pain in the ass to drive when the roads were slippery. I knew the highway and bridge would be well plowed and salted, so I took my car.

To avoid the congestion from parents dropping kids off at schools along Fourth Avenue, I turned right onto Twentieth Street and drove along the Greenwood Cemetery. It looked like a Black Forest postcard. I turned left at Sixth Avenue and right on Ninth Street, wasting five minutes crawling behind a garbage truck. The huge tires splashed through the slush, and pedestrians jumped away from the curb to avoid being splattered. It was five past eight when I arrived at the parking lot, five minutes late for the monthly meeting of the Departmental Quality Assurance (QA) committee. As I hurried to the meeting, my mind drifted to a conversation I'd had about a week earlier with a friend of mine...

After hearing my account of Mantzur and Sorki, my friend Nils, a guest professor from Sweden sat silent. Only after a healthy pause did he ask: "How can this be possible? How in the late nineties, in New York City and in a country where medicine is so advanced and controlled, where lawyers hide behind every tree—how can a bunch of surgeons keep up such an ongoing spree?"

"Very simple," I'd replied without hesitation. I'd been thinking about it for three years. "They do it by controlling the quality assurance mechanisms and knowing which patients can be safely disposed off. They are experts at using the system to their advantage." The ease of my answer was somewhat confusing. They do things quite a bit differently in Sweden.

"How is your QA system structured?"

"First, all complications are presented at a Morbidity and Mortality conference, noted in writing and accompanied by formal minutes of the proceedings. We're a teaching hospital, so in our case all the presentations have to be done by our residents."

"I see. It sounds like good opportunity to learn. But do you expect them to evaluate what happened?"

"No. They're not supposed to pre-judge the cases; they just have to offer an objective description of what happened. Part of my responsibility for the residency program consists of seeing to it that our residents prepare well-researched, accurate scientific presentations of these cases. And that's how I got onto this thing. After a while I simply couldn't help but notice the patterns in Mantzur and Sorki's cases on my lists."

"So what can you as an academic surgeon do in a case like this? Did you sound an alarm?"

This wasn't an easy question to answer. "Yes and no. Remember that our task is to present the facts and provide scientific background. We're not supposed to preempt the M&M conference's deliberations; we're supposed to provide material. The conference has to draw its own conclusions.

You have to avoid being subjective. We don't mention patients' names, and the summary of the M&M discussion normally concludes with either 'the standard of care was met,' 'technical complication,' and so on. Remember, the idea of the M&M is not to judge, but to inform, to learn—" Nils put up his hand, gesturing at me for silence. The look on his face teetered between dreadful comprehension and blissful ignorance. A healthy knot of flesh formed between furrowed brows.

"So, tell me something. Suppose you were guilty of a real fuck-up. I don't know—left a clamp inside a guy or something stupid like that. You'd have a resident standing up there talking about exactly how it happened, naming the doctor and describing the misadventure and that would be filed away as a technical complication?" I could see he was starting to appreciate my dilemma, and I hadn't even started.

"Anything short of removing the wrong organ will earn you a 'technical complication' at the most. Most of the problem cases are closed this way. The label doesn't really count; it's the process. The exposure is painful enough. Under normal circumstances it should send a clear signal."

"Can someone avoid being questioned by the M&M?"

"Yes. You simply don't show up when your case is scheduled for discussion. When this happens the case is automatically transferred to the next level, the departmental QA committee." Nils leaned back in his seat a bit, now that he was warming up a little to what I was saying.

"And that's where things get nasty for these guys, I suppose."

"That's the theory. But in practice our QA committee does almost nothing, it just clears everything. That's one of Mantzur's little tricks."

"What's that?"

"Mantzur hardly ever comes to the M&Ms, and never responds to any letters sent to him by the QA Committee. You see, all the serious stuff—like 'on table' mortalities or 'unplanned' postoperative returns to the OR—are automatically registered and referred to the QA Committee by the hospital QA nurse anyhow. That doesn't mean they are going to look into the matter. It is good enough for them to just note it in order to meet the formal requirements of the State of New York with its numerous laws and rules to improve practice, maintain standards and these sorts of things. As long as the hospital plays by the book everything is fine. One could almost say that because we have so many rules and regulations, the main role of the QA committee has become to make sure that the formalities are being followed. The quality assurance they provide is not quality of care but quality of paperwork because that's what determines the flow of funds."

"Is that all there is to it? Just these two departmental committees?"

"No, there's a third level, an external controlling body. It is called the QA Committee of the Medical Board."

"That group oversees all departments in your hospital, I guess. Like a joint controlling body reporting to top management. Am I right?"

"Exactly."

"So it cannot be bypassed or avoided?"

"No." He looked at me lamely.

"Then where's the problem?"

"The chairman of that committee."

"I don't understand."

"It's chaired by the terminator himself."

"You mean—Sorki?"

"Yes. But it gets better than that. Sorki and Mantzur—the other, more cunning terminator, Terminator Two, if you please—also sits on the Board of Trustees, which, in turn, controls the level of top management that Sorki's committee reports to. They've got Howard—our president—by the balls, and he knows it."

"Marc," Nils said, shaking his head with a look of downright amazement. "This is unbelievable. In our Swedish system this could not happen. True, we have disreputable doctors as well—everyone has them—but the magnitude of the problem is different. What about the patients? The families? The lawyers? I was told that in America there are more lawyers than doctors. How is it possible that Mantzur and Sorki are not sued?" I sat back and considered one of my favorite quotes, making sure I had it right before I spoke.

"'Doctors are the same as lawyers," I said. "The only difference between doctors and lawyers is that lawyers merely rob you. Doctors rob you and kill you.' Great quote, eh?"

"Who said it, Mark Twain?"

"No, Anton Chekhov, a Russian writer. He knew from first hand experience—he trained as a physician."

Nils laughed. "Still, I thought your lawyers would love to exploit those cases and make a buck—"

"—No, they'd rather focus on more promising cases. Besides, even if the patient uses a lawyer he's more likely to sue a highly trained and competent physician and not one of the negligent ones."

"Nonsense, Marc." When you think about it, it really does sound ridiculous.

"Take a solid and dedicated surgeon who promptly re-operates on a patient whose intestinal anastomosis has leaked. He re-opens the abdomen and finds a dehisced anastomosis and lots of pus. The patient dies, and the family sues the surgeon for the leak in the intestine and the failure to diagnose it earlier. OK? Now let's consider the bad, negligent surgeon. He does not diagnose the leaking intestine, does not perform the needed re-operation, and treats the patient with antibiotics. Right? His patient also dies, but the family will never know that his death was due to the anastomotic failure. His death will be attributed to 'natural causes' such as pneumonia or old age."

"That's ridiculous—" I carried on through his disbelief.

"—On top of which most lawsuits do not even concern true malpractice. As we know, bad outcome is not equivalent to malpractice. That a patient dies from a heart attack after the operation is not necessarily associated with malpractice, right? Listen, I know the figures, I researched them. An estimated 44,000 to 98,000 hospital patients die each year in this country because of medical errors. Do you believe that the majority of such cases result in lawsuits? The reality is that marginal practitioners rarely get sued."

"You mean that the lawyers are stupid and don't know who to sue?"

"Forget about lawyers. Lawyers care nothing about medical practice, about quality of care. Lawyers care about making money. Think about it this way: The litigation process is initiated by the aggrieved patient or family. Lawyers do not find cases in the street. Patients who consult a lawyer have three specific characteristics that set them apart from harmed patients who do not sue. First, they may be poor and need the money, but the poor are usually not insured or are badly insured—by Medicaid—and our terminators do not touch them. Or, second, they belong to a minority and want to screw the rich white doctor; but in our environment these are usually not insured or only insured by Medicaid—not 'their' type of cases."

"Does it matter if a person is white, black or Latino?"

"Of course it matters. I work in Brooklyn. If I am sued in Brooklyn by a black patient, my chances to win the lawsuit are almost zero. The jury is always non-white and sympathizes with poor patients who were allegedly harmed by the rich white doctor. So race does matter."

"And the third type?"

"The third type is well informed, intelligent people. The patient understands that he has been harmed. This type is not a common specimen here in Brooklyn. They are inclined to select doctors in the Ivory Towers of Manhattan. 'Their' patients, on the other hand, the patients on whom Mantzur, Sorki and similar types thrive, are old, from nursing homes, insured, low middle class, whites, and people who can be easily disposed of without attracting attention. Furthermore, 'they' have great charm. Mantzur and Sorki are on the 'best doctors' list of NY; very well spoken. 'I am sorry—we tried to save your mother's foot—the mother

91

being a 101 year old half-dead specimen anyway—but her poor heart failed.' Or 'The cancer was extensive—we tried to take it out, but—' People are not going to sue a surgeon for the lost life of an octogenarian, particularly when the surgeon is so 'famous' and 'kind.' Not to mention the fact that in some cases the family is actually relieved when the outcome is fatal."

"Marc, this is just appalling. How can you work and survive in such a crazy environment?"

I shrugged. "I don't know. I guess I shouldn't be so paranoid. After all, we're still talking about a minority. The vast majority of doctors try their utmost to do what's best. Still, I think it is absolutely crucial that someone stops these killings. Everybody here knows what is going on. But they all prefer to look the other way."

"Just keep out of trouble," he had insisted. "Do your job and leave it to the administration and your chairman."

▲▼▲▶▼▲

"I know," I said to myself in the hallway, now standing outside the door of Malcolm Rusk's office. I shook my head slightly to clear memories of a dozen similar conversations. One last deep breath. *Get some oxygen into the brain...*

I'm going to need it.

The door's well-oiled hinges didn't make a sound as it opened and closed behind me. A distinctive click was its only signature.

The departmental QA meeting was already under way. The committee's chairman was Dr. Malcolm Rusk, who had recently taken the position over from Dr. Winestone. Tall, lean, well groomed, articulate, and extremely politically correct, Rusk was a perfect choice for this role. A son of Polish immigrants, born and raised in Wisconsin, he had adopted and cultivated a 'waspish'—almost British—aura. The way he talked, the way he overdressed in tailored three-piece suits, and that white handkerchief in the breast pocket—I imagined Rusk was previously Ruskovesky or something similar. Rusk was one of the most benign surgeons I'd ever met. He would not harm anybody. He also could not discipline anybody. Sorki constantly laughed at him behind his back.

Rusk interrupted the meeting to welcome me: "Sit down, Marc. Heavy traffic as usual?"

"In a manner of speaking yes," I said, thinking about the lumbering and smelly garbage truck that had been in my path.

"You live too far away," Dr. Gotahedi commented. "Why don't you buy a house on the Hill just off the bridge? Took me fifteen minutes this morning," Gotahedi always liked to boast about his three million-dollar house on the hill that he knew I couldn't afford.

"Marc," Rusk said then, trying to get us on track. "Look at the agenda. We were discussing the first case that Judy brought to our attention." Judy Kennedy, sitting on Rusk's left, was the QA nurse. She was a middle aged, tall, fleshy Irish woman, both pleasant and soft-spoken. In her capacity Judy knew about any surgical disaster or mishap in the hospital. She knew what was happening; she wasn't stupid. I'd tested her a few times with small sarcastic questions or comments but she didn't take the bait. Instead she'd remained the correct and objective QA nurse. Was she spying for Sorki? Was she affiliated with the hospital mafia? Was she on their side? It was quite possible. She was a widow and widows need to survive just like everyone else.

Rusk continued: "To recapitulate, this is a patient who expired during an abdominal vascular procedure." The name of the person behind the case was never mentioned in the agenda or the case report. "Dr. Ilkadi, you reviewed the case. Please share your findings and opinion." I walked over to the coffee machine and poured myself a cup. No donuts today, which was good for my expanding girth.

I already knew what Ilkadi would say. I also knew that he took part in the operation, called in to bail out Mantzur, his old mentor. *OK, he is the Chief of Vascular Surgery—but how can he objectively review a case in which he took part?* Ilkadi started. "Colleagues, look at the second page, case 1999/12. It was an eighty-one year-old male, background of ischemic heart disease, congestive heart failure, COPD, a minor stroke three years ago, who presented this time with a large—six point two centimeter—abdominal aortic aneurysm. Pre-operative cardiac evaluation established him fit for an elective repair of the aneurysm; his ejection fraction was reasonable." *Sure, he must have been very fit,* I thought acerbically. According to Dr. Geddy, the chief of cardiology, all patients operated by Mantzur were "fit." *They have to be.*

I had researched this case myself, and I was interested to see what they'd say about it. I listened intently.

"To cut the story short, the patient underwent a routine graft replacement of his Triple A. After the completion of the proximal anastomosis he started to ooze a lot from the retroperitoneum, requiring a massive blood transfusion. Attempts to stop the bleeding failed, coagulopathy developed despite infusion of fresh frozen plasma and platelets. In total he required, let's see, he required twenty units of pack cells and fifteen liters of clear fluids. Eventually he arrested."

"Holy cow," Sam Glatman balked. Glatman was the second vascular surgeon on the committee. "The guy was wet!"

"Dr. Ilkadi," Rusk said with a sense of immediacy, trying to cut to the bottom of the thick layer of bullshit he was expecting. His eyes were focused and his lips trimmed tightly. "What really happened? What was the cause of the hemorrhage? Was the vena cava injured? The renal vein? Was there any technical problem with the anastomosis, which triggered the coagulopathy?"

"Malcolm," I said, unable to hold myself back any longer. "The guy bled to death because he received urokinase. They gave him urokinase, which blocked any effective clotting."

Rusk looked surprised: "What are you talking about? Urokinase is contraindicated in such operations."

Gotahedi jumped in to help his brethren: "Dr. Zohar, let Dr. Ilkadi finish his assessment. No one asked you to review this case or to comment. Anyway, you are not a vascular surgeon. Please Dr. Ilkadi, tell us why he died."

Ilkadi looked puzzled. "Urokinase? There is nothing in the operative report about urokinase. Our assessment was, that is—my assessment is—" he hesitated. He shifted ever so slightly in his seat. Subconsciously perhaps, he wiped the palms of his hands upon his stylish dark slacks. "The coagulopathy resulted from hepatic cirrhosis."

"Dr. Rusk, I am not a vascular surgeon," Gotahedi said quickly to take up some slack. "But all of us have had previous experience with similar cases. You start an elective procedure, you encounter a previously undiagnosed chronic liver disease—I mean cirrhosis—and these patients bleed like from a water tap. Nothing one can do. I don't see anything extraordinary here. Shall we move to the next case?" Gotahedi looked at his gold Rolex, "I have a case at nine-thirty, a cute little old woman with recurrent incisional hernia. She adores me."

"Listen to this little creep," Glatman whispered in my ear. "What a narcissist!"

I almost didn't hear him before I exclaimed: "The liver cirrhosis story is absolute nonsense. Dr. Ilkadi, is there any documentation in the chart? Any pre-operative liver dysfunction? Any liver biopsy showing cirrhosis? Could we look at the chart please?"

"Marc," Rusk said, interrupting my assault. "Time is out. Shall we move to the next case? Judy, how many cases left on the agenda?"

"Two cases and then the old business."

I continued, oblivious to what was being said. Pilots know this phenomenon as "tunnel vision" or "boresight vision." My field of view was so narrow all I could see were Ilkadi's pupils. "Malcolm, before we close this case I ask permission to review the chart myself. I know that this patient received urokinase intra-operatively."

"What is this?" Dr. Stig Rasmussen, chief of Neurosurgery spat in disgust. "Another witch hunt by Dr. Zohar? Until now we see Dr. Zohar conducting a witch hunt against Dr. Sorki. Now is he doing the same against Dr. Mantzur?"

"Stig, please, no names. We do not mention names here—" Rusk called out.

"—Rubbish, rubbish, names or no names, we know what's the matter here!" Rasmussen pointed a chubby finger at me. "This man conducts his personal vendetta against respectable members of our profession. This is unacceptable and has to be stopped."

Stig Rasmussen was a big, balding, red and sweaty Scandinavian with a huge head and a pair of penetrating, icy blue eyes. He was an impressive man with a remarkable curriculum vitae. A Finn, he had studied medicine in Stockholm, trained in neurosurgery in Sweden, Norway, the USA and Korea, where he also procured a local wife who later separated from him. Rasmussen worked virtually everywhere, including the United Emirate Republic and Saudi Arabia, where apparently all of the great Sheiks were his friends. He allegedly spoke numerous languages. He'd also passed through a few of Brooklyn's hospitals before he was recruited to the Park Hospital two years ago.

From my recollection he was warmly received by Sorki and associates at the Medical Board. Socially Rasmussen was charming. His tastes were oriental; including sushi and petite oriental women. He arrived with a different one on his arm at each of the hospital's parties. When complimented about the beauty of a concubine he would laugh heartily and often say: "Hey, should I arrange one for you? No problem!" We assumed that Sorki and Susman frequently enjoyed his hospitalities. What it was that brought Rasmussen to our institution at the age of sixty plus was not entirely clear to anyone. However, Winestone once admitted to me that Rasmussen had a Pandora's Box of nasty old stories to his credit. Evidently he was rushing to his friends' aid should he require the same assistance farther down the road.

"Dr. Rasmussen," I protested, "I am not interested in any personal vendetta. I just attempt to find out what happened. Isn't this the declared task of our QA committee, to investigate and then suggest corrective action?" Rusk stood up and started pacing a tight racetrack pattern between us all.

"Please stop it, both of you. As the chairman of this committee I hereby postpone this discussion. Was this case ever presented at the M&M? No? Very well then, we will let the residents review the chart and present it at the M&M. Dr. Ilkadi, any objections?"

"M&M is fine with me."

"Dr. Gotahedi?"

"Dr. Rusk, sure. You will present it at the M&M anyway. Be my guest. But in terms of QA, the case is kosher. I suggest to enter in the minutes that we accept the report by Dr. Ilkadi."

"Crazy idea!" I shouted. "All I want to do is see the chart!" My face was as red as a crab.

"I refuse to take part in this ongoing feud," Rasmussen stood up and paraded his large bulk out of the room.

Rusk winked at me as if nothing had just happened and said: "OK then. Let's look at case 1999/13. Dr. Falkow, you reviewed the case. Please go on."

Mitch Falkow was a private thoracic surgeon. The poor guy was currently in a big mess. Last week he operated on the wrong side of a patient's chest. No excuses for him...

▲▼◢▲▼▲

After the QA meeting Sam Glatman followed me into my room munching a ham and egg sandwich. I was starving—Where did he find it?

"Wanna bite?" Sam asked with a full mouth, probably noticing that my pupils doubled in diameter when my eyes locked onto it. I wanted a bite very badly, but I'd have probably just thrown it back up again. Stomach acid, egg and mayo were a bad combination. I shook my head no. "Gee, I'm famished! Won't Winestone supply us with food for these nasty meetings?" He took another bite and with his mouth half full continued. "OK, Marc, so what's the story? Urokinase? Where did you get that? You mean he executed the patient with urokinase? Is he crazy or what?"

I shut the door behind him. "OK, Sam, listen to this..."

Glatman wiped a piece of egg from his moustache with the sleeve of his white coat, looked at the ceiling and then at my phone. "Marc, your room is not bugged or anything? You have to be careful."

I shook off the thought. "I don't give a shit. Two weeks ago I sat here at my desk around five p.m. and Adams was standing at my door."

"Adams?"

"Jim Adams, the second year resident, you know, the Bostonian. Nice kid."

"Oh yes, yes. I know Adams. He's scrubbed with me a few times. I like him." Another big bite and some sloppy chewing noises. "Go on."

"Adams looked pale and exhausted. I asked him what the problem was. He said to me 'Dr. Zohar, we lost a patient on the table. We operated on him from the early morning until now, and we lost him.' Sam, you know how junior residents are. This was his first death on the table. The patient walks into the room on his feet and leaves in a box. Adams took it badly." Glatman looked at his watch. I didn't have his attention yet.

"Yeah, yeah. Stop commenting and give me the facts. I've got to go."

"Adams told me about the aneurysm case, how he bled from everywhere, how Ilkadi was called in, how they tried to patch the proximal anastomosis, all in vain. I tried to comfort him, saying something like, 'Jim, these things happen, if you operate enough you have to have complications.' You know, the usual spiel."

98

Glatman looked at his watch again. Damn it!

"Wait. Then Adams asked me something like this: 'Tell me, why did they use urokinase?' I almost jumped out of my chair! He said Mantzur injected about a hundred thousand units of urokinase into the aorta and then asked me if that was wrong." Sam sat forward in his chair. His head tilted slightly to one side, a sure sign that he was concentrating on my words. Now I had his attention! "I told him urokinase is a potent thrombolythic agent. It virtually dissolves all clots. You can use it in peripheral vascular procedures, inject it into the limbs to dissolve clots, but it is absolutely contraindicated in abdominal procedures, and especially when the entire ret-roperitoneum is opened and dissected—as in this case."

"No wonder the patient bled from everywhere," Glatman realized out loud. "He could not form clots. Did they try ami-nocaproic acid, or cryoprecipitate to abort the thrombolysis?'

"Not according to Adams. I told him that they killed his patient and asked him if he was sure of the dose. He said he was absolutely sure, and that it was Mantzur who asked for it from the circulating nurse. He figured she'd enter it into the chart."

"What made the old man use urokinase?" Glatman asked me. He hadn't looked at his watch for five minutes.

"He is confused, he is impaired. He uses urokinase in his fem-pops, to lyse residual clots. He forgot that this is a Triple A."

"And Ilkadi? Ilkadi isn't a fool."

"Ilkadi was called in later on. He was not aware that urokinase was given. The anesthetist sleeps, the nurses com-ply with the orders, the resident pulls on the retractors. It's the old story."

"Marc, who was the senior resident on this case? He could say something."

"The chief resident was Assad. He adores Mantzur. He just wants to cut. He won't say anything against the Padrino."

"I suppose so," he agreed. "Listen Marc, you know that I am not a big shot, just an average surgeon. I have my complications and problems. But this gives me nausea. And Winestone avoids confronting the issue." Sam sighed a deep, throaty sigh. "Something has to be done here, but I've got no idea what it is."

"Sam," I said pointedly, "you know what to do. You're a local boy."

"I couldn't do it without your lists. You know what I'm talking about."

"Not yet Sam. I cannot help you now. I'm being paid by Winestone. Do you want me to commit financial suicide? When the right time arrives I will act—but not now, it is too early."

"OK then," he said and then changed the subject. "What are you doing this weekend? Would you cover me? I am off to the Bahamas, have to satisfy my girlfriend." Glatman winked at me before I had a chance to answer. He already knew I'd say yes.

▲▼◢◣▼▲

Beverly, Winestone's secretary, was waiting for me by my open office door with a blue computer disk in her hand. She was wearing black high heels and a short skirt that left almost nothing to the imagination. It could have been the high heels, but I was pretty sure her legs looked even fitter than before. I tried to pretend I didn't notice, and was reasonably successful, I think. She followed me into the office and sat on the opposite side of my desk. I liked innocent-looking big women and she knew it. Except that she wasn't terribly innocent looking.

"Dr. Zohar, how are you today?" She fanned out her freshly varnished red nails. "Do you like them?" The bitch was teasing me. I tried to remain business-like. I could care less about the nails. But the rest of her?

"Looks great," I admitted, my eyes consuming her complete luscious package. "You've been waiting for me?"

"No particular reason. Just a social visit. Can I get you a coffee? Milk, no sugar, just as you like it? Any gossip?"

A social visit? And why is it that I remember closing my office door?

"Not really, how is your boyfriend?"

"Bruce is a darling. He's very good in bed but occasionally I figure he is too young for me. You know what I mean?" She flashed a beautiful white smile at me. *Dangerous!*

"Bev, Bruce is good for you. He loves you. Older men might be more experienced and bold, but we're also dirty and impotent. Now please forgive me, I have lots to do. You offered me coffee, don't forget."

"Yes, you're right. So what are you doing now? Busy writing one of your articles? You have to let me help you. I am an excellent editor. I worked on the newspaper in college."

"Thank you very much. I'll keep that in mind."

Bev stood up. I looked at her muscular legs contracting with the slight effort. Again, I tried to look like I barely noticed, but this time it was like concealing an enormous pimple on the end of my nose. I swallowed hard. Her voice was the backdrop to rapidly forming images in my mind that are better left unsaid. *Married? Yes. Buried? No.* "Will you be available at four p.m.?" *A personal meeting? In my office perhaps?* "Dr. Winestone wants you to see him in his office. Dr. Mantzur will be attending as well."

"What does he want now?" I said with irritation. I hated it when reality came snapping back so quickly.

"I don't have a clue," she admitted. "Have you seen my new earrings?" She flipped her hair to expose one ear. "Aren't they gorgeous? Larry's gift for Christmas. Real diamonds. He's such a dear!" She walked out, waving at me with the blue disk.

At four p.m. I knocked on Winestone's door. He was sitting on the black leather sofa. Mantzur—the vice chairman—was in one of the matching chairs.

"Hi, Dr. Winestone, Dr. Mantzur." I smiled as I greeted them.

"Marc, thanks for coming. Please sit down." Winestone offered me a handshake. I accepted his warm hand, and then I offered one to Mantzur as well. It was amazing how similar their handshakes felt. I wondered how a psychologist would analyze it. I didn't have a clue why I was there today; I was in and out Winestone's office every day, but this was my first formal meeting with both of them.

"Marc, do you have any idea why we asked you to see us?" Winestone was not smiling or joking as usual. He sounded serious. *Bad sign.*

"No clue."

"Well, Marc, the matter concerns a certain patient..." He looked at a scrap of paper. "Ah, yes. Mr. Jose Valez. Does that ring a bell?"

"Dr. Winestone," I smirked and almost laughed. Perhaps he wasn't being so serious after all. "I have seen thousands of Jose Valezes."

He was not amused. "Let us concentrate on the last Jose Valez you saw. You saw him at the clinic on January eighth?"

"I don't know what you are talking about." *What's their point?*

"I'm talking about the esophageal case. Carcinoma of the esophagus."

"Now I remember," I said, swallowing. "This was a young Hispanic man in his forties. He was referred to the clinic from outside with the diagnosis of carcinoma of the esophagus. If I remember correctly, the lesion was mid-esophageal, at around twenty-five centimeters. It was confirmed by biopsy as a squamous carcinoma."

Winestone played with his pen while he listened. "OK," he said, "what did you do with the patient? He hasn't been operated on as yet?"

It must have been that piece of shit Assad who ran to Mantzur. He idolizes Mantzur. The only difference between brown nosing and kissing ass is depth perception, and Assad clearly has none.

I looked at Mantzur, who remained impassive, and answered Winestone: "No, the patient has not undergone surgery as yet. According to the CT scan the lesion appears locally advanced. Hence, we referred him for chemo and radiotherapy, in an attempt to downstage it, you know—as suggested by recent literature—"

"—Dr. Zohar," interrupted Mantzur, "Cancer of the esophagus is a surgical disease. The place for it is in the specimen jar or the pathologist's table."

"Not really, Dr. Mantzur. Things are being done differently now."

Mantzur raised his voice one octave. "What literature? What changes? I've been removing those cancers for thirty years. At Upstate University, where I trained as a thoracic surgeon, we removed a few of them each week. Chemo? Radio? Nonsense. The patient has to be able to swallow, and to eat. Eventually all of them die, but they ought to die while eating. Patients who eat are happy!" I noticed with satisfaction that I had managed to irritate him.

"Marc," Winestone said, "Dr. Mantzur is our thoracic surgeon, our esophageal expert. We have to concentrate our experience in the proper hands. I suggest that he take over your patient."

Two in three of his esophageal cases die after the operation, seven out of his last ten esophageal resections died, and you, Winestone, call him an expert! I realized almost immediately that I didn't actually say that out loud. I wished I could have.

Instead, I said: "I do not think that this is a good idea. This patient can swallow. He is not totally obstructed, I think that starting with chemo-radio therapy is the way to go."

"And then, did you also plan to operate on him? You perhaps consider yourself a thoracic surgeon now?" Mantzur had never been sarcastic before. "Not a thoracic surgeon but an esophageal one. I consider myself an experienced esophageal surgeon. I am convinced that I have removed as many gullets as you, Dr. Mantzur, and it was not thirty years ago. And besides, I plan to invite Dr. Falkow." I knew that Mantzur hated Falkow, who was a private thoracic surgeon—and a busy one. But I also knew that I was losing this battle. It was obvious: Winestone wanted to demonstrate his support for Mantzur by forcing me to surrender my patient and by reprimanding me in front of him.

"Dr. Zohar," he said. "Look. Dr. Mantzur is our vice chairman. As a rule he will be taking all esophageal service cases. He is our esophageal surgeon."

By "service cases" Winestone was referring to non-private patients, particularly, the ones who were not insured or were insured by Medicaid. These patients were treated by full-time salaried faculty, not by the private surgeons who do not want to waste time on them. Mantzur forced hospital administration to top up the Medicare rates for his Medicaid cases, so the rates he got for a Medicaid case were similar to a private surgeon's rates.

I capitulated against my better judgment. "I see. The case is yours," I told Mantzur. "Anything else, Dr. Winestone?"

"Yes. I hope you understand that we must work together." He gestured towards Mantzur. The Padrino smiled and nodded like a wise grandfather. "Thank you very much, Dr. Zohar. I appreciate your cooperation."

At the end of the corridor I pressed the button and glanced at the panel above the elevator door to see the floor numbers going on and off as the cabin approached. The left cabin did not move; it seemed stuck on the second floor. The right cabin hovered in the upper floors where the top managers reside. After a moment of impatient waiting, I decided to take the stairs. A hollow metallic noise resonated through the staircase. It took me a couple of seconds before I realized that it was my office key clanking against the metal railing. It's a game we used to play when I was a child, when we lived in a run-down apartment house in Haifa. We all knew how it irritated Mr. Podnarski, our Polish neighbor on second floor. One day as I went down the stairs, clanking my key along the iron bars, I ran into Mr. Podnarski on the second landing. He was holding his hands to his ears, his manic eyes on me and wailing something in a foreign language. Then he started to cry. I ran by, finally realizing he was seriously mad, and that the noise of the key on the metal bars was enough to freak him out of his wits.

Funny how the brain works. I put the key in my pocket and shuffled down the concrete steps. Why was Winestone pretending to be blind to Mantzur's deeds? Of course we each kill a patient or two, some of us more than a few. Over-operating for money is the standard, not the exception. But one thing for sure was that the actions of the Godfather were on the extreme end of the spectrum—way beyond malpractice. Terminal patients with black feet undergoing open iliac endartrectomies, patients with brain metastases from lung cancer undergoing open thoracotomies for a "biopsy" or "decortication," dying Alzheimer's patients with large stinking sacral decubitus wounds undergoing huge excisions with flap closure to slowly die in the aftermath. The list was horrendous. In the old days the Godfather was apparently a cool and reliable surgeon, able to compensate for poor judgment with good technique. But his operative skills had long faded away, and almost any vascular case he did went back to the OR for re-bleeding or thrombosis. I had documented all of his complications over the past three years—it was my job to do so for the M&Ms. Looking at each case in isolation, one could pass many as a "mistake in judgment," a "technical complication," or a "misfortune." But in statistics you do not focus on individual cases. You look at patterns. True, some eighty patients of Mantzur's suffered a severe complication yet eventually survived. The problem is, another forty-two didn't. They were executed.

I thought of Mr. Valez again. A tune sprang to mind, and I began humming a line from a song in a Jack Nicholson movie. "Always look at the bright side of your life..." What was that movie? "As Good as It Gets." I liked Nicholson. His dry sense of humor and sarcasm were refreshing in small doses. Yes, indeed. Let's think positive: If Mr. Podnarski made it, so can Joe Valez. Even in Auschwitz the fatality rate wasn't one hundred percent.

▲▼▲▼▲

I left the physicians' parking lot and headed south on Fourth Ave towards the Southbound Gowanus Expressway. From there I'd make my way towards the upper deck of the Verrazano. As I looked over my shoulder before crossing over to the E-Z pass lane, I noticed a rugged looking individual driving a new looking F-350 Super Duty pickup near my blind spot on my right side. I'm not sure why his face stuck out like it did. Perhaps it was the rumors that Susman was talking about hiring some "contacts" to beat obedience into me. Maybe it was that I'd seen someone who looked just like him in the hospital the other day.

Maybe I was just imagining it.

The driver slowed down to let me in. I waved as I completed my lane change and slowed to fifteen miles per hour to go through the E-Z pass tollbooth. I checked my rearview mirror and took another look at the man driving behind me. I took a good long look.

He had an easily recognizable face, a really large forehead matted with curly, though thinning dark hair. His eyes were covered by one large, thick eyebrow and wrinkles inspired by age. I put him in about his mid forties. I noticed his shoulders were broad and powerful, while the one hand I saw resting on his steering wheel looked about as wide as both of mine side by side.

I tried alternating my glances from the road to my rear-view, but I found myself looking more often into the latter. His face was totally expressionless. He was concentrating on something. My stomach surged:

Was it me?

Were they not just stupid rumors and empty threats? Has Susman actually hired someone to physically harm me...

Snap out of it! You're just fucking paranoid.

We motored a few miles down the 278 West and took the ramp just shy of the Goethals Bridge to New Jersey. That took me to the southbound Westshore Expressway. His vehicle never lost more than ten feet from my bumper. I changed lanes a couple of times to maintain my speed around slower vehicles...

...He followed. Now he was flashing his high beams at me. He was gesticulating at me from his seat. It looked like, "Pull over, now!"

In between images of getting beaten almost to death and wondering why I'd been so verbally opposed to Susman and his mafia, I didn't notice that my steering wheel was shaking in my hand. Road noise in the vehicle doubled, and it sounded like I was driving along a rumble strip in the shoulder though I was still securely in the left lane.

I moved over one lane and then worked over into the shoulder. I wasn't going to let him follow me all the way home. If I was going to take a beating, it wasn't going to be in front of my wife. I braked slowly to a stop. Both hands were fixed on the wheel as I looked in my drivers' side rear-view mirror. He had pulled over behind me. *This is it. Time to pay the piper.*

Adrenaline pumped through my veins as I prepared for my first fist fight in fifteen years. I wanted to be brave and accept it like a man but it's so much easier said than done. I was scared. It was more a question of trying to make whoever this guy was think the opposite.

For some reason, it suddenly seemed important to me how much Susman had paid him. Hopefully not too much...

He knocked on the window. I looked up at him sheepishly. I hadn't ever been pulled over on the road for a beating before, so I wasn't sure how to go about it. Should I throw the door open and start throwing fists? Should I reach into the back and grab my solid steel wheel lock and wave it around like a light saber? Or would that just promote me from a beating to a bullet in the head? Should I scamper out the passenger side door and flag down traffic for help?

I rolled down the window slightly. If he wanted me, he could come in and bloody well get me.

"Bad luck," he said in a low voice not befitting a man of that size.

"Yes, indeed," I replied, trying hard to keep my voice even. I wasn't going to let him go back to Susman so that they could laugh about how I'd yelped and cried for mercy. If he reached in for me, I had a pretty good idea where my wheel lock was. I knew I could reach around and grab it and give him some good news with it. *But wait! I still have my seat belt on. As I turn around I'm going to have to unlock it... Maybe I should just stomp on the accelerator and drive away, or will I just be delaying the inevitable?*

"You realize of course that at this hour, nobody is going to come and help you."

He was right. Who in New York would want to interrupt a savage beating by the roadside? Everyone would much rather just drive on and pretend they hadn't seen anything. They could tell their friends about it later on at the bar. It'd make a great story. I yearned for a police vehicle to pass by...

"No, probably not," I admitted, looking up at him. He probably stood about six foot three. He was leaning over my window, his lips almost at the two-inch crack I had opened.

"Well," he said, sighing. "We might as well get it done."

"Yes, yes. We should." First, I unbuckled my seat belt. I then unlocked the door and opened it and stepped out of the car. I contemplated grabbing my wheel lock but then better judgment prevailed. *A guy like this never comes without a backup plan.* I suspected his would be something in the .45 caliber variety.

He moved to the trunk and turned to look at me. His face was just as passive as before. What sort of callous thug was I dealing with here? Could he be reasoned with? He didn't appear to be all that anxious to get started on me, so perhaps I could reason with him. I moved over towards the back of my car, trying to keep my shoulders back. I wanted to keep some dignity, although I was sure to lose some along the way.

"Well?" the man said.

"I can deal with this, but is there nothing I can do for you? Money, perhaps? I don't have a lot on me but—"

"No," the man shook his large head. "I do this for people all the time. Even if you had lots of money I wouldn't accept it. It's really simple. Do you want me to do it or not?"

"Beat me," I screamed defiantly my nose to his. "Kick me, punch me, but I will not change my stance! They will never have my compliance!" The large man winced and pushed me away from him. He stepped away from me and started sidestepping back towards the driver's side of his truck. He didn't turn his back on me this time.

"I have no fucking clue what you're talking about, dude. I just wanted to help you change your tire."

"What?" I spat.

"Your tire," he said humbly, pointing at the flat on my rear passenger side. It had a hole about the size of my index finger in the sidewall. "I just wanted to help."

I stood there for a minute contemplating exactly how stupid I'd just been. Then I reflexively roared with laughter. He stood there, beside his large, idling diesel truck. The look on his face was dumfounded, but it was clear that he appreciated the humor of the misunderstanding. "Yes, yes of course." I went to the front and popped the trunk. "I have a spare in the back…"

Naked, I ran to the open-air spa in our back yard. The fresh snow felt soft and frosty under my bare feet. I took off the cover and immersed my frozen body into the steaming-hot water. This was one of the pleasures of winter for me—soaking in the hot tub, the snow covered trees around, and above me the starry sky with the constant, soft hum of New-ark-bound airplanes emerging from the ocean. I sipped from a glass of brandy. The glass had almost frozen, but the liquid remained fluid and pleasantly burning. I closed my eyes.

Heidi arrived from the house, took off her bathing robe and lowered herself into the water. "Ah, it feels so good. The problem is that going out will be so traumatic. It's bloody freezing! They say we had twenty degrees today and that it's going to start snowing again later."

"We could sleep here tonight if you wish."

"We would drown." She sniffed at the air a bit and then almost stuck her nose in my glass. "What are you drinking—Schnapps? It stinks."

"Brandy."

"It still stinks." She watched as I took another quick sip, and then seemed to freeze in thought. "What are you thinking about?"

"The usual. You know, the hospital, the department—"

"—You are obsessed." She flicked a small amount of water on me teasingly. "You come home and sit at your com-puter, then you eat your dinner and all you talk about is Man-tzur and Sorki and Winestone and…who's the fat one again?"

"Susman."

"Whatever. And after dinner you go back to the com-puter and now you think about the same crap. It's not healthy."

"What do you want me to think about?"

"I don't know. Rub my foot. I hurt it at the gym today."

"OK, where is it?" I felt for her foot in the dark water. "You wouldn't believe what happened to me today." She plunked her legs on my lap, and I started massaging her sore foot. "I was on my way home from the hospital and this big

110

guy started flashing his lights at me and signaling for me to pull over."

"Oh," she said, clearly appreciative of the foot rub. "What was that about?"

"I wasn't sure at first. I guess I was getting a bit paranoid because I thought it was someone Susman had arranged to beat complacency into me."

"Do you think they would do something foolish like that?"

"No," I lied. "But the imagination can be a very convincing enemy. Apparently he had been at the hospital and we left around the same time. He recognized me because his father is, get this, a patient of Sorki's. I guess they had a meeting today and I saw him there. Automatically when I saw him again following me—"

"—You figured he was a hired thug." Heidi chuckled at me. "You and your imagination!"

"I know, but you never know with those guys. Especially Susman. I wonder how I can liquidate those bastards? They are much too powerful to be eliminated through conventional, civilized channels. Now, with Winestone almost in their hands they are untouchable. Basically I have only one remaining option. I have to report them to the State." She bolted upright, creating waves in the small tub.

"You are going to report nobody. They will destroy you!"

"I could do it anonymously. It is possible. The New York State Health Department encourages complaints from anybody who has a valid or even an invalid criticism or complaint. Remember that case of mine from two years ago? When I performed a colostomy on the wrong loop of bowel on that black woman with advanced cancer? The poor woman died. What an awful disaster! I had to appear before the OPMC? I never learned who reported me."

"You know I forget all of these acronyms. What is the OPMC?"

"Office of Professional Medical Conduct—or, I suppose it should be called medical misconduct. I was lucky. I was only admonished; it could have been much worse. Anyway, I could report them to the OPMC. With the lists I have on Mantzur and Sorki, it would trigger an investigation. They'd relish being able to land two big fish simultaneously."

"What about Winestone?"

"That is the problem. My action could start a domino effect. If they find out that Mantzur is a bad boy, they could ask why Winestone did not control him. This is complicated. A journalist writing for a newspaper or magazine is another possibility, but that might create more problems."

"Absolutely. Never trust a journalist. Once you start with them your case is their story. The more you suffer, the more they thrive. They are whores."

"What's new, Heidi? All professionals are whores to some extent."

Heidi's usual soft manner took on a tone of anger. "I won't tell you what to do," she snapped. "But before committing yourself to any crazy move, understand that we cannot survive without your salary. I pay the bills and I know. It's three thousand for the mortgage, two thousand for the cars and insurance, fifteen hundred for college, and then all the other insurances, and we are not even talking about food and clothing. We would not survive more than three months. Before you start to act like a hero, just get this into your head: I do not intend to take our sons and live on the streets for the sake of your stupid pride. In America when you stop earning money you are nobody. We've been through this before. Don't do anything without Winestone. He is not an angel, nobody is. But he likes you, and he is on your side. Get that into your head, Doctor. You don't know it all."

Heidi climbed out of the water and shuffled toward the house. I emptied the last drop of the brandy, wishing for more. *Perhaps she's right. Perhaps I am not that noble and unselfish. Nobody is.*

Take Winestone, for example. He was making big bucks. Nobody knew his financial arrangements, but cautious estimates were that he raked in up to a million a year. He was at peace, and nobody of significance bit at his bum. On the surface his residency program ran smoothly and was developing some reputation reflected by a better quality of candidates applying each year. His full-time team was easy to control. Rusk and Bachus were doing well for themselves, better than they could do elsewhere.

And then there was me. I was sure that Larry Winestone liked me in some fatherly way. He respected me and perhaps was even proud to have me around him. Sure, he needed me for the residency and enjoyed boasting about his growing list of published books. But what about hospital politics? He knew that I was controversial and physically unable to keep my mouth shut. He also knew that I depended on him and was still awaiting a full professorship. I was a newcomer to the U.S. with house payments eating into my cash flow. I couldn't afford more than a few months without pay. I could have applied for another job, but even then I would need the unequivocal support of the Chairman as a credible reference. I was his at least for the next few years, or so it seemed.

On the other hand, he knew I had a "list"—and more than one. He knew I despised Mantzur because I'd told him so several times. A few weeks ago—after he told me that the Godfather and Sorki were planning to get rid of the Chairman of Medicine and pass the crown to Susman—I told Winestone that the next step would be to get rid of him and crown Sorki as chair of our department. "You may be right," Winestone responded. "Let's wait a year and see."

I had told him nothing new. He was shrewd, no doubt about that, and he could afford to be. Winestone had a contract; it would cost the hospital a couple million to get rid of him. Not likely.

Me? I was on a three months' notice. Heidi was right. *Then why the fuck didn't I tell her so? I hate sleeping on the sofa.*

9

A Stubborn Group

Young men kill their patients; old men let them die.
—James Gregory, 1753-1821

"Joseph," Winestone began. Mantzur was sitting behind his own heavy desk, and Winestone was standing almost at his side. "I spoke to my full-time staff. They do not agree to take Sorki's cousin as a categorical resident. They are willing to consider him for a preliminary position. They are adamant about it."

Mantzur repositioned his eyeglasses and looked at his black notebook. Tomorrow was Friday. His operative list was not full, and he had to fill it somehow. Each Friday he operated until midnight. Then he would drive through the night out to the tip of the island for the weekend. He looked up at Winestone and smiled. A front upper tooth was missing. "Larry," he said, "are they crazy or what? They are playing with fire. Sorki will be furious."

"He'll have to accept it. You know my style. I involve my staff in the decisions surrounding selection of new residents. I cannot risk antagonizing them over this issue." Winestone appeared tight and nervous, not his usual benign self.

"Of course, Larry," said Mantzur. *And I thought we had brought the message across. Sorki will throw a temper tantrum, I'm sure.*

"Joseph, they're in the library. Why don't you go and talk to them? See if you can change their minds."

Mantzur sighed and put aside the black notebook. He had to find a major case for tomorrow. He threw a warm smile at Winestone and said: "I'll talk to them. The cousin has to be admitted." Mantzur was aware of the gradual decline of his practice. Only two or three years ago he was the king of surgery in this hospital, his lists extending from early morning until night. Carotids, aortas, fem-pops, lungs, chests, esophagi, colons, breasts, everything—it was common knowledge that Mantzur would operate on anything he could lay his hands on. And how he operated! Beautifully. Not too fast, not too slow; meticulously and patiently. Junior residents worshipped him, and the seniors adored him for he was dedicated to their operative education, allowing them to master each step. Mantzur never interfered too much; he would let you commit the crucial mistake, inadvertently cut that vessel, and only when the blood hit the ceiling would he take over. "You get excited only when you can hear the blood," was his motto.

To confirm Mantzur's status as the local maestro Howard built a private OR suite for him. But when he could not fill his lists it was no longer "his." What happened? Why were the referrals diminishing? Mantzur blamed it on the HMOs channeling patients away, the retirement or death of his old medical colleagues, and above all, the decline of his status in the hospital. People were no longer compelled to buy his favors by referring patients to him.

Prior to Winestone's era, the Chairman was a nobody. A puppet in his hands. Things were different now. Winestone was of a different caliber of manager and the least of his real problems. I was the one that bothered him the most. In his head, he was certain I was spreading rumors and lies about alleged malpractice and complications. At the same time Sorki and Susman were not as they were before. Mantzur, had elevated both of them from the gutters to key positions in the hospital, providing them with status, which translated into money, and now they were biting at his buttocks. It seemed that they lost respect for him.

Rusk and Bachus sprang to their feet when Mantzur entered the library. Rusk offered him a chair. Only I remained seated. *Like a well trained butler,* thought Mantzur, *What a phony WASP this Rusk guy is.* He smiled at them. He liked Bachus; he trained him. *Bachus would never stab him in the back. He was almost family.*

115

"Dr. Mantzur, could I bring you a cup of coffee?" asked Rusk.

"Thank you, Malcolm. I just had a glass of my herbal tea." He looked at me. "Good afternoon, Dr. Zohar. I see that you are busy writing another paper?"

"Hi, Dr. Mantzur." *How long will these pleasantries last?* "Yes, we are always writing something, you know."

Mantzur tapped on the polished table with his double diamond-ringed hand. He cleared his voice before speaking. "Guys, you know why I've come to you today. Dr. Winestone asked me to do so. He elected not to be present in order to let you decide on your own." Mantzur raised his hands. "Guys, this department needs peace. We have to satisfy everybody. There is enough space here for all of us, so let us compromise. Dr. Winestone tells me that you are somewhat resistant to the idea of accepting Sorki's cousin. I do not understand this. Sorki is the President of the Medical Board and a respectable member of this department. He was here long before you arrived. Shouldn't he have the privilege of helping his cousin, aren't we a family? I call on you to be reasonable which, in the long term, would benefit the department and each of you personally."

I looked up from my papers. I couldn't believe the audacity of his expectations. "Dr. Mantzur, personally I like Sorki Junior. I spent some time with him doing research and I assess him as a bright young man. But this does not mean that he can walk straight from the Immigration Passport Control into a US surgical residency program."

Mantzur cupped his ear. "What do you say?"

"I said that we cannot take someone who just flew in only because his cousin is Dr. Sorki. The guy has to learn English first."

Rusk joined in. "Dr. Mantzur, I have to agree with Marc on this point. Dr. Sorki's cousin has to learn spoken English. We suggested to Dr. Winestone to admit him as a preliminary resident this year. Should he perform well, and I am convinced he will, we'll promote him to a categorical spot the year after."

Mantzur looked at Bachus, sure that he would support his old mentor. Bachus shifted in his chair. "Dr. Mantzur, I have to agree with my colleagues. Admitting the cousin could harm our residency program. Each year we select three top candidates from a few hundred applicants. We cannot bypass the process. This would be unpopular among our residents. Let us take him as a preliminary."

Mantzur fought down his irritation. So that's the situation? Winestone wants to compromise, but Zohar has already poisoned the minds of these two. Suddenly he felt a strange sympathy for Winestone. *In a way Zohar is to Winestone what Sorki is to me: a troublesome son. What do you do with your son when he won't listen? You teach him a lesson. Perhaps Susman's suggestion wasn't that crazy after all...*

Mantzur picked up the thread. "Think about it again. Sorki won't like your decision. Even I am not able to restrain him when he is angry. Consider all that you could gain or lose."

Rusk, Bachus and myself looked at each other and then at Mantzur. We shook our heads. *No way!*

Mantzur walked back into his office. "Larry, they are a stubborn group—stupid, I would say. They said No to the cousin. A grave mistake."

"I told you so, Joseph." Winestone was standing at the window, apparently lost in thought, marveling at the distant Manhattan skyline. There were heavy clouds above; it had been snowing for days on end.

"Anyway, Joseph," he said, "we shouldn't worry too much about this minor episode. You are the Vice-Chairman, and you and I are running this department. We are the generals. Our task is to look at the bigger picture. I don't particularly mind if the young bucks squabble a bit. It'll help them to come to their senses." Winestone shrugged.

"By the way, Joseph," he continued, "I have a case scheduled for tomorrow afternoon, but it looks like Beverly double-booked me. I am giving a talk at the Jefferson Hospital in Manhattan at 6 p.m. I won't be able to make it, unless—would you by any chance—?"

Mantzur searched Winestone's eyes for a long moment. "I'll check my list," he said. "Perhaps I can slot it in. I'll let you know, Larry."

"Thanks." Winestone touched Mantzur's elbow with his usual gesture. "I knew I could count on you."

"What is the case?"

"A forty-five-year-old male. He needs a lymphnode dissection for testicular cancer. The patient had previous abdominal surgery. Dr. Wilkinson fears intestinal problems. That's why he asked me to stand by on the case."

"Wilkinson... The the new urologist from Chicago?"

"Yes. I haven't had a chance to introduce him to you; he only just started last week. He's a polite young man; you'll like him."

"Yes, course. Larry, I'll try and calm down Sorki. But you know how he is."

"Well, Zohar and the others will have to face the consequences then."

Mantzur extended his hands palms up in a gesture of resignation. "Young men—what can you do? Sons learn by making mistakes, eh?" His voice was pleasant, and his eyes returned Winestone's smile as they shook hands.

▲▼▲▲▼▲

I was trying to concentrate on a manuscript when Winestone entered my office. He moved behind me and massaged my shoulders with his skillful hands. While doing so his eyes scanned every piece of paper on both my main desk and the side one: Correspondence, rejected manuscripts, accepted articles, everything. Then the expected question came: "Marc, what can you tell me? Anything new?"

"Not really, Dr. Winestone." He could probably tell that I was up to something from the tension in my shoulders. "Other than that I had a rough night. I was called for an acute abdomen at midnight, when we had him on the table it was two a.m., finished at three, just a perforated duodenal ulcer, which we patched. And imagine—at four o'clock at night there was a traffic jam on Staten Island expressway; it snowed like crazy throughout the night. I am glad Heidi gave me her four-wheel drive today."

Winestone did not appear interested. "Marc, any news from the other side? How is Sorki?"

"How should I know? I thought that you have well developed lines of communication via our distinguished vice chairman."

Winestone ignored my sarcasm. "We did the correct thing," he said. "We could not compromise the residency. Sorki will be incensed, we know, but he will recover. Mantzur will see to it."

So now it was "we" who did not compromise. Amazing how Winestone's mood oscillated from heroism to submission to appeasement in about as long as it took most civilized people to eat a bagel. Barbara appeared at the door as he pumped me for information. She was a fourth-year resident, a graduate of Pennsylvania University Medical School, and the daughter of a surgeon. She was tall, blonde, and had thick ankles. Barb was a model resident—hard working, responsible, reliable, knowledgeable, articulate, polite and generally pleasant. In her green scrubs and white coat with blonde hair showing under the cap she could have easily played a role on television's "ER."

"Good morning Dr. Winestone," she said. "I'm sorry, I shouldn't disturb. Dr. Zohar, I'll come back later. There are a few things I've got to discuss with you."

"Come in, Barbara." Winestone grabbed her by the elbow and all but forced her onto an empty chair. "Tell us what case you did this morning."

"I did another vertical banded gastroplasty with Sorki. This was his fifth this week. As usual he does not let me do much—just cut here, cut there—he does most of the operation."

Winestone must have been jealous. Even after joining Sorki at the Obesity Center he got perhaps one case per month with most patients being channeled to Sorki. After all, he monopolized the referral channels.

"Barb," I said, "don't complain. Be happy that Sorki adores you and demands that you scrub with him. How was he today? Good mood? Bad mood?"

"When we were closing he told me that you guys refused his cousin. Then he gave one of his little speeches, like 'I'm the president of the Medical Board, I am a senior surgeon, I am a top gun, I'm going to get rid of Winestone and his useless full-timers, I'm going to destroy them.'"

Winestone and I both considered the news. Sorki was getting pretty vocal about this situation lately, and this was not the first time one of our senior residents had brought it to our attention.

"Sorki is angry with us, eh?" asked Winestone.

"It appears so," Barbara said. She wasn't sure exactly how serious Sorki was when he said "destroy them." It seemed like the typical political warmongering that she would have to expect at any hospital she would end up. She accepted the fact with humble determination. After all, it was none of her business— yet. "I will come back, Dr. Zohar. Have a pleasant day."

Winestone adjusted his green necktie. It was his green day: A green silk shirt, green wool Bavarian sport jacket, green flannel trousers, green socks, and thick soled leather shoes.

I tried to break some of the cloud cover that had set in since Barbara's announcement. "All you need is a green hat with a feather, and you could be a Leprechaun," I said. He almost smiled.

"I bought this jacket in Munich last year. Like it?"

"It does look expensive," I said, fueling his ego. He was looking a little pale.

"It was on sale, around seven hundred fifty Deutsche Marks." Winestone leaned back in the easy chair and crossed his legs. "Marc, Sorki obviously is flaming but we know what kind of personality he has. He'll get over it. Mantzur will see to it; it's in his own best interest. Now tell me, that article for the *British Journal*. Any responses from the editors yet?"

PART 2

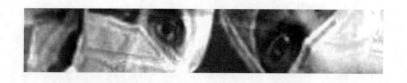

The Hunter and the Hunted

10

Skirmishes

*An operation is an assault on a fellow human being—
legalized, but nonetheless an assault. In a sense, today
the license to kill is given by society only to surgeons.*
—*Alexander J. Walt, 1923-1996*

February-April 1999.

The morning started with "nutrition rounds." Debbie, the hospital's chief nutritionist, Rusk and myself alternated in the task of supervising total parenteral nutrition in surgical patients. Today Debbie accompanied me. Our first patient was in the SICU, a ninety-something skeleton connected to the ventilator and a renal dialysis machine. "Dr. Garibaldi requested TPN on her," Debbie announced by way of an apology.

"Debbie," I said seriously. "This is a living corpse. Look at her! Eyeballing her from a distance of one hundred feet you know that her chances of leaving the hospital through the front entrance are much worse than your chances of winning the Miss Universe competition."

"Yes, my chances are much better!" Debbie, in her mid-thirties, was perhaps the best-dressed woman in the hospital.

"Seriously, Debbie, do you really think that TPN will help this poor dying soul? A combination of ninety years, plus the respiratory and renal failure, is lethal. She has no chance whatsoever." I sighed. She just kept on looking at me with her patented "Determined Debbie Look." I could have told her that her hair was on fire and she might have flinched. "Let's see her chart anyway."

Debbie handed me the chart and said nothing; my moans and groans were nothing new to her. "Debbie, look at all those consultations: medicine, pulmunology, endocrine, gastro, infectious diseases, renal, plastics—for the bedsore, I assume. Does she even have a bedsore? Look here, there are more: cardiology—"

"—Well, doctors ask for consults and give consults. What's new?"

"Come on, Debbie," I said impatiently. "Don't you understand what's happening here? This dying patient is on Medicare. As long as her heart beats the Medicare can be milked like a holy cow. It has been milked for years—first by her nursing home and primary physician and now by all of us. Now, even as she's dying, we surround her as vultures, each billing a few bucks. Let her die? Never! Why shouldn't we go on billing her? As long as she breathes—or the machine breathes for her—we can make money. Of course we say that it would be unethical to stop now and the family wants her to go on and all that crap." Debbie was not impressed.

"Please, Dr. Zohar, did you finish your speech—which I already know by heart? We still have five patients to see. Do you want to give her TPN or not?"

"If you want give her peripheral nutrition instead, it's cheaper and safer. And Garibaldi will provide her with TPN anyway. Let him poison his patients by himself. Do you think the patient needs a psychiatric consult as well?"

Debbie rolled her eyes. "Next patient is Mantzur's. Mr. Valez is in bed six. Should we see him first?"

We found our resident Galvitunyu at Mr. Valez's bedside. "What's up, Ron?" I asked as I entered the cubicle with Debbie in my wake. "Isn't this Jose Valez, my stolen esophagus?"

"It is, Dr. Zohar."

"Why is he still down in the ICU? I thought you operated on him a week ago."

"We did. He is very sick, however. Sick and septic."

"He must be leaking. Did you do a contrast study? A CT?"

"No." Galvitunyu shook his head. "Mantzur does not want any study."

"Sure. Mantzur never wants to confront his own disasters."

Galvitunyu said nothing. *I shouldn't involve him in this.* I continued: "And now you want TPN, eh? Why didn't you place a feeding jejunostomy?"

"Mantzur does not like feeding jejunostomies with his esophageal resections."

"Debbie, let's approve TPN here. Ron, you have to find out why he is septic and treat the cause. If not, he'll die."

"You're right of course," Galvitunyu answered solemnly. "But what can I do?"

I shrugged. "Talk to Mantzur. I don't want to be stepping on his toes."

I finished my nutrition round and caught the elevator to the department. The elevator was empty. *Fuck the bastard. He stole my patient and killed him. The esophageal expert. The bloody terminator.* In frustration I banged on the elevator walls with my fists and feet. People between floors must have thought there was a ferocious beating taking place. I was surprised security wasn't waiting for me when I disembarked on the proper floor.

I found Sam Glatman sitting in my office, chatting to Beverly. She left when I walked in.

Glatman winked at me: "Look at that arse of hers!" He said it much louder than I think he meant to. He was shameless and paid it no mind.

"Not so loud," I insisted. "She is poisonous."

"Marc, do you think that there is something between her and you-know-who, our fierce leader Larry?"

"Who knows?" I said as I moved around my desk and crashed into the seat. "Winestone likes young women. She spends hours with him behind closed doors, taking dictation and going over the mail. And those earrings he bought her for Christmas? I don't know, you tell me." We both had a bit of a laugh before Sam readjusted himself into a more determined posture.

"Marc, do you have a few minutes?"

"Yeah, why? What's up?"

"We have to talk," he said, standing up. "But not here. Come with me." I followed Glatman down the stairs to the hospital's library on the third floor. He greeted the chief librarian, an aging spinster, and opened the door to the dark and empty audiovisual room. "Marc, from now on we'll meet here. I do not trust the department, your room is surely bugged and Beverly is probably listening behind your door. I wouldn't trust your tiny secretary, Anne, either. She looks nosy."

"Anne is OK."

"Marc, no one is OK right now. Trust me. Now sit down and listen. I did what you suggested and it is not effective. I complained to the State about Mantzur. Six weeks and no results. I inquired at the Medical Records whether the State asked for Mantzur's charts. Nothing!"

"Who do you know at the records?"

Glatman laughed. I could see a twinkle in his eye. "Maria, that small Puerto Rican woman. I buy her lunch from time to time. You have to feed them for information, you know."

"As long as you feed them only with food."

"Marc," Sam retorted, "be serious. I sent the state an awful lot of material I'd collected during the M&Ms. They didn't bite. I also contacted Medicare."

"Why Medicare? What do they have to do with this?"

"Mantzur milks Medicare. It's obvious. For example, when he performs a bypass with a synthetic graft he bills as if it was performed with a vein graft. More money, much more money. Medicare has a fraud unit. The feds would love it!"

"Sam, perhaps anonymous whistle blowing is not what the lords at the OPMC fancy. Perhaps you should call them and schedule an interview."

"Face to face?"

"Yep. You want Mantzur dead? You have to go and see the guys personally."

"The lists, Marc. I need your lists. I need documentation. Nobody has what you have."

"OK. You go to see them, and I will give you the lists." Sam almost hugged me: "This is great. We might just rid this hospital from the grasp of the terminators. From now on we'll meet and talk only here, OK? Where and when do I get your lists?"

"Tomorrow, Sam. Ten a.m. Right here."

"I'll go now, and you wait a few minutes before you leave, OK?" Sam was kicking into cloak and dagger mode. It was probably unnecessary, but if it fueled his vigor I'd let him mope around the hospital in long overcoat with the Pink Panther theme song playing through the paging system. "See ya tomorrow."

I looked at an old issue of *Lancet* I had picked up from the shelves. The cover was missing, and a quotation printed in small italics at the bottom of the first page read: "Physicians must particularly try to avoid being quacks. The fact that medicine is not an exact science favors quackery." It was a quote by Chalmers Da Costa who lived between 1863 and 1933. Da Costa was a great surgeon from Philadelphia. A hundred years later and nothing had changed. *Will Sam be able to fix Mantzur? What should I do about Sorki?*

▲▼◢◣▼▲

Dr. Mahmud Sorki arrived in the auditorium at eight fifteen a.m. The M&M meeting was already underway and he saw Radezki standing at the podium. We had already started with Sorki's first case. Sorki signed his name on the attendance sheet and took a seat at the back row where he loudly greeted his neighbors to let everyone know that he, the mighty Sorki, had arrived. He put his reading glasses on and searched in the printed case report to synchronize it with what Radezki was reading. This was the patient he took from me. A simple operation cum mortality. How unfortunate that it was so predictable by now.

Radezki read on through Sorki's big entrance. "After the second gastrectomy the patient continued to produce fresh blood from the nasogastric tube, requiring eight units of blood during the postoperative night to maintain hemodynamic stability. His clotting parameters at this stage were within normal limits. Therefore, on hospital day four the patient was taken back to the OR and underwent a completion gastrectomy and a stapled Roux en Y gastro-jejunal anastomosis"

"Dr. Radezki," interrupted Winestone, who was chairing the meeting again that day. "Please describe the operative findings at the third operation." Winestone looked diminutive from above, and with his bulging cheeks he looked like a hamster wearing glasses. His thinning hair was an artificial reddish brown.

"Basically the same findings as at the previous operation—a distended gastric remnant, distended with blood. The patient was returned to the ICU hypothermic, acidotic and producing no urine. Four hours later he developed cardiac arrest and did not respond to CPR."

Usually Sorki was totally relaxed and confident during the presentation of his cases, but something had changed. He felt tense and sensed a strange hollowness in his lower abdomen and moisture in his hands. Was he afraid?

"Any comments from the floor? Anybody would do anything different?" asked Winestone. He ignored my raised hand.

Clever, thought Sorki. *Winestone wants to fly over the case. Good.* Sorki appeared overcome by a dim sense of relief. He was obviously content that Winestone was ignoring me on his behalf.

Winestone scanned the crowd, pretending not to see me. "Is Dr. Khouri around? Yes, there you are. You examined the pathological specimen?"

"Thank you, Dr. Winestone," Dr. Khouri said. She continued. "I got a few specimens from this patient. The first was two vagi nerves, which confirmed a complete vagotomy. From the first, second and third operations I received portions of the stomach, which on gross examination and microscopy demonstrated erosive gastritis."

Thank you, Dr. Khouri, Sorki was probably thinking to himself. Ten years ago the chief of pathology wanted to fire her for alleged incompetence. He and Mantzur removed the chief instead. He smiled to himself. She had been a dedicated friend ever since. It's like she read his mind: Her pathological diagnosis almost never differed from his clinical one.

"Dr. Sorki, it was your patient. Do you wish to comment?" said Winestone, still ignoring my hand. It was pretty clear to everyone what was going on.

Sorki stood up in his ever grandiose fashion. He addressed the crowd as if Winestone wasn't there. His voice was strong, loud and confident. After all, he was the President of the Medical Board: "This was a very unfortunate case and very frustrating as most of you would consider, very frustrating." He chuckled uncomfortably as the lies rolled off his lips. "Extremely labor intensive as well. Three major laparotomies. As Dr. Khouri pointed out, the patient suffered from severe erosive gastritis, his gastric mucosa had the appearance of a wet sponge—" Sorki stopped to let the audience absorb the message. With his thick lips pursed he continued: "—a wet sponge, which was bleeding like hell. Partial gastrectomy, then subtotal and he was still hemorrhaging. Eventually we were forced to remove the entire stomach, a rather heroic operation on a bleeding patient as you would all appreciate. I wish to congratulate Dr. Radezki for the excellent presentation of this most complicated case." Sorki fell back into his seat. His hands were wet, and he rubbed them inconspicuously on his trousers.

Winestone looked at the M&M outline. "Who is next? Oh, another case of Dr. Sorki's. Dr. Radezki, are you also going to present this case?

Sorki pulled on his finger joints. They relaxed with a loud click. *I knew it,* his expression sang. *They would not dare to attack me. They bite at Mantzur but not at me.* "Can I say something?" I said, dropping my hand and standing up instead. I was not going to let this one be overlooked. Not the one he'd stolen from me. "Dr. Sorki, didn't the patient bleed from a duodenal ulcer? Did you ever open the duodenum and control the bleeding vessel? Didn't he bleed from there while you were chopping away his healthy stomach?"

What is that Jew chirping about down there? Sorki's body language inquired. He leaned forward to hear what I was saying.

"Dr. Sorki, do you wish to respond?" asked Winestone.

"We can't hear what he's saying," shouted Rachman Gotahedi. "Speak up!"

"Dr. Zohar has raised the possibility that the source of bleeding was at the duodenum," explained Winestone.

"Dr. Zohar may raise any possibility he wishes." Sorki said, pronouncing each word slowly. "But the fact is that the patient bled from his stomach. Erosive gastritis, erosive gastritis, g-a-s-t-r-i-t-i-s! Do I have to repeat? Didn't he listen to what Dr. Khouri said?" Sorki raised his hands with mock desperation, "Come on friends, there is nothing more to discuss here." The audience remained silent.

I tried to say something in response, but my words were lost. At the same moment Winestone ordered Radezki to continue with the next case.

Sorki relaxed a bit and smoothed his moustache. Elbowing Stig Rasmussen, the neurosurgeon, who sat on his right side, he whispered loudly: "They want to teach us surgery, the academicians." Rasmussen nodded and joined in whispered laughter. Finally he mopped his sweaty forehead with a handkerchief and complained:

"Mo, it is hot in here."

"Wait, Stig. The next case will be hotter."

I should not have chaired this meeting today, Winestone thought, half listening to Radezki, who was presenting Sorki's second case. An old-time chairman, Winestone was not afraid of Sorki, nor was he threatened or intimated by him. He just detested direct confrontations, preferring to sting his enemies from the back. *I should have let Rusk chair today's M&M.*

Radezki read from his text: "This was an eighty-year-old female who previously underwent a hemicolectomy for Duke's B adenocarcinoma of the left colon. A routine follow-up colonoscopy demonstrated an irregular mass around a suture at the anastomotic site. A day later the patient was operated for a probable anastomotic recurrence. The anastomotic site was resected. Postoperative course was uneventful. The pathology reported mentioned a suture granuloma."

Clearly a non-indicated operation, Winestone was thinking. *But I have to send the message across in a moderate and elegant way.* "Dr. Radezki," he said, "what was the pre-operative diagnosis?"

"Anastomotic recurrence."

"Did you obtain a histological confirmation?"

"No, Dr. Winestone. It was based on the colonoscopic appearance."

"How could they have a histological diagnosis?" I barked from my permanent seat in the third row. "They did not even bother to wait for the histology. They operated the morning after the colonoscopy."

Here he goes. I wish he wouldn't. "Dr. Radezki," Winestone said, "why didn't you wait for pathology?"

Radezki's voice was cool and measured. "The decision to operate ASAP was taken by the attending surgeon."

A quiet tension seized the auditorium as the audience realized a confrontation between the chairman and Sorki was building. "Dr. Sorki, would you like to comment?" Winestone said.

Sorki usually spoke from a sitting position, but this time he stood up and straightened the sleeves of his navy blue

131

woolen jacket. "Mr. Chairman," he said, "I notice that Dr. Zohar has some problems with the timing of the operation, but Dr. Zohar is perhaps not aware that the patient was obstructed and that she had evidence of colonic obstruction at the site of the mass." He paused, took a breath, and said with an air of finality: "The operation we performed was an emergency procedure. We could not wait for the pathology report." Considering the discussion terminated, he sat down.

"Could we see a pre-operative plain abdominal X-ray?" suggested Dr. Rubinstein, a semi-retired private surgeon who was known to raise more money on the stock exchange than in the OR. Rubinstein was considered independent and vocal, afraid of nobody. "This will tell us whether she was obstructed or not."

"Do we have the X-ray? Could we see it?" Winestone asked the radiology resident.

The resident fumbled for a few minutes in a huge envelope of radiographs and then said apologetically, "Dr. Winestone, no such pre-operative X ray is available."

"It is not available because it has not been taken," I pointed out. "It has not been taken because there was no need to take a plain abdominal X ray as the patient was not obstructed!"

Sorki jumped up again and began talking before being acknowledged by Winestone. "I would advise Dr. Zohar to have his facts right before trying to mislead this respectable assembly of friends and colleagues, all distinguished surgeons. The truth is that the patient was totally obstructed. The colonoscopist could not pass the colonoscope beyond the anastomosis. After explaining to the patient that she was obstructed we performed an emergency laparotomy, as was necessary."

I was up again this time, addressing Dr. Winestone and ignoring Sorki: "How could she be obstructed? She received a pre-operative bowel preparation, which would have been impossible in a completely obstructed patient!"

Realizing that he was losing control of the meeting, Winestone resorted to time-honored tactic of removing the problem from the discussion. "Dr. Rusk, it appears, as a matter of fact, that we have a slight—how to say it?—we have some controversy here. I suggest that the proper place to discuss this would be the Departmental QA committee." The audience exhaled in unison. A confrontation had been averted before the explosion. Sorki and Winestone—as well as everyone else—knew that the "controversy" would be "solved" in a benign manner by Rusk at the next level.

▲▼◢▲▼▲

"Where is Winestone?" I asked Anne a couple hours after the meeting was adjourned.

"Locked away with his beloved Beverly—as usual." Anne shared an office with Beverly, but no love was shared between them. Was it jealousy? Anne was short and Beverly tall. Anne hid a scarred face behind layers of make-up while Beverly's skin was perfect. Anne was battered by a manic husband while Beverly's boyfriend sent her roses each day. As the Chairman's secretary Beverly enjoyed a salary significantly higher than Anne's. More than that, Winestone showered Beverly with warm affection while his attitude to Anne was almost rude. He had no use for women who did not serve him directly.

"How long has she been with him?" I asked.

Anne looked at her watch. "Since he came in. Maybe two hours."

"What are they doing?"

"I've got no idea. Last week I had to get him to the OR for an emergency. I knocked on his door and entered immediately. Do you know what position I found that slut in? No, I can't tell you. You'll think I'm crazy."

I sat down in my easy chair. It was entertaining, though not surprising. Nevertheless, I wanted to know more:

"Please, Anne. You have to tell me, I am your boss. Finish your story."

Anne blushed under her thick layer of makeup. "Well, he was sitting at that large, black easy chair, and she was kneeling at his feet. They were behind the desk. I could not see everything. I said, 'Excuse me, sir, the OR needs you urgently,' and left as fast as I could."

"Well, there is always a differential diagnosis. It may well be that she was looking for an object which dropped on the floor, or she was tying his shoelaces, or—"

"You don't get diamond earrings for picking up pencils and tying shoelaces, Dr. Zohar!"

Who cares? If the old man wants to have fun, let him. It's his risk also. She must be doing it well with her beautiful mouth. I smiled. *This is amusing.* "Now forget about what you saw. No word to anyone, understand? Don't give Winestone any opportunity to get rid of you."

After Beverly left Winestone's room I walked in and approached his desk. He looks as friendly and cheerful as ever in a black pin-striped suit.

"Good morning Marc!" He beamed at me, "Please sit down. What's new?"

"Hi Dr. Winestone. Nice suit. New?"

"Not new, I bought it in Rome. Pure Kashmir wool, not bad, eh?" he said feeling the delicate fibers.

"Yes, but the tie doesn't match."

"What do you mean? Rim said it matches perfectly." We both chuckled.

"Whatever you say. I came to show you a letter I want to send to Sorki."

"Show me." Winestone grabbed the letter and started to read. He was an extremely rapid reader, picking spelling errors better than a computerized spell checker. He had a remarkable photographic brain, like a human scanner. He mumbled aloud paragraphs he wanted to emphasize.

Dear Dr. Sorki,

I assume that you remember the case of an eighty-year old lady who in 1997 underwent a left hemicolectomy for adenocarcinoma of the colon by blah, blah, blah. On 11/21/98 she underwent a routine colonoscopy. Biopsies were obtained. A day later, you operated on the patient-resecting a minute segment of the colon. Histological examination of the specimen revealed a suture granu-loma (Dr. Khouri). On February 5, 1999 this case was presented at the weekly Mortality & Morbidity meeting. During the discussion the point was made that the risky and unnecessary laparotomy and bowel resection in this eighty-year-old female could have been avoided, if you would have awaited the biopsy results. You told then the gathering that you could not wait for the biopsy results and that the operation was performed as an emergency, because the patient was obstructed. To this I commented that to the best of my knowledge (I reviewed the patient's chart before the meeting) the patient was not obstructed and that the colonoscopist, in fact, examined the entire colon-which was not obstructed. You stood up then and told me not to misinform the meeting without knowing the facts; you added that the patient had a large bowel obstruction-the colonoscope not able to pass beyond the obstructing mass in the left colon. Review-ing the endoscopy report— (a copy enclosed) it is clear that the patient's colon was not obstructed-in fact the colonoscope passed easily into the cecum which was not dilated. Clearly therefore you performed an unnecessary and risky emergency bowel resection. You accused me of spreading inaccurate information while it was you knowingly misinforming the meeting. You—the chair-man of the Medical Board—are surely aware about the importance of an objective M&M as part of an ongoing quality assurance system. You—the elected leader of the hospital physicians—surely understand the serious implications of providing false information to this distinguished gathering of your own colleagues. Therefore, I call on you to do the following: Apologize to me, to the chairman of surgery, and to the surgeons present at the M&M meeting for mis-informing them.

Should you fail to comply with the above I will be forced to lay a complaint against you with the appropriate authorities.

Sincerely, Marc Zohar, MD.

Winestone lifted his eyes above his thick and scummy glasses. "CC to everybody, eh?"

"Yes."

"Marc, it's a good letter but you cannot send it. Let me talk to Mantzur. He's trying to pacify the situation. Aren't you going to London soon?"

"To Brighton. The British meeting is in Brighton this year, in May."

"Did I tell you how I drove with Mr. Goligher, the king of the rectum, from London to Brighton? You know that I trained under him?"

"Yes, Dr. Winestone, I know." This did not stop him from telling me the story.

▲▼◢◣▼▲

The next day, Bashir Bachus was standing at the door of my office. "Hey, Marc. Have you eaten yet?"

"No," I admitted. My stomach sounded like the inside of a bowling alley. I'd been listening to it for half an hour. "Why?"

"We would like to take you for some hummus and babaganush." The offer was positively tantalizing.

"You know I bring my lunch with me." I pointed to the small plastic container with my daily portion of carrots, celery and cashew nuts. "And who are 'we?'"

"Salman and myself." Salman Chaudri and Bashir almost never went out for lunch. It was clear that they want to talk to me or, more likely, that Winestone wanted them to.

"Why not? Middle Eastern food could improve my mood. Better than this," I said, motioning to my lame looking lunch box.

"Great, baby! I knew you wouldn't say no to hummus." In his mid-thirties, Bashir was tall and built solid. His aura of success, sense of humor, articulate tongue, steady income of over three hundred grand, BMW sports car and a house on "The Hill" made him the hospital's most eligible bachelor. Bashir was an Armenian who graduated from a medical school in Rome and trained in surgery at the Park back in the time when the department was under the boots of Mantzur and Sorki. When Winestone arrived, the bright and open-minded Bashir was the first to vow unconditional obedience to the new lord, for which he was rewarded with the directorship of the Surgical ICU, a source of a decent and steady income. Two years later, I was recruited by Winestone. Later Bashir told me that he was raised with the notion that all Israelis grew a horn on their head, but gradually, he said, as he noticed that I had no interest whatsoever in impinging on his territory in the ICU, he became one of my few friends in the hospital. "Let's go. Chaudri will join us at Fatima's Tavern."

Fatima's is a cheap Middle Eastern eatery at the south, less affluent edge of Park Ridge. The décor is set by a few large wooden tables, wobbly chairs, white walls hung with framed posters of Jordan-Air, and a large food counter with a huge refrigerator. I adored this simplicity because anyone who knows the Middle East understands that the humbler the restaurant is, the better the hummus will be. Salman Chaudri arrived just as we started looking at the menu.

"Hello guys!" Chaudri grinned, exposing a set of slightly bulging teeth under a black moustache and black eyes. His stocky frame was immersed in his customary dark suit, which he wore during both summer and winter months.

Chaudri was a Bangladeshi Muslim who trained in surgery at the Park under the old regimen but graduated after Winestone arrived. A talented surgeon, a shrewd businessman with an engaging personality, he rapidly developed a thriving private practice and became a key player in the hospital's community. Like Bachus, Chaudri chose to declare his unconditional support to Winestone and became the latter's personal adviser on the Park's affairs. He became my buddy and as such a communicating link between Winestone and myself.

"What shall we drink? Beer?" asked Bashir.

"I'll have diet Coke," said Chaudri, who, as a devoted Muslim, did not touch alcohol.

"Nothing goes so well with hummus as a cold beer but I have a hernia booked for two 'clock. I'll have tea with na-ana-fresh mint." I examined the menu, "Shouldn't we order a large, mixed platter—of everything?"

Bachus talked in Arabic to the proprietor Fatima, a large Arab woman. "I hope you told her to warm the pitas," I said. We carried on some pretty light conversation as we waited. Occasionally, silence embraced the table between the occasional slurping of empty glasses.

"...does she even understand your Arabic? Isn't she Palestinian?"

"No, she's is from Jordan."

"Isn't it the same?" I asked dumbly.

"You Israelis know nothing about Arabs and the region you live in. You are foreign bodies," joked Bachus.

"Peace, peace!" called Chaudri. "Here comes the food. I am so hungry, let's eat and talk later."

Bachus tore away a piece of a pita, dipped it into the hummus and brought it up to his mouth. He sucked it back and chewed anxiously. "Not bad. Fatima knows how to prepare a decent hummus."

I placed a hip of hummus on my plate and poured a generous quantity of olive oil from the small bottle placed on each table. I swallowed the dripping pita: "Six out of ten on the hummus scale," I said. "Hummus must literally swim in olive oil."

"I would grade it eight," mumbled Chaudri with a mouth full.

"What does a curry-eating Bangladeshi understand of hummus?" Bashir nudged him. "I ate the best hummus in the world in Damascus, at the old market, nine out of ten!"

"We are Muslims and almost Arabs," retorted Chaudri.

I bit into an olive. "The best hummus in the world is prepared and served at Abu Shukri, via Dolorosa, just off the Nablus Gate, the Old City, Jerusalem. Hummus making is an art, like surgery and Abu Shurkri's restaurant, a few tables in a shabby room, is the mecca for hummus."

Chaudri systematically eliminated a high pile of stuffed grape leaves covered with tahini sauce and wiped his moustache. "Marc, you've probably guessed why we asked you to lunch. You know that Bashir and myself are your friends and as good friends we want to tell you not to send your letter to Sorki."

"Why not?"

"Because no one has ever sent Sorki such a letter. Because Sorki and his friends are the kings of this hospital, and because if you intend on keeping your job and staying on you cannot send it."

Bachus took a sip from his tea glass and grimaced. "This is not fresh mint at all; this is local rubbish." He practically wiped his tongue to get rid of the taste. "Listen Marc, Chaudri and myself are a local product. We were trained under these guys and we know them inside out. Why do you think Winestone uses Chaudri as Roosevelt used Harry Hopkins? Sorki's and Mantzur's power base is wide and indestructible. Let's start from the top with the president, OK? Sorki is Howard's personal surgeon—he removed his gallbladder a year ago. The vice president, Dr. Farbstein, is enslaved to Sorki, Mantzur and Susman—a lot of dirt involved, of course. You want to talk about the Board of Trustees? Mantzur sits on the board as the only hospital doctor. The Medical Executive committee is in their hands. The chairmen of medicine, cardiology, oncology, radiology, pediatrics are all yes men. They are all on short-term contracts, renewable only if approved by the almighty Medical Board, which is Sorki and Mantzur."

"Guys, I know all of this. I am not stupid. Still, what those two are doing is outrageous. I bet that no one out of surgery realizes how bad those two are."

"Nonsense, Marc! Nonsense!" Chaudri almost shouted. "Those two are not monsters as you try to describe them. We agree with you that their mode of surgical practice is despicable, but otherwise they are respectable members of the medical community. They are not monsters. They have families, wives, children, friends, and they are popular socially and look after their trusted friends."

"What he is trying to tell you," interjected Bachus, "is that the two alleged monsters represent the community which most deserves them. Life is hard today, harder than ever. Malpractice policy costs around thirty grand and is always going up. Add this to the office's overhead and see how much one has to generate only to start practicing. And why should a doctor live worse than a Wall Street dealer? A few years ago Medicare paid two thousand for a gallbladder and now it pays a few hundred. So what do surgeons do? They must remove more gallbladders to maintain the same standard of life. Now, the number of symptomatic gallbladders walking in Brooklyn has not increased, eh? So what do they do? They remove asymptomatic gallbladders—doing what you call unnecessary surgery. Is it unnecessary? Not for them. For them it is necessary—to afford the new house, the Mercedes for the wife, the private law school for the kids. Do you understand? In this community everyone has skeletons in his closet. The deeper you dig the more you'll find. But once you start to dig you will be excommunicated, as in the church, capisce?"

"Capisce, capisce. Are you becoming Italian, Bashir? Is it your girlfriend's influence?"

"Shuddup! Don't interrupt when I'm talking." He took another sip from his tea and addressed me after wincing at its bitter taste: "Do you understand what I'm saying? Sorki and Mantzur are not an exception. They are part of a crowd, and the crowd is large. And Marc, everyone commits mistakes and tries to cover them up. Even Winestone does. Remember the Whipple he did on that old, blue obstructive lung disease? We all knew she didn't have a chance. We told him so, but he operated nevertheless. Did anyone say anything at the M&M? Of course not! And that huge fat lady with her entire gut outside her tummy, in a monstrous hernia. Didn't we tell him that hernia was inoperable? We did, but he operated and she died. Remember how long this case lasted at the M&M? One minute! Winestone managed to cover it up in a few seconds. Is Winestone a monster? Do you wish to fight with him as well?" We sat silent, contemplating what had just been said. He had a few good points; there was no doubt about it. Finally, he concluded: "Let's get some coffee."

"I'll have more tea," said Chaudri. "And order a few of your Arabic cakes. You call them Baklava? Marc, in a certain way you are an outsider. Your goals are different. We want you to stay because the department needs you. So forget about Sorki and Mantzur and concentrate on yourself. Teach, write, publish and make money. Going against Sorki is like committing suicide. You're not a suicide bomber, eh?" He pointed a finger to his temple. "Throw the letter away. Trust us. This is the way to go."

▲▼◢◣▼▲

I sat in front of the computer. Today's assignment was the epilogue for the book Winestone and I were editing. The ideas and words were not flowing as usual. The screen saver reappeared with the chubby, smiling face of Winston Churchill and the V sign in his right hand. Churchill is my hero. I am fascinated by the multi-faceted personality of the so-called "largest human being of our time" and read all he

141

wrote or said. Recently I discovered a passage by Churchill that could have quite easily been said about Mantzur:

> He presents to me ...the same mental picture as a great surgeon before the days of anesthetics, versed in every detail of such science as was known to him: sure of himself, steady of poise, knife in hand, intent upon the operation; entirely removed in his professional capacity from the agony of the patient, the anguish of relations, or the doctrines of rival schools, the devises of quacks, or the first-fruits of new learning. He would operate without excitement...and if the patient died, he would not reproach himself.

Winston Churchill must have had a certain surgical personality in mind when writing that to describe the WWI British military leader Douglas Haig. Surgeons both talented and ruthless—to the verge of psychopathy—have always existed. Take, for example, the leading European master surgeon between the world wars, Ferdinand Sauerbruch of Berlin, who late in his career was described to tear out brain tumors in living patients with ungloved fingers. Yes, surgeons like Mantzur and Sorki are to be found everywhere. They will always exist. Someone aptly described what they do as "eyebrow raising events."

Was this all we could do when confronted with their cases—raise our eyebrows to each other, wink a few times, and keep our mouths shut? Perhaps Winestone, Chaudri and Bachus were right. Perhaps I simply have to look away and concentrate on my own work. Work on improving my practice, getting more referrals, generating money, upgrading my academic appointment. People detest confrontation and arguments. A study I read in a recent issue of the *American Journal of Surgery* claimed that the most frequently suggested improvement given by residents for the M&M conference was to decrease defensiveness and blame. *How am I viewed at the M&M meetings by surgeons, residents and students? Do they read me as an aggressive, rigid, obsessed, or manic?*

Am I normal? What's my problem? I may be suffering from a chronic malady. Malpractice phobia, perhaps? I don't know.
Not long ago, a visiting guest professor from the Midwest, a giant of American surgery, told me after a dinner in Manhattan: "Marc, New York surgery is notorious. You cannot change local traditions and paradigms that took many years to develop. Look at myself. Do you know how long it took me to dominate the practice in my own Department, to mold the surgeons into my own pattern? It took thirty years. Winestone is a young chairman at the Park. He has to move cautiously. Stick to him and help him. Opposing the local private Mafia will bring you nowhere. You cannot change the world in one day." Clearly the giant's speech was promoted by what Winestone told him.

I touched the keyboard, and the screen saver disappeared. The blank epilogue file re-emerged. I looked at it lamely, and then switched over to a file containing an almost completed book. I went to the last chapter, "The M&M meeting."

An "ideal" and objective M&M meeting as featured above is not conducted in many places because of local sociopolitical restraints. If this is the case in your neck of the woods, it may be damaging to your own surgical education: how would you know what is right or wrong? Books and journals are useful but cannot replace a thorough analysis of specific cases by a group of educated surgeons. As you know, there are many ways to skin a cat, and it is easy to be a smart ass looking at things through the "retroscope." Our sick patients and the events leading to the M&M meeting are complex. But behind all this complex chaos there is always an eternal truth that should be and can be disclosed and announced. As Winston Churchill said: "Success is the ability to go from failure to failure without losing your enthusiasm. Failure obliges change—success breeds complacency."

Fuck Sorki, fuck Mantzur. Fuck all of them. Who cares what they do? Not me, not anymore. Am I the protector of Brooklyn's population? Stop being the constant rebel fighting against the rest of the world. You are almost fifty years old. Act mature and do what is good for you!
Fuck'em.

▲▼◢◣▼▲

Mike Silverstein stopped me in the corridor later that day. "Dr. Zohar, could I have a few words with you?"

"Sure, Mike. What's the problem?"

"Could we go into your office, please?

"Of course." Silverstein appeared nervous, unlike his usual self. Usually he was so laid back he was almost horizontal.

"Have a seat, Mike," I implored him in what I hoped was a relaxing tone. I was curious as to what he was upset about. "What's the matter? Your wife decided to leave you?"

"Not exactly."

"Your girlfriend decided to leave you?" He smiled a little bit, and even chuckled.

"No, not yet. I want to get your advice on a case. I don't know what to do."

"OK then."

"It is Susman's patient in the medical ICU," he explained. "He is around seventy-five years old, admitted last week with acute on chronic-renal failure. The renal team started hemodialysis. Chest X ray showed a poorly defined hilar mass, probably malignant—"

My phone rang. I picked it up, listened, and put it back. "Mike," I said with a degree of urgency he understood immediately. "My case is on the table. Is your story long? Can it wait?"

"It can't. To cut the story short, they did an abdominal CT."

"Why? Any abdominal complaints?"

"Not that I know of. Do you see any medical patient in the ICU not undergoing a CT for whatever reason?"

"Yep, you're right. Go on." I closed the door and started changing into my blue scrubs.

"So the CT showed a triple A, a small aneurysm about four point five centimeters."

"It is small and asymptomatic. This guy seems a wreck. I would leave it alone."

"I agree, and this is why I wanted to talk to you. Mantzur wants to operate tomorrow, and I am scheduled to do it with him."

I shoved my feet into the white wooden OR clogs. I decided I'd try my newfound indifference on Mike. "What do you expect me to do? I am only a humble full-time staff surgeon. Did you talk to Winestone? He likes you a lot. You can talk to him openly."

"I did. He appeared evasive. Told me that Mantzur is the attending, that I am a chief resident and should obey orders."

"So?"

"Well, today the poor wreck developed some cardiac arrhythmia and Dr. Geddy introduced a temporary pacemaker. And besides, his ejection fraction is fifteen. Can you believe it? Geddy cleared him for elective aortic surgery."

"Wake up, man! Geddy would clear his own father for elective triple A repair—provided, of course, that Mantzur's the surgeon. Look, Mike, I can't help you. God couldn't help you. You expect me to fight Mantzur alone, eh? What do you think that I am—Robin Hood?"

"What should I do? I don't want to repair a triple A in a living corpse."

"Do what your conscience tells you. You could tell Mantzur to go to hell. You could just become sick tomorrow. Or you could take a deep breath and tell Mantzur that the operation in this particular patient is unnecessary, not indicated and doomed to kill the patient. You are a chief resident; he can do nothing to you. You are out of here in a few months anyway."

"Dr. Zohar, I told him so—in different words of course. He said, 'Mike, you are wrong, this triple A may rupture. It has to be done.' Is he senile or impaired?"

"Both. But this is not my problem anymore. I am not the Chairman. Have fun, Mike."

I caught the elevator down to the third floor. It was empty again. I kicked its walls a few times with the wooden soles, grateful that there was no surveillance camera there. It was always the same elevator—another year of this and I'd probably destroy it.

11

The Investigation

*What we call experience is often a dreadful list of
ghastly mistakes.*
—*J. Chalmers Da Costa, 1863-1933*

May 1999.

It was eight thirty a.m. when Dr. Mantzur entered the
auditorium. This was when he always arrived at the M&M—
if he arrived at all. He walked slowly down the left aisle
towards his seat in the center of the second row just behind
the Chairman. He was dressed conservatively today, and as
he ambled by I picked up the scent of Paco Rabanne—so
strong that even the medical students at the other corner of
the auditorium could smell it.

Behind a permanent facial mask of Eastern calm, Mantzur was in a foul mood. First, his mouth was still aching from
the reconstructive dental job he'd had last week. Second, Silverstein had just notified him that the Triple A he did a few
days ago passed away at night. *Well, only those who do not
operate do not have fatalities.* Third and more significantly,
Dr. Albert Farbstein, the Vice President, had phoned him
early in the morning to announce that the State's Office of
Professional Medical Conduct (OPMC) had asked for fifty-
eight of his charts. What could it be? He never had to deal
with the State or the OPMC before. Fifty-eight charts! *Who is
behind this? We'll have to find the responsible party. I have
to warn Sorki!*

Dr. Moshesh was at the podium along with Winestone.
Another Sorki case? Winestone has to go easy on Sorki, Mantzur thought. The peace he had negotiated was so fragile—
especially after the situation with the cousin.

"This is a seventy-four year old female patient with
known metastatic rectal cancer state post chemo and radio-

therapy, who presented with intermittent rectal bleeding. CT scan showed multiple bilobar liver metastases, ascites and possible peritoneal deposits of cancer. Her bilirubin was two point seven."

"Could we see the CT please?" I asked in a voice loud enough for the auditorium to hear me.

"Would you show us the CT please?" Winestone intoned.

The radiology resident, a short Indian woman, placed the CT film on the overhead projector and began talking in a heavy Madras accent: "This is an abdominal CT taken before the operation. You can clearly see multiple lesions, which are disseminated diffusely throughout both lobes of the liver, suggesting an advanced metastatic process. Notice the large quantity of free fluid around the liver and in the gutters."

The resident changed the film and continued: "Coming down to the pelvis, we see ascites, and here we can see a large rectal tumor which appears to be adherent to the pelvic wall."

"Thank you," said Winestone, pointing to Moshesh, "Please continue. What did you do with this patient?"

Moshesh smiled. "We performed a full laparotomy which disclosed about a liter of ascites. The rectal tumor was fixed to adjacent structures and appeared to be non-resectable. The colon was therefore divided proximal to the tumor, the distal segment was closed and the proximal brought out as a colostomy. The postoperative course was complicated by a progressive hepatic failure, which led to death on postoperative day twenty six." Moshesh smiled again, apparently satisfied with his smooth presentation.

Embarrassed silence descended on the auditorium. It was clear to all present that this patient was laden with cancer deposits like so many holes in a Swiss cheese and that the operation was unnecessary—hastening the patient's demise. There was nothing to be gained by saying anything since Sorki was the surgeon. Besides, I was practicing being humble.

"Any comments?" asked Winestone.

"I don't understand the indication for surgery." I said against my better judgment. *If nobody else is going to say it*...

"We saw the CT, and it's clear that the surgeon knew prior to the operation that nothing could have been done for this unfortunate patient. So why the surgery?"

Can't he understand? Won't he learn that we do whatever we want in this hospital, Mantzur was probably thinking to himself. It wouldn't surprise me if he knew that I was behind the OPMC's request for those charts.

"Dr. Sorki," Winestone continued. "Would you please respond to Dr. Zohar's question?"

Sorki appeared combative. Too many of his cases were being presented, and he was probably a bit upset that I asked questions. After all, why should he—the president of the Medical Board—swallow this crap? Sorki stood up. His words were flavored with heavy sarcasm. "Mr. Chairman, I am not going to respond to the specific comment by my honorable colleague," he motioned down to me from his perch, "who should have carefully listened to the case presentation. The indication for operation was rectal bleeding. Isn't it clear?"

"What bleeding?" I retorted furiously, abolishing my previously humble stance. "A few drops of blood over twenty-four hours?"

"Do not interrupt me when I am talking. This patient lost a significant amount of blood and required multiple blood transfusions."

"Moshesh," I turned to face him. Sorki was herding himself into a corner. Like a chess player, I was thinking a few moves ahead and had his king in my sites. "Please look at the chart. How many units of blood were given pre-op? And what was her hemoglobin before the operation?"

Moshesh looked toward Winestone. Patients' charts are routinely brought to the M&M but never searched in public. The statements and claims by surgeons were always accepted as truths. Winestone had no choice. He was in a crossfire but had to play it objectively. "Look at the chart," he commanded Moshesh.

Moshesh paged through the thick chart, taking his time: "The pre-operative hemoglobin was twelve point three gram-percent. Transfusions? Let's see, transfusions? I do not see here any record that the patient received any blood transfusions during the index admission."

"Dr. Rusk, what is your opinion?" asked Winestone.

Malcolm Rusk cleared his throat. "Dr. Winestone," he said with half a glance towards Sorki, "it appears to me that it may have been an error in judgment to operate on this patient who suffered from generalized abdominal carcinomatosis. In addition, even if the patient was bleeding—and she wasn't—the source of bleeding could not have been removed at surgery. Furthermore, it is difficult to see how a proximal colostomy would have a significant effect on bleeding which in fact did not occur."

Sorki's face tightened. *Is Rusk crazy? What happened to him? Is he taking anabolic steroids or Viagra? Such macho talk!* Sorki rose again. "Dr. Rusk, please stop, please! You are an educated surgeon, one of the leading teachers of our residents." Sorki smiled and looked around, letting the sarcasm penetrate the ears of his admirers. Despite the smoke and mirrors, everyone knew he was nervous and agitated. There was the faintest hint of hesitation in his voice. People picked it out immediately because they'd never heard it before. "I am convinced that you understand the term palliation, pal-ia-tion. This patient's cancer bled and she was operated for palliation. I do not know why the chart contains no record of blood transfusions. The record can be rectified." He sat back down, satisfied with his answer.

Rusk was not intimidated: "Dr. Sorki, this simply is not true. It was a serious error to operate, and the statement that a major blood transfusion was given is not true. In fact it appears that you have provided this meeting with false information."

Sorki jumped from his seat like a snake had bitten him on the ass and shouted: "Dr. Winestone, stop these false accusations immediately." He looked down at Rusk and myself who, not coincidentally, sat side by side. "You think what you think and do what you do, but I am a big boy, I do what I want to do. Do you understand?" He pointed at Winestone with his index finger: "You are the chairman. You have to control your people and their lies. I can practice surgery as I find it appropriate, this is what we—" he pointed at the group of private surgeons who listened silently—"have always done." Winestone shrugged and did not respond. Sorki mumbled to himself as he chugged up the aisle and stormed out of the auditorium.

▲▼▲▲▼▲

"Come, Marc," Sam Glatman said to me about an hour after the M&M had been dismissed. He was standing at my door and had a childish look on his face. His cheeks were a fleshy pink, and he was almost gushing with joy. "Let me treat you to a latte. Let's go to Border's."

"Yeah, I think we could do that." We crossed the street to the bookshop, ordered our coffees, poured in half and half, sprinkled it with cinnamon and sat down at a small table.

I took a noisy sip. Hot! "Sam, exciting news about the Padrino. Imagine! Fifty-eight charts! I would've loved to see his face when he heard the news. How did you arrange it?"

Sam laughed heartily and wiped the foam off his mouth, "Your lists, my friend. Without your lists we would go nowhere. You are a genius!" I enjoyed the pat on the back. It'd been quite a while since I'd received such a bold compliment.

"Tell me more." I sipped more carefully. "I want details."

"Well, as you know, my anonymous letters and calls to the OPMC were ignored. After you gave me the lists I called them up and arranged for an interview with one of their top surgical boys—a guy called Carducci, Dr. Fausto Carducci."

"Another Italian?"

"A local boy, a retired surgical program director from Staten Island. We had an excellent talk. The guy seems knowledgeable and serious. He'll chew Mantzur's ass."

"He deserves it. Did you hear that his last triple A died last night? The guy did not have a chance—killed in cold blood. So Mantzur has been dealt with, or at least we think so. What about Terminator Two?"

"Jesus, what a show at the M&M! Did you notice how he treated Winestone? Like a piece of shit. 'I do what I do'—to talk like this to a chairman, this is unheard of. Winestone has to grab him by the balls and squeeze hard." Glatman grabbed his scrotum and demonstrated the act. "If not, he'll lose any remaining authority and respect and there can't be much of that left." The latte tasted so much better today. Somehow, I didn't think it was a coincidence.

▲▼▲▼▲

The elevator I caught on the second floor was loaded with passengers, including three huge Caribbean paramedics escorting a stretcher holding a shriveled, contracted ancient-looking white woman. She labored loudly for air with rapid and shallow breathing. *Why isn't she getting oxygen? She may die before arriving at the eighth floor.* At the corner of the elevator I noticed Dr. Katzen—a private physician. Katzen, in a dark suit, a large black yarmulke covering his scalp, avoided eye contact with me. We were not sure how orthodox Katzen was. Chaudri suggested that the yarmulke was part of a plot to lure his mostly local Hasidic Jewish patients. Katzen's patients—when in need for elective surgery—preferred the prestigious Mt. Zion Hospital in Manhattan. All Rabbis knew that the best surgeons worked there. The cases I received from Katzen were terminal, did not need any operations, or were not insured and arrived during the weekend. Then my waiting room suddenly filled with Yiddish talking bearded men in heavy black coats that smelled of kosher dills. I exited the stuffy elevator at the sixth floor and walked to Winestone's office where the war cabinet was holding a meeting. Bachus, Rusk, Chaudri were already seated.

Winestone picked up a black folder off his desk: "Malcolm handed me this a few days ago. I believe that you have a copy as well, Marc. Impressive work, Malcolm. Well prepared."

"Thank you, Dr. Winestone."

"As a matter of fact," Winestone continued, "I wish to discuss with you today what to do with this." He pointed at the folder summarizing the Departmental QA committee's investigation of Sorki.

After the confrontation between Sorki and Winestone at the M&M meeting Winestone gave me permission to send my accusatory letter to Sorki and instructed Rusk to conduct a "pattern of practice" investigation on Sorki—to look at all his complications over the last five years. The end result—the black folder—contained sixty-seven of his complicated cases in chronological order, a detailed summary of each case, an in-depth analysis by one of us, and a conclusion.

"This is a nightmarish folder," I said. "Have you ever seen such a collection of horror stories produced by one surgeon? Of course, Mantzur is no better."

"This meeting is not about Mantzur. It is about Sorki. I was wondering what to do with the results of this investigation, this folder."

During the investigation, which lasted a few weeks, Winestone was under extreme pressure to stop it. The entire hospital knew when charts of one surgeon were summoned up to the Department of Surgery. Drs. Farbstein and Mantzur and even Mr. Howard, the President, ran to Winestone and tried to convince him to "stop the nonsense" or "arrange for a meeting between you and Mahmud." Winestone oscillated. One day he told Rusk to abort it. We were appalled and threatened to go on alone. This, together with Sorki's loud, corridor campaign against Winestone convinced the latter that the investigation had to proceed.

"I entertained a few options," Winestone explained. "As you may know, the bylaws state that after the chairman receives a report from his QA committee, he has a few alternatives, based on his own interpretation of the committee's findings. In this case, the committee has identified serious problems in the pattern of practice of the investigated surgeon. According to the bylaws I, as a chairman, have to pass these findings to the hospital's QA committee. Unfortunately, this is controlled by the investigated surgeon and his friends."

"And Mantzur, of course," I added.

Winestone ignored my comment as he did everything I ever said that was related to Mantzur. "I called a few colleagues from Boston and Baltimore. I asked whether they would agree to review Sorki's cases and the findings recorded in this folder, functioning as objective, non-biased, external experts. They declined."

"Why?" asked Chaudri.

"They don't want to take the risk. Sorki may sue them as he may sue you. And me. And you." He was pointing at me.

"Can he sue me?" Rusk sounded anxious. "I was appointed to chair the QA committee by you. I report to you. Why didn't you warn me about this prior to the investigation?"

"This folder contains a heavy set of allegations. We have to be careful and calculate well our future course."

I knew what was in Winestone's mind. He wanted to temporize, to manipulate, to let the other side know about the existence of this incriminating document and to negotiate peace or productive co-existence with Sorki, to be bridged by Mantzur.

"Dr. Winestone," I said, trying to sound innocent. "What about the OPMC, the State? Why not simply send a copy of this folder to them?"

Winestone's eyes bulged behind his lenses. His face reddened, and his neck veins swelled. "Do not even talk about going to the State. If you do—you won't be able to find a job again in this town. As I said to you before, I won't be able to protect you."

"Be that as it may, I am going to the State. See this?" I removed a letter from my pocket and passed it to Winestone. "This is an invitation I received today from the OPMC. They are asking me to come and discuss Mantzur's cases."

"Why you?" There was suspicion in his voice.

"I don't know," I feigned ignorance. Over the years, I'd gotten quite good at it. "They may soon call you and the others as well." I motioned towards Rusk, Bachus and Chaudri. Winestone surely guessed that it was Glatman and me who had reported Mantzur to the OPMC. Chaudri knew everything and whatever Chaudri knew would not be unknown to Winestone for long.

"What are you going to tell them?"

"The truth, of course." I was enjoying upsetting Winestone.

"Obviously I can't tell you what to say, but you understand the potential consequences."

"Are you threatening me?" I stood up and leaned ominously over his desk. My hands were poised at slightly beyond shoulder width and my face was set. My jaw was tight.

"Not at all, Marc," responded Winestone avoiding eye contact. He was in a very precarious position indeed. Of course, he dodged and weaved his way out: "Not at all. If you fail to understand how important Mantzur is to our cause, there is nothing I can add now and there'll be nothing I'll be able to do for you."

I pointed an accusatory finger at him, almost poking him in the chest, and screamed: "You are threatening me! You are interfering with the State's investigation. You are treating two murderers differentially, which you cannot do! Don't you understand that you can't pursue the one while ignoring and even protecting the other?"

"Marc," Bachus, who had moved to my side, whispered. "Take it easy, will you? Sit down and apologize. You can't shout at him this way." I appreciated his concern, but this was way above him now. In fact, even I was finding myself in over my head. Better to learn exactly how tall I was, and I was about to find out.

"I have nothing to add." I about faced and marched out. The door slammed behind me.

I spent the afternoon extinguishing small fires. One was a little bigger than the rest. Andy, our biller, disappeared without leaving a trace. For three years Andy was billing for us, arriving each Monday with his secretary to collect the patients' details. A month ago Bachus decided to investigate a number of random unpaid accounts, finding that on many occasions Andy was cashing the checks issued to us by the insurance companies. It appeared that Andy's billing company—which he claimed to employ fifteen certified medical billers—was a hoax—including the address and the phone numbers. And the so-called secretary and her recent baby were in fact his girlfriend and child. Andy must have skimmed me of at least a hundred grand. Now I understood why he had given me twenty-five smuggled Cuban cigars last Christmas.

The second fire was minor. Mrs. McFee, the vice president for nursing, called me. "Dr. Zohar, I need to discuss a serious matter with you—a rather confidential and touchy one."

"Please go ahead."

"Well, one of your chief residents was seen by the security guard in his duty room with our nurse last night."

I lowered my voice to sound confidential. "And who was the resident, if I may ask?"

She sounded embarrassed: "Dr. Silverstein." *Mike!* I thought, smiling from ear to ear. *You dog you.*

"Mike is our best chief resident. He is married, you know, and his wife is pregnant. Could we keep it confidential, please? Would you let our chairman and me deal with it?" She hesitated briefly. "Please?"

Intimate liaisons between two hospital employees, on duty, on hospital's premises was against the bylaws. I could imagine her touching her heavy silver cross.

"Mrs. McFee," I said, adamant. "I promise that this will be the last time that one of our residents is involved in such a scandalous behavior. And what about the nurse? Was she forced into Silverstein's duty room or did she go there on her own accord?"

"I will deal with the nurse. You will discipline the offending resident?"

"Our chairman will discipline the resident. Thank you very much." I hung up. *What a stupid bunch of puritans! You are allowed to screw patients, but screwing nurses is a sin. Can't the chief resident have some fun?*

Chaudri walked into my room and took a seat. His black eyes looked warm and amused. He sighed. "Life is so difficult. I had such a hard night, one intestinal obstruction and a bleeding ulcer. God, I'm so tired. Who has the power for all these fights?"

I told him about the call from Mrs. McFee.

"What a hypocrite," he exclaimed. "Howard was bumping her years ago and then he dumped her." We hummed and hawed at the implications. "So," Chaudri carried on. "What else is up?"

"Well, your chairman has to make up his mind. He has to decide which side he is on."

Chaudri laughed. "Marc, give him a chance. He cannot cross the Rubicon so fast. Going to the State to report on colleagues was never part of his lexicon. Winestone is one of the boys, a member of all their clubs. Old boys do not solve their internal disputes before the State."

I was surprised at Chaudri's insight. "Yeah, so what do you suggest that I do? I am going to the State, you know. I was invited."

"Just say the truth—how things were and are. We'll say the same if we are invited. As for Winestone, he is under tremendous pressure to abort the investigation and dump its findings."

"What do you think? You know Sorki well."

"Sorki won't compromise," Chaudri pointed out dead seriously. "He is set out to kill us all. Your letter was like a stab wound to the heart. Winestone will be forced to cross the Rubicon. Just give him a chance."

"And what about Mantzur?

Chaudri laughed out loud. "Marc, it is absolute chaos. Mantzur is upset. He's practically locked himself in his office day and night going over the charts, probably adding notes and editing them."

"Isn't that like tampering with legal evidence?"

"Of course it is illegal, but everyone does it. The charts won't be sent to the State until Mantzur surrenders them to the record room. He'll take his time."

"Does he talk to Winestone?"

"Sure. It appears that Sorki tried to convince him that it was you and Rusk who stabbed him in the back. Winestone, on the other hand, is convincing him that it was the old general Lungetti who sent copies of the M&M meeting to the State, and perhaps it was even Sorki himself who wanted to screw the Godfather, a traitor who joined Winestone."

"Why Lungetti?"

"They've hated each other for the past thirty years."

"Salman, tell me, why is Winestone sticking with the Padrino? What is the reason for this bond between the two of them?"

"It is an enigma. I don't know. I do not have a clue what he sees in the Padrino. But do us a favor and play the game. Go to Mantzur and show him the letter you received from the OPMC, and tell him that you will do anything to help him."

"Is this what Winestone asked you to convey to me?"

"Yes. Screw the old man and at the same time smile at his face. Shmooze him."

"You talk like a Jew. Are you sure you are a Muslim?"

"During the last Ramadan Ilkadi wished me Happy Chanukah, hinting to my association with you guys. So go and shmooze him. He is bad, so bad."

I hesitated and then said, "OK. This seems to be the way to go."

12

Whistle Blowing

No patient is too sick to have his life saved.
—Mark. M. Ravitch, 1910-1981

June-July 1999

They stood against the green ICU wall as their father was wheeled away. The youngest of the three was about twelve years old, the eldest eighteen. The one in the middle, sandwiched between them, towered a head above his siblings. Fair, pale, freckled faces of Irish Brooklynites. There was something in the way the three boys looked away; their eyes avoiding the distorted, bloated, and unnaturally swollen face of their father. It discomforted me. They came to bid farewell to their father who was now being taken for his third re-operation for severe abdominal infection. Their tall, strong, powerful dad. The soft-spoken, mustached, middle aged man who only a few days ago was sitting at the head of their Sunday table and cracking jokes was now ballooned grossly by numerous liters of saline seeping across his leaky capillaries. With the endotracheal tube sticking out the denturesless mouth he was a picture from a ghastly nightmare. *Oh God Dad! What happened to your face?* Was this why the three boys were crying in silence? Was this why they remained glued to the green wall, looking away?

I, their dying father's surgeon, was taking him for his third trip to the operating room. I looked at the three sons from a distance, trying to appear detached. Families of dying patients made me nervous. "Leave that stupid wall!" I wanted to shout at them. "Hug your dying father. Kiss his disfigured face. This may be your last chance to feel his warm, living body. Move it!"

Nothing happened. I remained mute. We moved on, marching towards the electronic door to the OR. I threw a last glance at the boys, cemented to the floor, intimidated by fear. I thought they would remember that moment all their lives and would forever be haunted for not leaping on their father's bed, placing their lips on his cheeks, squeezing his immobilized hands. "Oh Dad," they would continue crying for the rest of their years. "Please don't leave us. Come back!"

As we approached the OR, I could feel a building up of wetness in the corners of my eyes. I was a boy, and it was my own father being taken away from me. Looking at other people's sorrows we sometimes cry, remembering our own. I removed my green cap and dried my eyes. I put it back on and started to scrub while trying to plan the procedure I was going to do on the boys' father. But the boys' image kept interfering. I couldn't extinguish their gaze. Was this the way I looked at my father almost thirty years ago?

On the morning of his own operation my father shaved painstakingly, rinsed his face and applied a fine after-shave lotion. He—a surgeon himself—kissed his own surgeon on both cheeks, wishing him luck. The same two-cheek maneuver was repeated with a long procession of friends and family members. I was the last, the last to feel his soft, smooth and perfumed cheeks—the smell and touch I can sense even today. A day later I was allowed to see him in the ICU, a tube emerging through his toothless mouth, his cheeks gray and sunken, his white whiskers growing. Horrified, I looked away. *Is this my father?* I did what those three boys did today. Why didn't I touch him? Even today I am tormented for not placing my lips against his distorted, unshaven face, bidding him adieu. A day or so later I saw him at the mortuary. His cheeks were cold.

I threw the scrub brush away, rinsed my hands and entered the room. I looked at the critically ill patient immersed in the macaroni of lines. I had to save this guy. With the dressings removed, his fresh abdominal wound looked horrendous—pouring pus, intestinal contents and necrotic matter. The scrub and circulating nurses looked at the scene with distaste. Yet another "frequent flier" from the ICU who was not going to survive, they probably thought.

"Christ, he looks like a yellow balloon," said one of the anesthetists while trying to disentangle the lines. "How many times do you guys want to re-open him? He is clearly finished."

We re-cleansed the abdominal cavity, removing stinking pus and necrotic tissue from the diaphragm into the scrotum.

"This guy is acidotic, pH six point nine," announced the junior anesthetist from behind his screen. "I cannot ventilate him properly, CO_2 is in the sky."

"Call your senior," I snapped. "Don't you know that he has wet lungs? They are stiff. Increase the PEEP for God's sake. Don't you know how to ventilate an ARDS patient?"

I closed my eyes in frustration. Why, why, why, do they want to kill my patient? Don't they know that his lungs are as wet as a sponge. Why don't they ventilate him properly? Why does the senior leave the room? Why does nobody care?

Being a general surgeon, treating patients who exist somewhere between life and death, one often feels like the whole world is against you and your patient. The nurse who accidentally removes your drains, the radiologist who uses barium instead of gastrografin—how many times did we tell him! The transporter who on the way to the OR accidentally disconnects the oxygen, and that resident—yes, it is always a resident—who does something silly without your permission.

But this was nothing new. We know that hospitals are dangerous places.

So we finished cleansing the filthy abdomen, leaving it open again and wheeled the man back to the ICU. It was late; these cases are usually scheduled at the end of the day when the OR is free from the daily bread and butter routines. I found the wife, a stocky, plain looking woman, sitting alone in the families' lounge. The sons weren't around anymore.

"Hi, Mrs. O'Neill"

"How is he doing, Doc?"

"Not too good, I must say. The infection is spreading as I explained to you yesterday. The perforation in the duodenum, which we sutured before, broke down, which is another problem, and the necrosis at the retroperitoneum, that space behind"—I pointed to my back—"has entered the scrotum. We had to remove the left testicle. The infection destroyed it."

She looked at me calmly, fiddling with a large gold cross dangling low over a white T-shirt. "How many times are you going to re-open him, Doc? Can he take all these surgeries? Look how swollen he is!"

"You work for a dentist, right?"

"Yes."

"When your dentist treats a root canal infection, doesn't he re-open and re-treat—a few times, at least—the infected canal—before closing it permanently?"

"Yes."

"Think about your husband's infection as a root canal. I am going to enter his abdomen as many times as I find it necessary. Anyway, his abdomen is not closed. It is open as are his two loins."

"Is he going to survive, Doc?" She looked hard into my eyes.

"I don't know," I answered gravely, but honestly. "I am not optimistic. The infection is not under control and his organs are failing, first the lungs and now the kidneys. If he doesn't start to improve or if he deteriorates further within the next day or two—then the outlook is grim."

I looked at her, trying to assess the impact of my words. Her features remained calm, almost stoic. I said, "Good night then. I'm off. I'll talk to you tomorrow."

"Just one more question," she said then. "It is about his scrotum." She hesitated. "Doc, when he recovers, would he be able to function, you know—"

A lame look was the only answer I could provide, but it seemed appropriate at the time.

I knocked on Mantzur's door and entered. He was sitting behind his desk, shifting through papers. *He's probably counting his money or planning new exterminations.* Mantzur peered at me above his reading glasses. This was the first time I have ever visited his office, but he did not look surprised. *Winestone probably warned him.*

He walked from behind the desk and offered a wobbly handshake. "Hello, Dr. Zohar, what can I do for you?" He did not invite me to sit down. I noticed that his missing tooth was not missing any more.

I got straight to the point. "Dr. Mantzur, I need to show you something." I handed him the invitation to the OPMC. He grabbed it and read to himself, his lips moving. The letter said something to the effect that, "The office of Professional Medical Conduct is currently conducting an investigation concerning the above referenced physician. I am informed that you may have information helpful to this investigation. It is imperative that I interview you with regard to this matter...."

Mantzur was taking his time. I knew he was not a great intellectual but never realized how slowly he read.

Mantzur looked at me expressionlessly and said: "Why you? Why did they invite you?"

"I suppose because I am the one who organizes the M&M meetings." I shrugged. "Dr. Mantzur, I just wanted to show you the invitation and to say that I will do my best."

"Absolutely. Thank you very much." He tossed me a foxy smile. I knew that he did not believe a word I was saying. Mantzur looked again at the document: "And who is this Fausto Carducci, M.D.?"

"Probably one of their medical men. I will tell you when I come back."

"Will you? Please. I do not know what they want from me—all those patients who died were so old. You know how the vascular patients are. One wanted to save their limbs. Who informed on me and why?"

"Who knows? One has not a few enemies. Everyone has," I said. *You killed all of them, and I informed on you and will do anything to destroy you.* I recovered the letter from him and left with a smile.

▲▼▲▼▲

Changing Mr. O'Neill's dressing in the SICU put me in a good mood. After his initial operations many days of multiple re-operations followed, first in the OR and later at the bedside. In addition to failing kidneys and lungs he developed deep jaundice, and his circulation required inotrope-support. This, in the intensivists' language, could be translated into "multi-organ failure," a marker of "no return." But on one of the days he stopped deteriorating, and his organs gradually improved, the pus thinned and the wounds pinked up. It was then when we realized that he might survive.

Cases like these are rewarding. I climbed the stairs to the department. *They're a partial compensation for the shitty things I have to deal with. Shouldn't I be spending my life saving lives, staying away from all that dirty politics? I should, but working in a crap house there is no escape from it.*

I found Winestone in his office, deeply immersed in several open texts spread on his desk. It was Thursday, and he was preparing himself for Friday morning's professorial rounds with the residents. Winestone was an excellent teacher, and excellence came through systematic and thorough preparation. "Good morning, Dr. Winestone. You wanted to see me?"

"Yes, Marc. Sit down." He motioned me to a chair opposite his desk. "As a matter of fact I was looking at these books, searching for guidelines, whether mesh should be used to repair hernias in the presence of contamination, but I can't find anything decisive."

"Textbooks tend to be hazy about such matters," I agreed.

"Shouldn't we include this controversy in our next volume?"

"We could, why not? A great idea." An awkward silence followed. "You know that today in the afternoon I am going to the State—OPMC, you know."

Winestone fidgeted with his red silk tie, which blended well with the white shirt and black leather blazer. "Yes. Mantzur told me about your visit. You did well, Marc. Perhaps you will become a politician one day."

"I'm learning from you, Dr. Winestone." He liked to be flattered. He didn't realize that I was learning to manipulate people too... Or maybe that's what he meant.

"Marc, I was thinking a bit about this. Sorki is a big problem. One cannot reason with him. He constantly parades across the hospital threatening to get rid of all of us. We have to do something about this, I was thinking that perhaps, you—"

"—Dr. Winestone, do you want me to take Sorki's folder with me to the OPMC?"

"No, no, no. Don't do that! Please let me finish. You know that he and myself share the Morbid Obesity Clinic. Did you notice that the number of gastroplasties I did last month was almost zero while Sorki does them like crazy, three or four a week?"

"Of course. He is stealing your patients." *How slow he is to realize this.*

"Exactly! I talked to the nurse in charge. She's saying that Sorki informed her that I don't do gastroplasties anymore. Can you believe it?"

"Didn't you know that he controls the whole hospital?" *He wakes up only if his personal interests are at stake.*

"Marc, I haven't decided yet what to do about him, but let us keep all options open. When you meet today with that Dr. Armani at the OPMC, why don't you—"

"—Carducci is the name, Fausto Carducci."

"Whatever. Why don't you ask him...why don't you— you know what—tell him that we have this small problem with one of our leading local private surgeons. Tell him what the problem is. You do not have to be specific, you know. Ask his

165

advice, what should be done or could be done. Do you understand what I mean?"

"Absolutely," I said, standing up and heading towards the door. "I agree. This is a great idea. I'll talk to the guy." The door didn't slam behind me.

Up to now Sorki had been murdering patients, but to Winestone, bringing him to justice seemed to be a crazy idea. And now approaching the State about Sorki would be OK because Winestone's pride and personal well-being had been disturbed. Mantzur was still useful, so he could continue with his rampage as he saw fit.

I headed to my office, gathered a few documents into my briefcase, replaced the white coat with a blue blazer and walked out of the hospital towards the subway station.

▲▼▲▼▲

The steamy Manhattan daylight struck me when I climbed out of the humid subway station on Thirty-Fourth street, soaked in sweat. The contrast between this street and the one I left in Brooklyn twenty minutes earlier always amazed me. The people—especially the women—looked so much better. I bought a bottle of water from a street vendor and proceeded towards five Penn Plaza. At State or Government offices one could not expect even a glass of water. The OPMC offices were on the sixth floor where the elevator opened to a spacious waiting room.

"Dr. Zohar?" A white-haired man in a plain gray suit called me from the door. "I am Dr. Carducci. Please come in." He shook my hand vigorously—an honest handshake—and held the door open for me. "Nice of you to come. I appreciate it very much." We entered a large meeting room, a woman stood behind a long table. "This is Mrs. Thompson. She will be present during the interview."

Mrs. Thompson smiled at me, showing white but crooked teeth. She seemed to be in her forties, had a heavy build and was already graying. She wore a cheap business suit and round owlish eyeglasses, portraying the classical image of a dedicated public servant in New York City.

I knew the drill. I had been there before—discussing my own unfortunate case. Mrs. Thompson's function was to serve as a witness to the conversation between Carducci and myself.

Carducci noticed my sweaty forehead. "It is hot outside. Unfortunately, we cannot offer you even a glass of cold water."

"I know. I brought my own water."

Carducci laughed. I liked his manners—like a fatherly, retired high school principal. His voice was deep and warm, tainted with Staten Island Italian accent. "Dr. Zohar, you know why you are here. This may take a few hours. Feel free to ask for an intermission whenever you wish. To start with, Mrs. Thompson will hand you this form which explains how the OPMC functions. Here, take your time. Read it."

It read: "Complaints: OPMC receives complaints from various sources: patients, family members, friends, other health care professionals, hospitals, medical societies, other government agencies, and out of state agencies. Every complaint is investigated."

Oh, sure. It took Sam Glatman almost a year to draw their attention to Mantzur. I continued reading.

"Investigation: some complaints are dismissed due to lack of jurisdiction. Others are resolved by OPMC staff. Some are administratively closed after investigation fails to find evidence to support a charge of misconduct. Some are referred, after thorough investigation to an investigative committee of the Board for Professional Medical Conduct."

I was familiar with this too. I knew the figures. In 1999, for example, NY State Medical Board received 6,690 complaints against physicians, the main source of which—about sixty percent—was the public; complaints about doctors by doctors are rare. Ninety percent of cases were closed after initial inquiry revealed lack of validity. Ultimately five percent of the physicians were disciplined. How they are disciplined is another story. I skimmed through the rest of the document.

167

"OK. I am familiar with all of this." I looked at Carducci, who was immersed in his notes.

"Very well then." He took off his reading glasses, "Let me introduce myself to you properly. I am Fausto Carducci, a medical coordinator of the investigation committee that will assess Dr. Mantzur's case. As stated in the form in your hands, this committee will examine all the evidence. We will then have a few options, which range from dismissal to referral for a hearing. We could also recommend to the State Commissioner of Health to summarily suspend the license of the physician under investigation, that is, if she determines that the physician represents an imminent risk of danger to the public health."

"That is extremely rare, eh?"

"Correct. This occurs very rarely indeed. The offending physician has to literally rape the patient or execute him, and this has to be clearly evident, of course. The OPMC cannot risk any counter-litigation from the accused physician."

"I understand."

Of course it is much easier for a surgeon to kill a patient than to prove that it was a killing.

"By the way," continued Carducci. "I am a retired surgeon, so you can talk with me surgeon to surgeon, OK?"

"Great," I said. "May I ask, Why me? Why did you invite me and not the others?"

"Dr. Samuel Glatman—your friend? He gave us this list that I believe has been prepared by you. A very detailed list. Congratulations. It saved us a lot of homework." He placed a copy of my Mantzur's list on the table. "Before we start talking about Dr. Mantzur, please tell us a little about yourself—current position, background, you know."

"I brought my CV."

Carducci paged through the document. "You like to write?"

"I enjoy it," I admitted. "It is my hobby."

"I see that you wrote a few books with Winestone. You and him are close, eh?"

"I guess so." *Seems that Carducci knows a little about the Park.*

He leafed through the pages again. "Editorial Board of the *British Journal.* How did you manage to get this?"

I shrugged. "I don't know. They invited me."

Carducci placed the document on the table and said to Mrs. Thompson. "Very impressive."

I had passed his scrutiny.

Over the next half hour Carducci questioned me about the structure of our department, who was doing what and who was friendly with whom. "Dr. Zohar, you have to understand," he explained, "that we are very careful not to be involved in personal vendettas between physicians. Your friend Glatman, for example, is a vascular surgeon like Mantzur. They must be competing for referrals and patients. Therefore, we evaluated his complaint very cautiously. Your list, which he provided us, impressed us, however. Here's a copy."

"I know this list almost by heart," I responded. "It's terrible. Did you notice the ongoing reckless pattern? The guy simply operates on anything he can lay his hands on. Did you see the results?" *Don't get excited. Be cool. Don't make the impression that you hate the man. Be academic and detached.*

Carducci listened patiently as if he had all day for me, which was probably the case. Mrs. Thompson took notes. "Dr. Zohar, can I call you Marc?"

"Sure." He put me at ease. Clearly he was on my side.

"Marc, you have to understand something. We cannot afford to talk about patterns. Yes, I know, your list is long and if we would go back another five years we could fish out another fifty similar cases. He was probably doing this when he started practicing. I know these characters; I was a chairman myself. Going over each case and studying the pattern is beyond our means in term of time and resources. It would be an expensive process, which the state cannot afford. You have to select the worst ten to twelve cases. Take this red pen and circle what you think are the most terrible cases—they will become our focus of investigation."

I studied the list, holding the red marker in my hand. This was easy. I talked as I highlighted the most nightmarish cases. "Eighty-five years old, asymptomatic carotid stenosis, technical mishap during endartrectomy. He tied the artery- which is unheard of! Stroke and death. A small triple A, prohibitive risk factors, no indication for operation, death. Another asymptomatic carotid, this one in a patient who couldn't swallow because of an undiagnosed esophageal carcinoma. Death. Femoro-popliteal bypass, horrendous graft infection, failure to manage appropriately, death. Diagnostic thoracotomy in a patient with brain metastases. Death."

I looked at Carducci to see whether he was as horrified as I was. He shook his head solemnly. "Please continue."

"One more carotid in a terminal Alzheimer. Death. Thoracotomy for an unresectable cancer. Death. Esophagectomy and radical nephrectomy for an advanced esophageal cancer and small renal cancer—why the nephrectomy? Mortality of course. Triple A—intra-operative urokinase infusion, bled to death. Distal splenorenal shunt on an advanced cirrhotic, technical mishap. He never did such a case before, did not know where to place the shunt. Death. Bilateral, staged, ax-femoral bypass, unnecessary on one side, bled to death from an anastomosis on the unnecessary side." I paused to take a sip of water. I should have bought another bottle. "Do you see the pattern? The wild negligence?"

Carducci nodded. "Leave the pattern alone. Please go on."

I highlighted the twelfth case and handed him the list. "I hope that this will remain confidential. Everybody knows that I was called to see you. Perhaps you could also interview a few of my colleagues—as a smoke screen."

"Whom should I see?"

"Dr. Chaudri, Dr. Rusk, Dr. Bachus."

"Will they talk?"

"I think they will. They know Mantzur well and are abhorred by his practice."

"We will have to invite the chairman, of course."

170

"Dr. Winestone asked me to talk with you about another confidential matter."

Carducci was beginning to show signs of impatience. "This is all confidential. What does he want?"

"This does not concern Mantzur. It is another matter about which I prefer to talk about only with you." I looked at Mrs. Thompson, who remained expressionless.

"Let's finish with Mantzur. Marc, we need your help. We are still waiting for Mantzur's charts and X-rays."

"They're locked in his office. He is working on them."

"They are all the same." Carducci sighed, crashing back in his seat and removing his thick glasses to toss them on the desk. He wiped his eyes with his left thumb and index finger. "They're always trying to add notes, to delete data, to tamper with evidence. Do you have access to the Departmental M&M summaries?"

"Of course. It is filed."

"You have the list of the twelve cases, then. Please send us anything you have about them."

"Sure." I committed his request to memory. "What happens next?"

"First we have to gather all the evidence. This takes time, and the hospital is not very helpful. Then we will send the evidence to external experts, according to the individual case, be it vascular, general or thoracic."

"Who are those experts? Are they independent, objective?"

"Sure. We use out-of-town surgeons. We pay them for reviewing the cases. It is an expensive process, as I said."

"And then what?"

"The experts will decide with me whether or not this deserves a hearing. A hearing is like a court case, with a judge and lawyers on both sides."

"What could be the end result of a hearing?"

"There are a few possible outcomes. A reprimand, or administrative warning, is the mildest form of discipline. Then there is probation, and there could be actual suspension of license—from a few days to six months or longer. The most severe form of discipline is a permanent revocation of license, which the physician may either contest or accept. Of course, a physician who wishes to save himself the expenses and humiliation by public disclosure may voluntarily surrender his license."

"What do you predict will be Mantzur's fate?"

"This is unpredictable. I guess that he'll be referred to a hearing and I've told you about the possible outcomes. How old is he?"

"Almost seventy."

"Impaired a bit?"

"He may be impaired now, but he was doing the same things years ago."

"My guess is that we'll offer him the last option—to surrender his license. It could save him a lot of money with the outrageous fees lawyers charge." Carducci looked at his watch. "You wanted to tell me something else?" He nodded to Mrs. Thompson as a hint to leave the room. "What's Winestone up to? What does he want?"

I told him all about Sorki and his practice and provided him with a copy of my "Sorki" list. We went into details concerning the association between Sorki and Mantzur and their brethren. "This is the president and vice president of a Medical Board in a large NY Hospital," I concluded.

"I read in the *New York Report* that your hospital was named one of the top ten hospitals in the city," Carducci said. "Tell me. That Winestone, wasn't he at the Jewish Island Hospital before?

"Yes, he was."

"Didn't he receive millions for leaving?"

"Yes, he did."

"Correct me if I am wrong, but according to what I hear from you, Winestone wants us to persecute Sorki but is friendly with Mantzur and more than that—he made him a vice chairman."

"It seems that there is a special bond between the two. We do not understand why."

"This doesn't sound kosher to me. Your distinguished chairman wants to destroy Sorki and spare Mantzur, eh?"

I nodded. I was really getting to like Carducci: He thought like I did.

"This is wrong." Carducci appeared disgusted. "Tell him that if he wants to restore quality of care, if he wants justice—he has to deal with both of them equally. He cannot have both worlds. He has to decide."

"I agree."

It was late afternoon when I merged with the home rushers on the street. I felt good. I had crossed the river. I had blown the whistle on the terminators. To celebrate the occasion I treated myself to a glass of drought beer at one of the Irish pubs on the way to the subway station.

▲▼▲▼▲

It was five p.m. when I emerged from the Fourth Avenue station in Brooklyn. At this time of the day Park Ridge, revived by the yuppies returning from across the East River, looked like Manhattan. I passed through the Emergency Room to assess a patient with an acute abdomen. I told Radezki to book her for the OR and went to my office. David Jacobs, one of our interns, came towards me. Dave—tall, fair, a square face with deep blue eyes, was very bright, but the chief residents often complained about his lack of consciousness—which they attributed to an excessive nightlife. I liked Dave nevertheless and kept an open door for him.

"Dr. Zohar, I was looking for you." He seemed a bit upset. "Could we talk in your room?"

I closed the door behind us. "What's the matter?" I moved towards the seat behind my desk as he answered.

"I just finished a case with Sorki. He performed a lumpectomy on a nine-year-old girl."

"What?" my head snapped around and I froze in stride halfway to my desk. "You must be kidding." I had had enough of Sorki and Mantzur today, but I couldn't ignore this. "You're not talking about a breast lumpectomy?"

"Dr. Zohar," Dave said. "Listen. There is this nine-year-old girl, apparently a daughter of Sorki's secretary, you know, the blonde woman from the Medical Board. Mike Silverstein told me to go assist Sorki. When I entered the room the girl was asleep. Even under the drapes I noticed that the chest wall and breasts belonged to a child. I asked Sorki: 'What are you doing?' and 'How old is this child?'"

"He said, 'She is nine and has a breast lump. We have to remove it in order to exclude cancer.'"

"I told him that the likelihood of cancer at that age is negligible. He said that the girl's mother—his secretary—drives him crazy. He then made an incision, grabbed the lump with a Kocher—I think it was the girl's breast bud, you know—the tissue from which the breast would grow. He took the knife and was ready to chop it off, but I stopped him. I said, 'Hey, Dr. Sorki why not take only a portion for biopsy?'"

"He said, 'OK' and removed half of the bud."

I was busy changing into my scrubs. I had a case in a few minutes. "Dave, the man is crazy. He cuts half of this poor girl's normal breast. He may have disfigured her forever. You saved her half a breast, maybe. Congratulations!" I slapped him on the shoulder. "The man is fucking mad, manic and almost unstoppable. There's only one way to end his stranglehold on this hospital."

"I trust you know the way?" he asked cautiously.

"Take good notes," I said as I turned and headed out of the office and down the hall towards the elevator. "Write down everything. Everything."

13

The Lists

We do not go to the operating table as we go to the theatre, to the picture gallery, to the concert room, to be entertained and delighted; we go to be tormented and maimed, lest a worse thing should befall us....The experts on whose assurance we face this horror and suffer this mutilation should have no interests but our own to think of; should judge our cases scientifically; and should feel about them kindly.
—George Bernard Shaw, 1856-1950

July 1999

Only surgeons understand how fast a disease spreads and how slowly it's contained, how easy it is to make a patient very sick and how difficult it is to make him better. On Monday morning the ICU resident called me. "Please come down. Your guy's awake."

Rushing down I found Mr. O'Neill in a bedside recliner, a long tube connecting his tracheostomy to the ventilator. As I approached him one of the nurses said: "Bob, look who's here. It's your doctor!"

I didn't think he would recognize me after so many weeks of powerful sedating and paralyzing drugs. But the patient lifted his head and smiled at me, motioning with his hands for me to come nearer. I did. He placed his hands on my neck and pulled me down into a tight embrace. The tracheostomy tube prevented him from talking, but I could clearly read his lips: "I love you." I swallowed hard a few times; I could see the nurses doing the same.

Up in the department I was told that Dr. Winestone's mother was dying in a Manhattan Hospital and that he was at her side. Dr. Mantzur came to my office. For almost four years the man had hardly looked at me. Now he was making regular visits. I motioned for him to sit down.

"No, thank you," he said. "I am on my way to the OR. Just wanted to check out how your visit to the OPMC went yesterday."

"It was exhausting, Dr. Mantzur. They kept me for three hours."

"What did they want to know? Was it that guy Carducci? How is he?"

"A nice guy," I said earnestly. "Seems decent. As for what they wanted to know? Everything. These guys have a lot of information already, Dr. Mantzur. They know all about your problem patients. They have piles of material." What pleasure I had digging at the old fox.

"Who could have done it?" Mantzur looked straight into my eyes. "Who could be such a traitor?"

I shrugged. If he was really uncertain, perhaps he'd made more enemies than even I knew of. I wish I could figure out who they were. His enemies would be my best friends. "Only God knows, Dr. Mantzur. You have a few enemies, no?" He was silent for a moment, pondering the question.

"What did you say?"

"I said you've made a few enem—"

"—No," he interrupted. "What did you tell them yesterday?"

"I didn't say much," I tried to look as honest as I could. I wasn't sure how well I was bearing the brunt of his suspicious looks. "Most cases are thoracic and vascular, and I understand almost nothing in these fields. How can I judge? I told Carducci so."

Suddenly Mantzur looked frail and old, like an aging, benign uncle. *Do I really want to harm him? How many years would he go on operating anyway? Perhaps Winestone is right.*

Mantzur knew he was in trouble. There was nothing left for him now but a long uncomfortable wait. "They were all so old, bad vascular cases, you know. One cannot save everybody." He looked at my shabby furniture. It gave him an avenue to change the subject. "Marc, we have to renovate your office. I have to talk with Winestone. This is unacceptable." We talked briefly about what I'd like to see in there, and after a few minutes his dreary old frame had shuffled out of my office and out of sight.

A pleasure to see the old monster disintegrate.
Or was it?

▲▼▲▼▲

It was six p.m. when I finished my last case, a tracheostomy requested by the medical team for an elderly emphysema patient who most probably has no chance to come off the ventilator. When I entered the corridor of our department Dr. Winestone was storming towards the elevator. I ran after him. "Hey Dr. Winestone!" I shouted. "Where are you off to in such a hurry?" No answer. "What's the matter? How is your Mom?"

Winestone looked flustered and breathless, his face was red and drops of sweat covered his forehead. Waving his hands he hopped into the elevator shouting: "I must go. I'll call you."

That night Winestone called me at home. He sounded calm and calculated, like a general. That was the Winestone I knew. "Marc, this is Larry Winestone speaking. How are you?" This was how he usually started.

"Fine, thanks. How is your mother?"

"She's comatose. We are at her bedside. It does not appear that she'll hold on until the morning. But, as a matter of fact, the reason I am calling—" his tone became more urgent "—is that they have your lists."

"What lists?"

"The lists, the lists, your lists of course. They have them." A scalpel ripped into my abdomen.

"Dr. Winestone, I have many lists. Would you please be a little more specific?" *Fuck it. How did they get hold of them?*

"Marc, listen," he said, talking faster. "Yesterday afternoon Farbstein paged me, said he needed to see me urgently. I left my mother and drove in. Howard was there as well as Farbstein waiting for me. They showed me the copy of your lists, one Sorki's the other Mantzur's. Farbstein asked me: 'Do you have any idea what these are? We know Zohar has produced it. Did you know about the existence of such lists? Does he have more of these?'"

"What did you tell them?"

Winestone sounded amused for some reason: "I gave them the list back without looking at it. I said, 'Look, my mother is dying, I cannot concentrate. I have to go back to her. I will talk to you when it is over.'"

"And—?"

"—And I left them. How many times did I tell you not to respond immediately to any challenge, but to go home and think—to sleep on it?" He spoke ponderously, as if quoting a dignitary.

"Dr. Winestone, I went to Carducci yesterday. Mantzur is in big trouble."

Silence. "Did you ask him about Sorki?"

"Yes, I did. We have to proceed with him. There is no other option. Now that they have the lists they will be after us. They have evidence of who did it. We cannot afford not to give a copy of Sorki's folder to Carducci—before it is too late. They may be digging in your room now, as we are talking. You know Susman and his local dark connections."

"What do you suggest we do?"

"Let me go to Carducci again tomorrow with a copy of Sorki's folder."

"How many copies do you have with you?"

"You have two, Rusk has one and I have two. I'll give one to Carducci."

"OK. Will you call me tomorrow?"

"Yes, of course."

"Good night."

Outside on the deck it was a pleasant July evening. Warm and dry, free from the suffocating New York mugginess that we experience each summer. Surrounded by flowery plants, and with the fresh foliage obscuring the neighbors, I could pretend it was the Adirondacks. Only the ongoing rumble of the nearby highway hinted that this was a huge metropolis.

"Who was it?" asked Heidi, leafing through a women's health magazine.

"It was Larry." I said, mocking his Romanian accent. "His mother is dying." I flipped over the hamburgers on the gas grill, enjoying the sight of the fresh parsley peeking between the chunks of the red meat and the smell of grilled cumin. "And they found my lists." The last comment deflected off Heidi. I don't think she even knew what I was talking about.

"Larry's mother was dying ever since we arrived in New York, but she always recovered. She must be a tough cookie."

"Well, she's dying now. He says she won't live until tomorrow. He is a remarkable son, very dedicated. Did you hear what I said? They found my lists!" *Missed again.*

"Just don't burn those hamburgers. Why do you always serve me charred shoe soles instead of hamburgers?"

I uncorked the red wine and poured myself a glass. "Do you want some?"

"Perhaps later. First a diet Coke. What lists?" *Finally!* "I thought that you gave them to the guy at the State?"

"They have a copy of my complete lists. The horrible cases of Sorki and Mantzur—the whole spiel, including patients' names, hospital numbers, diagnoses, operations, complications, outcome and, most significantly, my interpretation of the events—whether the operation was indicated

179

and whether the treatment was appropriate. Do you understand?"

"Yes. How did they get it?"

"Only one possibility. The lists exist only on my home desktop and on a few backup floppies that I carry with me. Before going to Carducci I printed a few hard copies. The printer is not in my room; it's in my secretary's."

"Anne did it? That tiny mouse?"

"No way. Beverly sits in the same room, near the printer. I was in a hurry and must have left one copy behind. She brought it to them. I am almost sure of it."

"At Winestone's party—just a month ago—Beverly was all over him. Isn't she sort of the perfect secretary who adores her boss?"

"I think she hates Winestone. She just manipulates him. I'm sure that she did it. We'll find out tomorrow." I hadn't been concentrating on what I was doing, and thick bluish smoke was belching from the barbecue.

"Marc, look at the smoke!" Heidi laughed as I tried in vain to save the newly created hockey pucks on the grill. "The hamburgers are burnt again." I took them off the grill and headed over to our outdoor table. Heidi followed behind me and continued talking. It wasn't the first time I'd overcooked a meal. "I told you that Beverly is a phony—much too friendly and overly polite," she said. "I have this sixth sense about people. I am always right. I have the same feeling about Winestone. I wouldn't trust him. He's spooky."

The burgers were a little black on the outside but delicious inside. I replenished my wine glass and filled my pipe with tobacco—Davidoff Scottish mixture. *Fresh air, red wine and a little smoke, This is life. I wish I could retire.*

"This wine is sour," complained Heidi.

"I have to return tomorrow to Manhattan. I'm going to deliver Sorki's folder to Carducci, the OPMC guy."

She sipped from the glass and grimaced again. "This is disgusting. Pass me the Coke please." I did so, trying to enjoy the meal despite her concerned questions. "Aren't you tired of this? Sorki, Mantzur, Winestone, Susman, Farbstein, Howard, wars, manipulations. How many years do you want to continue? So now you are the whistle blower. Why you? Why not the others? Why can't you go to work, do your job, write your papers, and leave the chaos to others?"

I stared at my wife in awe. It was yet another one of her rare speeches I was hearing with more and more frequency lately. I puffed on my pipe, relishing the aromatic Latakia blend. "As you know," I said, "my personality is problematic. People can't figure me out because I have a character flaw that makes me a non-conformist, a perpetual rebel, an ongoing troublemaker. I have a sharp intellect, a solid body of knowledge and clear medical judgment, but when it comes to what they call emotional intelligence I lack a lot. And so I'm a puzzle."

Heidi laughed. "You are so full of yourself. Tell me, how does it feel reporting these people? They may lose their income. They have families. Don't you have any doubts?"

I broke off a piece of feta cheese, poured some olive oil on it and brought a bite into my mouth. It went well with the red wine. "Do I feel anything for Mantzur and Sorki?" I asked with my mouth full, then swallowed. "Do I have any empathy left for them? Absolutely not. I believe that the two are severely flawed psychopaths. You know that I have been observing them for almost four years now. I hardly ever spoke to Mantzur. The man will talk to you only if you are of some use to him, and I was not. Sorki—on the surface appears human. You saw him at the parties, how jovial he is when drunk. We even exchanged small talk, the usual stuff about women, booze and opium. But you could see the cold arrogance in his eyes. The personality disorder. Families? Don't cry for them, both are millionaires, gold made off their victims—like the Swiss Nazi gold. They could lose their licenses now and live well for the next hundred years. They are loaded!"

"Suppose you stop them, which I do not believe will be the case. What's next? What's your next crusade going to be?"

I emptied my third glass of wine. "Who knows?" I started pouring another. "For now, I'll use my etho-stat and my bullshit meter on these two." I stopped to enjoy my own neologism.

"What's an etho-stat?"

"An ethical thermostat. I am obsessed with the need of stopping their killings. I am proud to be the whistle blower. I know the dangers of whistle blowing—it has been well described in the literature—but I have to go on. Some places have an effective 'three wise men' system to control such criminals, but at our hospital all the 'wise men" are part of the system. I have nowhere to go."

"Do what you want. But understand that we can't move again. We cannot change cities every few years."

I emptied the remaining drops of wine into the glass and carried it with me into the study. "I know," I said to her over my shoulder. "I know."

Do I really?

▲▼◢▲▼▲

The following day I was told that Beverly had left her position to become the Administrator of Cardiology, with a significant hike in rank and salary. Anne had ceremoniously unlocked the chairman's office to show me Beverly's exotic farewell note written with red lipstick on Winestone's fancy desk: "Larry, you are a jerk!!!" No signature.

"I told you she is a spy," Anne gloated, celebrating the disappearance of her arch enemy.

"Leave it as it is. He has to see it for himself." I wondered whether Larry had to wash off her lipstick from other sites as well. Beverly had been working for them for some time now. When she exposed herself by providing them with my lists, she had to go. The kick upward into Cardiology was easily arranged since the Chief of Cardiology, Geddy, was an established ally. *Why did she do it?* I asked myself during the ride on the F Train on my way to the OPMC. Winestone was so nice to her—treating her as his own daughter. I saw the Christmas card she sent to him: "To the best Boss I ever had. Many thanks for the charming gift. xxx, yours, Bev."

But he was also such a pedantic and demanding old man. We will never know what passed between them behind those closed doors. *And why am I going to the OPMC with this heavy black folder in my briefcase?*

▲▼▲▶▼▲

"Marc, what do you have for me?" asked Carducci. This time we were sitting alone. I'd sent him an urgent message the day earlier and stated that I needed to see him ASAP. He motioned at the folder I had in my hand. "Let's see."

I opened it and laid it on his desk. Then I moved into a position beside him. "This contains a complete documentation and critique of Sorki's sixty-seven M&M cases from January 1994 to date."

Carducci browsed through the pages, asking now and then for clarification. He exhaled air noisily from his lungs and exclaimed: "Remarkable, quite remarkable. A solid piece of research. You did it alone?"

"No. In fact, the cases were reviewed by Drs. Rusk, Bachus, Chaudri, a few private attendings and myself. Rusk organized the folder and wrote the introduction—all being approved by Winestone."

"Remember what I told you about Mantzur? I need only ten or twelve bad cases. Sit down and make a list. Take your time. I have a few calls to make."

I stared at the folder. The evidence was horrendous for what can only be called serial killing. *How do I decide which murder is the worst and deserves the harshest punishment?* Is killing by a stab wound to the heart a bigger crime than asphyxiation? Carducci needed me to help find him cases that could be proved as outright killings rather than the result of "unfortunate complications" or a "slight deviation from the standard of care."

I grabbed the red marker. In 1994 a laparotomy and common bile duct exploration for jaundice caused by multiple liver metastases. Death. Restoration of bowel continuity after colostomy in a septic patient with multiple organ failure—which is crazy: Death. Common bile duct exploration for jaundice caused by cirrhosis in an eighty seven year old man, bled to death. A ninety-five-year-old bleeding from a small anastomotic ulcer, unnecessary re-gastrectomy: Death.

I became angry as I skipped through the cases. The pattern was as revolting as it was obvious: Eighty-five-years old, ninety-seven-years old, metastases everywhere, non-resectable tumors being resected, big operations performed on patients who cannot tolerate it and when non-operative treatment may have been appropriate, complications developing after the operations and are not solved. Carducci reappeared: "Marc, are you done?"

"Dr. Carducci, I can't select a few patients. You have to look at all of them and see the overall picture by yourself."

"We've talked about this, Marc. We have to focus on cases he won't be able to defend. He'll buy the best lawyers in town and bring expert witnesses to claim that the management of the case was OK. Descend from the Olympus, will you? Don't you know how easy it is to find a whore expert?

"What?"

"Exactly what I said—a whore expert. His lawyers will go to California or Texas and fish out a semi-retired professor of surgery who, for a few bucks or more than a few bucks, will travel to New York and say, 'Yes, this was an unfortunate complication, but the patient was high risk and it was a lifesaving operation and there were a few therapeutic options in such a scenario but what Dr. Sorki did was acceptable.' Do you understand? You have to pick up cases that are non defendable, those that represent an absolute crime!"

"I understand. Listen to just this one. I want to explain to you this one case to demonstrate how Sorki's monstrous mind functions—or dysfunctions."

"Go ahead." Carducci sighed, bracing himself with a deep breath.

"Look at this saga," I began. "This case was presented at one of the first M&Ms after I joined the Park. This was when I understood the insane phenomenon called Dr. Sorki. An eighty-one-year-old woman is admitted with a breast cancer. She was also cirrhotic with evidence of hepatic dysfunction. He, of course, does a mastectomy. Lumpectomies or partial mastectomies are not on his lexicon. Anyway, up to now it is acceptable. But then it starts. Her mastectomy wound becomes infected; she is cirrhotic and so does not heal well. He goes on and performs an open cholecystectomy and cholangiogram because she becomes jaundiced—not due to gallstones but because of the cirrhosis, which deteriorates due to the stress of infection. Then he notices she has an umbilical hernia, which bulges because of the ascites, which complicates the cholecystectomy. By the way, he could have fixed the hernia during the cholecystectomy. Anyway, he fixes it now—another operation under general anesthesia in a patient who slides down. At the same time he inserts a permanent venous line for chemotherapy. Why not? He can bill for it separately. A few days later—surprise, surprise—her abdominal wound opens up, and the gut falls out. Another operation. Later, the abdominal closure opens up again—this time only partially, and the intestine is well contained, yet he operates again. At this stage she is in a deep liver failure with pus pouring from everywhere—the breast, the axilla, and the abdomen. By now Sorki has done what Sorki had to do—five unnecessary operations. He finishes his job, although his oncologists are still busy administering chemotherapy to this dying and infected woman." I couldn't hide my disgust and hatred, and they fed my eloquence.

"Remarkable, quite remarkable. That case should be on your twelve list. Carry on. Give me the list." Before I left, he asked, "What did Winestone say about Mantzur?"

"I didn't get a chance to talk to him. His mother passed away this morning. I believe that he'll insist on sparing Mantzur. Not only won't he cooperate with you, but he'll try to assist Mantzur."

"Your friend Winestone is making a hell of a mistake! One can't strive for partial justice. Marc, you are going to send me the documentation concerning Mantzur, eh?"

"Sure. But Winestone shouldn't know that I am involved. He may suspect it, of course, but he mustn't know. How long will it take—the whole process?"

"It takes time. First comes the struggle to collect the data, but you are helping us with this. I've explained the process to you. If they come to a hearing—which I hope they will—it won't start for at least six months."

One and a half years later, as I write this chapter, Sorki's hearing is still underway; Mantzur's never started.

14

The Virus

I think all of us who have worked years in the
profession understand that many very skillful
operators are not good surgeons.
—*William J. Mayo, 1861-1939*

July 1999
Winestone entered my room and closed the door.
I shook his hand. "Dr. Winestone, you shaved."
He touched his cheek, a question mark in his eyes.
"Nothing, only that—you know, Jews do not shave during mourning. They grow a beard—at least during 'shiva.'"
"What's that?"
"Shiva means seven, the seven official days of mourning."
"Listen, Marc," he said, brushing off my emotional small talk. "Farbstein and Howard are breathing down my neck. So is Mantzur. Your lists—how should we explain them?"
"I've been thinking about that. Let's just say these lists were only a small portion of our QA database, gathered by me as directed by you. You, as chairman, have the authority to investigate the quality of care of any surgeon in your department. Tell them that we have a similar list for each of the surgeons."
"Do we?"
"Of course not, but it wouldn't be hard to come up with samples. We have all the M&M records."
"Go on."
"The lists were stored on my PC, and Beverly stole one of them."
"How could she do that?"

"By telling them that they were stored on the G Drive, which is accessible to everybody." Winestone knew nothing about computers. I tried to explain things another way: "She knows all the guys from the computer support team. She has all the men in the hospital around her little finger." His face remained emotionless. "They could have helped her to break my password."

"I will try to sell them this version. Sorki is working hard on Mantzur, organizing an onslaught. We'll see what happens when he realizes that he is under investigation by the OPMC. By the way, I was invited as well, coming Thursday." He showed me the invitation signed by Carducci.

"Dr. Winestone, this is about Mantzur. Carducci will ask you about Mantzur. Mantzur, not Sorki. What's your plan?"

"Let me tell you what I told Howard and Farbstein. At this stage of my life I will do what is right."

Right for whom? I wondered.

"Did you see what Beverly wrote on your desk?" I asked.

He was not amused by that comment. "Remember, you do not fight two fronts," he said. "During the Yom Kippur War, didn't the Israelis first contain the Egyptians before moving their forces up north to the Golan Heights to finish the Syrians off? Her turn will come." In his eyes I could see he had expelled Beverly from his heart and his life.

▲▼◢▲▼▲

Dr. Sorki gazed at the clock. *Fifty-five minutes skin to skin. Great.* It was his second gastroplasty that morning. The first one was even faster. No doubt he was the fastest knife around. He looked at Barbara, the fourth year resident: "Dr. Bernard, two gastroplasties before lunch. Let's close up. Hurry. I have a meeting to attend. Politics, you know." A burst of staccato laughter. To the nurse he said: "Lisa, get us some number one Vicryl. We are closing."

"Dr. Sorki, shouldn't we use a longer lasting suture material. Perhaps PDS or Prolene?" Barbara dared to ask, though hesitantly.

It was Barbara's tenth gastroplasty with Sorki, who accepted only fourth and fifth year residents for assistants. Barbara entered into her fourth year of residency on the first of July. Residents scrubbed with him reluctantly because he didn't let them do too much.

"Barb, I've used Vicryl as long as I've been a surgeon. PDS, Prolene, forget that junk. Do Winestone and Zohar also poison your mind?" Sorki liked Barb, appreciated her rich, dark blonde hair tucked under her cap, her handsome square face, her tall stature. Her ankles were rather thick but he wouldn't mind having her. This thought prompted another burst of laughter.

"What's so funny, Dr. Sorki?" Barbara started closing the abdomen, taking big bites at the edges of the fascia.

"Not so big, not so big," he shouted and grabbed the needle holder from her. "When you operate with me you do what I do, understand?"

"Yes, Dr. Sorki."

Sorki didn't mind getting a high rate of post-operative abdominal hernias in his fat patients. Why should he? He could bring the patient back a few months later for a repair of the ensuing hernia—another thousand bucks.

"Continue." He returned the needle holder to her. *You have to be tough with these young buggers.* "The State is investigating Mantzur, did you know?"

"I heard about it," was the short reply. Residents prefer to stay away from politics.

"Must've been Zohar. We found his lists. We'll fry his little ass until it's a nice pink and red. Did you hear about the lists?" Sorki liked to chat with the residents during the relaxing phase of abdominal closure. He flattered them by divulging a little hot gossip, hoping to be paid back.

"No, Dr. Sorki. Please maintain tension on the suture."

This WASPY bitch is not interested. "You know, your mentor Zohar could report me as well." He laughed and removed his gloves. "Use staples for the skin, three days of antibiotics. I want her out of bed tomorrow." He bowed theatrically to the admiring OR team. "Thank you, ladies, for yet another most pleasurable day."

Sorki strolled towards the Medical Board's suite. It was one of his axioms that surgical leaders rushed only in one place—the OR. In his right hand he swirled his car keys, an old habit from the old country where dignitaries use to swirl "worry beads" or rosaries. As he walked he rhythmically tapped on the corridor's wall. At the Medical Board meeting room all were seated along the long, heavy table. Sorki sank into his mammoth chair at the head of the table and nodded to everybody. "Cappuccino? Espresso anyone?"

He gestured to Kate, his secretary. Her false teeth were a little too large for her cigarette smoke-wasted face. Kate had been working on the Medical Board with Sorki and Mantzur since graduating from high school in Park Ridge. "Kate, I need a triple espresso." To his colleagues he said: "While you were talking and masturbating I did two gastroplasties." There were a few polite chuckles, but most of the laughter came from Sorki himself. He shouted after Kate: "How's Erika? How's her wound?" He pursed his lips. "It's Kate's little daughter, just a tiny biopsy." He looked at his watch: "OK, let us start. We can't drink coffee all day, I've got to go to the gym."

Sorki emptied the espresso with a rapid gulp, looked around, sucked in his cheeks and started pompously: "Friends, you all know why I called you to attend this emergency meeting. I see here only my oldest and most loyal friends. We have been together for many years, always working for each other, always united. But now we have a virus in the hospital, perhaps even a few viruses, which infect the atmosphere and sooner or later may infect us. In fact, our dear mentor and friend—" Sorki looked affectionately at Mantzur. "—Joseph, you are like a father to me. As you know," he said to the others, "Joseph is already infected. I'm proud to announce that we know the identity of the virus. His name is Zohar, Marc Zohar. On this occasion I promise you that the virus will be autoclaved. I'll protect you. This is my responsibility. I don't know how well you remember the virology lectures from the medical school, but I still recall that there are two kinds of viruses: RNA and DNA. Let me suggest to you that Zohar is a minor type RNA virus. You know—the RNA messenger. The key virus, the DNA one—the father of viruses—is Winestone." Sorki was impressed by the sudden gleam in his mind. "Hey Herb," he said to Susman, "Did you know there is a messenger RNA?"

"Fuck you, Mo," murmured Susman. After Susman suffered a minor myocardial event a few months previously, his cardiologist Geddy implemented harsh dietary restrictions. He had lost weight, and with it his sense of humor.

"Take it easy, Herbie. Let's discuss it. Albert, you are the second to the king on the eighth floor. What do you have to say?"

Farbstein rubbed his short beard. "Gentlemen, this is serious matter. Don't forget for a moment that we live in modern USA. This is Brooklyn, but Brooklyn at the end of twentieth century. Dr. Sorki makes promises to annihilate the viruses. I agree with this goal. I agree in general, yet I must warn you that modern viruses are deadly drug-resistant mutants. Winestone is extremely well connected at all levels. Can we afford to lose him together with the residency program? No way! First we have to prepare a suitable replacement for him. This takes time. You do not find chairman material in the street. Zohar, on the other hand, is a relatively minor virus, which is nurtured by Winestone, but there are symbiotic relationships between the two. First, we have to neutralize Zohar before we come to Winestone. And, let me tell you something. Winestone is a reasonable man, despite what you—Sorki—think. I believe that Zohar started the spiel and dragged Winestone into it. By the way, Mo, while we sit and talk, it may well be that Zohar has already complained about you to the OPMC. Do you think he created his lists to be used as toilet paper?"

"Let him complain. I have nothing to fear. Are you done? You sound like a...what are they called? A cantor. You sound like a cantor in the synagogue." He looked at his comrades and laughed. They smiled politely. *You must be brave to use ethnic remarks in Brooklyn—unless you make fun of your own ethnic group.*

"Mo, you know when I last attended a synagogue? Better not ask!" Farbstein waved with his hand. "Dr. Sorki, let me tell you only this. If Zohar brings you and Dr. Mantzur to the OPMC, you two will be in a prolonged and painful legal battle. As to Zohar and Winestone, whatever we plan to do about them it has to be legal. Do you understand? It has to be legal! Otherwise, in the long run, we're going to lose and pay a lot of money."

"Now you sound like a lawyer. Herb, tell him to shut up and sit down. We heard you." Sorki's voice was sharp, though he spoke with a smile.

"Dr. Farbstein, please tell us what Mr. Howard's position is on all this," requested Dr. Ajay Gavikumar, a prosperous private surgeon and Sorki's neighbor.

"Ajay, Howard is pragmatic. We are all familiar with his usage of the hotel metaphor. He has succeeded—with your help of course—to transform this pile of garbage to a five star hotel."

"What are you talking about? Are you out of your fucking mind?" shouted Susman. "This hospital stood firmly when we accepted you as a refugee from your previous shithole—"

"—Calm down. You don't want another MI." Sorki was laughing. Rapid shifts of mood—from outraged to benign—were trademarks of his.

"Herb, say what you want, but Howard and I transformed this hospital." Susman refused to calm down.

"Yes, and you brought in Winestone and Zohar."

"Gentlemen," said Farbstein. "As things stand today, I would not compare this place to a hotel but to a Las Vegas casino." He had apparently inherited from his father a dry, cynical, Old World sense of stetl humor, which he used to his advantage when dealing with this bunch of immigrants he considered inferior. "Zohar was recruited by Winestone," he continued. "The chairman is permitted to choose his own staff. I admit that hiring Winestone was a mistake. We didn't know he'd be so independent. But what's done is done. Please let me finish. You asked what Howard wants. He wants to maintain a flourishing hotel loaded with patients. You are responsible to bring the patients in and provide the services, so you have Howard in your pockets. A hotel business needs peace. Tourists avoid war zones. Howard needs industrial peace to increase revenues and satisfy the Board of Trustees. In order to achieve a reasonable state of productive calm, Zohar has to go. Let me work on it using legal pathways. I'm sure that Howard will be supportive. Later we'll deal with Winestone using your domination as key admitting physicians to tilt the balance in our favor. Meanwhile, confidentially of course, I'll be searching for a replacement chairman."

"Excellent, Albert! Excellent," said Sorki. "Get rid off the small virus. Use your lawyers. At the same time we'll let Winestone sweat for his salary. Joseph, you are quiet today. Don't let us think that the OPMC thing depresses you. You are Winestone's Vice Chairman. Tell us what we should do with him."

Mantzur tapped on the table with his diamond rings and cleared his throat. "Dr. Farbstein talks sense. I agree with him. First, we have to get rid of the small fish—Zohar. He is like a cancer in our flesh. Then there is Rusk—polite, correct, but I do not trust him at all. I do not think that Farbstein and Howard will have any trouble laying them off. The big fish—Winestone—will sink to the bottom of the pond if left alone. Chaudri and Bachus are our boys; we trained them." Mantzur smiled. "Don't forget that Winestone and myself are

193

good friends—very, very close. As close as is needed to support our interest. Whatever a few of you may think, I am one of you."

Sorki yawned, banged both fists on his chest and then stood up. "Enough. Anybody want to say something? Dr. Gotahedi? Dr. Ilkadi? Dr. Rasmussen? Ajay? No?" He named everybody around the table. "Herb, are ya coming to the club with me? You could sit at the bar."

"Just a sec," Susman growled. "Guys, I'm not buying your pacifistic shit. While these shitheads are screwing us we need to hold them down. We've got to start a war of attrition. For Christ's sake, guys, we have the full weight of the Medical Board and the gospel of the bylaws at our disposal, and you're talking all this metaphorical shit about viruses. Remember Senator McCarthy, the one who was active when I was a kid? How did he manage his enemies? Committees, committees and subcommittees. Mo, appoint me to chair a subcommittee to investigate who disclosed Joseph to the OPMC, and I will serve up Zohar on a frying pan."

"Special subcommittee of the Medical Board? Why not? All agreed about a subcommittee chaired by Herb?"

There was a collective murmur: "Aye."

▲▼◢▲▼▲

During morning rounds I saw Mr. O'Neill, who had been discharged from the ICU after his tracheostomy tube was removed. Now that his duodenal fistula had sealed, we could start feeding him by mouth. He clearly bore the look of a man who had returned from hell.

"What would you like to eat?" I asked.

He sighed. "A whiskey and cold water. I dream about a good diluted cold Scotch."

"Which is your favorite? Blended or single malt?"

"Doc, I stopped drinking eighteen years ago. I was a heavy drinker. Not a drop since, but I can still remember the taste. A cup of Irish black tea with a lot of sugar would be just fine." Sitting on the edge of his bed watching him gulping the hot tea, each gulp followed by a deep sigh, made my day.

"Doc, do you have children?" he asked me.

"I have three sons, same as you. Same ages more or less."

"How do you know that?"

"I saw them around the ICU when you were out. Nice kids."

"Doc, is that why you worked so hard on me to save my life?" He paused. "I mean...having three sons as I do, you felt what it would mean for them to lose their father?"

"I don't know."

"Doc, I will pray for you."

"Thanks, Mr. O'Neill. I appreciate it."

"I am serious, Doc. I am going to pray for you every day."

"I believe you. I will be grateful—I certainly need somebody to pray for me. It may help."

▲▼▲▼▲

Farbstein's gray beard appeared at my door just as I started to re-write another manuscript. I turned around on the swivel chair to address him: "Dr. Farbstein, how can I help you?" I surely was popular all of a sudden. First with Mantzur, and now Farbstein.

Farbstein was wearing his lab coat, a paper cup in his hand. Farbstein always carried a cup of coffee, ever ready to lecture you about which brand his secretary brewed for him that day. He was also a connoisseur of malt whiskey and literature, not to mention sailboats and pulmonology, his medical specialty. "Marc, could I have a word with you? Actually, I came down to see Winestone, but they tell me he went to town."

"Yes. He was invited to the OPMC."

Farbstein shrugged. He closed the door and sat down. "Marc, I've been in this hospital for thirteen years now." He sighed. "I came from Brooklyn's Jewish. This was another type of hospital with the chairmen of the departments running the place and the private attendings keeping their heads down. There was no abuse of power, and I think that the standard of medicine was fair. Now, this place is different. The private guys rule it; we had to adapt and we did. We are worried about this entire affair. We have to stop it before things are going out of control. Those lists of yours—why do you keep them and where are they? Could I see them?"

The jerk. The minute Winestone is away, he comes down to threaten me. "As Dr. Winestone probably told you," I explained, "we have a list of cases for each surgeon. This is part of our QA system. The lists belong to the chairman and are classified so no, you can't see them! And by the way— please do tell me how do you know about the lists and tell me also who broke into my PC? It's outrageous that the privacy of a surgeon in this hospital has been violated."

"Marc, you must stop this whole thing before it is too late. Let me have the lists."

"Forget it! Now let me put things into perspective for you, Dr. Farbstein. Dr. Mantzur is under investigation. It is very serious. A few of the patients whose cases are under review are out-and-out homicide. Those cases are indefensible. Do you understand? And the other guy—Sorki—he is in big trouble as well. Dr. Winestone is still investigating him, but I suspect that sooner or later we will have to report him to the State. Do you understand that we are dealing with two surgeons who have a good chance of losing their licenses? You ask who reported Mantzur? I don't know, but he and Sorki have many enemies. When you are arrogant for years, repressing people and ruling as ayatollahs do, sooner or later someone will seek revenge."

Farbstein listened, speechless. The paper cup was frozen in his hand. I had his attention, so I continued. "I know that you told Winestone yesterday, that you'll have to fire Zohar in order to calm down the situation. Go ahead—fire me. Please. Help yourself. But do understand. You cannot stop anything now. It is too late. Fire me, but at the end we will win!"

"Whatever." Farbstein had had enough. "We have to stop it. Winestone can investigate whomever he wishes. That is his prerogative as a chairperson but he cannot report Sorki to the OPMC. There are well-defined layers of QA mechanisms in this hospital."

"Frankly, I don't see how he can stop now. This is either Sorki or Winestone. We simply cannot co-exist with Sorki. Before it is too late, why don't you join with the forces of light and distance yourself from the forces of darkness?"

Farbstein yielded a tiny smile. *Light versus darkness. Only fanatics think and talk in such terms.* "I prefer the forces of gray," he said. "I appreciate shades."

"The gray of Russia under Stalin?"

Farbstein shrugged his shoulders and his face remained expressionless. He rose from the chair and walked out carrying his now cold cup of coffee.

▲▼▲▼▲

"Dr. Zohar?" The OR night supervisor was whispering into my ears through the telephone. "Sorry to call you at this hour, but Dr. Gavikumar needs you at the OR ASAP."

It was twelve o'clock. I'd slept ten minutes. If I left now I wouldn't be back in bed before four or five am. I also had a few cases booked for tomorrow morning. "What's the problem?" I suppressed a yawn. *Why does Gavikumar call on me? He has his own bunch of compatriots. Why doesn't he summon them at such an hour?*

"Dr. Gavikumar is performing a colectomy and encountered severe bleeding that is difficult to control. He wants you to come."

Funny. Uncontrolled hemorrhage during a colonic resection? Unusual. I moved myself to an upright position. "How long has he been operating?"

"Since three p.m. The case was booked as an elective left hemicolectomy. Can I tell him that you're on your way?"

"Yes, I'll be there." I hung up. In the bathroom I splashed my face with cold water. I rinsed my mouth — checking for any residual smell of the small cognac I had in bed before falling asleep. None—only the garlic from dinner. I looked at myself in the mirror and said loudly: "Fuck, fuck, fuck! They are a bunch of fuckers."

When I returned to the bedroom Heidi was awake. "For a doctor, you've got a pretty broad vocabulary," she said with a smirk.

"I know. I was saying that they are stupid fucking fuckers." I'd seen a T-shirt at a street vendor that said words to that effect. I'd almost bought one. *It could have been my new work uniform. "Can't I talk to myself?"*

It took me twenty-five minutes to cover the twenty miles to the hospital. My car was in the shop because some computer chip had started acting up, so I had to take my wife's Jeep. Luckily all the lanes were open. That was a bit unusual. The nights are used to mend our chronically tortured roads and bridges. At the hospital, I changed my clothes upstairs in my office and rushed down to the OR. I found Gavikumar pale and drenched in sweat in the OR lounge with the night supervisor hovering over him.

"Dr. Gavi," (She dropped the "Kumar," as many Americans did). "Please drink this tea. I put lots of sugar in it. Look, your hands are shaking. You must be hypoglycemic."

Gavikumar seemed over agitated and tremulous. "Marc, what are you doing here?" he said.

Is he out of his mind? He brings me across the Verrazano in middle of the night and asks what I'm doing here? "Dr. Gavikumar," I said. "I see that you're in trouble, and I came to help as you requested." The night supervisor standing behind him rolled her eyes. I looked at Gavikumar: The last time I'd seen a look like that was many years ago on the face of a friend of mine during a fire fight on the Suez Canal. *Should we call this "OR shock?"*

"It started well," Dr. Gavikumar explained slowly. "It was just a routine left hemicolectomy. Then we had an ooze from the left upper quadrant." He gestured towards his rib cage with the teacup and spilled tea on his scrubs. He jumped, "Bloody hot!" he yelled as pain and frustration collided. He then placed the cup on the table. "We tried to stop it but somehow I could not get an adequate exposure. I left a few packs. Moshesh is with the patient."

Moshesh! The blind leading the cripple across the freeway! "Just sit down here and drink your tea," I told him. "Let me go inside and fix the problem."

"No, no. Wait. I'll come with you."

"You just rest here. You deserve it after battling six hours with horrendous bleeding. You did well. The patient is alive!" I was treating him like a psychiatric case, giving him plenty of warm and authoritative reassurance. The last thing he needed was to be told how badly he'd fucked up.

Through the glass above the sink I saw Moshesh's head pumping up and down and to the sides while I was scrubbing. *What's he doing? Dancing?* The sound of loud techno-music welcomed me when I opened the door. Moshesh continued dancing, clapping with his gloved hands. The two nurses were laughing. The anesthetist, a resident, appeared to be dozing behind at the head of the sleeping patient.

"Hello, Dr. Zohar! Welcome to the disco. Join the club!" shouted Moshesh above the deafening booming of the music.

"Hi everybody!" I performed a few dancing steps myself to satisfy Moshesh and the nurses and then said: "Could we turn it down just a little bit and finish this case? Moshesh, please move to the left side. Let us be done with this so we can go to sleep."

"Sleep, sleep, sleep, hallelujah!" shouted Moshesh.

I removed the blood-soaked packs from the abdominal cavity. The anesthetist was suddenly awake. I asked him: "Doc, how is he?"

The anesthesia resident reported the following: "He is stable, BP OK, urine output so-so, 30ml last hour, last hemoglobin four. He is cold, very cold. The faster we go from here to the ICU, the better."

Are they crazy? Why don't they give him blood? With a hemoglobin of four he could hardly carry any oxygen to his tissues, "You mean four or fourteen?"

"Four, crit is twelve."

"Why don't you give him blood?" I shouted. My eyes passed along the violent message because my hands were too busy.

Moshesh looked at me, his mocking eyes staring at me above his mask. "Didn't they tell you? He is a Jehovah Witness. No blood for him, man."

Gee. Why did he fuck around for six hours losing blood in a Jehovah Witness before calling for help? Blood was oozing from left and above. The guy was obese. The blood must have been coming from the spleen—injured during the mobilization of the left colon. We had to move fast. With each drop of blood the hemoglobin would fall to levels incompatible with life.

I extended the incision. "Pull hard on the retractor," I told the medical student. I placed my right hand deep under the costal margin, felt the spleen and blindly mobilized it with my fingers. It came up. I placed a few clamps on the vascular attachments and let Moshesh tie it with ligatures. I put a few packs into the empty space that recently held the removed spleen. It was white and dry, not a trace of blood. Done. "Would you close?" I asked Moshesh, "I'll be outside. Please do not dance while closing, and take deep bites."

From her elevated nursing station the night supervisor said: "Already done? That was quick. What was the problem?"

"Just the spleen. It's out now and Moshesh's closing. Where is Gavikumar?"

"In the lounge. He's sleeping, I think." She lowered her voice as if someone could hear. "What was he doing there for six hours? Couldn't he deal with an injured spleen?"

I shrugged. "The patient was very deep, and the spleen was so far away. Not to mention that the resident is not at the top of our list. Poor Gavikumar suffered from what I call a 'surgeon's block,'" I explained. "Just like 'writer's block.' I know how it feels. You want to do something, but the operation simply does not go forward. You want to dissect out this vessel, but it becomes non-dissectible, and then everything bleeds. You know what has to be done, but you are frozen. You cannot proceed. All eyes are on you, everyone waiting for you to solve the problem, but you can't, and you don't know why. You start to sweat under your scrubs. Under your cap drops of sweat emerge and drop onto the patient. It is even worse if you wear eyeglasses, because you do not see a thing. All becomes foggy." *I do know how it feels. I dream about it even today.*

It was too early in the morning for this. She wasn't even listening to me. "Good night," I said.

I found Gavikumar in the lounge watching late night TV. I told him what we did and tried to make him feel better: "Your patient is huge. I wonder how you succeeded in removing his colon. You must have struggled with Moshesh, but you know, you should have arranged for another assistant. I am going home to get some sleep. I have a case at eight a.m."

Gavikumar sat up. His face went from emotional exhaustion to dead seriousness when he stood to his feet and said, "Listen, Zohar. I have to tell you something. I was at the Medical Board today. Sorki called a special meeting to discuss you guys. My advice to you is, be careful and watch your backside. Those guys are not playing cards. They are dead serious."

"What do you mean?"

"Well, as an example, if I were you I would watch my back at night in the parking lot. Understand what I mean?" Gavikumar placed his soft hand on my arm.

"Thanks for the advice. I'm off." I didn't trust him. *Why did he bring me here tonight? Is there someone waiting for me?*

It had been raining most of the previous night. I hadn't had the presence of mind to grab an umbrella, yet the rain felt refreshing that early in the morning. As I moved through the parking lot towards my wife's Jeep, water began crawling down my collar. *Why don't they just provide everyone with covered parking?* A solid breeze blew through the lot, knocking the hanging lights back and forth. One second they blinded me, and the next second I was in the dark. It was a spooky backdrop to an awkward night.

I was confused. There were just too many things about my having been called out that didn't make sense. *Had Gavikumar actually called for me? Had I been brought here for another reason?* Not even the cold rain tiptoeing down the nape of my neck could distract my train of thought.

Ridiculous. This is just as silly as when I blew that tire. I took a deep breath and tried to exhale the tension in my chest as I took the last few steps to my black Caddie. Suddenly it occurred to me that this black Cadillac Deville was not mine. I stood there for a second looking at it, half grinned at myself for my mistake and turned to walk back to Heidi's Jeep just across the lane and down a few stalls.

"I've done the same thing," someone said from behind me. I turned to see Dr. Wilkinson, our new urologist. Unlike me, he had an umbrella to shield himself. "Seems we share a taste in old Caddies."

"And what a good taste it is!" I grinned at him. "What are you doing here so early?"

"Ah, had to come in for a bleeding patient. After a prostatectomy, you know."

We sort of half waved at one another as he unlocked his driver's side door and climbed in. A few steps later and I was doing the same thing. I had been outside maybe a minute, but I was drenched. I took a minute to wipe off my face and squeeze a little water out of my hair. I noticed a set of brake lights in the rearview mirror as Wilkinson eased his vehicle out of the parking spot and shifted into drive to proceed out of the lot. I turned my head slightly to get a better look at his car as it approached the automatic gate and signaled right to turn onto Fourth Ave. The only difference I could see in our cars was the—

—It happened so fast it took me a couple of seconds to realize what I had just seen. I was watching Wilkinson ease his vehicle onto Fourth Ave followed by a quick burst of brake lights, and the next thing I knew the vehicle was shaking violently from a massive impact on the passenger side. A large five-ton truck had reversed from the right straight into the Cadillac like a sledgehammer and wrapped the driver's side around the brick pillar at the gate. I hadn't even gotten out of my Jeep before the truck had geared up and sped off. It was long gone by the time I got there.

A few other people had seen the accident and hurried over to help. Wilkinson was trapped behind the steering wheel and bleeding badly from a deep cut above his temple. Ambulance personnel from the hospital rushed out to help, and together we wrestled him out of the vehicle and into the ER.

Everything happened so fast I have almost no recollection of exactly what happened as we were fighting to extract Wilkinson. I remember standing at the swinging doors into the ER, my clothing dripping wet from blood and knowing that it could have been me. Should have been me.

As the doors swung shut on Wilkinson, I knew he would live. He'd lost some blood, but I of all people understood how resistant the human body was to damage. What I also realized was that the stakes in my pursuits were climbing higher than even I might have been prepared to pay. It had finally come down to the bottom line: My morals or my life.

15

Witch Hunt

*Surgery, like aviation, is in itself not inherently
dangerous. But to an even greater degree than the sea,
it is terribly unforgiving of any carelessness,
incapacity, or neglect.*
—*Francis D. Moore, 1913-2001*

August-December 1999.
Unlike the Battle of Stalingrad when subhuman cold
weather did not halt the onslaught and killing on both sides,
hospital wars in New York come to a standstill during
August. All major players in the saga escape to their respec-
tive mansions at the Hamptons, Island Sound, or Jersey's
shore. Each to his pool, tennis court or boat. Those like Dr.
Carducci, the state investigator, who are not blessed with
waterfront property, spend the high summer in France. Even I
escape with my family from the filthy beaches of Staten
Island to the immaculate beach dunes of Cape Cod.

Burdened with the uncertainties and anxieties as to the
final outcome, the key figures in the story did not entirely
enjoy their vacation. According to Chaudri—who knew
everything—Winestone and Mantzur visited each other's
estate on the Island. What the two of them discussed we have
to leave to our imagination. Did they discuss Wilkinson's
parking lot accident which was brushed off by the police and
hospital authorities as an incidental hit-and-run mishap?
Maybe. After the accident Winestone reassured me: "No way
Marc, they would never try to do such things to you. As a
matter of fact Mantzur promised me, confidentially, of
course, that this could not be connected to Sorki or Susman,"
but long ago I had stopped believing him.

As September neared the combatants re-emerged into
the final and conclusive phase of the struggle. Winestone was

204

planning for the "world after Hitler." That is, when Sorki had lost his license and was out on the street. He toyed with the idea of promoting a "weakened" Godfather as President of the Medical Board.

"You see, Marc," he told me, "this is what Howard and Farbstein want—a weak Medical Board so they can rule us all. We need a strong Medical Board with our own man there." He was alluding to Mantzur.

That was ridiculous. It was as if Churchill would appoint SS leader Himmler, or in our case Dr. Mengele, as the President of New Germany after the Allied victory. I was amazed by Winestone's jumbled personality.

So where did we stand at this point? Both killers were under State investigation. There was a good chance that Sorki would lose his license, but we didn't know when. I hoped that the same was true for Godfather unless Winestone managed to save his skin somehow. Meanwhile we were under attack by Sorki. The Department of Medicine had been instructed by its new Vice President Susman not to refer any patients to us, which was deadly to our practice. The emergency room had similar instructions. Mantzur continued to practice as he did before, and so did Sorki.

I didn't think my job was in danger. As long as Winestone hung in and as long as the investigation went on, they wouldn't touch me. But I was far from popular. Would the situation improve after we'd won—when we had crushed Sorki? Perhaps, but I was not convinced at the time. Something was amiss. I was anxious about Winestone's plans for Mantzur. I did not want to continue working with the killer. Was it time to find another job and move on?

▲▼▲▲▼▲

Dr. Johnson, a chief resident, presented the case of the nine-year-old girl who underwent biopsy of her breast mass by Dr. Sorki.

"What was the indication to operate on this young girl with early asymmetric breast development?" Chairman Winestone looked fresh and vigorous this morning. Even his hair had undergone metamorphosis: The white had turned to fresh brown.

"I talked to Drs. Kosai and Rosenberg—both of them world-renowned breast pathologists. I asked them to review this patient's histological slides. Both were convinced that we are dealing with a variety of early breast development and that the surgical biopsy clearly risked future breast asymmetry."

This was not an ordinary M&M case. Winestone did not usually interpret the case presentation with definitive statements that belonged in the discussion phase. The auditorium was exceptionally crowded; when two prominent gladiators confront each other the crowds always turn up.

"Dr. Johnson," Winestone continued. "You reviewed the relevant literature, right? Will you share your findings with us please?"

Johnson used the overhead projector. "Dr. Winestone, I looked at a few key sources. In Haagensen's classic Diseases of the Breast the author wrote: 'When the mother of a little girl discovers a "tumor" beneath the child's nipple she is apt to overlook the possibility of the precocious or early puberty and rush off to her local surgeon.' He also wrote this: 'I cannot condemn too strongly any kind of surgical procedure upon the breasts of children...the hazard of damage to an abnormally early developing breast is great.' Then I found this editorial in the *British Medical Journal* from 1978. I quote: 'Surgical interference in such a case is a catastrophe.'"

Today's M&M was well orchestrated and pre-planned by Winestone. He was laying an ambush for Sorki in an attempt to disgrace him in front of everyone. Rumors that Sorki had removed half a breast of his secretary's daughter had circulated through the hospital for months. An anonymous letter to the secretary described in scientific language what actually happened to her daughter and advised her to search legal advice against her boss. Farbstein and Susman hired a private investigator to figure out who sent the letter. I was naturally the prime suspect. They sampled my printer and took fingerprints from my office, but nothing had been proven. Winestone instructed me to lock my mouth during today's discussion, so I sat behind Sorki and took notes.

"Thanks, Dr. Johnson, for this useful review," said Winestone. "We have to conclude that the biopsy performed on this child may be associated with potential future problems—" Winestone raised his hands and added in a sad tone, "—which is very unfortunate."

Sorki got to his feet. "What's the problem? What problems? I would like Dr. Tenya, our chief pathologist, to show his slides. Let's look at the slides and learn!"

"I discussed the case personally with Dr. Rosenberg from the Memorial Hospital. He told me that this is a case of prepubertal breast development. I have his report in writing."

"You investigated this case?" Sorki shouted. "You quote books. What is the purpose of all of this? We listened to you, we gave you a chance. Now let's listen to our chief pathologist."

Winestone was obstinate. "No point to watch slides. We are not pathologists. I have the reports in my pocket."

"Dr. Jacobs scrubbed with me on this case. I told him that there is a good chance that the biopsy will be negative." He shouted again, "Now let us see the slides!"

"Dr. Sorki, I want you to be calm and scientific. Don't tell us what to do. You had the chance to lead this residency and you lost it."

"I am just a private surgeon," said Sorki putting on an air of modesty.

"Let us see the slides!"

"Show him the slides!" called voices from the audience.

Dr. Tenya sent his deputy, Dr. Khouri, to the battle. "We sent the slides to three experts. There was no disagreement. "As you see here," she pointed at the slide with her laser marker. "The lesion represented benign hyperplasia of the breast due to excessive estrogen stimulation. There is a predominance of ducts. This should resolve spontaneously, and there is no need for further surgery."

"Dr. Youngman, any comments?" Winestone resorted to heavy artillery now. Youngman, whom he had summoned to fight Sorki this morning, was a distinguished and nationally well-known Professor and Chief of Pediatric Surgery at the Manhattan University.

Youngman went to the podium. With prematurely white hair and a lean physique, he had the stereotypical look of a medical academician.

"I am a pediatric surgeon," he said with an authoritative air about him. "I am pleased to be here today to comment. I am heavily involved in surgical education, and I think that the M&M meetings are very important. We must learn from our mistakes how to treat a similar case next time. I am pleased that we could eventually see the slides—it has all a role in education. Now, Dr. Sorki, I know that you are an experienced surgeon. I respect you. I also know that you had many similar cases before so please tell me, what was in this case that convinced you to proceed with the biopsy?" This guy was a magician, and put Sorki at ease almost immediately.

Sorki put on his civilized tone: "In fact, Dr. Youngman," he said, "this was the first such case I have seen in my life. This was a fast growing and painful mass and it was unilateral. I watched it for a few weeks. The mother became a nervous wreck. Malignant sarcomas are not unusual in this age. I did a tiny biopsy removing ten percent from the mass." With his thumb and index finger he demonstrated how tiny the piece was. "They talk about a mastectomy." He laughed. "We only tried to calm down the mother. There are many articles about this topic, very educational." He laughed again. "If this case is unnecessary then all we do in adults is unnecessary as well. How many breast biopsies that we do are negative? Let us present all these cases? Ha! We would spend our days and nights discussing all our negative biopsies in adults."

Youngman spoke slowly, seriously. "What you did, Dr. Sorki was dangerous. Biopsy of a mass in a fully developed breast is different: It is to rule out malignancy. The issue is different in a prepubescent child—"

"—She could have had a malignancy," Sorki interrupted. "I've told you. Why don't you listen?" He waved his hands in frustration as if brushing off the expert in the said field.

Youngman did not lose his calm. I was gaining more and more appreciation for his talents. The man was a diplomat. "I have seen hundreds of such early breast buds. Parents are always anxious and frightened. We must calm them down, check the pressure. How many times do we find a carcinoma in a painful breast? Never! No pathologist in this room has ever seen a carcinoma in a prepubertal girl! The residents should remember this case and learn to exercise judgment. Never interfere surgically in a premature breast. What you, Dr. Sorki, did is a hemi-mastectomy. We'll have to wait for the consequences."

"OK," Sorki sneered. "The mother even got a letter warning her about all of this—"

"—Dr. Youngman, was there a role for a needle biopsy?" asked Sam Glatman.

"Our role here is to reassure, reassure and reassure—"

"—Let me tell you something," said Sorki. "Now, a few months after the procedure the other breast is normal. Give me your address. I'll send you the follow-up in five years." Disproportionate laughter followed his offer.

Youngman turned to Winestone. "What did he say?" Winestone shrugged his shoulders. Then Youngman whispered into Winestone's ear, "Larry, that guy's a psychopath." His task completed, Youngman left the auditorium. Winestone would have to pay for that favor.

"Dr. Sorki, did you think about asking for a second opinion?" asked Chaudri.

"I watched her for two weeks. It was still growing."

Dr. Gelfand, a local pediatric surgeon asked, "Dr. Sorki, you said that you have never seen such a case. So why in God's name didn't you ask for a second opinion?

"Look who is talking," Chaudri whispered to me. "Why didn't he ask for a second opinion himself last week?" He was referring to an incident in which Gelfand removed the normal kidney of a newborn suspecting it to represent a tumor. Further to that, it was the child's only kidney.

Sorki had enough of this. "Dr. Jacobs, you scrubbed on the case with me. Why don't you tell them that we did only a tiny biopsy?"

Jacobs stood up and spoke as requested. "This was a while ago, but I remember the case very well. Immediately after the case I went to one of the full-time attendings to discuss it with him. We removed half of the mass, around fifty percent if not more."

"We did not remove that much." Sorki disagreed emphatically.

Dr. Smith, a plastic surgeon, quickly joined in the Sorki bashing: "As a plastic surgeon, I saw more than a few young patients with marked asymmetry of the breasts after trauma or surgical procedure during development. The breast scars interfere with normal development. The final outcome is unpredictable."

Winestone attempted to take the reign of the meeting into his hands. "I see a hand there, Dr. Tischler. Last comment!"

Tischler, South African trained, was the local chief of pediatric surgery: "Could I show a few slides? As you see here, this case does not represent abnormal development of the breasts but a normal one. The pathologists do not have enough experience with normal breasts in that early phase of development so they define any tissue as abnormal."

"This is absolute nonsense," grunted Sorki, dispatching the words with another flicked wrist. "Where did you learn pathology? In South Africa?"

"Since there is no general consensus we refer the case to the Department's QA committee," concluded Winestone.

"He looks like Napoleon," Chaudri whispered to me again.

"Bonaparte was thinner," I half joked. It was true.

I met Bachus in the elevator after the M&M. "We gave Mo a devastating blow. Not even one of his cronies stood up to defend him. What do you say about that?"

Bachus was not impressed. "It was too much. It may have generated lots of sympathy for Sorki. Those guys just sit there and think, 'Look how they're crucifying him. Tomorrow they may do it to me.'"

▲▼▲▼▲

At the West Wing, third floor, I saw Herb Susman leaning against the wall. When I faced him he averted his eyes towards the ceiling. We were alone waiting for an elevator. He was clearly uncomfortable about being there. I wasn't sure if he wanted to hit me or run away from me. "Hi, Dr. Susman," I said, happy to see him writhing as he was. He ignored me and stared with interest at a spot behind me. I said, "Hello in there! Earth to Herbie—"

"What the fuck are you talking to me for?" he barked, continuing to avoid eye contact.

"Because I have good manners," I replied and jumped into the first elevator that arrived. Susman stayed behind. I can only imagine what he said as I disappeared behind the glossy metal doors. I had some words of my own for him, the fat bastard.

"What a rude pig," I said as I sunk into a chair opposite Winestone.

"Who?" he asked irritably.

"Herb Susman." I recounted the incident.

"I wouldn't worry too much about that. I'd be more worried about meeting with his subcommittee next week."

"Dr. Winestone, this subcommittee is a joke and a paradox. The bodies which were elected to maintain the standard of care in a hospital are under State investigations and at the same time they continue witch hunting those who they think sold them out."

Winestone picked up the phone and then slammed it down. "Wrong number. I need a personal secretary. These women are useless."

"Didn't you interview a few candidates yesterday?" *None of whom, I think, could have Beverly's legs. A bitch, sure. But what a thoroughbred.*

"Yes, but nothing that I like."

Chaudri had told me that President Howard vetoed the one person Winestone wanted to hire. The story was that the woman had previously resisted Howard's amorous advances.

"Now listen," Winestone continued. "About the subcommittee, they have the power to investigate you and ask you anything they want. Your appearance is crucial. You have to be cool, deny everything, respond in a courteous way and say the minimum. No accusations, no declarations, no objections. Just 'Yes, sir,' 'No, sir,' and 'I don't know, sir.'"

"But why should I play the passive, humble, innocent guy? Why not put up a fight?"

"Listen, Marc," he said, adopting that fatherly overtone again. "I just came back from Howard's office. He and Farbstein kept me there for three hours; they want me to get rid of you. They believe that you reported Sorki and Mantzur. Clearly, they do not have administrative grounds to let you go, so they are pressuring me to fire you on professional grounds." There was a serious fire burning under my ass.

"So—" My blood was boiling. I was surprised I could even talk.

"—So I told them that this is impossible, because, as a matter of fact, I am satisfied with your professional performance," he said.

"Thank you very much," that was a bit of a relief, but there was more than a hint of sarcasm in my response. "You are so kind. I am so relieved that you are happy with me." *We reported Sorki together and now he—Winestone—is distancing himself from me, presenting himself as my savior.*

"As a matter of fact, Farbstein had your personal file, and he read a few complaints against you. One was about sexual harassment and the other about an incident when you assaulted that black secretary."

"Come on now. You know that this is rubbish. I never assaulted anybody."

"I only know that there were complaints against you."

"Well, if they are so desperate to satisfy Sorki and let me go, why shouldn't I admit that we blew the whistle—and agree to resign for say, a minor sum of money. Maybe a million or so?"

That irritated him. "They will never give you so much out of their own hospital pocket. At best they will give you a year's salary. They care less if you sue and even win two million. Then the insurance company would pay, not them. In addition, you should never leave a job before you have another. Unless of course you want to retire and have the means to do so, which I don't think you do. Wherever you go they will ask why you are out of work. Even if a local chairman wants you, his CEO may have spoken with Howard in one of their meetings." Winestone grabbed me by the elbow. His grip was loose. "Marc, didn't I promise you that next year you'd be promoted to full professor?"

I sensed that Winestone was adamant that I should stay to fight along him, but I decided to test him anyway. "Dr. Winestone, we were thinking of buying another house. This would entail a large mortgage. Do you think the time is right?" I searched his eyes.

He returned my gaze. "Absolutely. I see no problems."

He had passed the test. Years ago another boss looked away, and I knew that I had to move on. This test was only valid, however, in non-psychopaths or evil persons.

Winestone accompanied me to the door. "Marc, whatever happens I won't fire you. Just listen to my advice. Go there and be quiet. Take a valium if you have to, but sit down and shut up."

I met Carducci at the OPMC for the third time. He invited me to help him go over Mantzur and Sorki's charts. Carducci opened a thick chart. "Marc, look here. See this long paragraph squeezed into the bottom of the page. See how the handwriting is different, smaller, and more careful. He probably used another pen. It is hard to assess the ink because these are all photocopies. Just read it." In that particular paragraph, dated prior to the operation, Mantzur explained in great detail why the high-risk patient would need his small abdominal aneurysm to be repaired.

"This is not his style. He would never use such scientific terms. Someone dictated it to him. It could even have been Winestone," I suggested.

"All his charts underwent such improvements," said Carducci. "There are new pre-operative notes-explaining the indications, and there are new post-death notes justifying the mortality—"

"—No wonder he locked himself in his room for two months before handing the charts to you. What do you want to do about it?"

Carducci ignored my question. That was unlike him. "Now let me show you a few of Sorki's charts. Tell me, does he ever write detailed notes? Does he dictate the operative cases by himself or let the residents do it?"

"They say that Big Mo carries no pen."

"So look at it. Look at all those beautifully written statements and follow-ups. Look at the immensely detailed dictated operative reports—by Sorki himself."

I laughed. "Dictation services worked overtime for Sorki last month. But this is easy to prove; it is all computerized, and you could find out when these notes were dictated. A dictation of a 1997 case—typed last week—would prove that the chart has been meddled with."

Carducci nodded his head. "And each of his charts has a few new notes by the referring physicians and other consultants which support the need for the operation despite the prohibitive risks."

"By Susman, Geddy and—"

"—Yes, these names are everywhere."

"But Dr. Carducci, isn't tampering with charts a criminal offense? Surely you have scientific methods to prove that these notes were inserted post factum? You could prosecute those guys based only on this."

"Marc, we are not the FBI. We do not have that ability. Tell me, how are Mantzur and Sorki doing? Behaving themselves?"

"Mantzur is his old self," I admitted. "You know, continuing to bypass healthy limbs. Sorki has undergone a metamorphosis. He has stopped doing emergencies and cancer surgery. He concentrates on morbid obesity procedures and hernias—playing it safely. He appears calmer and more introverted. I bet his Albany lawyers are telling him what to do. He also went—for the first time in his life—to the annual meeting of the American College of Surgeons, although he is not a Fellow. Again, to boost his image."

"I will be interviewing both of them very soon," Carducci assured me with a degree of finality befitting the conversation.

▲▼◢▲▼▲

A week later Chaudri and I returned to Staten Island. On the way there, we talked about the situation. "How was the subcommittee meeting?" he asked. "Did you take any valium?"

"No. I was cool. But it was sort of a kangaroo court, you know. You should've heard Susman's opening speech. It went like this: 'Nothing, nothing should leave the hospital." I was doing a pretty good Susman impersonation, if you ask me. I had my gut puffed out like the fat slob he was, and I swore like a biker. "We wash our dirty laundry ourselves. I don't give a shit whether you all bang your fuckin' heads against each other—but do it in the hospital and not in the street. We'll eradicate any traitors. We'll find them and they'll have to go.

Never, never in my many years in this institution has a doctor complained about another—and to the State!'" Chaudri was almost amused. "This tirade went on and on."

"I can imagine." He shifted in his seat, "What did you tell them?"

"I denied everything," I said. "When Susman asked me what I thought about Sorki, I said I had academic differences with him on the way surgery should be practiced. Then Susman asked me about my past. Why did I come to the US? Did I have any prior involvement reporting doctors to the authorities or the media? They must've done some research about my past. I told them that as a senior surgeon I had contacts with the authorities and on a few occasions communicated with the media as required by my status."

"Was Sorki there?" Chaudri asked.

"No, he wasn't. His buddies probably advised him to calm down and not stir the shit."

"The others said nothing?"

"Nothing. Winestone sat there quiet as a lamb. Schwartzman wanted me to elaborate on my academic differences with Sorki, but I declined. Look at these chairmen, how they play the game. Take Schwartzman, for example. He's Chairman of OB Gyn, ex Vice Chancellor of Upstate University, ex President of the American Association of Gynecologists. He won't do anything to irritate Sorki and Susman. This is unbelievable."

"Schwartzman, like Winestone, suffers from the same syndrome. He is old and wants to protect his chair. Why should he fight for justice if at the age of sixty-eight he can continue doing nothing for half a million a year?" As we crossed the upper level of the bridge we saw the sunset beyond Staten Island's beaches and the Jersey shore. "Zohar," Then Chaudri said, "You never told me about your involvement with the media in Israel."

"Salman, who cares about that shit? Whatever happened there happened." It was too painful to talk about, and besides, he wouldn't understand.

16

Unnecessary Operations

*The real problem isn't how to stop bad doctors from
harming, even killing, the patients. It's how to prevent
good doctors from doing so.*

—*Atul Gawande*

Tuesday, 9 November 1999

That morning's M&M meeting was memorable. It was
one of Mantzur's typical cases: an eighty-six-year-old female
with palpable femoral pulses on both sides, plus an ischemic
ulcer on one foot. No pre-operative angiography was done,
but from the physical examination it was clear that she didn't
need a bypass from the aorta into her femoral arteries. Mantzur, however, did an aorto-bifemoral bypass, injected urokinase, and let her ooze to death. There was no longer a hushed
and embarrassed silence with people afraid to talk against the
Godfather. Accusations of medical malfeance poured out
from Sam Glatman and other private vascular surgeons.
Mantzur—angry, sweaty and red-faced—backed down.

"In retrospect," he said, "I should have done just an
amputation—but the family refused." He denied administering urokinase although it was recorded in the chart.

Only his protégé Dr. Ilkadi tried to support him: "There
was no need for a pre-operative angiography with the Duplex
scan showing iliac obstruction," he said.

After the meeting Mantzur approached Glatman and
hissed at him. "You're going too far, much too far. I'm warning you—" It seemed to me that we were progressing. The
"green wall" was crumbling.

I met Winestone in the department. I realized that he chose not to attend the meeting because Mantzur's case was going to be discussed. "Morning, Dr. Winestone," I said cheerfully. He resisted my charm and carried on with conspicuous gloom. "You missed an excellent M&M. They presented Mantzur's case," I said as if I didn't realize he already knew that. His face turned a darker shade of gray. "He came under a lot of scrutiny, and it was embarrassing to hear him trying to justify such stupidity," I continued.

Winestone ignored my provocative words. "Poor timing," he said. "We must give him a break. Let him breathe. Otherwise he'll join Sorki's camp."

"He belongs to that camp already."

"Not really. As a matter of fact, he was our guest Sunday on the Island. He is very supportive of us and I think that we are able to help him."

"Only God can help him now." I wasn't kidding. Once the OPMC was finished with him, he'd never practice medicine again and for a man like that it would be like being choked on a rope, not unlike many of his former patients.

"Not really. Monday I went to meet Dick Kelly. He is going to save Mantzur."

Dick Kelly was the President and CEO of the Manhattan University Medical Center, a towering figure in a local medical establishment.

"I am not sure how he can save him," I said. "There are heavy allegations against the man."

"As a matter of fact, Kelly helped Donald Moore." Winestone was referring to a recent event covered in the news. Moore, the Chairman of Surgery at the Manhattan, left residents to close up the abdomen of his patient, told the family that the operation was finished and that everything was OK, and went to the airport. When he returned the patient was dead. "Moore was almost fired," Dr. Winestone said. "Kelly saved him."

"Yes," I agreed, but he could tell I differed from him by the aggressive shaking of my head. My right hand waved pointedly with my index finger extended. "But this was an isolated incident. Moore is a great surgeon and educator, and it was an unfortunate incident. Mantzur is not Moore. And even if Kelly helps Mantzur, that is not the end of the story. There are senators, the media. Nothing is absolute."

"Are you planning suicide?" He cleared his throat and adopted a conciliatory tone. "Marc, you know how much I like you. I respect your ethics and morals. But you have to make peace with Mantzur. Next week you, Mantzur and I will have dinner together. He'll take us to a Persian restaurant."

"Let me think about it."

I left the room recalling that a year ago, during one of his political tutorials to me, Winestone said, "Marc, when you reprimand anybody or, in general, before you say anything painful, start with a few kind words. Like 'you know how much I like you.' It works!" *Perhaps too well,* I realized as I walked away quietly.

▲▼▲▲▼▲

That day was more promising. I met with a special agent from the Office of Investigations, U.S. Department of Health and Human Services, in the library's audiovisual room at his request. He was dark and slim, in his thirties with a big gun bulging under his suit. He showed me his gold badge and started to take notes on a legal pad—like a paralegal clerk, but slower. It took him a minute to complete a sentence. He was interested mainly in the methods used by Mantzur to milk Medicare. He told me that Dr. Glatman had tipped them off. *Is that how confidential they are?* I explained that Mantzur used synthetic grafts such as Gortex to bypass diseased or non-diseased arteries in the limb but billed for the more complicated and more expensive vein bypasses. I told him how easy it was to prove this fraud. I also drew his attention to Sorki, who demanded a cash payment of a few thousand from obese Medicaid patients who come to him for a gastroplasty.

"This is clearly against the law, eh?" I said.

The special agent filled almost a whole pad with his small handwriting. I was not impressed with his intellect or drive, and I wasn't too sure that this was the way to terminate the two crooks.

At the department my secretary Anne was crying at her desk. "What's the matter?" I asked.

She said nothing. She just kept crying.

Julia, our administrator, was ready to jump in. "Dr. Zohar, let me explain." We moved into her room where Julia showed me a few slips of paper. "These are mail orders we found in Anne's desk. She has been ordering merchandise from catalogues for personnel who no longer are with us. She's the one who collects the mail, right? She was intercepting the merchandise in the mail room."

I looked at the slips. "This is hardly evidence that she is responsible. What are you going to do with her? Why is she crying?"

"She's to be terminated with three months' severance pay. It has already been decided by Human Resources. She has to vacate her desk immediately."

"Just a minute. You can't get rid of a person with so little evidence. She's working for me, my patients like her—"

"—Don't talk to me about it. I can't do anything for you. Talk with Farbstein or Human Resources."

Winestone was my first stop. "Forget about her," he said after I explained the situation that he was already fully aware of. "I warned you that the war would be bloody and full of casualties. They know that she is useful to you. Be happy that it is she who was terminated and not you. Do not create too much fuss about this."

Anne was waiting in my room. "Dr. Zohar, Julia planted these slips in my desk. I swear I know nothing about the mail order thing. She has had it for me since I found her doing it with that creepy security man. Remember I told you about that? She hates me."

"Relax, Anne. Let me call the union for advice, and then we'll go together to Human Resources."

▲▼▲▼▲

"How would you define an unnecessary operation?" asked Mr. Wells, a young malpractice lawyer from upstate New York. (His client injured the bile duct during a cholecystectomy, and I had agreed to serve as an expert witness for the defendant.) Wells seemed unfamiliar with surgery-related litigations.

"It is easier to define a 'necessary' operation," I replied. "That is a procedure for which there is substantial medical evidence to suggest that the patient will benefit from it. For example," I continued, "an appendectomy for a ruptured appendix or the repair of a bulging and painful hernia. These are necessary. On the other hand, in a patient with an arterial occlusion that has already caused the death of the foot from gangrene, an arterial bypass is unnecessary. An amputation is needed but not a bypass. In your case, the patient had asymptomatic gallstones. Thus her cholecystectomy may have been unnecessary."

"Is the definition of unnecessary operation simply the opposite of 'necessary?'" asked Wells.

I laughed. "If it were so simple you would not need the opinion of experts. You would not be paying me four hundred bucks per hour. The definition of an 'unnecessary' operation as used in 1950 by the American College of Surgeons was 'an operation, which is not supported by clinical reasoning and judgment.' In other words, it would be impossible to find expert surgeons to claim that the operation performed in a specific patient could have benefited him or her. On the other hand, such experts, if polled, would undoubtedly suggest that the risk of harm caused by this operation was far greater than its chance to benefit the patient in any way. This introduces us to the concept of benefit- risk ratio. This term is key!"

"Aren't most operations necessary? Why should a qualified, well-trained and licensed surgeon recommend and undertake an operation that is not necessary? Isn't our medical system considered the best in the world?"

"Let us look at a few figures." I opened a book and flipped to some previously marked pages. "In 1976, a total of 9,000 operations were performed per 100,000 Americans. In the same year only four hundred operative procedures per 100,000 individuals were performed in England, and 6,200 in Canada. Do Americans live longer than the Brits or Canadians? Do they enjoy better health or quality of life? Not according to the statistics. The excess number of operations performed on Americans may, in fact, be termed as unnecessary."

"Do we have exact U.S. figures about the number of operations that would be defined as unnecessary?" asked Wells.

"Estimates vary among geographical regions and between the various procedures, a conservative assessment being that between fifteen to twenty-five percent of operations performed are unnecessary. Now imagine that at least twenty-five million operations are carried out each year in the USA; this translates to 3.75 to 6.25 million unnecessary operations every year." I enjoyed lecturing this lawyer although I was not sure whether his interest in the topic was genuine. I suspected he had a four hundred dollar an hour interest.

"So what? Most operations are necessary; a few are not. Big deal. But people sometimes die after unnecessary operations. In 1976 doctors in Los Angeles staged a work slow-down, including a stoppage of all elective operative procedures. The number of deaths in that county steadily decreased during the strike, only to increase as soon as the operating rooms returned to function in full steam. In 1973, doctors in Israel went on a prolonged general strike, addressing only 'emergencies,' and the country's death rate dropped by half. During a fifty-two day doctors' strike in Brazil mortality figures dropped thirty-five percent. We have no data to support the claim that withholding elective operations would have eventually increased the number of deaths when those denied proper surgery started to die."

"How risky are unnecessary operations? Can you estimate such risk?"

"The risk of dying after an operation varies. It is negligible for some minor procedures such as operations on varicose veins, for example. It may reach half a percent for removal of the gallbladder, a cholecystectomy. And it may be as high as five percent for major operations such as that performed on large abdominal arteries. For the sake of the discussion let's assume that the average risk of dying after an operation is one percent. This implies that, in this country, up to 62,500 people may die each year following unnecessary operations. By comparison, the official U.S. toll of casualties in the Vietnam War was 58,184. And think about the costs! At an average direct cost to the patient or his insurance carrier of $5,000 per operation, the 3.75 to 6.25 million unnecessary operations performed each year may represent an expense of $18.7 to $31.25 billion per annum! The price of pain, suffering and amount of personal tragedies is immeasurable. Impressive figures."

Wells looked at his watch. Perhaps he was thinking that he came here only to discuss his case and not to be educated. Or maybe he was interested. I continued, regardless. "Surgeons abhor the term, 'unnecessary operation.' You never hear them uttering this horrid phrase, at least not in public. Try to stand up during a Departmental Morbidity and Mortality meeting and say, 'Doctor, I think that the operation you performed was unnecessary' and watch anger and commotion evolve. Indeed, much has been written about this phenomenon but almost never by surgeons. This is, of course, understandable; generals become as touchy when told that their war was unnecessary. And what do butchers think about vegetarians?

"The problem lies with the culture, the surgical culture. In a culture brain fed on a notion that the surgical knife always heals and if occasionally it kills—what the heck—the burden to prove that an operation is unnecessary rests on anyone but the operating surgeon. In other words, an operation is necessary until proven otherwise. Any qualified surgeon can come up with a new operative procedure, claiming it to be beneficial. You think it is unnecessary, dangerous? Prove it! Numerous examples of such procedures exist in all fields of surgery and pop up every week."

"What about the term 'inappropriate operation?' Is it the same as 'unnecessary?'"

"No, the term, 'inappropriate,' is much less irritating to the surgeon than is the term, 'unnecessary.' To establish an operation as appropriate, the surgeon needs to present evidence that it is worth doing—that its predicted benefits exceed the negative consequences, and by a wide margin. Most operations performed are appropriate, a significant number are not, and not a few belong to a poorly defined gray zone, with indication and value disputable."

"This is interesting," the lawyer said. "Last question. Why do you think that surgeons are engaging in unnecessary or inappropriate surgery?"

"Three chief reasons: greed, ignorance, and behavioral disorder. Usually it is a combination of two or three of these, but greed is probably the dominant factor. Little is written about this, especially not by surgeons. There is a Russian proverb that states, 'When money speaks, the truth keeps silent.' As early as 1732 Benjamin Franklin wrote that 'God heals, and the doctor takes the fee.' Obviously, the surgeon is entitled to his fee, but the problem arises when tempting remuneration is the motive for the planned operation. That financial incentives generate 'bad practice' was perceived by Bernard Show, who blamed the fee-for-service system: 'It is not the fault of our doctors,' he wrote. 'Fee-for-service-is the crux of the matter. You do more you get more.' Simple. Managed care, HMO's, Medicare, Medicaid did not alter significantly this fundamental reality. Medicare reimburses the surgeon much less per operation than a private insurance company does, but still, less is better than nothing, and doing no operation brings in no money. For a surgeon, operating is significantly more profitable than managing the patient without an operation. Do you want to see how?"

"OK."

"For a forty-five minute office visit trying to avoid an unnecessary operation I bill the patient $250. His insurance company may pay me $110. For the forty-five minutes it takes me to repair a non-existing hernia I can bill $2,000 and receive $750. An old aphorism says that the decision not to operate is much more exacting than the one to operate. The dollar does not make it easier. The system punishes the surgeon who chooses not to operate, rewarding the 'aggressor' with many times the amount of money. But do understand that this motive is usually justified by the fact that we have to pay malpractice insurance, the office, the lease, right?"

"Now the ignorance?"

"Ignorance, OK. How can surgeons be ignorant? Four years at college, four years in medical school, five years of surgical residency training, numerous accrediting and other examinations. How can anyone be ignorant after thirteen years of practical and theoretical study? 'Ignorant' is perhaps too strong. Shall we call them instead misinformed or outdated? Try to keep updated in an ever-evolving profession if, in order to produce three hundred grand per year you have to run day and night between clinics and hospitals. The average surgeon emerges from his training program knowing when and how to operate. To maintain state-of-the-art knowledge, surgeons must constantly update themselves using the available continuous medical education venues. Those who chose to stagnate within their daily practice by surviving on knowledge gained during their training years may fall behind rapidly and practice within the framework of yesterday's surgical understanding. Not aware that matters are constantly changing, they continue to perform operations which are no longer considered appropriate. I could give you many examples but let's move on. What was the third motive?"

"Behavioral disorder?"

"Yes. Look at this book." I took it from the shelf: *Medicine On Trial*. "Look at this chapter called 'Cut and run.'" I read from the text: "'The big ego of a surgeon who wants to strut his stuff can lead to unnecessary operations.' The authors, non-surgeons and only one of them a M.D, have hit the heart of the matter. Surgeons love to do what they know best—operate. As professional soldiers need combat, surgeons need to operate. For most surgeons, including myself, an operation is a fulfilling and satisfying experience. The bigger the operation, the greater the satisfaction. Do you know the exhilarated sensation felt by a mountaineer after reaching a snowy peak? Do you ever experience the fervent feeling at the end of a marathon? That sweet feeling of exhaustion mixed with triumph? That is what surgeons are after: The successful completion of a seven-hour abdominal operation like a complicated removal of the pancreas. This specific surgical behavioral disorder may push even a solid, well trained and ethical surgeon to do more than is needed."

"This is fascinating. The theory behind doing too much—"

"—It is not theory. Look at your gallbladder case. She did not have any symptoms. Her cholecystectomy was therefore unnecessary and inappropriate, and now she is a cripple with an obstructed bile duct."

In one sentence I'd summarized his case and probably given him the answer he was looking for.

PART 3

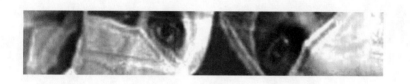

Wheels of Justice

17

The Matching Game

*The surgical resident is like a mushroom: kept in the
dark, fed shit, and expected to grow. And he does....*
—Anonymous

December 1999

"Mr. Huang, do you have any hobbies?" Mr. Huang was
one of fifty out of a few hundred applicants selected to be
interviewed this year for our residency program. We would
select the candidates based on their qualifications, including
which medical school they attend. (Winestone did not wish to
consider non-US medical graduates) We also considered
exam scores, letters of recommendation and, of course, the
interview itself. After the interview we graded the candidates, who in turn graded us within the National Surgical
Matching system. Around March we would be notified which
three geniuses have matched with us.

"Sure. I jog, I scuba dive. I do mountain climbing. I
cycle. I am a gourmet cook. What else? Yes, I play acoustic
guitar and—"

"—Great." I said, interrupting him. *Diverse talents,* I
noticed. "I see that you also mentioned 'languages' in your
CV. What does that mean?"

"I love foreign languages. I speak several."

"Such as?"

"German and—"

"OK," I said, putting his CV down and looking him
squarely in the eye. "Sagen Sie mir bitte irgendwas auf Deut-
sch. Sagen Sie mir warum Sie Chirurg werden moechten."

Silence.

"Verstehen Sie mich?"

An embarrassed smile. "I must be out of practice. At high school I was three months in Munich, an exchange student. How time flies."

"Indeed." I moved on, letting him stew humbly in the pot he had heated himself. "Mr. Huang, you have managed to acquire an impressive resume. Under 'volunteering' I see reference to an AIDS clinic in Puerto-Rico. What was this?"

"It was during summer vacations. You know—kind of support work with indigent AIDS population. Testing and treatment. It also helped my Spanish."

This is also when you practiced scuba diving. "Could you name a few complications of AIDS for me?'

"Infections…"

"Who paid or is paying for all these hobbies and international volunteering, including the fighting alcoholism project in Finland?"

"My parents."

"They're generous indeed! Tell me, any doctors in your family?" Studies showed that doctors' children make better residents than others. Sons of surgeons make excellent surgical residents. Nepotism? Yes, but we want to train surgeons, not sissy morons no matter how cultured they think they are.

"Not really. My parents run a Chinese takeout restaurant in Preoria."

"Where is Preoria?"

"Illinois, an hour or so out of Chicago."

I looked at this tall, handsome, well-groomed young Chinese American and thought about his presumably shorter parents slaving day and night in their tiny greasy suburban Chinese restaurant so that their talented son could add "high altitude medicine" in Nepal to his resume. These candidates impress me with their hugely inflated multi-faceted resumes—a product of obsessively dedicated scholastic and social activities, and at the same time they depress me for how stereotyped they have all become. The sons of immigrants from Bangladesh or Vietnam, Jewish girls from

Brooklyn, and athletic WASPS from Boston, all sporting white smiles. They all talk alike with a lot of "like" in mid-sentence. To me, the obsession of these youngsters with building impressive resumes is pathetic. Do you need to para-glide or fly a Piper in order to be a good surgical resident? I know that after a sleepless month on call many of these multi-talented prodigies will walk around like zombies. *Give me a simple but intelligent boy who during his summer holi-days is helping his father on the farm, and I will make a decent surgeon of him.*

Mr. Huang sat upright on the edge of the chair and stared at me with intelligent, eager to please eyes. I threw my customary final question at him. "Do you read? I mean non-medical stuff?"

"I used to. But now in medical school, there is so little time." This is what many of them say. They do not read. Those who don't read don't think. Do we need to educate another robotic human surgical machine?

I stood up. "Thanks for coming, Mr. Huang. It was a pleasure talking to you. Good luck." We shook hands. I wrote in his file: "Average candidate" and the number 3.

Afterwards, a bunch of us moved into the library to dis-cuss the candidates. Rusk—the one who organized the pro-cess—read from a file. "Ms. Finkelstein, this was the little, black-haired girl from Philadelphia. Bachus gave her three point five and thinks she is solid. Winestone gave her four point five! Hey Dr. Winestone, you really like her?" Chaudri and Bachus smiled at me. We knew that Winestone adored little, well-educated women candidates. Rusk continued: "And our friend Zohar gave her a mere three points."

Winestone threw his hands in the air and trumpeted: "Three! Why? Three means average. She's not average. Her scores are in the ninety-fifth percentile and and—" he sput-tered, searching for his next point of proof. "Have you seen what her dean wrote? She is clearly at the top of her class—and you give her three?" Winestone was angry because my score would lower her final average, affecting her position in our matching list.

"I gave her three because she is a phony. I asked her what kind of surgeon she wants to be. She said that she might be interested in breast surgery. So I asked her a little question on breast cancer. She knew nothing!"

"You're not supposed to ask them medical questions," said Rusk.

"We can ask whatever we want. Dr. Winestone, this woman is a bullshitter. I wouldn't like to have her as my resident."

"Guys, let's not start a fight," Rusk requested. "Chaudri gave her three point six, and I gave her three point five. Her average is thus, let's see, three point six. Next is—."

Winestone was clearly unhappy. "She deserves much more than that. She's at the top of her class—."

"—Next is Mr. Wilkins, the tall, blond guy with a mustache. He is from the University of Illinois. Dr. Winestone gave him three points, I gave him three point three. Marc, you gave him four. Why so high?"

"I like him. He appears trustworthy and hard working, albeit not a star. When I asked him how he would treat shock he responded better than any of our first year residents would."

"Marc, you do not know how to score," said Winestone. "The man was average, no spark at all. Dull. Did you notice how slowly he responded to questions? And his scores were in the fortieth percentile."

"I disagree. What are we looking for? TV anchors or surgical residents? He answered the questions slowly and methodically. Thinking before he spoke. At least I feel that this guy is not a psychopath as Roget was." Roget, who graduated last July, was greatly appreciated by Winestone but scorned by the rest of us. According to our chairman, a senior resident was perfect as long as he looked well after the chairman's patients.

We finished the meeting and moved into the corridor. Winestone asked Chaudri: "Salman, any news otherwise? How is Sorki these days?"

"Operating like crazy. He senses that he may lose his license. He tries to generate as much money as possible to pay for the lawyers and survive during a dry year or, hopefully for us, the dry years to come. I heard that Howard fired Dr. Berger. Do you know how it happened?" Berger was the new Chief of Radiology, a professor brought in last year from Philadelphia.

Winestone was beaming. He seemed to revel in tales of people being fired or displaced. He must have been trying to show us how resilient he was. "Berger did not play to the expectation of the Medical Board. Sorki wanted him to come openly against us. He refused to do so, and Farbstein was instructed to get rid of him. Unfortunately, his contract did not protect him."

"What was Farbstein's excuse?" I asked.

"They played the classical trick. Radiology was in shambles before Berger arrived. Berger tried hard to improve the mess. But when he asked for money to digitalize the system, Howard ignored him. Next they send Gavikumar and Gotahedi to Howard to complain that the file room is chaotic and nobody can find X-rays. Howard continued refusing to see poor Berger and eventually he was told that everybody was complaining that his department was disorganized. So they gave him three months salary and good-bye." Winestone smiled with satisfaction. "They would like to do the same with me," he added. This he found a little less pleasing.

18

Pressures

The Department of Surgery is like a boat at sea: I'm
the captain and my responsibility is to steer. You are
the oarsman; your responsibility is to furnish the
power without rocking the boat too much.
—Owen H. Wangensteen, 1898-1981

January 2000.
From January on, events took sharp twists and developed in rapid succession. Our clinical practice was collapsing. ER physicians had instructions to divert surgical patients to Medicine, which in turn sent them to Sorki and company. Medical patients who needed surgical care were prevented from being seen by us, as orchestrated by Susman. I couldn't get a secretary to replace Anne; Farbstein had frozen the position. Sorki went to Howard to complain that my conversion rate of laparoscopic cholecystectomies was excessive, so Howard demanded an explanation from Winestone. I provided the data to show that nineteen out of the twenty of my conversions to open cholecystectomy suffered from acute cholecystitis or needed bile duct exploration. Alas, it was useless. The issue was referred to another special subcommittee chaired by Susman. Winestone's morbid obesity practice ceased to exist, with all patients kidnapped by Sorki. Also, the chairman of the OR committee was replaced by one of Sorki's cronies.

Winestone was summoned to Howard and Farbstein, who gave him an ultimatum to fire me by the first of July. They also suggested replacing Mantzur with another vice chairman and apparently had a candidate in mind. Howard said, "Larry, we need you as a senior chairman, we want you to stay. But we think that you should leave minor issues—micro-management of the department—to somebody else."

The plot was simple. Fire me, and Winestone would be alone to fend for himself. Force another Brooklyn-made "academic surgeon" on him to actually run the department and let Winestone serve as a puppet. Sure, they could fire Winestone, but he had a long contract; it would cost them five million dollars to pay him off. But they also knew that Winestone wouldn't function as a puppet, so when Sorki and the new vice chairman started suffocating him—he'd leave on his own. Cheap! This was a good plot by Sorki and Farbstein. So what about Howard, who had recently been playing as one of Winestone's buddies? Why the 180-degree change?

I asked Chaudri. He responded by saying that Sorki was just terrorizing Howard. "OJ Simpson survived, right? Anything is possible in this country, and Howard acts as if Sorki would survive the OPMC. Sorki's been traveling to Albany. He's hired the best lawyers. You know that money buys justice, right?" Chaudri chuckled darkly. "Big Mo knows how to manipulate the system. Suppose he has contributed to a party, suppose he was taking part in fund raising for Rudi. On "the hill" where he lives, all of his neighbors are big shots. Suppose one of his neighbors is a certain State Senator, and he calls the big shot in Albany and says. 'I am sending you my friend Sorki who is a great surgeon. See how you can help him.'"

"OK," I said, thinking about it briefly. "But why has Howard changed so suddenly, so dramatically? He might know that Sorki is off the hook. He might know that Sorki could survive and then make his life difficult, but what's the rush? Why wouldn't he wait for the final outcome at the OPMC?"

Chaudri laughed. "Because Howard is subjected to blackmail by the troika of Sorki, Susman and Farbstein. Money? Always possible, but Howard is a rich man. So what's left—as usual—is sex. It is well known that Howard has steady relationships with three women in the hospital: a white secretary, the tall woman on the fifth floor. Then there is that pretty Chinese nurse in the clinics. And finally, a black administrator—she is quite attractive. They may have evidence? An allegation of sexual harassment may destroy the career of this successful hospital administrator—do you think he wants to remain in this shit hole forever? Surely his eyes are on Manhattan. And his wife—" I had a lot of information but no definitive answers. Everything was a mire of politics and bureaucracy. The wicked web was getting bigger, with influences spreading farther than I'd ever imagined. I was sure a few people were playing both sides of the court. The only problem was I couldn't identify them.

Winestone did not give in and refused to fire me. He understood that if he did, his own days would be numbered. I entered in my diary:

> Sorki looks like Saddam Hussein, talks like Saddam and behaves like him. Like Saddam he manages to threat, bully and blackmail everybody around him. Like Saddam he survives—the ever-successful psychopath. We thought that he is dead, that the justice system will prevail. We were wrong hitherto. Will he really win? A year ago—after we did not accept his cousin to our residency—he promised to get rid of us. Will he?

19

Going Down

*One reason why academic conflicts are so brutal is
because the stakes are so low.*
—*Arthur Baue*

February 18th 2000

Today's front page of the *New York Report* dealt with a
New York neurosurgeon who was being investigated by the
OPMC. The State's commissioner of health declared:

> After a preliminary investigation it is my belief that
> there exists a potentially grave risk to patients at the
> Shore Island Hospital in connection with surgery per-
> formed by the surgeon. The surgeon's license to practice
> has therefore been suspended until the end of the inves-
> tigation.

The State Commissioner of Health also declared:

> When this department brings information to my atten-
> tion indicating that patients are at risk in any way, I will
> act swiftly and decisively to ensure that patients are pro-
> tected and that they receive only the highest quality of
> medical care.

Why was this surgeon suspended and Mantzur and
Sorki were still operating? This was the enigma we had to
solve.

I established email contact with Jane, the health corre-
spondent who wrote about that neurosurgeon for *The New
York Report*. She wrote back, "If you have a strong paper trail
and want to discuss it with me at some point I would be
happy to meet with you."

Although it was too early and risky to share data with
her, an open channel with the *Report* could become useful if

our situation became critical. But my friend Daniel from Dallas thought otherwise and emailed me his opinion on the matter:

> In a way, this neurosurgeon case is a blessing for you because it enables you to have a free shave on someone else's beard. It is a great test case both for the quality of this reporter and for the power of the newspaper when the editors decide to run such a story. It is a free simulation for you.

> One of the key lessons is this: Think about yourself in Howard's shoes, assuming he reads the New York Report despite his active sex life. He sees a big scandal, one of the biggest possible stinks a private hospital can face: head of neurosurgery in deep shit, a series of bad cases, hints of bad blood, personal vendettas, a big fine by the state. It really is as bad as it gets.

> The comparison to the Sorki and Mantzur cases is obvious. Howard picks up the latest edition of the New York Report, expecting to see how the hospital president commits hara-kiri in public. But to his delight, he is surprised to find that the reporter of the mighty newspaper comes to interview this doctor and—lo and behold— they come out of the whole thing smelling great. He defends his doctors, showing that they have investigated the cases thoroughly.

> The hospital is presented as a small hospital striving for excellence. Sure, there are problems, like everywhere else, but they are building, investing resources, bringing talent from Manhattan—they want to do good. The bottom line is that in the court of public opinion, the hospital comes out smelling like roses. Or at least this is the impression gained from the article. No difficult questions asked by the reporter, long citations of what was

said, lots of info he—the President—fed her on side issues.

So Howard or any other of the decision-makers who are your enemies (Susman, etc.) at your own institution sits down and thinks, "What does it mean for me?" And the answer is not to think much of your implied threat that you are going to the press to tell your story if you're fired. It's just not that much of a threat. It can be a bit unpleasant, but basically the whole incident can be smoothed over because the fucking journalists don't know what the hell they are doing. I am trying to tell you to factor this into your calculations. For example, if the situation was reversed following these reports (all on the front pages and high visibility) and the Shore-Island hospital were closed, the top administrator fired—then your "golden parachute" out of your hospital would have to be made of platinum. And if you eventually decide to go to the press, do not go to Jane. Find another serious investigative reporter if you can, or go to another newspaper.

▲▼▲▼▲

Howard and Farbstein met with Winestone for another biweekly pressure meeting. Howard talked this time. The gist of what he said was this: "Larry, we may have been too harsh on you. We want you to continue as a chairman and a program director. The gynecologists are moving away from the adjacent offices—you'll get all their space. Hire a vascular guy, get a new thoracic chief, and create a trauma unit. Mantzur is old, complains about back pain all the time. How old is he? Seventy? Seems to me he's seventy-five. He is going downhill, has complications. Why don't you investigate his performance and let us get rid of him? Larry, why do you involve Dr. Dick Kelly? He called me yesterday. I told him that this is a family matter and none of his business. I know you met Carducci again. This is a mistake. Rusk can stay if you need him. But Zohar has to go. He is the troublemaker. We can't keep him."

A few days later Winestone was summoned to Farbstein's office. He stopped at my door on his way, his face red and sweaty. "Marc, if they come down and tell you to go home, do not fight, do not shout. Simply ask. 'Why? What is the reason?' Be cool." Apparently he'd figured that my end had arrived.

When Winestone returned from Farbstein's office he found me with Chaudri. He smelled like he does after a six-hour gastric bypass. Basically, like a carcass. "Marc," he said. "I have to negotiate with them; I can't just go on refusing. They will agree to keep you here until January 2001 if you sign the resignation letter now."

"Do you think I'm crazy? Why should I resign? Did I do anything wrong? Forget it!"

Winestone's eyes did not meet mine. "Marc, I would suggest that you think about signing the resignation. By January things may change. By then Sorki may be dealt with and if so, your resignation won't mean much then. If you won't sign they will fire you on administrative grounds. You know, like downsizing, that sort of thing. Then you'll have to leave now. By signing you can buy time."

I didn't want to be rude to the chairman while Chaudri was present, but I did hold my ground as politely as I could. "I can't sign anything. I don't see any reason to sign."

Winestone's voice sounded distant and detached. "Perhaps you should go and see a lawyer," he said. "I may have one for you, not too cheap—but effective. I used him when I left the Jewish Island—"

"—Hold on a minute!" I exploded. I didn't care if Chaudri was there or not. I opened my briefcase and got the copy of Sorki's file we gave to Carducci nine months ago. "You see this? You prepared it with us. It was given to Carducci by me together with you." I removed a floppy diskette from my pocket, "You see this? It contains what you dictated

to me about Sorki for Carducci. So, dear Professor Winestone, irrespective of what you think, we float together in this
boat. Now you want to dump me?"

Silence.

I looked at Chaudri. He appeared to be enjoying the
show. Nobody talked to the Chairman of Surgery that way.

I continued. I had some inertia and like a body in motion
I stayed in motion. "You want me to sign this fucking resignation form? OK. You want me to be the scapegoat? OK, I
will do that—but you have to arrange the payout. Go get me a
deal, get me a million and I will sign it and leave this shitty
place. You suggested that I go see a lawyer? Not me—we
must see a lawyer. If you do not want to be with me on this
one I will fight alone using my own methods. First thing I'll
walk up to Farbstein and Howard with this file and diskette
and tell them that you reported Sorki. I'll also tell them that
tomorrow morning all Sorki's and Mantzur's cases are surf-
ing on the Internet with their numbers and names for America to see evidence that they—and you—protected those
killers for years."

Winestone didn't even blink. "Marc, relax. Sit down.
Did I ever tell you to sign the resignation? You need a lawyer.
They can fire you on administrative grounds—nothing to do
with Sorki."

I laughed at him just as Bachus walked in. He knew by
the maniacal tone of my laughter that he'd dropped like a
paratrooper into the middle of a fire fight.

Chaudri joined in. "How can they want to downsize and
at the same time instruct you to hire new faculty? How can
they talk about hiring a trauma surgeon? Marc is a trauma
surgeon. Did you ever ask them for any instruction in writing? They want you to organize Marc's resignation? Fine.
Ask them for written instructions."

"They'll never give anything in writing," Bachus
pointed out as Rusk entered the room and took a seat. "They
talked to their lawyers and were instructed not to be involved
in Zohar's removal. They want to dump it on you," he said,

motioning to Winestone. "If they wanted to fire Zohar, they would have done it a long time ago. They are scared."

Rusk spoke next. "Dr. Winestone," he said. "You are the admiral of the fleet. You sent us to the battle, and now the fight is on and we are taking heavy losses. Are you leaving your sailors behind? You should talk to a good employment lawyer because nobody is going to put up with this."

Winestone held fast. "I offered Marc the phone number of a lawyer—"

"—It is your problem!" I jumped to my feet and raised my voice additional octaves. "You get a lawyer and you pay." I was pointing aggressively. "You can't dump all of this on me!"

Winestone shrugged, looked at his watch and left the room. He had another meeting to attend. Meanwhile, the smoke settled behind him. We all remained silent. The grim realization of what was materializing from months of diplomatic maneuvering hovered around us like air pollution.

Chaudri finally broke the silence. "Marc, he's under tremendous pressure to provide them with your head on the plate. I don't think he wants to do it, but he has to."

"By letting me go he'll be digging his own grave—and very soon—"

"—He knows that," said Chaudri. "By the way, Farbstein is spreading rumors that you are a racist."

"What?"

"He claims that you hate blacks, that his wife overheard you during one of the parties making racially derogative comments."

"That is ridiculous. Who is his wife anyway?"

"It's his third wife, from Senegal. Marc, it doesn't matter what you said. What matters is that Farbstein is after you. He'll use any argument to bring you down. Call it a smear campaign if you will." We discussed this for a few more minutes before they had to attend different appointments. When they were gone, I placed a call to Carducci. It was time for an update.

"Winestone is in the same boat with you," he said after my detailed explanation. "There is no way he can dump you.

Within four weeks Sorki will probably be invited for hearings because, as you know, the experts are almost through with his cases. The hearing may take a year, but the outcome is almost always against the accused doctor. Marc, understand that the law is on your side. You did the right thing according to the law. Why do you want to continue working there anyway?" That was a good question to which my silence suggested I had no answer.

That night I carried with me a good dose of single malt to my study. I generated an update of my situation and emailed it to a few friends around the world. I concluded with a rhetorical question. "So who is Winestone? Is he Churchill, Chamberlain, or simply an old, tired, self-indulging Jew?" Twenty minutes later an email arrived from my friend Daniel:

> It seems to me that Winestone is joining a long series of historical figures, all of which had the good fortune of being associated with you. Marc, you do not seem to realize the old rule that proximity breeds contempt. Everyone is a giant until you get closer and see that he has bad breath and perhaps does not change his underwear often enough. You must be more tolerant. You want Winestone to fight wars. He is not a Napoleon. He is a survivor. Given his personal history, he has made a remarkable career. He strikes me as a clever person, and although he is not the kind of person I would like to have at my side on a dark night, he is basically honest. He is a master of the art of the possible and a shrewd politician. Yes, he may be getting old, and the last thing he needs is a big blow-up at the end of his career. Nevertheless, until you have a better option, you are stuck with him. He may not be the fighter you wish him to be, but he likes you a lot. Believe me—you can use someone like him. Don't lose his friendship at any cost. Not at this stage in your life.

We sucked out all the feces and pus from the peritoneal cavity and took a last look at the large bowel anastomosis. *Looks fine. Did we forget anything?* "Barb, cover the anastomosis with some omentum, OK? It will reach, see?"

"Dr. Zohar, why don't you go? I can close alone. Sorki trusts me." Barbara's eyes were twinkling from above her mask.

"Barb, not only does he trust you. He wants you!" I removed the soiled gown and gloves and left the OR. I threw a lab coat above the blue scrubs and headed towards my office.

Not too much later I was reading *The New York Report* when Chaudri showed up at my door. "What're you doing?" he inquired politely. "Don't you have patients to see?"

"Did you see this?" I pointed to the page on the newspaper. "A gynecologist carved his initials on a patient's skin. Must be crazy, some sort of psychopathic disorder."

"Show me—" He grabbed the newspaper. "Jane's the reporter—your friend, eh? When is she going to write about us?"

"It's too early, Salman. Let's allow the OPMC do its job. Just keep reading. The Commissioner of Health suspended the gynecologist's license and fined Mount Zion Hospital."

"Great." Chaudri read on. "This should scare Howard and Farbstein. Marc, last night while I was waiting together with Jacobs in the OR lounge Sorki joined us. He started to pick on Jacobs, asking him if he thought Winestone was going to advance him to the third year. I told Dr. Jacobs that he would be advanced. Then I told Sorki that his cousin could have been advanced as well if he had taken Dr. Winestone's generous offer instead of declining it. When I said that Sorki screamed, 'My cousin was better than Jacobs! And tell me Chaudri, why are you Winestone's puppet? I was your teacher. I bought you books, invited you to my home!'" Chaudri continued, dispensing with the Sorki impression.

"I told him I still have the books and that I wasn't his resident anymore and that I could tell him when he was wrong, and he was wrong. This provoked a long monologue. He had a lot of venom in his speech. He said things like, 'Fucking Howard, stupid Farbstein. I told them to fire Winestone and Zohar, but they are frightened to touch Winestone because they do not want to lose the residency. They are afraid to fire Zohar because they do not want to appear in *The New York Report*. Well, tomorrow I will have lunch with Howard, I'll tell him that seventy-five percent of the hospital's physicians will stop admitting patients.'"

Chaudri was having too much fun to stop the description. "I told him he was wrong again, and that the medical people were not with him, and that they were only bullied and frightened by his friend Susman. Then Sorki exploded, shouting something like 'Susman is my best friend! And Howard and Farbstein went to the guy in the State—what's him name?—Carducci. They told him that I'm the best surgeon here, that I have operated on them and their wives.'"

"You must be kidding," I said, balking. "They went to Carducci to actively support that psychopath?"

Chaudri didn't hear me. He had more to tell and was trying to remember every detail. "I told him not to be over confident, I said, 'This is not the time to get rid of anybody, better spend the energy defending yourself.' But he just continued screaming, 'Zohar, Zohar, why do you support him? Winestone would have gotten rid of him a long time ago but Zohar knows the entire dirt about Winestone, he knows about all the skeletons in his closet. Winestone is afraid to touch him.'"

"That may be a valid point," I allowed.

Chaudri continued. "You know what I said? I said, 'Dr. Sorki, tell us what you know about Howard that obliges him to protect you.'"

"Salman, it's good to see how well you can stand up to him now," I said. "By the way, have you seen the last issue of *Pulse?*" I handed him the newsletter on health care in New York. "See how much they earn? Howard's base salary is $644,202 and Farbstein takes $337,202! This is only the base pay; you have to add to it the bonuses, the perks, the payoffs from contractors, the side profits, the kickbacks. No wonder Howard and Farbstein strive to save Sorki. Why disturb the balance? Life is so good."

Thea, Winestone's new secretary, appeared at the door. "Dr. Zohar, the Boss wants to see you now. He's not in the best mood. He's just had a long meeting upstairs with Farbstein."

"Salman, come with me. I might need a witness." Chaudri followed me to Winestone's office.

Winestone appeared grave sitting behind his large desk. His red neck seemed in danger of being choked by his thick white shirt.

"My, aren't you looking serious today!" I said, pretending to be aloof.

Winestone picked up a document and said: "As a matter of fact, this is very serious. Let me read you from a letter I was handed by Farbstein just a few minutes ago. The first paragraph says, 'We have defined a need to develop a trauma center...we have urged you to proceed in a concerted, timely effort to recruit the surgical team that will be needed for this program...'" Winestone read this in a flat tone devoid of emotion. "Second paragraph: 'As previously discussed as well, we are quite concerned with the current economic status of the Park Hospital and find it necessary to make staff reductions to decrease our expenses. Reductions in personnel have already occurred in management and non-management positions. Unfortunately, we have concluded that our physician organization must also be reduced and that Dr. M. Zohar's— your name is misspelled here—where was I? OK, 'and that Dr. Zohar's position will be terminated on July 1, 2000. Similar reductions in salaried physician staffing are currently planned in the hospital for this summer. Kindly inform Dr. Zohar of our intentions to terminate his position on July 1, 2000. I am available to meet with you and Dr. Zohar at your request to discuss this matter.'"

Winestone put the letter down and studied me. I knew he was expecting me to explode, but counter to doctrine this time I did not. I took a few deep breaths, contemplating the implications.

Finally I spoke. "That is an excellent letter. I was waiting to see this—stupid Farbstein digging his own grave."

Winestone shrugged off my optimism. "I advised you to sign a resignation. If you had done so, we would have had time to breathe, at least until the end of the year. You did not take my advice."

I have only three months left. I have miscalculated. I did not believe they would dare to fire me. And where does Winestone stand? Is he playing their game now, trying to save his own butt? I have to start looking for a new job ASAP. What will Heidi say? We have to start being careful with money.

I stood up to leave. "Dr. Winestone," I said, "so they are firing me. Whatever. After three months I won't be here. Do you think that this will solve the problem? Do you think it will save Sorki? Do you think that this will save your vice chairman?" My voice was shaking.

"Marc, Marc," Dr. Winestone said in his calming tone. "Please sit down. In these places a person is fired only if he does not arrive at work the day that follows the day of termination. You know I will not allow this to happen. But you have to help me fight them. You have to calm down and help me deal with them. Our main goal should be to revamp the department. We need a new vascular surgeon to take over Ilkadi's position and to develop endovascular surgery. Your friend Morton from Detroit would be ideal, and I want you to continue working on him. Now Howard wants a trauma unit, and we have to assemble one for him. We need an established academic trauma surgeon. I think that your friend from Dallas, Daniel, could be perfect for this purpose. Marc, our priority has to be to establish a strong department. You have to help, and in doing so you will be helping yourself."

Chaudri remained passive. I didn't move or speak.

"Let us continue functioning as if nothing happened," Winestone insisted. "And Marc, you are going nowhere. You'll stay with us. Remember that recruiting your own friends is good for you and us. It will increase our power. They will fight for you."

In the corridor after our meeting I sneered at Chaudri. "How stupid does he think I am? He expects me to find a perfect replacement for myself. I'll find him one, all right."

▲▼▲▼▲

Farbstein's eighth floor suite occupied an entire wing of the pavilion. I entered it unannounced at eight a.m.—before his three secretaries arrived. Farbstein sat behind his massive desk, the Metro pages of *The New York Report* spread before him. A cup of coffee was in his left hand, and the phone receiver was in his right.

"Morning, Dr. Farbstein."

He looked up. The look on his face remained passive, as if my visiting him was a regular occurrence. With the cup he motioned toward the secretaries' room. "Coffee's there, fresh Colombian. I brewed it myself. Please help yourself. I'll be with you after this call."

I poured myself a cup and strolled back into Farbstein's room. It was four times bigger than Winestone's. The windows offered panoramic views of South Manhattan and Brooklyn bathing in the morning March sun. In a few weeks spring would be here. I looked at the pictures on the wall: Farbstein on his sailboat in shorts and baseball hat, Farbstein in tuxedos with Sorki, Mantzur and Howard at a social event. A picture of the late great Rabbi Menachem of Brooklyn, inscribed, "To Dr. Albert Farbstein, for his contributions to the well being of our community, May the Lord bless him." I examined Farbstein's bookshelf. *Harrison's Textbook of Medicine, Fishman's Pulmonary Diseases and Disorders, Hurst's Diseases of the Heart,* and a few non-medical books. Apparently Farbstein read a lot. I picked up Hamill's *A*

Drinking Life. What a lovely book! Hamill was born and grew up in this neighborhood when it was predominantly Irish.

"Dr. Zohar." Farbstein interrupted my mental tour. He motioned me to a chair on his side of the desk, "Like the coffee?"

"It's excellent, as usual," I said before taking another small sip of the dark brew.

"How can I help you?"

You bastard. You know exactly why I am here. I removed the copy of his letter to Winestone. "Dr. Winestone showed me this letter, and I have a few questions. First, could you explain why you are firing me?"

"Well, Marc, we are re-arranging the hospital, adding PA's, hiring new people, and we decided to let a few people go, including yourself."

I forced myself to remain cool. "OK, I understand, but why me? What did I do wrong?"

"Nothing. We just decided to let you go. Did you see your contract? We can let you go without any reason. We didn't give you a contract for life. People come and go."

"Yes, I understand." *This fool! He'll dodge and weave until I tire myself out.* "But why did you single me out? Why me? Why not, for example, Rusk or Bachus? You want to downsize. OK, but how did you decide to choose me?"

Farbstein maintained his composure, but I sensed that he had had enough. "This is what we decided. We need physician assistants, and we are short of money."

"Dr. Farbstein," I finally erupted, sick of his bullshit. "Why don't you stop hiding behind empty words and discuss this matter openly? A normal procedure would be for you to instruct the Chairman of Surgery to fire a person and let him decide who that should be. But you singled me out, which is evidence that this is a personal vendetta against me."

Farbstein looked away. "No vendetta. Just an administrative decision. We just decided that we don't need you anymore. We tried to tell Dr. Winestone this for six months. He did not understand."

"Winestone is not stupid. You wanted him to fire me so I would sue him."

"I don't know what you're talking about—"

"—Well, look at the top paragraph of this letter. How stupid it was to add it here. It says you want Dr. Winestone to build a trauma unit. Do you know that I am the only so-called qualified trauma surgeon in this hospital? You're looking for trauma surgeons and yet you fire me. Is it a joke? What is the punch line?"

"Yes, we need a trauma center. We'll need PA's—"

I laughed out loud. A real tumultuous belly laugh. I needed it! "That is a good one! I'll have to write that down." My eyes weren't watering from laughter, but I did the motions anyway. I wiped my left eye, then the right. This was too much. It also bought me some time to think through what I was going to say next. "But Dr. Farbstein, to have a trauma unit you need a chief of trauma and a few trauma surgeons to take calls. You need to hire new trauma surgeons, and you are firing the only trauma surgeon you have. This is clearly a personal vendetta on your side. Could you explain to me the reason?"

"Look," he said. "We decided that we do not need you in your present capacity. We do not consider you to be a trauma surgeon. Look at your contract."

I got back to my feet and raised my voice. "This is a clear vendetta, and so it will be judged in court."

"Court? What court? Who's talking about court?"

"I'm talking about it. You are pulling this hospital down. For unknown reasons you're serving Sorki, who is the main reason for all this mess. You are firing me at the time when the State is investigating this hospital. You are accusing me of being the major whistle blower with no evidence. Think about the consequences in court."

Farbstein attempted a sip from his empty cup. He, too, was trying to buy some thinking time. "I know nothing about that. We are letting you go because we have decided to hire new people. We offered to keep you until January 2001 if you were willing to resign. You didn't, so you're—"

"—I came to you to straighten this mess out, but you're hiding behind your technical jargon and empty words. Next time, Dr. Farbstein, we'll meet in different places, but we'll meet. I promise you that. Have a nice day."

▲▼▲▼▲

What now? Winestone is faltering. What is his deal with Mantzur? The OPMC is procrastinating. Howard and Farbstein are in Sorki's pocket. I surely need a lawyer now, at least to negotiate a buyout. Go to the media? Only as a last resort.

I looked at my father's portrait on the wall. He was holding a cigarette in his right hand, and his right eye was closed, probably as a result of the smoke shown in the picture. The left eye looked down on me. I wondered what he would have done, but there was no way to know. Eventually I'd win. Mantzur's and Sorki's fates were sealed by destiny from the first day we met. Farbstein was a prick. All he wanted was to maintain his big office and sailboat. Winestone misjudged me. He thought of me as a small dog that would bite them when he ordered. From inside the hospital or outside, I knew I'd win.

Eventually.

Dr. Farbstein had handed the top one to me just a few days ago when he rolled into my room saying, "Dr. Zohar, according to the rules I have to hand your termination letter to you ninety days in advance." The letter said,

Please be advised that the Department of Surgery is in the process of reconstructing. In view of the proposed changes, this letter is to inform you that your salaried position as an attending surgeon is being terminated on July 1, 2000. This decision has been previously dis-

251

cussed with Dr. Lawrence Winestone, Chairman of Surgery. Very truly yours, Albert Farbstein, MD. Executive Vice Chairman for Medical Affairs.

"Thank you, Dr. Farbstein," I said. He continued towards Winestone's room, handing him a copy of the letter.

That same afternoon Winestone and I met at his library. He was holding his copy of the letter. He said, "Clearly the hospital's lawyers have drafted it in an attempt to incriminate me as an informed collaborator. I have to distance myself from their decision; I have to oppose it firmly but at the same time not to sound insubordinate. I do not want to give them any excuse to fire me as well. I will seek legal advice, and it will cost me money."

Oh, you are so poor. "I am going to see a lawyer on Friday, a big shark—the one who killed you on the Sudkumar affair.

Winestone flinched. "Marc, that is a good choice. Rothman is a very good lawyer. But you should think very carefully what you are going to disclose to him. I would not advise telling him that it was you who sold Sorki to the State—"

"—I am going to tell him everything. And by the way, it is not me who gave Sorki to them. It was us."

"OK, OK." Winestone wavered. "I won't deny it, but remember that at the subcommittee of the Medical Board you were asked who reported Sorki and you said that you did not know. A transcript of that meeting exists. The hospital lawyers will bring it up in court, and it will appear that you lied."

"Come on, Dr. Winestone. That subcommittee's aim was to harass suspected whistle blowers. I do not care what they say. I am going to tell the whole truth to the lawyer and to the media if necessary."

"That may be a grave error on your side."

"Dr. Winestone, at this stage I am alone. I am going to the lawyer alone, and I am the one who is paying. I offered to see a lawyer with you. Now I am alone, and what I say and how I say it is my problem. I don't want to discuss it further with you."

Chaudri joined us in the library. "John Howard stopped me in the corridor this afternoon and asked if Zohar was looking for another job. I told him you were running out of time and could potentially do a lot of damage to the administration at the hospital. I also made the suggestion that they let you stay one more year until you find something else. You know what he told me? He said he doesn't care about another disgruntled employee and that he doesn't care if you go to the media. He gives it six months before everything will be forgotten anyway. He figures it would be worse on you because no other hospital in the city will take you on."

Winestone was not amused by Chaudri's prophecy. "As a matter of fact, we have to change our focus. Sorki is no longer our main foe. Yes, he is still crazy and dangerous, but Howard and Farbstein are our enemies. We have to focus on them!"

When we left the library Chaudri said to me, "Winestone is blabbering. He repeats himself, has big plans but does nothing. You have to fight your own wars from now on. Go and see the shark."

20

War of Attrition

When I take up assassinations, I shall start with the
surgeons in this city and work up to the gutter.
—Dylan Thomas, 1914-1953

April - May 2000.

The notion that spring had arrived in New York struck me with the warm breath of outdoor air when I emerged from the subway into the corner of Forty Second Street and Fifth Avenue. I was much too early for my appointment with the lawyer, so I looked around for something to take up the extra time. Across the street I saw Nat Sherman's cigar shop and couldn't resist. I bought myself three medium size Dunhills made in the Dominican Republic—how long will that silly boycott on Cuban cigars persist? I found a cup of coffee at the nearby Starbucks, then strolled into Bryant Park and located an empty bench bathed in the early afternoon sun. I noticed the fresh buds on the trees; a few weeks and it would be all green. After a sip from the hot coffee, I lit the cigar and observed the curls of blue smoke floating effortlessly above me.

Where should I start with the lawyer? Should I give him the whole story from the first day or concentrate on recent events? William Rothman would have already been familiar with our hospital and the personalities involved. Only recently he won a few million for Dr. Sudkumar, a former resident of ours who sued Winestone and the hospital for racial discrimination. Her firing occurred just before I arrived. It was Chaudri who told me, "You have to see Rothman. He is a master shark!" According to Chaudri, Rothman effectively incited the Brooklyn jury against Winestone and his team, presenting them as useless and clueless—and sexist, surgical educators victimizing a talented, dark-brown, Indian immigrant. "Go and see Rothman," Chaudri said, laughing. "You should have seen him in court tormenting Rusk. He looked into Rusk's face with his one eye—the other was missing and covered with a black patch—and asked 'Dr. Rusk, please tell us how many times you had to take the board exams.' I never saw Rusk so flustered before."

I opened my briefcase and examined the bunch of documents, trying to organize my thoughts.

▲▼▲▼▲

I crossed Fifth Avenue opposite the public library and entered a tall office building. The elevator took me to fifty-seventh floor directly to the law firm of Rothman and Epstein. A polite secretary ushered me into a spacious meeting room, "Something to drink, Doctor? Coffee, tea, water?"

I showed her my Starbucks cup. "Thanks. I still have a few sips left."

She smiled. "Mr. Rothman is on his way from court. His assistants will be joining you in a moment." I walked to the windows. What a vista! One could control the three New York City airports from there. I looked at a brochure on the table. "Bill Rothman has been in practice since 1970, he has degrees from Cornell College, the University of Washington Law School, and Cambridge University, England, where he was a guest Scholar. He concentrates in commercial litigation, dispute resolution and antitrust counseling. Bill has written extensively on litigation procedures and teaches in continuing education programs for the profession. He is a director for the civil legal aid program for the indigent in the western counties of New Jersey." The Cambridge Scholarship and the *pro bono* activities impressed me.

Two staff members joined me, a black woman in her mid thirties and a younger white woman. They introduced themselves, shook hands, and sat down at the opposite side of the long table, producing blank legal pads. "Mr. Rothman instructed us to listen to your story," one of them said.

I was just beginning when Rothman arrived. He was around fifty years old, lean, with a sharp face, a dark inquisitive left eye and a fleshy nose. The right eye was missing and covered with a large black patch a la Moshe Dayan. *An injury?* We shook hands,

"Dr. Zohar, it is my obligation to warn you that this firm is currently representing Dr. Sudkumar's discrimination case against your hospital and that anything you'll be saying may be used by us in that case. Furthermore, I assume that Dr. Winestone dislikes me. You know, nobody likes me after I have cross examined him." A dry chuckle.

I liked his genuine tone. "I don't have any problems with that."

The three hours of briefing went smoothly because Rothman was familiar with the local hospital scene and knew the leading characters in my story. He interrupted my narrative with many questions and paged through the documents I produced. When I finished Rothman said, "Dr. Zohar, we in this firm are well aware of the immense corruption, sleaze and dirt in this type of New York hospital. Your hospital—the Park—is one of the worst of the bunch. We do not understand it. The chaos and intrigues are too complicated to comprehend. Howard and Farbstein are clearly criminals who abuse and steal federal funds. They should be behind bars. But let's concentrate on your urgent needs. What is your objective?" He answered his own question. "First, to keep your job until you decide to leave. Second, if the latter is impossible, to arrange for a reasonable severance deal—at least a sum which will pay for a college education for your sons."

"What about revenge?" I asked. I regretted it almost as soon as I said it. But we have to be realistic. After years of abuse, I was no different than any other human being. Like a dog pushed into a corner, like a bear separated from its cubs, I would lash out, too.

Rothman's single eye burned into me regardless. "Revenge? Revenge is a term that we do not use here. We are in the business of finalizing disputes legally. Revenge is a destructive term which does not exist in our lexicon."

"OK," I said, but I didn't dare believe him. Whatever vernacular you want to use, revenge is in the dictionary. It was in mine, and it had more than likely been in every one of his preceding clients. He knew it as well as I did.

He continued. "I am appalled that you, a senior surgeon, are employed without at least a one-year contract. Is this slave labor? Anyway, I see here two potential venues, which we'll examine. One is the whistle blowing statute, which usually applies to public servants. You are not a public servant, but the State or the Federal Government insures the patients harmed by those you exposed. Thus, there may be some opportunity here." He pointed at the studious one. "Clara," he said, "would you please find the statute for us?"

He looked back at me, slammed his fist on the desk and chuckled. "By the way, the losing side in the Federal court pays the other side's legal fees as well."

"And what is the other venue you had in mind?" I asked.

"The option of using the issue of national discrimination. You are foreign? You are a Jew, right?"

"Sure, but at least one third of the population in this town is Jewish, so what's the point?"

Rothman looked at me as if I were a fool. "Dr. Zohar, your enemies are largely Muslims, right? I would wager that if you were one of them, they would have welcomed you with open arms—"

Clara returned with photocopied sheets. Rothman snatched them with his right hand. "Here it is. Thanks, Clara." He then read from the sheets. "Statute #740, retaliatory personal action by employers, prohibition. Look at this, what a bunch of idiots run your hospital. 'Section 2, prohibitions. An employer shall not take any retaliatory personal action against an employee because such employee does any of the following. Paragraph a. discloses or threatens to disclose to a supervisor or to a public body an activity, policy or practice of the employer that is in violation of law, rule or regulation which violation creates and presents a substantial and specific danger to the public health or safety. Your buddies Sorki and Mantzur kill patients and bill Medicare. Right? You reported this, so you are protected!"

Rothman dropped the paper on the desk, his face expressing contempt. "And didn't they consult their army of lawyers before firing you? But then their lawyers are a bunch of imbeciles"—he smiled at his associates—"as we learned during the Sudkumar's case."

"So what's the procedure?" I inquired.

"My team will research the topic further. Then we'll draft a letter to those clowns delineating the case against the hospital and warning that a lawsuit is imminent. This will force them to rescind your dismissal."

"How much will it cost?"

"Nothing," he said with a smile. "We are not like all those doctors requesting money up front. Seriously, if you decide not to hire us, today's consultation is free. If you decide to retain us, we'll ask for an initial down payment of $5,000." That sounded like money up front to me. "I charge $400 per hour, my associates charge less, and then there are special fees for research and the time invested by the paralegal team. It all depends on the amount of work required, and we'll send you details with the contract."

I could almost feel my entire salary melting away. "Say I am fired anyway. How much will it cost me to sue them?"

"Well, our billing is always the same, per hour and continuously. No, we don't work on contingency basis if that is what you have in mind. Others do, we do not."

He is assuming that I am one of those rich surgeons. Sudkumar's case must've been managed on a contingency basis. How else could she have paid him more than a million bucks? Access to justice is expensive. I stood up. "OK, I want you to represent me. I'll mail the check."

"Dr. Zohar," he said, "do not even think of any contact with the media as long as our negotiations with the hospital are under way. You do not negotiate with a man and shoot him at the same time." Perhaps he was right, but threatening to shoot someone could quickly lead to more successful negotiations.

When he offered me his hand I pointed to his Moshe Dayan eye. "How did you get this? An accident?"

"A childhood accident," he said dryly. I imagined the pain of growing up without an eye. Now I understood the source of that fierce compassion in his sad remaining eye.

▲▼▲▲▼▲

In the afternoon I saw Mantzur shuffling along in his scrubs. He looked pale, unshaven, exhausted and didn't even notice me. A few minutes later I learned why. While operating on an asymptomatic carotid stenosis, the endartrectomy thrombosed in the recovery room and the patient became aphasic. In an instant Mantzur became an old man who couldn't operate. Disaster followed a disaster. What was the difference between him and Dr. Harold Shipman, the British country doctor who proved a mass killer of elderly women? Or the notorious Dr. Michael Swango, the good-looking doctor from the Midwest who got his high from poisoning patients? A few of our residents called Mantzur "Dr. Kevorkian" behind his back. But Kevorkian did what he did out of compassion for the dying patients. Mantzur was definitely not another Kevorkian. Winestone had to stop it or he'd fall because he was blind to Mantzur's endless chain of horrors. Looking today at the Padrino's drained face I hardly felt antipathy towards him. *Is this how Dr. Mengele looked at his last years? Is this is how one loses hatred and contempt against a defeated enemy? But is he defeated?* Time to call Dr. Carducci.

"Dr. Carducci, our friend Mantzur continues eliminating a patient per week—if not more. Last week he excised the hemorrhoids of a patient who then bled to death from the colon above. Two weeks ago he sat for two days on a patient with a huge leaking triple A. The guy had excruciating back pain, but Mantzur decided to schedule it on his elective operative list. The patient decided not to wait. His aneurysm ruptured, and he died. Dr. Carducci, are you there?"

"Yes, Marc. I'm listening."

"You want more? Three weeks ago he performed an elective arterial bypass on a terminal cirrhotic patient—tense ascites, jaundice—he could not even survive the anesthesia."

"What can I say? Marc, I can't talk to you about this. I can't give you any inside information. The case is under investigation."

"Dr. Carducci, I didn't call you to ask questions but to tell you that almost a year ago we brought his cases to your attention, but today the carnage continues. Do you want us to sit down and watch him? The guy is impaired. He has no judgment and no insight. He has to be stopped."

I sensed his voice softening. "Marc," he said, "the reports from the external reviewers about Mantzur arrived. Tomorrow we'll have a meeting to decide whether to continue with the hearings."

"It's taking much too long. And what now? Do you want us to go to Albany, to the Commissioner of Health?"

"No," Carducci insisted. "She'll send you back to me. She'll tell you that we are still busy with the case."

"Why don't you suspend his license immediately?" I was getting impatient. I was almost ready to accuse the OPMC of being guilty for Mantzur's executions.

"The cases are not so clear as you indicate. Most were old and sick anyway. It is not like an operation on the wrong side of the brain—"

"—Come on Dr. Carducci," I interrupted. "do you mean to say that an elective fem-pop bypass on a Child C chronic liver is not a clear kill? What about his impairment, that ninety percent of his cases are presented at the M&M meetings?"

"Your friend Winestone has to stop him. He is the chairman, but unfortunately he is defending him instead."

"Winestone can't do anything. He is obstructed by Sorki. Dr. Carducci, you have been in this business a long time now. What do you predict will happen to them? I have to know."

"They will both lose their licenses. Give me another six months."

"This is what you told me more than a year ago. Did you know that I have been fired?"

Silence. And then, "No. Who did it?"

"Howard and Farbstein. They obey Sorki."

Silence. Then, "Just hang in there, OK?"

"I'm trying."

Six months. A patient per week could perish at the rate Mantzur was going now. Twenty-four more deaths rested in the hands of the OPMC. I just hoped something happened soon.

▲▼▲▲▼▲

While I was changing from scrubs to civilian clothes, Dr. Winestone stormed into my office. I'd heard earlier that he was in a meeting with Howard. He ignored the fact that I was only in my underpants and collapsed in one of my chairs. "Marc, they are retreating. Tomorrow morning you'll get a letter from Farbstein rescinding your termination." I could see tears in his eyes. *It had been a long battle for him, too. One that he'd asked for, mind you.* "Come, let me call Heidi. She has to know."

"She's not at home." The news did not excite me. I knew that they would bend or pay the price for their stupidity. "What happened?" I started to dress.

"My letter did it. I worked on it for two weeks and got legal advice. What do I tell you always? Think, think, wait, sleep over it and think again. And only then act. Now you know that my diplomacy works." I knew about his letter. He'd showed it to me before sending it to Farbstein. It said:

> I was both surprised and disturbed to receive a copy of your memo to Dr. Zohar terminating him. Although you spoke to me about the necessity to downsize the Department of Surgery and identified Dr. Zohar as the only physician to be terminated, I clearly stated to you that I did not agree with this decision. Dr. Zohar makes significant contributions to the department as a clinician and academician. In addition, Dr. Zohar is an experienced trauma surgeon and would be an obvious choice for membership in the newly planned trauma center for the Department of Surgery. It is my responsibility as Chairman of Surgery to explain to Dr. Zohar the reason for his termination. There are no issues regarding his performance for this action and there was no process specified in regard to downsizing the Department that resulted in identifying Dr. Zohar as the appropriate candidate for termination. I am therefore asking you to rescind this unilateral decision. I am willing to discuss the need to downsize the Department of Surgery and present you with an appropriate plan to accomplish this goal.
>
> Yours sincerely,
> Lawrence Winestone, MD, FACS
> Professor and Chairman

"Yes. It was a solid letter. I told you so."

Winestone seemed satisfied. "This morning Howard asked me if this was my final stance on the Zohar problem. I told him it was and that I would present the contents of the letter in court when there is a lawsuit."

"And he will sue you," I told him. "Howard has identified Farbstein as the chief crusader against us. I knew they were going to bend. And I was not wrong, for an hour ago they asked me up to Howard's room. Farbstein was there as well."

"I wish you could reconstruct what was said."

"Sure, let me have a dash of this bottle. I need a drink." He pointed at a bottle of Lebanese Arak on my shelf. I had never seen Winestone accepting a drink in the hospital.

I poured a finger of Arak into a tea glass and topped it with some non-carbonated mineral water, watching the transparent fluid turning an opaque, milky white. I handed him the glass, and raised the bottle to him. "Lechaym." ("to life"). I took a sip from the bottle. It tasted great in its pure form. Winestone gulped and continued.

He explained to me how the conversation went, probably verbatim. This was where Winestone's photographic memory came in handy.

"I told them that if they fired you, I'd have to tell the court the whole story. That of course, would lead to the media. He had no choice but to rescind your termination indefinitely." Winestone explained that Farbstein was understandably appalled at the implication and pleaded with Howard to reconsider the situation. "Farbstein said, 'Who is Zohar anyway? Is he nationally known? Why do we need him?'"

Farbstein is right. He is smart. They'll be sorry, I thought. Winestone continued: "But Howard had already made up his mind. He said they couldn't do it, that he didn't need court proceedings and media sniffing around us. He said he didn't need to spend a few million on lawyers. 'Just be realistic,' he told Farbstein. 'Larry is the Chairman, and he decides whom he wants to work with. It is his department, not yours.'

"Then I asked Farbstein if I could go down and tell you that a letter rescinding the previous one will be delivered to him tomorrow morning."

"And how did he respond to that?" Although I was skeptical at first, I was getting great pleasure out of hearing

263

this. They were squirming. Oh, how they were squirming. *Like little worms with hooks up their asses!*

"He was pale but nodded, and here we are. This is the way to win. The residents can write as many petitions on your behalf as they wish, but this is not democracy. My letter did the job. Please call your wife and let her know."

Winestone could be so be warm and caring—and equally cold and callous. I sensed that he was genuinely happy for saving my job even though by saving me he had saved himself as well. I watched Winestone drain his glass and knew that now Farbstein was the dog pushed into the corner. And an injured dog, at that.

21

The Feeding Tube

*Let man learn to be honest and do the
right thing or do nothing.*
—*James Marion Sims, 1813-1883*

August-September 2000.

Lake Algonquin was covered by dense mist. It had
been drizzling on and off since we arrived a week earlier for
a summer break at the Adirondacks. After lunch I kindled a
large log fire on the lawn overlooking the lake and perched
myself with a diluted whiskey and a laptop. Heidi
descended from the kitchen stairs with a tea mug in her
hands. "What're you writing now? I thought we're on vacation."

"I'm going on with my book. When do you want me to
write? In the car on the way to Brooklyn?"

"You can write as much as you wish, but who would
want to buy such a book? Do you really think that people
want to read about wild doctors and chaotic hospitals? Do
you believe that laypersons would have the patience to follow your long M&M transcripts? Too many foreign sounding characters butchering old Brooklynites. Go on, have fun
but I doubt if anyone will publish this book."

"Heidi, do you know how many hospitals exist in this
country? Thousands. Some are better, many are the same,
and some are even worse than ours. Most hospitals have
their own versions of Sorki, Mantzur, Farbstein, Howard
and even Winestone. There is nothing new under the sun.
Be assured that there are not a few Zohars around who
would like to deal with their Sorkis but don't know how or
are shit scared. Don't you think that doctors would love to
read such a book? People love to read about themselves.
Don't you think so?"

Heidi added a log to the fire. "But what about the lay public—would it interest them?"

"People read Clancy and love his technical jargon. They want to learn about his submarines and radar. People read John Grisham, too, pondering the intricacies of the court system and law. So why shouldn't they want an inside glimpse of the surgical world? Not the usual success stories, but a picture of the real world."

"I'm not convinced. You will lose credibility if you are too negative in portraying the local medical system. No one wants to hear that our doctors are not the best in the world." She looked at the sky. "I hope the sun will come out. At what point are you now? I mean chronologically."

"I'm writing about the present now, after my termination has been rescinded. I'm writing about the current skirmishes between Winestone and myself."

She took the laptop and reviewed my notes. Shaking her head, she put the laptop down and sighed. "I don't understand why you have to irritate Winestone. Can't you see that he's the only friend you have? Why do you have to fight so much?"

We looked up to see the mist lifting itself off the lake. I explained the situation to Heidi. "We are both to blame, I suppose," I began. "He is a one-man show, a captain who wants to navigate the ship into friendly waters and senses that I'm in his way. I may have been useful in eradicating Sorki, but in the post Sorki era I will be an obstacle. He may be preparing the grounds for sacrificing me as a scapegoat so that he can tell Howard, Farbstein and Sorki's friends, 'See? I got rid of Zohar. Now we can start again a peaceful and productive co-existence.' In his mind he probably thinks that he saved me."

"What are you going to do?"

"Nothing. Just wait and see."

"I noticed that you've been sending emails to Jane at *The New York Report.*"

"We chat a little. She has a keen interest in the medical scene in New York and wants to know about the hospital—so I tell her. She knows about Sorki and Mantzur but until the OPMC comes up with a decision she can't write anything. You know how journalists are. They ask many questions and offer nothing in return. We'll see."

▲▼◢◣▼▲

I had an emergency consult on the medical floor at twenty past seven that morning. The nursing station was crowded with physicians in suits running through their morning rounds before going to their offices. Many started at five thirty, rushing from hospital to hospital. A glimpse at one of their patients, a brief good morning, a superficial glance at the chart—no need to examine the patient as this would be done by the residents. And—and now to the most important task—entering the daily note. Medicare wants this to be substantial, reflecting a significant contribution to the patient's care. *No note—no money.* I looked at stressed physicians hysterically filling pages with notes no one will read, and if anyone wanted to, who could decipher the handwriting? *Is this modern medicine?*

A bunch of medical students were hanging around the station. "What's up guys? Cheer up. Aren't you enjoying your rotation in medicine?" They smiled back weakly. I don't blame them for being disenchanted and depressed. I entered a brief note in the patient's chart—*his acute abdomen is caused by a congested liver. He needs diuretics—not surgery.*

Seven fifty-five a.m. I rushed to the auditorium for the M&M. When I arrived, Dr. Mahmud Sorki was seated in the second row from the back with Radmunsen, the neurosurgeon, on his left and the former army General, Dr. Lungetti on his right.

The M&M handout said his case would be the third, starting in another thirty minutes. *The old woman decided to die immediately after his operation,* Sorki probably thought.

So what? She was sick. Susman asked him to perform the operation. He should have refused, but it was too late now. Sorki looked around. He wasn't expecting me to sit in the back, so he probably figured I was not attending. I could see his broad shoulders almost heaving with relief. Howard had more than likely told Sorki that the affection between Winestone and myself was fading away and that I was looking for another job.

The meeting started, and Bachus was moderating. He'd fly through his case and more than likely wouldn't go through details. Winestone hadn't arrived yet, probably to avoid frontal confrontations.

Sorki winked at Radmunsen. *"Allahu akbar,"* he muttered to reassure himself. "God is greatest." The recent events had rekindled in him the belief in Allah. Last Friday he had visited the Mosque for the first time in twenty-five years. *"Allahu akbar,"* he repeated to himself. "Allah will destroy those infidels." With Allah's help he'd overcome the OPMC and "these two Jews." Sorki smiled—amused by the thought that among the hundreds believers who knelt at the Mosque on Friday he was undoubtedly the only one who returned home to a bottle of Vodka. Allah accepted all his children.

I don't know what motivated me to sit so far back—just behind Sorki. He noticed me and seemed to be covering up his nervousness by joking and laughing with Radmunsen in loud tones. *What's he doing here?* he was probably thinking. *He never sits in the back. What's he up to?* I knew he couldn't stand having me just behind his back. Waiting for Sorki's case to be presented, I saw Winestone entering the hall.

The third case was a classical case in the Sorki mode presented by Jim Adams, our fourth year resident. He read from the handout. "Mrs. S. H., eighty-nine years old, was admitted for poorly controlled diabetes, severe respiratory and cardiac failure and arrhythmias. On admission she was disoriented—"

"—Susman's patient, a bedridden wreck," whispered a junior resident in my ear.

"On hospital day fourteen," Adams continued in a monotone voice, "due to the inability of the patient to tolerate any oral intake, she was scheduled for a percutaneous gastrostomy by the gastroenterological service. Seven minutes into the procedure it had to be terminated due to desaturation to seventy-eight percent and an arrhythmia." Adams paused as if waiting to be asked a guiding question by Bachus. None arrived so he continued: "The medical attending then requested an open gastrostomy. Four days later the patient was cleared by the primary medical attending, pulmonary attending and cardiology attending, for the procedure."

"What type of anesthesia was given?" asked Bachus.

"Epidural. The open gastrostomy was performed without difficulty. The patient was transferred to the recovery room and then discharged to the floor with PCO2 of sixty and saturation of ninety-two percent. Two hours later the resident was called because there was no tracing on the monitor. She was found unresponsive and in an asystole."

"What was her arterial blood gas prior to the operation?" asked Bachus, not looking up from the handout.

"Saturation was ninety-five percent, PCO2 was eighty-two."

Clearly she was in a respiratory failure when taken for this elective—and unnecessary—procedure. Let's see who'll dare to say anything.

Deep silence. Bachus looked around. "Dr. Winestone, any comments?"

The chairman stood up and cleared his throat. "In general I don't have an issue with the indication for gastrostomy in this case. But the timing was wrong. Gastrostomy is at best a semi-elective procedure. This patient was not in the best condition to undergo the procedure. I would have wanted to prepare her for the operation, to improve her respiratory status. Meanwhile I would have fed her via an alternative route—a nasogastric tube, for example."

"Any further comments?" asked Bachus. I was sure he wished it were over. "Anyone? Dr. Rubinstein?"

The retired Rubinstein was afraid of nobody. His words were clear to everyone: "I do not know what the hurry was. Why not feed her IV or place a feeding NG tube? It was a wrong time to operate. Gastrostomy was not necessary—not in a septic patient in respiratory failure."

"Nasogastric tube could not be passed. She had a large tongue!" exclaimed Sorki.

Rubinstein raised his voice. "Nonsense. If you can pass a scope, you can pass a tube."

"Dr. Rubinstein, why don't you switch on your hearing aid? I told you, NG tube would not go down."

Rubinstein was obstinate. "I do not accept this."

Sorki looked around. "You can accept or not but I'm telling you that this poor patient needed the gastrostomy to provide her with drugs, antibiotics, and nutrition."

"Dr. Sorki," said Rubinstein. "You could have placed a soft tiny feeding tube with the aid of an endoscope. You could have fed her via this tube and given her antibiotics."

"Three attending physicians cleared this patient for surgery and you tell us that she was not ready. Why didn't you invite the gastroenterologist to this meeting? He'll tell you that endoscopy would have been difficult. And where is the anesthetist who agreed to the operation?" Everyone could hear the anger in Sorki's voice. *Is he losing his self-control?* more than one person thought.

I walked to the aisle and raised my hand. Bachus ignored me, mumbling the closing words. I approached Sorki until I was two feet from him. Then I spoke up: "I have two questions to Dr. Sorki. First, I want to know how was the patient being fed during the fourteen days in the hospital prior to the operation? I see here that her pre-operative albumin was three point nine grams percent. She was not malnourished. And second, Dr. Sorki, why do you like to operate on patients who are already dead?"

Silence descended yet again. "Dr. Zohar, would you please repeat the last question?" said Bachus.

"I asked Dr. Sorki why he has made a habit of operating on patients who have already died. We know that this is not the first case."

Sorki shouted: "I don't agree to further discuss this case. This was not my case. I was asked to do a gastrostomy and I did. To discuss it properly we need to have the anesthetists and the referring physicians here!"

"Why do you always blame others?" I inquired loudly. Everyone in the auditorium heard me. "You were the surgeon. It was your responsibility. This is not the first time that you inserted gastrostomies in dead patients," I said. We were so near to each other—I was ready for a fist fight. Almost five years ago, when we first met each other in this auditorium, I knew that I had met my archenemy, my moral antidote. My nemesis. I'll bet he perceived it as well. Now our mutual loathing exploded. Sorki pointed at me and then pointed with his index finger at his brain. "He is crazy, absolutely crazy." He stood up and raised his hands, gesturing at his friends, and walked toward the doors of the auditorium.

"Why can't you have an open academic discussion for once?" I shouted at his back. "I asked you a question! Answer it. Tell us why you operated on this dead patient?"

Sorki's face twisted with contempt. "Ha!" he laughed. "An academician is what you are. An A-C-A-D-E-M-I-C-I-A-N." At the door he turned and spat out: "Why don't you report me also to the State for this case?"

"Good idea. Why not?" I took a deep breath. Finally, I had accused him of murder in public. I saw that the meeting had been disrupted. Surgeons standing in small groups were discussing the events. I heard a voice trying to control the situation. "This is unacceptable. This is not the way to address a colleague at the M&M meeting." Winestone exited the auditorium without looking at me. He was probably pissed off at me again.

I found them all in Winestone's office a bit later. Winestone was grave, and Bachus was pale. Winestone attacked me as soon as I entered. "Why? Why? Why did you do it? This was a grave mistake!"

I shrugged. "Well, he operates on dead patients, no? So I asked him why. Big deal. What's the problem?"

"No, no, no!" he shouted. "This is a big problem, Zohar. I can't protect you if you continue this way. You can't be emotional at the M&M. Scientific, yes—emotional, no!"

"Dr. Winestone," I blurted. "I can't be emotional? I have no permission from the chairman to be human? Please forgive me, but I suffer from an unfortunate psychological disturbance. I become emotional when observing how patients are being killed at a rate of greater than one per week."

"Bashir," Winestone urged, "talk to him, explain to him. Make him understand."

Chaudri spoke instead. "Marc, the private surgeons are very upset. Forget about Sorki's friends. I'm talking about the guys who wrote letters to Howard calling on him to rescind your termination. Even your buddy Garibaldi who cooks pasta for you said that what you did today is unacceptable. Marc, the private guys are afraid of you. Each of them has a few skeletons in his closet. As they watched you attacking Sorki each of them was thinking, 'This is not an unusual case, I did a few gastrostomies on dying patients, everybody does,' and then they think you are crazy and after you do Sorki you may turn your fury on them. So now they are definitely against you. They wish you would leave this hospital. You are a threat to them."

"Chaudri is absolutely right." Winestone wanted to share his wisdom with me now. "While Sorki is being dealt with by the OPMC you grant him an aura of martyrdom. A grave error."

"Well, Dr. Winestone," I sneered, "you are the chairman, and you should have stopped him doing what he does long time ago. But at the meeting today you were just sitting there looking at your shoes and then standing up to say you don't have a problem with the indication. He does these things again and again and no one opens his mouth—so I have to do this. But I am fed up. I am not going to play your games anymore. Want me to leave? Fire me now. I want to be fired."

In Winestone's blank eyes I could see that I'd exhausted my usefulness to him. More than that, I was a burden. When I closed the door behind me I heard him saying to Bachus: "Did you see the deep scratch in my Porsche? On the Island they wanted eleven hundred bucks to fix it. I went to the Palestinian on Atlantic Avenue. He did it for five hundred and fifty dollars." I didn't need to see the Chairman's face to know it glowed in self satisfaction when he recounted the story.

Each of us had a role in Winestone's puppet theatre. Each of us played a different marionette. Rusk—the only US-born one among us—functioned as a foreign minister. Chaudri was the spy and the advisor on local psychology. Bachus was the boy for all purposes—taking the Boss's night and weekend calls and offering an ear for his repetitive car talk. What about me? My task was to liquidate Sorki, but my fire now threatened too many bystanders. It had become so uncontrolled that it may have even endangered the Boss himself. My role as Winestone's marionette was over. It had been over for a long time.

Back in my office, I changed to scrubs and climbed into my white Swedish OR clogs. As always, my father smiled at me from his portrait on the wall. I looked at him and an idea struck me: *Why shouldn't I save Sorki? I am out of here, so let me help him to survive—let him live. Let them all kill each other.*

22

The Beginning of the End

Those who speak the truth are regarded with fear and aversion. Abuses accumulate...Ignorant neglect is tolerated in some, the best effort is censured in others...There is an outward appearance of the highest efficiency, when in reality the institution is a whited sepulcher...No man is appointed to the staff purely for fitness, but personal reasons sway the result. On one side we see the suffering poor, on the other the foul and loathsome rule of the system...If I had my way, I'd strike that thrice accursed system dead.
—Chalmers Da Costa, 1863-1933

November 2000—May 2001.

Espresso tastes best after an operation. Sorki emptied the small porcelain cup and shouted: "Kate, another espresso!" He snuggled and stretched in his new leather chair. When he moved to the new Medical Board suite he ordered the largest desk and chair available in New York City. He looked around. Even Howard's office was smaller. *Screw Howard. The Irish man was still scared of him now that—finally—he was busy getting rid of Zohar.* At last Howard forced the Executive Committee to censure Zohar for his outrageous show at the M&M, and Winestone did not dare to utter a word. Even Winestone was getting tired of Zohar. *But eventually Winestone would be unprotected, like the Shah without American support and condemned to a lonely death in Egypt or—in Winestone's case—on the Island.* Another espresso arrived.

"Thanks, Kate. Your espresso is fantastic."

It was more than a year since that stupid operation on her daughter's breast. *Is her breast developing a deformity?* He didn't dare ask. He emptied the second espresso in one gulp, throwing the hot bitter fluid into his throat like a shot of vodka. It was ten a.m. and he was thinking about vodka. *"Allahu akbar,"* he muttered. *"Allahu akbar."* He had to be careful. He muttered too much.

Susman noticed it. The day before he'd said, "Hey Mo, what the fuck are you mumbling there?" People did not understand, but Allah gave him the strength to persevere, to push on as usual—as if all he achieved and fought for was not melting away. He removed a nail file from his drawer— better to file than bite them, and it helped with the thought process. *Allahu akbar. What to do with Zohar's proposition? This is unbelievable. Zohar claims he could provide information that may change the course of events at the OPMC hearings. He refuses to disclose details or motives and asks to meet face to face with Sorki and his lawyers. Howard said that a black cat passed between Winestone and Zohar. Was that Zohar's motive? Or perhaps he wants to extract money? Jews are always after money—even the Koran says so. When was the last time he looked at this holy book? How could Zohar possibly help him? Surely he knows everything about Winestone. That is how he kept Winestone in his pocket until now. But something has happened. What?*

"Dr. Sorki," Kate buzzed through the intercom. "The OR just called. Your next gastroplasty is on the table. Five minutes to go." Sorki put the nail file away and massaged his eyes and forehead in an effort to relieve the dull headache boring his skull since he woke up. He hadn't slept much since his lawyer called. Sorki was thinking about what to do with Zohar's offer. His wife believed it was a plot—a trap. "Mo," she said. "How can you believe that a Jew will help you in order to screw a fellow Jew? Can't you see that they are conspiring against you? Even the state prosecutor employed by the OPMC is Jewish."

"And what about Farbstein? He would auction his family for a few grand. Zohar too may want to sell Winestone for a few green bank notes. Why not?"

"I don't think so. Zohar is a zealot—a psychopathic zealot. I saw him once at a dinner party. He reminds me of those Catholic monks who taught at our church school. He is not the type who suddenly changes his direction for a few bucks. I warn you—no deals with him. We can manage even if you lose your license for a year or two. You could practice in Teheran—they adore you there."

Sorki put his green cap on his head and started walking toward the OR. His wife was right. She was always right. That's why he married her. She was bony, cold to the point of frigidity, but her Italian shrewdness compensated.

"Hello Dr. Sorki," people called out to him as he walked by nursing stations, patient rooms and down the corridor. "How you doin'?" he returned with a smile and a polite nod. Here and there he stopped and hugged an orderly or a floor cleaner. "Hello Uncle Joe, how you doin'?" He was hugely popular and he knew it. This was his hospital, and the people adored him and respected him. *Yes, it is my fucking hospital!* he thought.

They believed in his leadership and rightness. He had to fight on. He'd lose with a smile on his face like a proud martyr. *No deals with Zohar. Whatever will be will be, and yes, with Allah's help, I'll come back. They'll see. Allahu akbar.*

Sorki entered the OR and stopped at the scheduling desk. "Enjoyed the cake?" he asked the secretaries. His wife baked a cake for them each week.

Dr. Rao, a third year resident approached him. Sorki fumed. A few years ago it was always a chief resident, last year a fourth year and now—a lowly junior. He clapped the resident's shoulder. Nice guy, Indian—from the North, just a few fingers on the map from the old country.

"Dr. Rao, are you ready for the magic? I bet you could not sleep last night. Man, you are going to watch the greatest gastroplasty surgeon in the State of New York. Let's scrub."

"Dr. Sorki, there is a small problem which I wanted to discuss with you before we start," said the resident cau-

276

tiously. "An ultrasound report mentions a large anterior abdominal mass."

Sorki brought his heavy, hairy arm around the resident's neck. "Don't worry. When you're operating with me you mustn't worry. Forget about the fucking ultrasound. The woman who reported it is a virgin. Today you're scrubbing with Sorki. You'll learn that I can deal with any unexpected abdominal findings—with anything. Just scrub and leave the rest to me—the virgin and all."

▲▼▲▲▼▲

"Is this line secure?" said my lawyer Bill Rothman. "I hate to call you at the hospital."

"Yes, Bill, I hope so. This is not my private line." I looked at my watch. Talking to Rothman meant money for every minute. Divide $400 by 60—a minute costs $6.66. Heidi moaned that I worked only to pay off my debt to my lawyer. In this city, however, you are dead without a good lawyer.

"Dr. Zohar, you have to move to Manhattan ASAP. We are negotiating your contract. Now about your hospital. We drafted a petition to the Public Health Council of the State. We faxed you the first part, you know—the events that led to your censure, the background. So let me now read to you the final parts:

> Despite these requests and without further notice to Dr. Zohar, on October 24, 2000, the Hospital's Medical Executive Committee met and conducted a hearing and deliberation upon Dr. Sorki's complaint. They then voted that Dr. Zohar's criticism of Dr. Sorki at the morbidity and mortality conference was "misconduct" and formally censured him for that criticism. Dr. Sorki participated in the meeting both as complaining party and committee member. Neither the Chairman of his Department, Dr. Winestone, nor Dr. Zohar was present.

A major basis for the censure was a statement made at the meeting by the President of the Hospital, John Howard, who noted that, unlike many of the attending physicians, Dr. Zohar was a hospital employee and thus subject to the hospital's power to hire and fire. He requested for a ruling that would result in Dr. Zohar's firing "in such a way that the hospital is not hurt." A censure by the Executive Committee, issued from its professional perspective rather than an employer-employee perspective, would "have a lot of weight in the way we view it administratively...

In other words a censure would serve as a justification for the president, as a non-medical administrator, to fire Dr. Zohar in the near future while defusing the kind of departmental and faculty resistance that had arisen the last time the hospital had attempted to discharge a troublemaker.

During the meeting several participants questioned the issuing of a censure without allowing Dr. Zohar or Winestone to be heard. "It would be called a kangaroo court," one Committee member argued. "These individuals should be given opportunity to speak!"

"Why didn't you mention that none of the other distinguished members of the committee—the bread, salt and cream of the hospital—dared to open their mouths and ask why I attacked Sorki? They all sat there as dummies—Sorki's dummies."

"Let me continue."

Dr. Samir, the Committee Chairman, suggested in response that Dr. Zohar would have a right of appeal. But Mr. Howard, the President of the Hospital disagreed. There was no need for due process and certainly no right of appeal because, in his view, "censuring is not an appealable action." Besides that, Howard continued, pursuing legalisms would be a "waste of everyone's time with no different conclusion." At the end of the process it was still going to come back to an employer/ employee situation. Dr. Zohar was employed by the hospital. The change would come relative to his status through that employment equation.

In short, according to the President of the Hospital, the entire purpose of the censure was to set in motion the termination of Dr. Zohar's employment. It was a first step from the medical side of the hospital and would be picked up in due course by the administrative side, which could then fire Dr. Zohar for supposed "misconduct." In the meantime, the hospital could deny Dr. Zohar any opportunity to be heard on an appeal of the censure by claiming it did not affect his privileges.

At this point Dr. Zohar complains to the Public Health Council that the Hospital's censure on him constitutes the kind of 'improper conduct' that is barred by Public Health Law §2801(b). The censure is a tactic aimed at justifying the termination of Dr. Zohar's employment without an opportunity to be heard and without any right of appeal. Such conduct tarnishes Dr. Zohar's record of professional employment and diminishes his privileges within the hospital (no matter how much the hospital's administration may deny it).

"Bill, this is very nice and well written, but what about the money? Who'll reimburse me for your fees?"

"When we file the complaint they'll eventually agree to settle and pay your damages," he said with satisfaction.

"I don't know," I said cautiously. "It seems to me that Winestone and Howard are not worried by my threats."

"They are bluffing," Rothman assured me. "They've been bluffing all their lives, manipulating people and doing wrong. They are used to being threatened and living in constant conflict. They take your threats seriously but play it cool."

"Now that I know that I am going and they won't pay very much, should I start to destroy them? Is it time to go to the media?"

I heard him chuckle on the other end of the line. "What would Marc Zohar gain from slowly destroying the famous Park Hospital? Half of its doctors are marginal, but by destroying them the best you can do is perhaps save a few patients and gain nothing personally. You might even just destroy yourself."

God, how bloody calculated are those top lawyers! Everything was translated in money value. One thought I'm sure hadn't occurred to them was that I'd get a lot more enjoyment from revenge then I would out of a year's salary. I would gladly give up a new Jaguar for an old Ford to have the pleasure of seeing our enemies annihilated. For that bittersweet feeling of revenge. To see the surgical mafia at the Park crumble into the depths of non-existence. I wanted to destroy them! To see them burn in hell.

Whoa, I thought. *Take it easy.*

"Dr. Zohar," Bill continued, oblivious to my dark thoughts. "One more question. The other hospital, the one you are heading for. Is it OK? Have you checked it out thoroughly?"

"I think so. It seems OK to me. It's not exactly the Mayo Clinic, but OK. Why do you ask?"

"Because I don't want you to go there and start another crusade," William Rothman said. He sounded amused. For some reason I liked the man who, despite charging $6.66 a minute to talk to me, made me feel grateful for talking to him at all. That was double the current rates for sex phone.

▲▼▲▲▼▲

"Dr. Zohar, how nice of you to come up. Do sit down." Behind his immense desk, Howard's gigantic stature shrank to a normal size. I looked around his huge office; it was much bigger than Farbstein's a floor below—which, in turn, was larger than Winestone's, three floors down. I noticed golf trophies and group pictures on all walls.

"You are a golfer, Mr. Howard?"

"Since the age of thirty-five. The best anti-stress remedy one can find." He smiled at me. "You should start now. Never too late."

"I could use it," I admitted lamely.

Howard leaned across the desk. "What's up? What do we need to discuss?"

"Well," I began. "As you know, I am the problem-maker, the 'virus,' some call me." I used fingers on both hands to emphasize the quotations. "If this is the case, I thought perhaps I should be leaving, so I came to discuss this with you again. Do you remember what I said the last time? You never got back to me."

"Yes, you are a good man," Howard said. "You're a good writer, a good researcher, you have an excellent future—"

"—And a good surgeon."

"Yes, absolutely. Dr. Winestone tells me that Dr. Gershon in Manhattan's Village Hospital wants you badly. They are very short of people of your caliber. Dr. Winestone told me that he has highly recommended you to Gershon."

"Oh sure. Dr. Winestone wants to get rid of me. Another reason to leave."

"What better way to get a glowing recommendation!" Howard allowed himself a throaty chuckle. "I thought you and Winestone were buddies. Am I wrong?"

We were at one time, I thought.

Howard sighed. "So when do you want to leave? Next month?" He obviously didn't care about what passed between Winestone and myself. "You don't want to hang around too long. You don't want to raise your flags, waiting for the outcome, do you?"

"No, I don't need to hang around. I know that Sorki will eventually collapse. Do not forget that it was Winestone and myself who sold him to the State. And I was the one who reported Mantzur; you must thank me for this, Mr. Howard. I did a great favor to you and the hospital."

Howard grimaced, but then appeared to ignore my comment. "When are you thinking of leaving?"

"I don't know yet. I'm still negotiating a contract. June or July. I'll let you know."

"Great. I like your openness and your decision to go to a hospital that really needs you. I might add it lacks the political background of this place so you'll be more at home there. The Park is special, you know. Dr. Winestone doesn't understand that this is not his old Jewish Island Hospital." Howard leaned back in his chair. "It's a very special place. It's the third major hospital in my career. When I was second in command at Short Island we had a few problem surgeons there. One must learn to deal with it and live with it. Morals and ethics have no business in hospital surgical departments. Ten years ago when I came here I knew that a hospital like this could either grow or regress to the size and stature of, say, Victory Cross Hospital. So I pushed it up. I knew that wars such as we have now would be inevitable. People such as Sorki and Mantzur arrived from far away and then trained locally to become the leading local professionals. Those were the people I had to work with, to rely on, but they were only interested in money, not education."

Why is he telling me all this? Is he trying to justify himself to me? Why now? For almost five years he totally ignored me, then tried to destroy me, and now he was talking to me as if we were buddies.

Howard looked at the ceiling and carried on as if talking to himself. "Yes, they became the local top knives. I knew that when I brought people such as Winestone or yourself there would be struggles."

So now he is the one who brought me. Sure. My look of disagreement turned into a smile when I considered how

282

hopeless my situation was. Nobody understood what was really going on here. Or, I reconsidered, everyone but me understands!

Howard bent forward again. He didn't like my smile. "I'm not kidding," he said. "This is serious. I know Sorki has problems, but he's a good man and a good surgeon. Yes he made mistakes. He should have recognized that Winestone is the chairman and cooperate. Sorki has some problems with his judgment. If he'd asked Winestone for advice we could have prevented the whole mess."

He looked at me, and I saw a glimpse of kindness in his blue eyes. "And you, Dr. Zohar, you were also mistaken. Yes," he reiterated. "Even you made mistakes. You had a point, but there was no need to take the dirty laundry outside. You could've come to me. I wish we'd had an open communications channel between us."

So why the bullshit?" I imagined myself saying. *"You are profiting on the back of these criminals. You have confused me with one of the local rats you hire for peanuts and fire without compensation. You didn't realize that I'm a bigger sociopath than you are—and unpredictable!*

Instead, I chose diplomatic channels. "But Mr. Howard, you are an administrator, not an M.D. Wasn't it Dr. Farbstein's role to monitor the practice of Sorki and Mantzur, to see that matters don't deteriorate to such an extent. Don't blame yourself, blame Farbstein!"

No reply.

I continued: "You know that Farbstein actively supported Sorki all the way. Didn't he know what kind of practice he and his cronies conduct?

Howard proceeded with his monologue, again ignoring me. *Some open channel!* "It is sad for me to see how the OPMC treats this hospital. At Sorki's hearings the prosecutor made fun of his referring physicians. Sorki didn't use to enter any notes in the charts—all notes were entered by the referring physicians. But they don't understand surgery. They sent the patients for operation with the best intention. Why blame them? There are seven hundred good doctors in this hospital—why blame them for the sins of a few? I admit, they are not interested in academics, they are not as well read as yourself or Dr. Winestone—."

"Interested, yes, but only in money—"

"—What's that?"

"I said that they do what they do for money only." *As you do.*

"Dr. Zohar," he said with finality. "You can stop working now and we'll pay you until July." His lecture was finished. Now it was back to business.

You cheap bastard, you make a million a year and want to pay me off with a few bucks.

"Mr. Howard, do you remember what I asked for?"

He looked at his notes. "Yes, we agree to fully vest your pension fund. You'll be able to take it with you. No need to pay any tax." He scribbled this down.

"Then I would like severance pay equivalent to at least three years' salary."

Howard raised both hands in disgust. "An employee who resigns is not entitled to a severance fee. You know that."

"I do. But I'm not just an employee. I may decide not to leave on my own. I told Dr. Winestone that it would be better for me if he fires me. I could sue him then."

"You don't want to sue him. It could take years."

"Of course I don't want to sue him or anybody else. But I've worked here for five years and all was not well. You know the history. By the way, did you have a chance to glance at the draft of the petition my lawyer is preparing?"

"Yes."

"Tell me why Winestone suddenly decided in 1998 that Sorki is such an awful surgeon. Wasn't he just as awful in 1995, 1996 and 1997? And what about Mantzur? Why did Winestone try to save him all those years? Considering the amount of turbulence I've saved the hospital in the future by eliminating those two murderers, don't you understand why I feel I deserve the golden handshake?"

Howard smiled. "Dr. Zohar, do you think I'm an heir to the Rothschilds? This is a non-profit city hospital in Brooklyn, New York. We do not have generous sums of money! Here's what I can do for you. Leave now and we will pay you for the next six months with benefits."

You're not getting this, are you Howard? Am I corruptible? Sure I am—as is anybody else—but only for huge sums of money.

Howard could buy me for a three year-salary because it would make me financially independent of the organized medical crime system. I could educate my kids and do what I wished. But I couldn't be corrupted for peanuts. I was a psychopath as Howard was, but of a different kind—one he had never encountered before. I was a medical vigilante. Sorki was correct.

I'm a virus.

Howard was waiting for my reply. My silence unnerved him. "OK, this is a final deal," he said. "You stay with us until the day you start in Manhattan. We continue paying you a full salary for six months after you leave. It's a lot of money, you know. We never do such things, and we must not advertise it like the Firestone balloon."

I nodded to indicate understanding but said nothing. Howard goes on. "So we have to draft a termination agreement—."

"—No, I'm not being terminated, I'm resigning."

"Whatever. In addition, we'll have you sign a small non-disclosure document. The standard."

"I'll have to show it to my lawyers."

"Of course." He paused. "You don't want to go to the media. We are going to support you with the best references wherever you go. Your only enemy here would be Sorki, perhaps, but otherwise you can leave without a grudge against anybody." He stood up and walked me to the door. "I am glad you didn't bring up one of your cigars," he said. "I miss smoking so much."

A firm handshake. I knew he'd immediately call Sorki to announce the big news. "Hey Mo," he'd say. "I got rid of Zohar for you."

I descended the few floors to our department. Winestone's office was open, and I heard Thea calling: "Dr. Winestone, Mr. Howard for you on the phone."

▲▼▲▲▼▲

Carducci sounded warm and friendly instead of defensive as he had the last time. "How are you Marc?" he asked. "What's up?"

"Did you get my recent fax?

"Yes. Thank you. We are working on it."

"I've heard that for almost two years. While you guys are 'working on it,' our friend continues damaging patients. The last case is criminal—he takes a fat lady for a gastroplasty, opens the abdomen and finds a large mass. He knows that there would be a mass because the resident tells him so before the operation, based on the ultrasound study. So he removes the mass together with a piece of omentum but doesn't send it for a frozen section. He doesn't even put his hand into the pelvis to see if perhaps the source of this mass is in the ovaries. He doesn't feel the liver to find out whether there are additional metastases. No, our friend doesn't do what any reasonable surgeon would do. He simply continues with the gastroplasty. And—as you know—the pathological report of the mass describes a metastatic adenocarcinoma. So now we are left with a patient who is doomed to die. She will need another laparotomy perhaps. Think about chemotherapy in a patient who can't vomit. It's difficult to vomit after a gastroplasty."

"Marc, we know," Carducci tried to assure me, although there was no sense of any real urgency in his voice. *It was just business as usual: Some poor fat woman was riddled with cancer and was probably going to die. Big deal.* "We read your fax. May I advise you to keep your head down. You did enough. Now leave it to us."

"The guy is crazy, keeping up with what he does while undergoing hearings by the OPMC. Why don't you suspend him immediately?"

"We are working on it, Marc."

"What about our second friend?"

"Mantzur?"

"Who else?"

"He is busy surrendering his license. I hear that someone in your hospital offered him an administrative job." Carducci sounded disgusted at that. Perhaps he wasn't callous after all. "Take care and good luck."

What did he mean by "Keep your head down"? Why did he say so? Perhaps he suspected that I was responsible for the recent *New York Report* article by Jane Rosenberg. It appeared on the first page: "Doctors punished by State but prized at the hospital; seventy-five percent quickly resume working." Everybody was talking about it. I am sure that what hit Howard and Farbstein the most was the following paragraph:

> According to data from the State Health Department, New York Park Hospital has more doctors who have been disciplined or investigated for negligence than does any other major hospital in the city…
>
> Two surgeons are now under investigation by the Health Department. One is the president of the hospital's Medical Board.

Did Carducci worry that the next article would criticize the OPMC for procrastination?

"You've got mail!" my PC announced. Email from Daniel. The message was jumbled. It read something like this:

Once you approach Sorki' s lawyers, the game is out of your hands. You may think you want to say X, but you are not their client. They will get you on the witness stand unprotected, and they will twist and turn your testimony until you will not recognize it yourself, producing not X or even Y but Z. You are wrong if you think that without cover of your own bunch of lawyers you can control the situation. Once you started talking to Howard about leaving, they are in familiar territory. You're another "disgruntled employee." Many people resign seeking extra monetary compensation or revenge believing they have enough evidence to cause trouble. The administrator deals with this situation based on what he learned in Management 101. You always say, No, just as the government always ignores the requests of terrorists. He knows that if you say Yes, you are a target for every employee who decides to extort money when he or she goes away. The worst damage you can do is to trigger a big scandal with a short half-life. The worst scandal is forgotten within three or four days. By the time the scandal blows by, with accusations and counter-accusations involving press agents and people hired to mitigate the effects of the scandal, nobody remembers the original reason.

The other side also has defenses. They can start an immediate lawsuit against you. The underlying basis can be ridiculous, but it will force you to pay large attorney fees until you face financial ruin. They can sue you time after time to engage you in an endless legal battle that will consume your time and resources...

I knew all of this. Besides, Sorki's lawyers didn't get back to me. *Let's forget about it. Why is everybody a prophet of doom?* Regardless, I had to force myself not to delete the message. I read on.

…Whenever you make a move, sit down and think not only about the scenario that you wish would happen, but also about other scenarios that may happen. They may not be as scared as you think. I cannot give you specific advice, but in the situation you are in, assuming you have decided to move to the Manhattan hospital, there is value in ending things well with Winestone. If for some reason things do not work out well for you at the Village Hospital and you begin looking for another job, you will need his support. Besides, your next hospital will come back to Winestone for information about you before they give you privileges. Go to the Manhattan as you've decided. But don't burn everything behind you when you leave. Ending well, as opposed to ending badly, has value.

Daniel

Great preacher. Beautiful. Real words of wisdom. But each of us has a different set of inborn and acquired values and temperament. If I would be what you want me to be—my dear friend, Daniel—I would be an established Chairman of Surgery and not a refugee knocking on the door of a less than average hospital in Manhattan. If I had followed your advice I would be sitting at this moment drinking champagne with Winestone, Mantzur and perhaps even big Mo.

"Dr. Zohar, Dr. Zohar, please go immediately to the ER. Dr. Zohar go to the ER."

That stupid public address system. What now? Probably some brain-dead corpse undergoing an experimental and futile thoracotomy by the ER residents. Cracking open chests of dead patients. Educated by ER on TV! I entered the elevator and made sure I was alone before I kicked the wall.

"Adams is busy with a stabbed heart," said a blonde ER resident, pointing with manicured index finger toward the closed door of the trauma room.

A huge man was lying on the trauma table, barefoot, his underwear soaked with urine and feces. His hands were tied to the table side bars, his chest was open and dripping blood. At the head of the table, Jacobs—a junior resident—was bagging oxygen into the endotracheal tube. An ER resident was squeezing the Ringer's lactate infusion bag.

Adams's gloved hands probed deeply into the patient's chest, his scrubs splashed with blood. He turned his head to me and announced: "Knife injury to the left of the sternum. Arrested on arrival. Had to crack his chest before calling you." He continued to squeeze the heart rhythmically with his right hand. *Probably a waste of time.*

"His pupils are reacting," Jacobs said anxiously. Some oxygenated blood, at least, was reaching the victim's brain. The EKG traced a coarse ventricular rhythm. We didn't have much time left.

I reached for a pair of gloves.

Who is not familiar with the twilight of life in a slowly dying patient? Delirium, blurred vision, loss of sphincter control, and the air's typical fetor announces the beginning of the end. Then there's the tiny event that triggers the cessation of life. The sweet old lady lying in the ICU after a myocardial infarction suddenly needs to move her bowel, and her heart stops. The man recovering after a laparotomy who—no one knows why—suddenly grows excited and then collapses from a massive pulmonary embolism. One remembers those cases. Their faces are so clear, but their names forgotten.

It is said that every surgeon carries with him a little cemetery. But we are haunted most by the patients whose deaths we carry responsibility for. Like that middle-aged executive, hemorrhaging like a tap from esophageal varices, slowly fading while the esophageal balloon just won't go down. Could you have operated and saved his life? Yes, you know now. And the teenager on the ventilator, her muscles paralyzed. You were a junior resident then, and you practically executed her by botching a tracheostomy. And the Russian man, fifty-something, with a carcinoma of the stomach. By mistake, you ligated the main artery that supplies the intestine. Eventually the entire bowel necrotized. He, conscious until the end, watched you calmly with his febrile eyes. He would have died anyway, you told yourself. But it didn't help. And the car dealer whose vena cava you damaged while repairing a triple A. He bled and bled; you opened him three times; he still died. Then the white, ashen body expired and multiple pairs of eyes focused on you with sympathy, indifference, cynicism, sometimes reproach. You were exhausted, you wanted to escape, lie down and close your eyes, but the family waited beyond the doors and you were so lonely. Errors occur. Shit happens. It was never negligence, only unfortunate errors.

Hands gloved, I took my place opposite Adams, pushing his hand away from the hole in the heart—replacing his index finger with my own to dam the flood rushing through the heart's wall. Now Adams was suturing the hole under my finger.

"Careful," I hissed. "Jim, be careful. Don't take the coronary in your bite."

Jacobs administered O-negative blood. The wound was almost closed, the empty organ filling with blood. A few more squeezes of Adams's hand and the heart resumed its beat, the EKG tracing nearing normal...

Then, the unbelievable happened:

The man woke up. His dirty hands free, because of loosely tied knots, groped for his chest. The oily stained nails—he must have been a mechanic—reached for the excruciating pain. His large hand penetrated the open wound and almost enveloped the heart.

"Fuck!" I yelled out in astonishment and horror. "Give him twenty milligrams of morphine, now!" Our huge patient stirred, sat up on the table and grabbed for the retractor spreading his ribs. The sutures began to gape. Blood splashed my glasses.

"Jump on him!" I hollered. Everyone was on the move, but nobody seemed to know what to do. Hell, even I was working purely on instinct. "Move your ass!" I screamed at the small group of ER residents. Four of them leaped on the patient forcing him down. We knocked him out with a round-house punch of morphine. My sweat poured directly onto the exposed heart, my necktie hung into the open chest. I tightened the suture, put in a few more stitches and tied the final knot. "OK, wheel him to the OR, we'll need to clean the entire mess and close him up." I turned to Adams. "And give him some antibiotics. Look at all the shit on his fingers."

"Systolic one hundred, sinus rhythm, pupils reacting," reported Jacobs in the background.

"Great," I said. "Another life saved." I discarded the stained gloves and washed my hands at the sink. Looking at the mirror I noticed blood on my glasses and forehead. When I was a small boy I once saw my father removing his trousers, exposing a large red stain on his underwear. "It's from the operation," he explained. "He bled like a pig—soaking everything."

I was impressed then, and even more so now that I knew the feeling. To be a real man you must soak in your patient's blood when necessary. I rinsed my glasses. I've done lots of stabbed hearts, but I've never had a patient grabbing his own heart with his filthy hands. I followed Adams and Jacobs to the OR. *Gee, how tiny is the span between life and death.* I felt goose bumps on my back. *How satisfying is life-saving surgery when we have to deal with so much crap?*

▲▼◢▲▼▲

Through the open door of our library I could see Wine-stone in council with Chaudri, Bachus and Rusk. The oblique afternoon sun almost blinded me when I entered. I blinked. "What's up? Why is everyone so serious?"

"Dr. Winestone has been invited to appear at Sorki's hearing," said Rusk.

I joined them at the table even though the chairman would probably rather I had not arrived. "What's the big deal? Is it customary that the OPMC invites the chairperson of the department."

"Not the OPMC," explained Chaudri in his new capacity as Winestone's right-hand man. "Sorki's lawyers invited Dr. Winestone."

"Dr. Winestone," I said, trying not to smile. "They will fry you!"

"I know." He was not amused.

I saw an opportunity to dig at him. Naturally, I grabbed a shovel. "You want to know what Sorki's lawyers will ask you? They'll say, 'Dr. Winestone, you have known Sorki since 1994. Why did you wait five years to report him? Were his cases kosher until now? And was it actually you who reported him? And if not why weren't you the one who reported him if his practice was as awful as you claim it was."

Winestone avoided eye contact. "No problem," he said. "It's a trend, a pattern. I will emphasize the trend. One or two complications are OK, but over the years I was able to see the trend. One needs time to comprehend a surgeon's pattern of practice."

"Dr. Winestone, the State, the OPMC don't care about trends or patterns. They care about individual cases."

"I care about the trend. It doesn't matter to me what the State wants or cares about." *As obstinate as ever.*

Rusk looked at his watch. It was four p.m.—time to go home.

"You know what?" I continued. "They'll also say, 'Look at this case from 1995 which you reported to the State in 1999? How come it was presented at the M&M and passed as 'appropriate?' You chaired the meeting, eh? Who signed the minutes that described the treatment of the case as appropriate?"

Winestone said nothing. Rusk was seething. Would he explode? No. Rusk was responsible for the M&M minutes but was only following orders based on Winestone's political agenda of the day.

I continued. "To save Sorki's ass they may also mention Mantzur's cases. 'Why, Dr. Winestone, didn't you report Mantzur—whose practice has been as awful as Sorki's, if not worse? Is it because Sorki competed with you on those morbid obesity cases?'"

Winestone's thick lips closed tight. I think he was brooding. *He must hate me now. I'm digging at him in front of the others.* I carried on, disregarding his discomfort. "Surely they'll try to show that all of this is a personal vendetta by you against Sorki. The big chairman wants to destroy a poor private surgeon. That is how they could paint it—or how I would have painted it if asked for advice by Sorki's gang."

"Dr. Winestone, before appearing you have to talk to a lawyer," Rusk said.

"I'll be represented by hospital lawyers."

Sure. When the chairman is in trouble he's supported by the hospital's legal system. And I—I am forced to defend myself out of my own pocket. That irritated me. "Dr. Winestone, if I were you I wouldn't trust the hospital lawyers. Remember how well they helped you with the Sudkumar affair. I could arrange a discount from my lawyer—Rothman. You know him?"

The others laughed. Even Rusk allowed himself a giggle. Winestone stood up. "I have to pick up my car from the garage."

"What's the matter with it?" Bachus asked, anxious to change the subject.

"One of the rear lights—you know how much they charged me? Twelve hundred bucks! Not covered by insurance." Winestone disappeared around the corner and the meeting was dismissed soon after.

In the corridor Chaudri asked, "Marc, why did you dig at him?"

"Salman, for five years I fought on his side, but now all he wants is to save his own thick skin. He has dumped me. He functions now as Howard's expert on Zohar—helping him to save a few cents as in 'Zohar will leave anyway, why should you pay him? At the end he'll be forced to agree to a few peanuts.'"

Chaudri twirled the cap of a ballpoint pen in his hand. "This is becoming more and more interesting. Like in a soap opera, things become dirty towards the end. By the way, are you still working on your novel? Is there any sex in it?" I laughed, but shook my head. We made small talk for a few more minutes before heading in different directions.

As he left I realized that out of all of us Chaudri was the only one whose situation—both politically and financially—had improved during those turbulent years. And significantly. *Is my best buddy in the Park Hospital a double agent?*

▲▼◢▲▼▲

In the mid morning hours Time Square appeared surprisingly calm, although I had nothing to compare it with. During my five years in New York City I never visited the Square at night. I walked westward to Forty-Third and entered the vast lobby of *The New York Report*. I picked up one of the black phones near the security desk and dialed Jane's extension.

"Dr. Zohar?" she said. "You're on time." She sounded surprised. A young voice. I'd never talked with her except through extensive email correspondence over the last year. "Let's meet at the cafeteria on the seventh floor," she said. "My cubicle is too small. I'll clear you with Security. Please take the elevator to seventh floor."

The elevator was intercepted on the third floor by a young woman. "Dr. Zohar?" she said, showing me a faint smile. "I'm Jane Rosenberg."

This is the famous health reporter for The New York Report? The ride the rest of the way to the seventh floor gave

295

me enough time to scrutinize her. She seemed to be in her early thirties. She was wearing expensive Italian high-heeled shoes, a modest green patterned skirt and a matching blazer. I was sure she was a New York Jewess. Definitely upper middle class.

The elevator discharged us into a huge cafeteria. Journalists sat around in groups engaged in lively discussions. So this was the premiere newspaper in the world?

"Seems that this is your newsroom, eh?"

She didn't smile back but pointed at a large empty table. "Let's sit here. Plenty of space to spread all the paper you're carrying with you."

"Any coffee?" I nodded towards the counter.

"Sure. This direction."

"I'll pay."

Ms.—*or is she a Mrs.?*—Rosenberg pulled out a tiny notebook. "OK," she said, "let's see what you've got. The issue is unnecessary operations, correct? Mainly in elderly patients."

I emptied my leather bag on the table. "I have everything you want to know about these two guys—a folder for each. Everything is here, including all the cases that are being investigated by the OPMC."

"Do you have hospital numbers? Record numbers? We could run them through our computers. We have access to their billing systems."

"Jane, billing is a minor issue here. The concern is the fact that the system allowed two surgeons to abuse it, to milk it, harming patients and, even killing them for years."

"Show me a few examples. Take me through a few cases—use laymen's terms."

Patiently I described a few of Mantzur's vascular exterminations and Sorki's patients' faithful expeditions to the other world. She shook her head in disbelief. "And you have other cases?"

"Tons. Look at these files. Copy anything you wish. Another major issue is that while these two guys—by the way"—I allowed myself a wicked smile—"we nicknamed them Terminators One and Two" Still no smile; my sense of humor didn't touch her. Either that or I'd become more callous than even I realized and it instead horrified her. "While they are under OPMC's investigation and hearings they continue their spree. See this file from the last eighteen months." I selected the top case. "For example, a nine-year-old girl…" I recounted Sorki's notorious breast case.

She picked up the file and read it carefully. I could see she was interested. An unnecessary and mutilating breast operation on a child—*this is sensational,* she was probably thinking. This was what journalists are after. It was almost as bizarre as carving the doctor's initials on the patient's skin and possibly more interesting than removing the wrong half of the brain. *Mass liquidation of elderly patients—who wanted to read about it? A breast of a nine-year-old child? Great story!*

We went over the material and the key players in the hospital. She was evidently a pro—sharp and knowledgeable. "If what you're telling me is true, and according to what I've read it is, it's scary in New York. How is it possible?"

I emptied the last drop of coffee. It was disgustingly cold. "Jane, do you watch the Sopranos?"

She nodded.

"Think along similar lines. This is a similar soap opera. You see how Toni Soprano runs the business—then think about Sorki and the rest. Different accents."

She stood up. "I need to copy some of this stuff and to do some homework. We have interns as well to do the scat work." Her first smile. "Let's go down to the newsroom." In the elevator she asked: "What was the reaction at the hospital to my last piece?"

"Howard and Farbstein were surprised by it—perhaps a little shaken. They entered into a defensive position, I suppose, waiting to absorb the next attack. If it comes…"

We walked across the huge newsroom, which at noontime was buzzing with activity. "This is the national section, here's the international desk, and this is my cubicle—here, in the Metro section." She stopped. "Next attack? Yes, it could come soon, depending on whether you wish to come forward."

"No way!" I exclaimed. "You know that the documents I showed you from the M&M's and the QA committees—are protected by law from public disclosure. Not only that, but if you feature me as a hero in uncovering this affair, my professional career in this town is *finito—passe.*"

"At the Report we treat our sources with confidentiality, not only as an ethical obligation, but also because we know that a journalist who betrays his sources very soon finds himself without any. However, we have to cite a source—unless we wait until the OPMC comes up with a verdict."

"I can't afford to serve as your only source. Why don't you try the others?"

"Let me see what I can do with what I have, and then I'll explore different avenues. I'll keep in touch." She escorted me back to the elevator and I headed back towards the subway.

Times Square was crowded with Japanese tourists hunting for lunches, overpriced but available at the local eateries. The early spring breeze was mildly cool. For a change one could walk in Manhattan's streets not freezing to death or melting. My mood was elated. I felt unloaded, as if things were finally rolling forward—as if the house of cards I'd been trapped in for so many years was collapsing. I knew that timing was crucial—that the house could collapse on me as well.

I felt strong and confident nonetheless.

23

The *New York Report*

In some hospitals there is a certain evil tendency. Now it slumbers—now it turns uneasily in sleep, dreaming of power—now it wakes to harmful deeds...That evil tendency may be called 'the system'...it means that certain medical men improperly and unjustly acquire supreme power for selfish interests not for the public welfare...In an institution in which the system is in full sway, some of the staff get more than they deserve and most get less than they need...
—Chalmers Da Costa, 1863-1933

June –December 2001.

The bulky Saturday edition of the *New York Report* was delivered before 7 a.m.—landing with a heavy thump at the doorsteps. Heidi picked it up and sorted out its multiple sections on the kitchen table. The article we expected started on the front and continued in the Metro pages. We sipped from our coffee mugs and read.

"License of Prominent Doctor Suspended During Inquiry," by Jane Rosenberg

The New York State Commissioner of Health has suspended the license of the president of the Medical Board of New York Park Hospital in Brooklyn, calling the doctor, who has a large surgery practice there, a danger to patients. The doctor, Mahmud Sorki, is under investigation by the Health Department on numerous negligence and incompetence charges stemming from his surgical practice at the hospital, where he has worked for roughly 30 years and is among the top administrators and money makers. Colleagues at the hospital, including the head of surgery, have complained to administrators about Dr. Sorki's care of patients for at least four years, according to doctors there, including those who support Dr. Sorki.

Dr. Sorki is the latest, and most prominent, doctor to be brought up on charges of negligence at Park by the Health Department in recent years. The hospital has more doctors who have been disciplined or investigated in negligence cases than any other major hospital in the city, according to the State Health Department. The health commissioner opted, with a power she uses infrequently, to suspend Dr. Sorki's license while his hearings continued. "Dr. Sorki constitutes an imminent danger to the health of the people of this state," said the order issued by the health commissioner. A final conclusion to the hearings could range from a total restoration of his license to its final revocation.

The state began its investigation last year after complaints from hospital staff members regarding numerous surgical cases. In suspending Dr. Sorki, the commissioner cited two of the cases. In one, the state accused the doctor of attempting dangerous and unneeded stomach surgery on an 89-year-old patient who was being treated at the hospital for congestive heart failure."

"Which case was that?" asked Heidi.
"The last gastrostomy. The one for which I was censured for telling him that he operates on dead patients." I continued reading.

In the other, the doctor was accused of inappropriate treatment of a patient who came to the hospital for weight reduction surgery. According to a sonogram taken before the operation, the patient had a mass near her abdominal wall, but the doctor proceeded with the elective surgery anyway. The patient, who was later found to have cancer, should never have had the elective operation, according to the state. Dr. Sorki's lawyer, Hubert Baker, said in a written statement: "We are surprised and dismayed at this unwarranted decision by Health Commissioner and are considering all options, including a court challenge. Dr. Sorki has never been the subject of any charges of any kind. Dr. Sorki has denied all of the allegations against him and looks forward to the opportunity to clear his name and his reputation."

Administrators at the hospital did not answer e-mailed questions regarding Dr. Sorki yesterday and did not return repeated calls.

Through the years, a variety of doctors have complained to hospital administrators about Dr. Sorki's surgical practice, but he has never been sanctioned by the hospital, said nearly a dozen people who work within the department and who spoke only on the condition of anonymity, for fear of being fired. One doctor, Marc Zohar, had complained repeatedly to the chairman of surgery at the hospital, Dr. Lawrence Winestone, and was fired last March. Dr. Zohar was inexplicably rehired a few weeks later, letters between the doctor and administrators show. Dr. Zohar would not comment, citing a legal agreement with the hospital not to discuss his situation.

Tensions between Dr. Sorki and those who have expressed concern over his care have erupted over the years in a variety of ways. At conferences that are held for the medical staff to objectively and privately evaluate cases with poor outcomes, tempers flared and arguments ensued, which is unusual in that type of setting, according to several participants. In a meeting involving a case in which Dr. Sorki operated on the healthy breast of a 9-year-old girl, several doctors contended that the surgery was unneeded and wrong-headed, according to minutes from the meeting, and several people who attended it, and Dr. Sorki was reported by some who were present to be "furious" and "defensive." "What you did is dangerous," said a doctor who was brought in as a guest from Babies and Children's Hospital of the Manhattan University, minutes from the meeting show. That case is one of those being investigated by the state.

"The whole atmosphere in this department is hard to deal with," said one medical resident. "It is very unpleasant."

Supporters of Dr. Sorki agreed that the atmosphere had been increasingly toxic in the department, but blamed his detractors. Dr. Rachman Gotahedi, a surgeon in the department, called Dr. Sorki "an excellent surgeon." Dr. Winestone, the chairman of surgery who was brought in to save the residency program, which was close to closing in the mid-1990s because of poor quality, denied that his department was in turmoil. "The department is in good condition," he said yesterday. "There is nothing to defend. We have high standards." He declined to comment further.

By all accounts, even among his adversaries, Dr. Sorki is a respected member of the hospital. Several members of the board of directors and hospital administrators have sent their family members to him for surgery. As the president of the Medical Board, Dr. Sorki oversaw the hiring of all doctors at the hospital and the quality of care being given. He also was among the top 10 percent of money makers at the hospital in 1999, according to state data. Many concur that his technical skills are unrivaled at the center, but contend that he makes errors deciding which patients require surgery and who should be left untreated. "Technically he is excellent, just unbelievable," said one surgeon, who echoed the comments of four others. All five agreed, however, that Dr. Sorki's choices of when to operate were sometimes poor.

According to numerous accounts, the tensions between Dr. Sorki and others in the surgical department intensified four years ago, after Dr. Winestone recruited Dr. Zohar. Critical scientific evaluation of cases did not sit well with Dr. Sorki and others who have controlled the medical staff over the last few decades and who prefer to view surgery more as an art form in which successes cannot be quantified by scientific measures, said several people in the hospital.

The goals of the department have to do with education, developing good quality of care, working to get better," said one doctor. "Things here would be a lot better, insofar as that goes, without this controversy." Some doctors at Park said they believed that Dr. Sorki had been undone by jealous rivals. "I have known Dr. Sorki for 30 years," said Dr. Fakir Aprahamian, an obstetrician. "If any loved one in my family gets sick, I would trust him with my heart. He is a good physician and a caring physician. Obviously there is a lot of animosity and jealousy, and I believe the major reason for the state's case is that."

"See what your beloved gynecologist says?" I teased Heidi. Aprahamian changed her uterine device each year.
"What could he say? What do you expect him to say? He's scared. And why do they mention your name? I thought that she promised to leave you out of it..."
"She doesn't cite me. The quotes are all of others. Whatever these reporters do they try to seem objective and balanced."

In recent years, several doctors practicing at Park have been sanctioned by the state but retained by the hospital. In the obstetrics and gynecology department, two doctors have been disciplined for botching cases. Another doctor at the hospital was sanctioned for sexually harassing a patient. Another prominent surgeon has been under investigation by the Health Department and recently retired quietly.

Community hospitals are a little less than optimally vigilant about these things," said one surgeon who has been critical of Dr. Sorki. "And it is really too bad because Park has a great spirit. It is full of great people who put patients first. But the hospital also has a tremendous responsibility because when people show up off the street, they believe they are always getting physicians of quality."

"Yes, a great spirit indeed." I sighed.

"And Mantzur, what about him?" asked Heidi.

"Oh, the old fox is smart. He knew when to take off his surgical gloves. He understands that he has lost the war. It seems that the Padrino will never decorate the pages of the *New York Report.*"

"And what now? What will Howard, Farbstein and Winestone do?"

"They'll just wait to see how things develop. They call it damage control, waiting for things to cool off, hoping there will be nothing further in the papers about it—they know that papers turn yellow and people forget."

▲▼◢▲▼▲

At night with the lights of the southern tip of Manhattan slowly retracting, the stern of the Staten Island bound ferry's is perhaps the most glorious place in New York City. I breathed with pleasure the smell of the sea and exposed my face to the kind cool breeze blowing from the north. I felt elated. Perhaps it was the wine I'd just I sipped with my meal at the South Sea Port. The truth is that I was happy with myself. I wouldn't tell anyone, but I was rather proud. I did it! I had managed to destroy the invincible Mafia almost alone. Why did I do it? Certainly not for personal gain. I lost time, health, position and money. Didn't I do it to let justice prevail? Wasn't that my prime motivation, to do the right thing? No. That's just a cliché.

Maybe it was my kamikaze reflex, the tendency to take risks. Some may call it courage, but it is not. Kamikazes do not follow the reasonable paths of others, and they are dangerous to the "organized" world, but they are not used to people who put their personal motives and interests aside and are driven by uncontrolled inner forces. They thought I would be easily disposed off. Even then Howard thought that because he was giving me a few bucks I would forget everything.

The lights of the Statue of Liberty were showing on the starboard side, and a young tourist took a picture of his girl. *I'll miss Brooklyn—the sight of this statue from my office window, the aroma from the ethnic restaurants on the avenue.*

Farbstein was the only one who realized my zealotry and could have bought me. The small managers from Brooklyn used to dealing with the local scum were too cheap. They wanted to get rid of me without spending a dime. But even if they'd chased me off with huge sums, the money wouldn't have satisfied me. I would have remained a person who was driven by an ego that thrived only on victory—an ego that wouldn't be bought or deterred by threats.

Perhaps Howard wanted me to liquidate the Mafia, destroying them and myself in the process. Chaudri, my good friend, played his cards well and replaced me as Winestone's right-hand man. His private practice benefited enormously from the vacuum left by the departure of Mantzur and Sorki. Heidi believes that Chaudri will be popular, wealthy, and busy and in ten years will materialize as a benign replica of Mantzur.

And Garibaldi, my pasta-making buddy, has become the new Sorki. He's the president of the Medical Board and in the OR is finishing off old Italian ladies. The ferry changed course and slowed its engines. I left the open deck and descended to the disembarking ramp, standing among the crowd that was eager to rush forward.

I resumed my reflections. Drs. Rusk and Bachus? They will stay on with Winestone at the Park Hospital at least as long as he survives there. Both honest and decent surgeons, they were caught within the rush of events neither benefiting nor suffering from the outcome.

The ferry bounced heavily against the ancient and crumbling wooden jetty, and the crowd rushed forward. I let them pass by and walked peacefully behind a slender black girl in shorts, enjoying the sight of her athletic lower limbs. For some reason this view reminded me that Winestone addressed our residents at their last graduation banquet on the subject of "Ethics in Surgery."

EPILOGUE

Nor is the public aware of the temptation, which men of our profession withstand. Credit for great abilities, gratitude for services performed, and high emoluments are ready to be bestowed for a little deception, and that obliquity of conduct, which does not amount to actual crime.
—*Charles Bell, 1774-1842*

I was sitting in my study when the phone rang. I picked it up on the third ring.

"Dr. Zohar, it's Dr. Carducci here."

"Hi, what's going on?"

"Well, I just thought you'd like to see this web site—"

"—Hold on a sec, let me grab a pen." I reached over my desk and plucked the first pen out of the holder. "OK."

"All right, here it is." He listed it off, then continued: "Search by name, Mahmud Sorki, MD." I wrote it down.

"What's on that page?"

"Just go there. Let's just say it's the fruits of your labor, I'm just sorry it took so damned long. The wheels of justice turn slowly on the rich and influential."

"OK," I said. "Thanks for the address. I'll take a look at it."

"Thanks for your persistence, Doctor. Good-bye for now."

I hung up the phone and twisted in my chair to access my desktop computer. With a few mouse clicks I was in an Internet browser. Carefully, I typed in the address:

http://www.health.state.ny.us/nysdoh/opmc/main/htm

Then I typed in "Mahmud Sorki, MD" in the search window...

Action: License revocation

Effective Date: October 12, 2001

Nature of Misconduct: The Hearing Committee sustained the charges finding the physician guilty of incompetence and negligence on more than one occasion; gross negligence; providing treatment which was not warranted by the patient's condition and failing to maintain accurate records.

Then, just on a hunch, I typed in Joseph Mantzur, MD:

Action: License limited precluding the practice of medicine

Effective Date: September 26, 2001

Nature of Misconduct: The physician did not contest the charge of negligence on more than one occasion.

These guys were finished. Sorki was advised by his lawyers not to appeal and left New York to practice in his "old country." The *New York Report* published a brief statement about the verdicts and nothing more. After watching the local hospitals and keeping doctors and administrators on their toes, Jane Rosenberg had been transferred from the newspaper's health desk, and the newspaper did not bother to replace her.

Farbstein changed skin colors a few times but kept walking between new administrative camps, serving and crossing all of them. Apparently he was telling everyone that the terminators should have been suspended years ago but among friends, after a drink or two, he lamented the loss of Sorki—"the greatest surgeon this hospital ever had."

As for Mantzur, Larry Winestone could not save him. He tried in a letter to Dr. Carducci—writing about his high regard for Mantzur as both a teacher and clinical surgeon, not to mention his role as the vice chairman of the department. Winestone also stated categorically that if he ever needed vascular or thoracic surgery, then Dr. Mantzur would be his number one choice as a surgeon. It did not help.

Herb Susman lost about two hundred pounds. After Sorki left he was kicked off his political high ground and the

Vice Chairman of Medicine position. And the OPMC had the noose around his neck: they were more than interested in all of those cases he shipped to Sorki for execution.

▲▼▲▲▼▲

"Shouldn't you include in the epilogue something on how to fix the system...some useful suggestions? Publishers would appreciate it, no?" Heidi asked, browsing with limited interest through the manuscript.

"You know how many scholarly non-fiction books and articles have been written about bad medicine, medical errors, about the influence of money on doctors, about the impaired physician, about the potential solution to the pollution—"

"—Yes, but there must be some way...I read somewhere that if surgeons were subjected to a rigid and regular scrutiny of their performance like that used for commercial pilots, then the rate of errors and disasters would decline."

"Boeing jets or Airbuses are complex but do not suffer from cardiac failure, Alzheimer or an unstable angina. If they did, they would be sent to the junk yard. Pilots usually fly healthy machines. Surgery is different. Sorki for example, would have passed any test on a surgical simulator. He knows to operate. The problem is he does not know when not to operate and when to stop or do less. There is no simulator to assess complex surgical judgment. Besides that, who would decide about the minimum performance required and who would enforce the new rules?"

"Well, the professional organizations, the hospitals, the State agencies—"

"Come on, Heidi. You know how many rules there are and how much of it is just lip service. No rules are effective if people such as Howard, Farbstein or even Winestone, do not comply and do not pay for the consequences. Take for instance the NPDB—"

"—What's that?"

"The National Practitioner Data Bank. According to the Health Care Quality act signed by President Regan years ago, hospitals are required to report 'lemon' physicians to the state licensing agencies, which in turn has to notify the NPDB. The NPDB should function as a database for impaired or dangerous physicians. But who is reporting? Do you think that Mantzur's or Sorki's names were in their files? Forget it!"

"You are pessimistic, Marc. You want to say that there is no easy fix, no solution?

"It is hopeless! We doctors can't control ourselves effectively, and the authorities' futile efforts to reinforce controls involve more and more red tape and bureaucrats. Look at our hospitals where there are more administrators trying to justify their existence than doctors. Look at the huge bureaucratic machine called Medicare. Did you know that Medicare regulations are six times more voluminous than IRS tax regulations? And everybody is cheating them, like our friend Mantzur did."

"OK. It's enough. When you start with your useless statistics it's time to quit." She dropped the manuscript on the desk. "Just write whatever you wish."

"But listen to this. Another thing I have to mention is that the huge and often contradictory and grossly deficient regulatory mechanisms in this country are very expensive. It has been calculated that twenty-eight percent of the total cost of health care in this country goes to pay the bloody bureaucrats. That's two or three times the rate of administrative costs in most developed countries such as Germany. Reducing US health care bureaucratic costs to the level of Canada or the UK would provide full medical services for millions of uninsured Americans."

When I finished the sentence I noticed that I was alone in the room.

The M&M meeting at the Manhattan Village Hospital takes place on Thursday afternoons. The auditorium is small and modest. The seats are worn, and the wallpaper is fading. I prefer a hospital that invests its money in a digital X-ray transmission system rather than spending millions trying to resemble a five-star hotel. I walk in and select a seat at random. I don't know yet who sits where. Looking around I recognize my new chairman and a few of the full time attendings. The other faces represent the usual ethnic admixture of New York.

The meeting is chaired by the vice chairman, a tall freckled middle-aged man. An Indian-looking resident presents the first case. I don't know his name. He reads from his notes but no handouts are available. *They are cautious here, leaving no material to be collected.*

The resident reads fast, and I try to concentrate to pick up the details of the case. Surely they would want to hear what kind of wisdom I—their most recent acquisition—could provide. The case involves a middle-aged man who underwent a segmental small bowel resection for a perforation, which resulted in diffuse intra-abdominal infection. We are told that after the operation he developed multiple organ failure and slowly—over a period of fifteen days—faded away and died. The case presentation is over in three minutes.

There are a few questions from the floor: "What type of anastomosis was performed?" asks the chairman. Another comments about the antibiotic therapy, and the vice chairman asks the resident: "Was an autopsy performed?" Answer negative.

My heart is pounding rapidly, and my hands are clammy. I am suffering from *deja vue*. I want to stand up and attack, to blame, to preach. I don't know the surgeon but what a fool, what a stupid fucker. He takes a guy, removes his bowel, performs an anastomosis within a pool of pus, prescribes a few antibiotics, places the poor man in the ICU— and bang—he thinks that his job is finished. Now he can go and chop on another victim while this one is being chewed to death by the free shit in his abdomen. What an idiot. No CT, no re-operation, nothing! My right hand pinches the left until I feel pain. *Just shut up, shut up, shut up. This is your last chance in this town. Breathe deeply and relax. It means nothing, it means nothing—who bloody cares. Life means nothing. It is not your business. Shut up!*

The Vice Chairman looks in my direction. "Gentlemen, I want to introduce to you a new member of our team, Dr. Zohar, who joined us early this week. Dr. Zohar is a Professor of—" His voice faded away in my consciousness.

Rusk, I command myself. Talk like Malcolm Rusk would have. I stand up and address the vice chairman: "Thank you Dr. McGregor for this kind introduction, which I do not deserve. Let me say how proud I am to join this reputable institution." Another deep breath. *Just bullshit them. Life means nothing. You're doing well.* "As we all know in surgery there are many ways to skin a cat. There are many options which are correct and within the standard of care. If one looks at today's literature dealing with surgical infections, one reads about people who would be more aggressive, who, in this particular case, would look for persistent or recurrent intra-abdominal infection. Then there are those who would have re-operated this patient. Yes, there is a wide spectrum of options, which could be used by the individual surgeon. The secret is to tailor the management to the individual patient based on the specific clinical findings. The unfortunate patient under discussion succumbed to severe systemic inflammatory response triggered by severe abdominal infection. Whether he was salvageable we'll never know."

You are doing great. Just keep bullshitting. Talk crap. "What we know is that the surgeon and his team did a great job trying to save this critically ill patient whose prognosis was guarded from the beginning!"

Silence. *They are impressed.* "Dr. Smith, you were the surgeon on this case. Any comments?" the vice chairman asks.

Smith stands up. I note the long white hair, and even from where I sit I see dandruff on the collar of his navy blue blazer. He smiles in my direction. "I have nothing to add. Dr. Zohar said it all. I'm familiar with Dr. Zohar's multiple contributions to the literature dealing with this topic. I'm happy that he approved our management. We clearly did everything we could."

The next four cases are vascular and thoracic. I won't be asked about them. I shut myself off and relax. I like this hospital. It will be fun.

After the M&M meeting a few surgeons approach me. "Welcome. We've heard much about you. Our residency has been craving for a man like you."

Dr. Smith comes to me. "Dr. Zohar. Marc? He shook my hand. "I'm Jack. Marc, we must get together for lunch one of these days. We have a lot to discuss. How about Friday lunch at the University Club? I'm a member."

In the corridor the Chairman puts his arm around my shoulder. "They like you, Marc. I'm happy you are with us. We'll have a great time together." As we walk towards the elevators he looks at me slyly and adds: "Marc, rumors reach me that you and Winestone did not love each other much. He gave you an excellent recommendation. I rarely see such an enthusiastic endorsement. I'm convinced that whatever he said about you was correct. I met Winestone on a few occasions. How could you work so long with such a character?"

I smile but say nothing. The chairman continues. "Marc, everybody reads *The New York Report,* and they all know about you and will be watching you. Administration has heard about your Brooklyn story and they asked me to warn you that this hospital does not fancy features on the pages of the *Report.*"

"Of course."

The chairman continues chatting as we entered the elevator. "By the way, Marc, Jack Smith—whom you just met at the M&M—is our number one private surgeon, immensely busy. To tell you the truth, between you and me, he is not one hundred percent kosher."

The chairman says no more. I know that Smith is the born-in-the-USA, board-certified version of Sorki. *Allahu akbar. Life means nothing.* I smile to myself. I am going to become their ally. Once I am dismissed by the Chairman, I turn on my heels and head in my own direction. I arrive at an elevator and wait for the cabin. It arrives momentarily and as I step in I notice that it isn't as nice as those at the Park, but it does the job.

How long will this elevator survive?

Glossary

Abdominal Aortic Aneurysm (AAA): An extreme dilation of the main abdominal artery—prone to rupture.

Adenocarcinoma: A cancer arising from any glandular tissue. (see carcinoma)

Anastomosis: The junction created between segments of intestine or blood vessels, sutured or stapled together.

Aphasic: speechless

ARDS (adult respiratory distress syndrome): A lung condition in critically ill patients causing "wet lungs" and respiratory failure.

Arterial blood gases (ABG): A test measuring the amount of oxygen, carbon dioxide, and acid in the blood.

Ascites: A diffuse collection of fluid in the abdominal cavity, usually due to chronic liver disease or advanced cancer.

Asymptomatic: Associated with no symptoms, e.g. no pain or other complaints.

Asystole: Same as cardiorespiratory arrest (see below)

Atrium: One of the two thin walled, low pressure- chambers of the heart.

Attending surgeons: Fully qualified and licensed surgeons.

Autoclaved: A process of sterilization of surgical instrument, which destroys all microorganisms.

Barium: A radio opaque solution used for contrast studies (see below).

Bilirubin: A substance measured in the blood –elevated in patients with jaundice.

Billroth I or II: A type of partial surgical removal of the stomach named after Theodor Billroth—a famous 19th century Austrian surgeon.

Carcinoma: A type of cancer (always malignant).

Carcinomatosis: When the whole abdomen is laden with cancer deposits.

Cardiac arrhythmia: An irregular heart rhythm or pace.

Cardiorespiratory arrest: When the heart and/or lungs stop functioning.

Carotid artery: One of the two main arteries supplying the brain.

Celiac plexus: A net of sensory nerves supplying, among others, the pancreas.

Chest drains: Tubes inserted into the chest to treat punctured lungs.

Cholangiogram: X rays to visualize the bile ducts.

Cholecystectomy: Surgical removal of the gallbladder.

Coagulopathy: Disturbed clotting of the blood due to various causes.

Coded/code: A term used to describe the death of a patient in the hospital.

Colectomy: Surgical removal of large bowel.

Colonoscopy: Endoscopic-fibro-optic visualization of the large bowel (colon).

Colostomy: An "artificial anus" with the feces evacuated through a segment of large bowel sutured into the skin of the abdominal wall.

Congestive failure: Congestive heart failure-- when the heart pump fails.

Contrast study: A radiological study in which radio opaque contrast solution is installed into the bowel and x rays are taken to outline its lumen.

COPD: Chronic obstructive lung disease—an "emphysema," lung disease usually caused by cigarette smoking.

CPR: Cardio-respiratory resuscitation-attempts to revive a dying patient.

Crit: Referring to hematocrit—a measurement of red blood cells.

CT: Computed tomography- a radiological imaging technique.

Distal: Below.

Duke's: A grading system used to stage colonic cancer.

Duplex arterial scan: A non-invasive test to visualize blood vessels.

Ejection fraction: A measurement of the pumping function of the heart.

Endartrectomy: An operation to "clean" and open up partially occluded arteries.

Endovascular surgery: Operation performed under X ray guidance inside the lumen of the arteries through tiny skin incisions.

ER: Emergency Room.

Erosive gastritis: Inflammation of the inner lining of the stomach caused by drugs or stress.

Extubated, extubation: Referring to the removal of an endotracheal tube used in artificial breathing.

Fistula: A hole in the bowel which communicates with the skin.

Fem-pops: Femoral-politeal bypass—an operation to create a communication between two arteries in the lower limb—bypassing an occluded segment.

Frozen section: A rapid pathological examination of tissues during the operation.

Gastrectomy: The surgical removal of part ("partial") or the whole ("total") of the stomach.

Gastrografin: A water soluble contrast solution used for contrast study (see above).

Gastroscope/gastroscopy: An instrument to visualize the inside of the stomach, performing "gastroscopy."

Gastroplasty: A weight reducing stomach operation.

Gastrostomy: Placement of a tube through the abdominal wall into the stomach for feeding purposes or decompression.

GI: Gastrointestinal: Used also to describe the specialty which deals with the stomach and gut.

Gutters: The lateral posterior spaces of the abdominal cavity.

Hemangioma: A benign vascular tumor.

Hemodynamic stability: When the blood pressure and circulation are normal.

Hemoglobin: A measurement of red blood cells—a low level denotes anemia and/or blood loss.

Hemorrhoidectomies: Operations to remove enlarged, painful or bleeding anal piles.

Heparin: A drug which prevents the clotting (thrombosis) of blood.

Hepatic failure: When the liver function fails.

Hilar mass: A shadow seen on chest X ray in the central region of the chest-usually a tumor.

HMO: Health maintenance organization—a US-based provider of health services.

Hemostasis: The surgical attempts to stop bleeding.

Hepatic cirrhosis: Chronic liver disease leading to scarring of the liver and its failure—caused by excessive alcohol consumption or chronic viral hepatitis.

Hypothermic: Cold—of low body temperature.

ICU: Intensive care unit.

Inotrope-support: Administration of drugs to increase the pumping of the heart.

317

Intra-peritoneal: Within the abdominal cavity.

Ischemic heart disease: Heart conditions caused by blocked coronary arteries—such as "angina" or "heart attack."

Jejunostomy: Surgical placement of a tube through the abdominal wall into the small intestine for feeding purposes.

JFK: One of New York's airports.

Laparotomy: Any operation during which the abdominal cavity is entered.

Lübscke knife: An instrument used to cut the sternum—the breast bone.

Lumpectomy: The surgical removal of a lump. Usually used to describe removal of a breast mass.

Mastectomy: Surgical removal of the entire breast.

Medicaid: A jointly funded, US Federal-State health insurance program for certain low-income and needy people.

Medicare: US Federal Health Insurance Program for people 65 years of age and older, some people with disabilities under age 65, and people with End-Stage Renal Disease (permanent kidney failure requiring dialysis or a transplant).

Metastases: Spread of cancer to remote organs and sites.

MRI: Magnetic resonance imaging- a sophisticated imaging technique.

Multi-organ failure (MOF): A condition in which many organs fail—occurring in critically ill patients and commonly leads to death. A common "final pathway" in surgical patients.

Nasogastric tube (NG tube): A tube inserted through the nose into the stomach for decompression or feeding purposes.

Nephrectomy: Surgical removal of kidney.

Non-resectable: Not amenable to surgical removal—denoting an advanced cancer which cannot be cured by the knife.

Omentum: Fatty tissue which is attached to the stomach and hangs down as an apron covering the abdominal contents.

OR: Operating room. Also known as the operating theater.

Packs: Referring to large gauze pads used to absorb blood and fluids during surgery.

Pack cells: Blood for transfusion-containing mainly cells with almost no plasma.

PEEP (Positive end expiratory pressure): A special mode of mechanical ventilation used to mechanically breathe for patients with wet lungs (ARDS).

Pericardium: The envelope of the heart.

Perforated ulcer: A spontaneous perforation of an ulcer of the stomach or duodenum, leading to abdominal infection.

Peritonitis: Infection of the abdominal cavity.

Pneumothorax: An accumulation of air between the lung and the chest wall.

Portocath: A catheter implanted into a large vein for long-term administration of drugs-usually chemotherapy for cancer.

Postoperative hemorrhage: Bleeding occurring after the operation.

Proctoscope: A short metal pipe used to visualize the anus and rectum.

Prophylactic: Preventive.

Prostatectomy: An operation on the prostate gland.

Proximal: Above.

Pyloroplasty: An operation to divide the muscle which controls the opening between the stomach and duodenum.

Renal failure: When the kidneys are not functioning properly.

Retroperitoneum: The space at the back of the abdominal cavity-which contains the kidneys and "great vessels."

Ringer's Lactate: An intra-venous fluid solution used to treat blood loss and dehydration.

Roux en Y: A technique of intestinal reconstruction in gastric surgery.

Saturation: Referring to the amount of oxygen in the blood.

Semi-comatose: Badly altered consciousness.

Short gastric arteries: Blood vessels which connect the spleen and the stomach.

SMA 12 test: An automated blood test measuring multiple blood components.

Shunt: An artificial, and usually temporary, surgically created blood vessel.

Silk: A non-absorbable suture material.

Splenectomy: Surgical removal of the spleen.

Stenosis: Narrowing, of a blood vessel or the lumen of any anatomic structure.

Sternum: The breast bone.

Suture granuloma: A benign tissue growth developing around a suture material.

Suture line: The junction between two anatomical structures-- sutured or stapled together.

319

Thoracotomy: Any operation which opens the chest wall.

Thrombolysis: The dissolution of thrombus or clots.

Thrombus: A blood clot.

TIAs, transient ischemic attacks: Intermittent episodes of brain dysfunction caused by poor blood supply.

TPN: Total parenteral nutrition—artificial feeding infused into the vein.

Tracheostomy: Surgical insertion of a tube through the neck into the trachea (the wind pipe).

Triple A (AAA): Abdominal aortic aneurysm—see above.

Vagotomy: Surgical division of the vagi nerves to heal peptic ulcers.

Vena cava: Refers to the inferior vena cava (IVC) --the chief vein which drains the lower part of the body.

Ventilator: A machine breathing for the patient.

Vicryl: Self absorbable surgical suture material.

Upper GI: Upper gastrointestinal tract, the digestive portion which includes the esophagus, stomach and duodenum.

Urokinase: A clot dissolving agent.

QA: Quality Assurance.

Whipple: A very large operation in which the head of the pancreas and the duodenum are removed—named after Allen Whipple, a late New York surgeon.